Kidnapped Nation

by

Braxton DeGarmo

Christen Haus Publishing

COPYRIGHT

Kidnapped Nation – Copyright © 2017 by Braxton DeGarmo. All rights reserved under International and Pan-American Copyright Conventions. By payment of the required fees, you have been granted the non-exclusive, non-transferable right to access and read the text of this e-book on-screen. No part of this text may be reproduced, transmitted, down-loaded, decompiled, reverse engineered, or stored in or introduced into any information and retrieval system, in any form or by any means, whether electronic or mechanical, now known or hereinafter invented, without the express written permission of Braxton DeGarmo.

Paperback/eBook Edition Publication Date: April, 2017

Paperback ISBN: 978-1-943509-23-2
EBook (mobi): 978-1-943509-24-9
EBook (epub): 978-1-943509-25-6

This is a work of fiction. The characters, incidents, and dialogs are products of the author's imagination and are not construed to be real. Any resemblance to actual events or persons, living or dead, is entirely coincidental. The use of real places and companies is done to add a sense of reality, but the circumstances surrounding such use is also fictional. The employees of such companies, their actions, and their comments are fiction and should not be construed as implied or explicit endorsements by or the beliefs of said companies. The use of public figures, such as politicians, is also done for the purpose of realism. Actions or comments attributed to them may be fiction, but may also come from public records, such as their own writings.

Cover design by Rocking Book Covers
For more information, go to **www.braxtondegarmo.com**

DEDICATION

This book is dedicated to those families that have lost their homes and their land to the aggressive tactics of the federal government.

TABLE OF CONTENTS

ACKNOWLEDGMENTS

As always, I again want to acknowledge and thank my dear wife, Paula, for her valuable proofreading skills, help and encouragement. Many thanks as well to Lenda Selph for her expert proofreading.

I'd also like to give a shout out to the staff at the August A. Busch Memorial Conservation Area—a.k.a. Busch Wildlife—for their assistance with information on the area. This area is truly a gem for those who enjoy the outdoors.

Finally, a big thank you to my editor, Patrick LoBrutto, whose suggestions always improve my books. I think you, the reader, will appreciate the final result.

AUTHOR'S NOTE

There's a good chance that you've already heard about the armed protest at the Malheur National Wildlife Refuge in Oregon in January, 2016. It was one of the latest incidents in what has been termed the Sagebrush Rebellion, a movement that began in the 1970s by landowners in the western states who wish to see reduced federal control over the territory in the 13 western states.

Since over 50% of the U.S. population lives in the Eastern Time Zone, most people have no idea what it means to have the federal government own or control the majority of the land within their state . . . or to be subject to the federal government's strong-arm tactics when it wants *your* land for the mineral rights. This story highlights what it's like to be a victim of such tactics by our government, using the Malheur protest as one premise for the story. I hope the story opens your eyes to these practices by our government, as well as entertains you.

One

The moonless but starry night provided perfect cover as the dark SUV pulled up to the single metal bar that served as a gate to the facility. Streetlights were non-existent in this "neck of the woods." Only the straying light from a passing vehicle's headlamps had a chance of revealing the two men who emerged from the late model Ford Expedition, whose driver had used night vision goggles for the last mile.

"Got it," said the younger of the two as he snapped the padlock with a pair of bolt cutters.

Together they swung open the gate. Then the older used his cell phone to broadcast a message to the group waiting for his word. He waved the driver through the gate and met him by the driver's window.

"Go on up to the main building. You know what to look for, right?"

"Yessir. We'll get 'er done."

"Good. Check it out and then start setting up."

The SUV, lights still extinguished, crept along the narrow, paved road and disappeared around a bend, hidden by tall pines. The man returned to a spot near the entrance where he could see the road as it stretched out both north and south. He turned to the younger.

"Go ahead and close the gate. Stay close by. We

need to move folks in as quickly as they get here. We have three hours before dawn."

Over the next two hours a ragtag caravan, of sorts, arrived at staggered times. Each arrival was noted by a preset signal with the headlights. Only two cars passed by that did not belong.

The assortment of pickup trucks, SUVs, and older sedans would not have appeared out of place for this remote location. Even the generator in the bed of one pickup and the small fuel tanker were typical for the traffic expected along that rural highway. What would seem strange to the locals was the wide collection of states represented by the license plates on those vehicles. Besides the locals from Oregon, Nevada, New Mexico, Utah, Colorado, Arizona, Idaho, Montana, and Wyoming were well represented, too. Even one vehicle from each of the Dakotas arrived.

The western states were under siege. These people, men and women, intended to get word of that siege out to the rest of the country . . . before it was too late.

As each vehicle moved into the area around the main building, men removed the license plates. Only the plates of the Expedition and a Chevy Tahoe were left in place.

"Got 'em all?" asked the older man, as the last of the vehicles lost its obvious means of identifying the owner. "We expect they'll be using drones to watch us within two days. Don't want to make it easy for them to ID any of us."

"We have them, except for yours and Adam's."

Their leader nodded. "That works. They'll know who I am soon enough."

They would indeed. The Feds who would soon descend upon this place already knew the name Simon Slattery. They didn't yet know he'd left his ranch in Nevada to lead this protest over land seizures by the federal government, and to support two local ranchers whom the Bureau of Land Management had targeted and were now in jail on what Slattery saw as the latest in trumped up charges against private landowners.

He walked over to a small group of men talking around the camp lantern one of them had set on his lowered tailgate. He glanced from face to face and saw serious commitment. But then, he knew *that* about each of them. They'd already driven hundreds of miles to participate in what Slattery hoped would remain a peaceful protest. Should the Feds turn it otherwise, he also knew each man was willing to become a martyr for the cause.

Yet, he knew that saying you'd die for the cause was easy to say and not so easy to accept if you felt the burn of lead in your chest. He prayed that none of them would take on that level of engagement.

"Hanson, no rush, but take Brandy and secure the southern access road. Use that beat up Fairlane we nearly had to tow here to block the road and then take up a suitable observation location. You'll have company sometime tomorrow I'm sure. The Feds will make sure they have eyes on that road."

He turned to two of the others. "Buddy, you guys take that hay trailer and block the main road in. We need something we can move in and out of position easily, and that should work. And find two people to man the fire tower. Make sure they have binoculars. They need to be in place by the time the sun rises." He paused and looked around. The lone security light over the main building illuminated the area well. Most of the people who had joined him that night took advantage of it to perform their initial tasks.

"Any of you guys see the electrician from Montana? Forget his name."

"Busby."

"Yeah. Him."

"Helped him position the generator near the meter box. I think he joined Comer and Thompson. Looking for an active alarm system before someone accesses the building."

Slattery nodded. He loved that these guys knew the plan and took the initiative. They made it that much easier for him.

"Good. We should be ready come morning." He smiled. "BLM staff is in for one hell of a surprise."

To most western landowners, their biggest enemy wasn't some foreign-born terrorist allowed into the country by the politically-correct crowd in Washington. Their enemy had become Washington itself. Ranches that had been in their families for generations had become targets for the government, which used the Bureau of Land Management to push those families off their land under the guise of protecting the environment. The real goal wasn't hard to see. The government elites wanted full control of the resources under those lands to pass on to their cronies in Big Business. The Edmond Ranch was the latest target . . . after the U.S. Geological Survey discovered oil, natural gas, and uranium in the valley.

Two

"Hi. My name is Brad . . . and I'm a terrorist."

The scene panned out to show Bradley Graham sitting in a circle with eleven others, an image reminiscent of Alcoholics Anonymous or any other twelve-step program. But this was no rehab meeting.

"You see, I'm a conservative, Bible-believing, patriotic American. I am pro-life, pro-freedom, pro-democracy, and pro-jobs. And because I'm pro-jobs, I'm also pro-business because that's where jobs come from. I believe that you must be self-reliant, hard-working, and sometimes sacrificial to become successful. And I believe in American Exceptionalism because it is this God-given political experiment called the United States of America, a republic based on liberty, equality, and individualism that allows you to reach for the stars and strive for your dreams. For these beliefs, our government and the United States military now label *me* a terrorist."

The camera zoomed out further to reveal armed soldiers surrounding and guarding the seated group. The ad continued.

"Where do you stand?"

Brad stood up and the camera zoomed in for a

close-up.

"I'm Brad Graham and I'm running for President under the banner of the American Party. Do you believe in America? If so, join us. *Support* the American Party and *vote* the American Party. It's time to *Take Back America*!"

Lynch Cully, the American Party's Chief of Security, stood behind the scenes in the studio and watched the production, amazed at what they required to produce a 30-second spot. They'd been there all afternoon, and Lynch had lost count at the twentieth take.

Brad wandered from talking with the director to a refreshment table someone had just set up, and then to Lynch. He carried two bottles of water and extended one toward Lynch.

"So, how'd that one look? This is tiring."

Lynch shrugged and took the water being offered to him. "No wonder feature movies cost so much to make. This is just a simple scene without any action and you're the only one talking. I can only imagine what it takes to produce a minute from an action movie."

His boss raised his brow. "And . . ."

Lynch didn't catch on for a second. "Oh. You looked great and you nailed the words. Again. You had your part down after five takes. There's always something else that requires a retake."

Lynch saw the director look up from his monitor with a scowl on his face. Lynch had seen that look a dozen times already.

"Uh-oh, boss. Get ready to do it again."

Brad sighed, and his shoulders sagged. "What now?"

The director began to yell. "Who put that refreshment

table there? It's reflecting in the backdrop windows. Somebody move it!" He looked toward Brad and gave him a 'Sorry' look. "Okay, folks. One more time."

Lynch's cell phone vibrated in his pocket. He retrieved it and walked toward the back of the studio. "One minute."

He needed to find a place to talk without disturbing the next shoot. He stepped outside, knowing that in a moment he'd be locked out as the studio began to record again. His security men, Mack Gilmore and Tony Tornatore, sitting in the SUV, jumped up as if expecting the boss next. He waved them down.

"This is Cully. Sorry, had to leave the sound stage. What's up?"

"No problem, Mr. Cully. Mr. McGonagle told me you'd be there and I could reach you at this number. This is Thomas McWhorter, with the Oregon campaign office. I was told to call you directly if the situation out here began to heat up. Well, it decided to boil over about fifteen minutes ago. The local authorities called in the FBI."

Lynch glanced at this watch. Oregon was two hours behind them and the earliest they could get there would be around midnight.

"I got a call from Lacy Edmond. She denies that they're involved with the protest, but she's asking to talk with Mr. Graham."

Lynch asked for a few more details and hung up. He needed to alert Brad. He turned and found the door locked.

*   *   *

Amy Gibbs paced between her front room and dining area. She'd had a long day that consisted of teaching six continuing education classes to the flight nurses and paramedics at MedAir Evac Services, where she worked as the director of education. In addition, she'd had to deal with a stubborn bureaucrat about their upcoming accreditation. She had looked forward to the end of the day and talking with her fiancé, Richard Nichols.

But now? She felt like throwing her phone against the wall, but that would be counterproductive and potentially expensive. Besides, the phone wasn't the problem. The man on the other end was.

"Grrrrrrr," she uttered to the otherwise empty room. She checked her watch for the fourth time. "He said five minutes . . . ten minutes ago. He is . . . slowly . . . driving me . . . mad."

Now she was talking to herself as well.

Three minutes later, the phone rang.

"Richard, that's enough!"

A familiar male voice on the other end said, "Umm, more trouble in paradise?"

Amy rolled eyes and sighed. "Dad. I thought it was —"

"Let me guess."

She shook her head and sat on the near end of the couch.

"I know it's probably not my place to say anything, but you two need to get your act together. Either you move there, as I've suggested before, or you get a clear commitment from him as to how long he plans to stay in D.C. and resolve yourself to wait it out. Without the bickering."

Amy felt as if she'd had this conversation before. A few times.

"I know. You're right. You've told me the same thing already, but he's *not* committing. I don't want to move to Virginia or Maryland if he's planning on coming back here once the election is over. And he's not —"

Her phone signaled another call coming in.

"Dad, that's Richard. Can I call you back?"

"Sure, just called to see if you wanted to come over for dinner tomorrow. Your brothers and their families are coming, too."

Her phone buzzed again.

"Sure. I'll call you back for details. Bye."

She signed off and switched to the call coming in.

"Hello." She wondered if she sounded frosty enough, or had her father's call softened her tone.

"Sweetheart, I'm sorry. I know that seems like the number one word in my vocabulary right now, but my job is, like, 24/7 now that we're just weeks away from the election. I can't guarantee how long I can talk this time either."

That did it. Now she felt the ice returning.

"How long we can talk? We didn't get past hello before you broke off the first call this evening. Let's see, on the second call twenty minutes after the first interruption, we lasted to your telling me your day was swamped and I just started to tell you I managed to get some flight time. The third call? Oh yeah. It consisted of 'call you in five minutes.' That was fifteen minutes ago. Should I set a timer?"

"Amy, look, it's my job and the nature of the season we're in. I can't stop the interruptions. It seems like there's always something, some fire to put out."

"Well, there might indeed always be something, but it's up to you whether you let it interrupt you or not. You *do* have that option. If this is the priority I get as a fiancée, I'm questioning what I'll get as a wife. To me, it's God, family, job. Not the reverse."

She wanted to hang up on him, but she'd been raised to be better than that. Throwing her phone against the wall remained an option, however.

He said nothing for what seemed like forever. Finally, he replied, "I . . . You're right. I need to work on priorities. Right after the election." His voice took on a pleading tone. "Look, if I don't do the job they expect of me, I'll lose it. I love this job. And it will support a family well. Even if you choose not to work. Even if we live here, near the capital."

That caught her off-guard. This was the first time Richard had mentioned living near Washington. She had never accepted the possibility that to marry Richard would *actually* lead to leaving St. Louis and her family. That had always been something off in Never-Never Land as having a remote chance of happening, but now he brought the Crocodile right to her doorstep.

"Are . . . are you saying you want to live there, even after the election?"

"Maybe. Uh, sure. I've really grown to like the area. The countryside's beautiful. The ocean is close. History surrounds everything here. Yeah, I could see living here. I haven't had time to really explore the area, but what little I have, I've enjoyed. I think you'd like it here."

If my family was there, she thought.

"Besides, if Graham wins, and his poll numbers keep rising, there's a great chance I'll have a job at the White House. If he doesn't, I've been getting feelers from other conservative groups here that might offer me a position."

Amy didn't know what to say. The Crocodile he'd brought to her door was no longer there. It was in her living room, sitting next to her on the couch, and she could hear time ticking away in its belly.

Richard hung up with Amy, feeling guilty that he hadn't been totally forthright with her. Yes, his job as Chief Social Media Strategist for the American Party focused now on the Bradley Graham campaign, as its first ever presidential candidate. As a conservative, Graham continued to fight against the Washington "Establishment" and the mainstream media with their liberal, progressive bias. Republican or Democrat, it made no real difference to their end game. That made Richard's job all the more difficult, and he *was* on-call 24/7. He remained truthful about the demands of his job.

Still, he should have told Amy he was looking for a house, to buy, not rent. He wanted to tell her. He almost got the words out, but she'd been so upset he didn't want to . . . well, he'd already overturned the apple cart. He didn't need to scatter the apples further. In the ideal world, talking about a house purchase should be done in person. But who lived in the ideal world? Not him. If he found a house, he'd make sure to get her involved.

He stepped to the curb and opened the door of the waiting SUV. As he climbed in, he looked at the trim, middle-aged, brunette woman sitting in the driver's seat. She looked just like the images on her billboards that sat strategically located around the metro area.

"Ms. Walther, thank you for working with me and being flexible about the time."

"Very pleased to do so. I'm used to it. Very few people here have typical nine-to-five jobs. Besides, Summer Stanton speaks highly of you."

That comment caught Richard a bit off-guard. He and the redheaded journalist had found themselves as targets of a blackmailer just months earlier. That had been a curious "match up," as their ideologies at the time were, and still were, polar opposites—like James Carville and Mary Matalin with their affiliations reversed.

"She did?"

The woman nodded. "It seems you and Mr. Graham made something of an impression on her. You can even see it in her reporting. The venom toward your candidate is gone."

In reflection, Richard had to admit that he had noticed that, too. He just hadn't paid that much attention to it. Yet, as he thought about it, while her work still tilted left and pushed the progressive agenda, she no longer spoke harshly of his boss.

He studied the woman next to him.

"May I ask you a personal question?"

She raised one brow and looked him directly in the eye. "If it's about politics, no. I work with people on both sides of the aisle and I never share my own beliefs or how I stand on issues."

He could understand that. "No, not that. Are you personal friends with Ms. Stanton? Is she the reason you took me on as a client?"

She smiled. "*That* I'll answer. Yes and yes. I sold her the condo where she used to live and then the home where she now lives. We've become friends. We have lunch together, oh, easily twice a month. And we're often at the same social events . . . events on both sides of the aisle, mind you. She mentioned that should you ever call me, not that she expected you to do so . . . but, should you call, she asked that I take you on. You have to realize that most people I work with are in, shall I say, higher tax brackets than you."

"Actually, I do realize that. I wondered why you agreed to work with me."

"Well, now you know. Shall we proceed?"

"My tax bracket, as you put it, isn't going to be a problem, is it?"

"Nonsense. Real estate is real estate. We all have the same multiple listing service. Plus, I might know of some sweet deals the other realtors don't have access to. So, let's go."

The Director sat at his desk fiddling with his pen as he read the latest brief about the situation in the Middle East. Using his ties with the Muslim Brotherhood, he had convinced it to work *with* The Assembly, not against it. He still had to compartmentalize them away from the factions of Hamas and Hezbollah they already utilized, but the Brotherhood's acceptance of The Assembly placed him one step closer to controlling the peace process. Could a second Nobel Peace Prize be within his grasp?

If only he could make inroads within the leadership of ISIS, or IS, as he preferred to call it. While he supported the creation of a caliphate, the barbarism of IS created a major PR problem, to put it mildly. The time would come soon enough, under the control of The Assembly, to rid the world of undesirables, to work toward the mandate of U.N. Agenda 21 to more than halve the world's population.

He initialed off on the brief and picked up the next item. A knock at his door caught his attention.

"Sir, I have one item that requires your immediate attention, and another that you might find of interest."

His secretary walked up to his desk and placed one piece of paper before him. He laid the papers in his hand back on the desk and picked up the single sheet. She turned and left the office as he began to scan the paper.

"FOR IMMEDIATE REVIEW—Armed protesters have taken over the buildings and property of the . . ."

He finished reading the short, but detailed, briefing. The FBI had already dispatched agents to contain the protesters while negotiating their surrender. They had learned from the 1985 MOVE bombing by Philadelphia police, Ruby Ridge in 1992, and the incident with the Branch Davidians near Waco a year later to take their time and try to end the standoff peacefully. IS had its PR issues; the FBI had its own.

Yet, he had a different concern. The group behind the protests persisted in bringing to light the government's continued "land grab," as they termed it, in the western states. They could not understand the need for sustainability of the world's natural resources. What they saw as a "land grab" was the government protecting the resources there. This, too, was well described in the Agenda 21 report. However, the U.N. and The Assembly needed to continue the implementation of Agenda 21 without public scrutiny. These self-branded patriots threatened that secrecy.

He would need to take time to mull over this turn of events. With luck, the protest would stall, the organizers could be prosecuted and jailed, and the public interest in their case would wane.

The Director stood and stretched. He walked to the windows of his office and looked out over the bleak adjacent garden as the gardeners made their final preparations for winter. Dead wood pruned. Seasonal plants removed. Mulch and weed preventer applied. Some saw only the starkness of winter coming, but the gardeners prepared for the emergence of new growth and the beauty of the coming spring.

He saw world events in the same light. While some saw their preparations for a new world order as dark and foreboding, he preferred to focus on the emergence of a beautiful new era for mankind—an era of enlightenment and humanity reaching new heights, a time for leaving behind the superstitions of religion and of man's fulfilling its evolutionary destiny.

He lifted the paper in his hand and flipped it over to read the FYI section. He smiled. *Finally, some good news,* he thought. The American Party had refused to move its headquarters to Washington, where the "movers and shakers" could begin to influence them, bring them into sync with reality. The party had, however, opened an office here. Karolus Karling, the previous director before his untimely and unexpected "suicide," had tried to blackmail Richard Nichols into working for them. That had failed. Yet, Nichols remained in their sights as the most easily influenced member of the party's upper echelon. Unlike Karling, he would not get directly involved. The Director would leave him in the capable hands of Maggie Walther.

Three

Lynch scanned the terrain and surroundings as he exited the SUV provided to them by their Oregon campaign headquarters. Three other men stepped out of the vehicle as well and took up positions around it. They each nodded to Lynch, who in turn nodded to Bradley Graham, the last to leave the vehicle.

Lynch had not been comfortable with the small security detail, but his boss had insisted upon it. So far, his boss's intuition seemed correct. There appeared to be no threat here.

As he looked about, though, it was the 'here' that troubled him most. The two-lane road disappeared before them down a broad valley between, well, between nothing. Lynch could just make out far distant mountains to his north, west, and south—perhaps the reason 'valley' was the term used by the locals for this area. But the immediate land was flatter than Kansas and drier than most of Texas. He had read that the semiarid terrain was that of a volcanic plain that received less than six inches of water a year. The place appeared so desolate he expected vultures to circle overhead while tumbleweeds the size of a school bus drifted across their path.

Barbed-wire fence rows stretched along the road with the occasional "No Trespassing—Private Property" sign tacked to one of the wooden posts. If something happened to them there, he would have no red-light or business security cameras to provide backup surveillance. Or worse—those barren plains could hide bodies where nothing but grazing cattle would ever stumble upon them.

On the positive side, the air was crisp and cleaner than he'd ever experienced. He'd only been in the area for 30 minutes but already knew he'd miss this air upon returning to the city, any city. And, in reflection, he realized they hadn't encountered a red light since landing. Another plus.

Still, to him, the area looked as if it were some giant volcanic caldera, and they were smack dab in the middle of it. The place was about to erupt. Just not in the sense of molten lava and pyroclastic flow.

He followed close on Graham's heels as they approached the roadblock. A stout man, maybe late thirties, stepped around the side of the barricade and took two steps toward them. His freshly pressed uniform identified him as the county sheriff.

Graham extended his hand. "Sheriff Wilde, I'm Bradley Graham."

The man shook his hand and nodded. "Yes, sir. I know who you are. Your campaign office notified me that you'd be coming, although I don't see how the Edmond case qualifies as a national campaign issue. We don't want a bunch of press and trouble here. In fact, lots of folks around here would prefer you head back to your campaign and not stir up any more problems."

"Sheriff, I can assure you the last thing we want is to

stir up trouble. The Edmonds asked me to come to their home to talk with them, not the other way around. As for the press, they'll be arriving by the busloads, but not because of me. And you already know that."

The sheriff glanced at the pavement, telling Lynch that he *did* already know that.

"Mebbe. We hope to get that under control before it becomes news. Folks around here just want to live their lives in peace . . . and quiet. You could help that and make my life easier by turning around and heading to wherever your next rally is scheduled."

Lynch saw something in his boss's eyes that he'd begun to see more frequently on the campaign trail— his displeasure with a public servant who looked out for himself rather than those people he was supposed to serve.

Graham didn't flinch. "Well, Sheriff, it won't be *me* making your life uneasy, unless you refuse to let us past this unlawful barrier of a public road. We have some of *your* constituents to visit and then I'll decide how much of a national campaign issue to make this. *Your* name could become a central one in the debate, or not. Up to you."

Wow. Lynch was impressed. Graham was usually laid back and easy to get along with. The man had steel in his voice this time. Lynch had a feeling the sheriff wouldn't know what hit him if Graham decided to take him to task publicly.

The sheriff said nothing, but Lynch could see the mental gears working to evaluate the risks of taking on a national candidate for president. Ten seconds later, those calculations ended, and the sheriff stepped back and waved to his two deputies to move the barricade.

"Thank you, Sheriff. Hope you have a quiet day." Graham turned on his heels and headed back to the SUV.

Lynch lingered to make sure the sheriff didn't have a change in heart, and then headed to the vehicle. Seconds later, they continued down that two-lane road and Lynch resumed marveling at the scenery, or rather, the lack thereof.

"Yes, sir. It appears they took control of the property on Sunday, three days ago, when the office was closed, and no one was around. They built barricades at the entrance and other obvious access points, and the local staff discovered them when they arrived for work Monday morning. The local authorities were called but were ineffective in removing them, so we were called yesterday afternoon."

Special Agent Art Tanner paced behind a row of cars, most without markings—but clearly shouting "Feds"—and a few marked "Sheriff Deputy." His week had promised to remain uneventful until these screwball protesters showed up. If they could convince them to leave, maybe he could get back to his routine in Bend, have dinner with his family, and sleep in his own bed.

Or maybe they'd be at home now had the staff called the FBI *first*. The protesters had taken over a federal facility, after all. Instead, they had called on their backwoods sheriff to deal with the problem. He could kind of see their position. The sheriff had been one of them, a BLM employee, until running for election. That didn't alter the fact that they had broken protocol by involving him.

He saw someone trying to skirt the police line with a camera. "One moment, sir," he said into his cell phone before placing it against his chest to muffle his yell. "Weaver! Get that screwball reporter over there! Get him back behind the line and beef up the cordon. We don't need someone setting off an incident here!"

He shook his head. Screwball protesters. Screwball press. Even a few screwball deputies he'd have to keep a close eye on. This was to be his word of the week—screwball.

He put the cell phone back to his ear. "Sorry, sir. Some guy with a camera broke through the police line."

"Do you have any idea what we're up against there?" asked the voice on the other end.

"Not yet, sir. There are two men at the entrance armed with hunting rifles. A handful of other men have been seen near the other access points, but we don't know for sure that they're armed. We can only assume so."

"That means at least 20 men. They can't guard the access routes 24/7 with fewer than that. What about food, communications? Have they made any demands yet?"

Tanner sighed. "Again, sir, we can only assume what they have. I can't imagine they'd do this without a stockpile of food and water. And no, no demands yet."

"Well, cut off their electricity."

Tanner wondered if he would soon have to add "screwball special-agent-in-charge" to his list. Did the guy think Tanner had just graduated from the academy?

"Already done, and the phone landlines have been intercepted so they only go to us. All roads into the area have roadblocks to screen people coming and going. Sir, we know how to do this."

"Get a drone in the air. Find out what we're up against."

Tanner shook his head. Yes, screwball S-A-I-C.

"Sir, we don't have a drone at the Bend satellite office. We're waiting on your guys in the Portland field office to send one. That's why I called, but they routed me to you. We were supposed to have that drone this morning."

"Oh. Okay. I'll make sure you get one. And I think I'll join you tomorrow. This may become more of an issue than we'd like to see. I got word that Bradley Graham, you know, the presidential candidate, is visiting the Edmonds. I wouldn't be surprised if he shows up on your doorstep, too."

"Yes, sir. I'll keep an eye out for him."

That was a given. He'd already received word that the screwball sheriff hadn't succeeded in turning the man back. Tanner took a deep breath and closed his eyes. *Great. Add a screwball politician to the mix. That's all we need.*

A half mile away, at a point overlooking the southern access point to the wildlife refuge's headquarters, the man felt his phone vibrating in his pocket. He rolled from his belly to his side to retrieve the device from the cargo pocket of his tactical pants. He glanced at the caller ID before answering.

"What?"

He kept his voice low but felt no need to whisper.

"Hey. Got word that we have a special visitor in the area. Bradley Graham, the American Party presidential candidate."

The man smirked. *Who cares?* he thought.

"He's visiting the Edmonds. Sheriff says *they* asked him to come."

The man saw no importance in this.

"So?"

"So, we might be tasked with a special mission. Be prepared."

The man frowned.

"What special mission?"

"Don't have a clear word on that yet. I was just informed to alert our group. But, if you ask me, I think they want him to disappear."

The man thought on that. Such a prominent "disappearance" could certainly aid their cause and guarantee front page headlines. But only on one condition. His disappearance from visiting that ranch wouldn't amount to much. To make it count, he'd have to vanish while visiting the protest.

"Think of the press coverage that would bring," the caller continued.

"Yeah, I see that, but only if he disappears while at the protest. You say he's visiting the Edmonds."

"Yeah. So, if he accepted *their* invitation, why wouldn't he accept one from the protest's leaders?"

Four

❦❖❖❦

"Dad, I'm gonna do it. I'm taking your advice, and I'm going to take the bull by the horns."

Silence dominated the other end of the phone.

"Seriously, Dad." Amy didn't know if she was trying to convince her father or herself. "I'm caught up at work and don't have any classes scheduled for over a week. I've cleared it with my boss, and I'm taking three days vacation to go to D.C. I've purchased my air ticket and reserved a rental car."

The silence persisted. Had they been disconnected? Was she talking to dead air?

"Dad?"

"Amy, I'm here. I guess I'm just shocked you're going to actually do something I suggested." He laughed.

That stopped Amy like a crash dummy hitting a cement barrier. Was she *that* strong-willed? Maybe. She tried to think of a rebuttal, but nothing flowed into her mind.

Her father continued. "I think the last time was when you agreed to summer college courses so you could graduate a semester early and save me some tuition money." His chuckling resumed.

"I'm not that bad. I listen to you." That came out too defensive.

"If you say so."

Now he was needling her—one of his favorite pastimes. He'd told her it was in the job description of being a dad.

"So, why a rental car? Can't Richard break away long enough to pick you up at the airport?"

"I don't know. I figured I'd surprise him."

The silence returned.

After a while, her father said, "You sure you want to do that? If he's as busy as he says, it might be you who gets surprised . . . and wastes a bunch of money on airfare and a car rental."

Amy had thought this through. She would need a rental car one way or the other because Richard would need his car for work and she didn't want to get stuck at a hotel depending on him for transportation. Besides, it would be a *good* surprise.

"I'm going to need a rental anyway, so why not surprise him? My flight gets in late afternoon, so I can be at his apartment as he gets home from work. He says he works from his place in the evenings. He told me he insisted on that with his bosses. Otherwise, he'd be at the office 20 hours a day."

She heard her father sigh.

"Okay. You'll do it your way no matter what I say, so be careful. D.C. traffic is a nightmare. Been there, driven it."

"I will. I'll let you know when I get home on Sunday."

* * *

"Thank you," said Bradley Graham, as he took another blueberry muffin offered to him by Mandy Edmond, Lacy Edmond's daughter-in-law. "These are delicious."

Lynch waved off what would have been his fourth muffin.

"So let me see if I'm getting this straight. This ranch was started in 1872 and remained in one family until you bought it in the early '60s. When you purchased it, you bought 6,000 acres, four grazing rights permits on public land, the house, and three water rights. Within ten years, the U.S. Fish and Wildlife Service, along with the Bureau of Land Management which was taking over from the wildlife service, cancelled 32 of 53 grazing permits with the reason that grazing was too detrimental to the environment even though grazing over the past hundred years hadn't caused the harm they alleged it would. This forced most of your neighbors out of business, leaving as their only recourse the selling of their land to the BLM. And at this point, your ranch is surrounded by the wildlife refuge and they want your land."

Lacy Edmond nodded. "In a nutshell, yes. All of that started after the geologic survey folks discovered evidence for oil and natural gas throughout the valley and uranium in our southern portion of the valley."

"And in addition to revoking the permits, they raised the fees for the remaining ones. That forced others out of business and some of those ranches still remained in the original families that settled them," added Mandy.

Graham took a sip of iced tea and looked contemplative. He rarely took notes, but this time he pulled a small notebook from his jacket pocket and jotted something into it.

"Tell me again about the water rights issue."

Lacy folded her hands in her lap and began to repeat that portion of her narrative. "This area in the 1870s had no water to speak of. The early settlers devised an amazing irrigation system from the mountains that brought water to the meadows and allowed farming and ranching. It also attracted migratory birds. There'd be no wildlife here without the man-made irrigation system. So—"

Mandy cut in. "So, when they cancelled the grazing permits, they also laid claim to the irrigation system and took control of it. They wanted the private lands on the Silvers Plain next to us, too, but no one would sell. So they diverted the water and flooded the plain. It doubled the size of Malheur Lake and washed away homes, barns. Folks there lost everything and the BLM bought them out for pennies on the dollar. Then, they re-diverted the water, the plain dried up, and they had the land.

"Mom, tell him about the land-use study you found."

Lacy stood up and began to pace about the room.

"By the mid-'90s we were one of the few remaining ranches. I found a study by the wildlife service, done in 1975, that showed their policies were failing. They insisted on a 'no use' policy where no activities were permitted within the refuge. And funny thing, the wildlife left, too. Private land like ours had four times more ducks and geese and the migratory birds were 13 times more likely to land on private property than on the refuge. We were a better refuge than they were and that pissed them off. After I brought that to their attention, the abuse and persecution really began."

"How so?"

"We filed a claim on an existing livestock water source and obtained a deed for that water right from the State of Oregon. When the bureau learned we had obtained a new water right near their refuge, they took us to court over it. Cost us a pretty penny, but we won in court."

Mandy stood and joined her mother-in-law. "So, being vindictive, in 1994, the bureau began building a fence to block us from our water. My father-in-law tried to stop the contractor from blocking our lawful water rights and the bureau had the local sheriff arrest him on two felony counts of disturbing and interfering with federal officials. He spent a night in the county jail, was taken to Portland where he spent another night in jail, and then appeared before a federal magistrate who released him without bail and never set a court date.

"Then they attempted to restrict our use of our own land. The upper portion of our property can only be accessed by a road that now goes through the refuge. They barricaded the road and threatened us if we used it. We removed the barricades and continued to use it because we have that right of access. It's a county road, a public road, and when we proved that to them, it riled them up even more and they revoked our upper grazing permit without cause or a court ruling. Oregon is a traditional fence out state. That means we have no obligation to keep our livestock fenced in or to control their movement. They found a federal judge who ruled that the federal government doesn't have to observe the Oregon fence out laws. So, we had a choice, fence in and maintain miles of fence, which would cut our ranch in half, or remove the cattle. We couldn't afford the fence, so we removed the cattle."

Graham stood up as well. "I see where this is going. They want your land so they keep attacking you. Now they've restricted your use of your own land and the ranch can no longer support the head of cattle you need to thrive. You're in financial hardship as a result."

Lacy nodded. "It was so bad, we had to sell our ranch and home so we could buy another property that had enough grass for our cattle. That property included two grazing rights. As soon as we closed on the property, those grazing permits were revoked."

Lynch shook his head. This simply wasn't right. The government wasn't supposed to fight its citizens and deny them their land or livelihoods. He stepped away from the window where he'd positioned himself.

"Excuse me for interrupting, but you said you sold your ranch. Isn't this your ranch?"

Mandy nodded. "The man who bought it died and his relatives traded us our original ranch for the one we'd bought. My husband and I live here and work it now, while Lacy and Lamont have a small house in town and help out."

"Boss, this isn't right. I thought we had a government of the people and *for* the people, not *against* the people."

Graham shook his head. "Wish that was the case today, but the elites in Washington want total control over our resources. It's part of their U.N. Agenda 21 goals. It's like the case of the guy in the next state over who got state permits to build a livestock pond for his small herd of cattle. He built a pond about two acres in size, used it for his cattle. Wild ducks and geese found their way to it. Fish flourished in it. And then the E.P.A. comes along and orders him to tear down his dam, claiming they held jurisdiction over *all* U.S. waterways. His pond was fed by a creek that anyone of us in this room could jump over and the E.P.A. claimed jurisdiction. The guy refused, obviously, and the E.P.A. began fining him to the tune of thousands of dollars a day. He wouldn't pay, so they took him to court. The court ruled in his favor and even made the agency pay his legal fees. That's what the current government is coming to and why we need major changes."

Lacy stepped closer. "Would you gentlemen like something to eat? We made sandwiches for everyone. There's plenty to go around."

Lynch was happy to see his boss nod his head. His stomach had begun to growl.

"I'll take food out to your men," said Mandy.

"Thank you," replied Lynch. He would have preferred eating with his guys, but Brad had requested he stay with him, as a witness to what was being said. They moved to the dining table where Lacy Edmond set out a spread worthy of working ranch hands.

After a blessing, they began to eat and Graham resumed his questions.

"So, what happened to get your husband and son in prison?"

Tears welled up in her eyes and she looked away to gain her composure.

"A . . . a little backstory first. The fall of 2001, my son

informed the fire department that he was going to do a prescribed burn. After he set it, it got out of control and burned just over 100 acres of grass on public land. We put it out. Nobody got upset. BLM said nothing. Prescribed burns were a standard practice and these things happen. Fast forward five years. Several lightning strikes on public land started fires that came together into a big fire that covered thousands of acres and threatened both our winter range and our home. Our son started a backfire on *our* property that worked. It saved our range, our home, and stopped the fire from burning more public land, too."

Lynch spoke up. "So, that was a good thing, right?"

She gazed at him. "You would think. My husband and son were arrested by the county sheriff and a BLM ranger on multiple state charges. The county district attorney reviewed everything and dropped all charges. Well, let me tell you, that didn't sit well with the BLM, but they couldn't do anything with the people who filled certain offices. The sheriff wouldn't file new charges, so they worked hard to get a new sheriff, the man you mentioned who stopped you on the road. He used to be a rangeland specialist with federal land management and was a witness against my husband on those state charges. About the same time, our joke of a president put an ex-hippie lawyer with no prosecutorial experience at all into the position of U.S. Attorney in Portland. Five years after that successful backfire, the new U.S. Attorney brought federal terrorist charges against my husband and son under the Federal Anti-terrorism Effective Death Penalty Act of 1996. Their mug shots were all over the press as arsonists, accused of starting the 2001 and 2006 fires. People we'd known for years shunned us."

Graham took a deep breath. Lynch could see his boss's anger trying to surface.

His boss took the story from there. "I think I remember the rest from news accounts. The judge thought the minimum five-year sentence was cruel and unusual punishment and overruled the minimum sentencing law. The judge retired immediately after the sentencing. Your husband and son served their time, were released, and then the refuge's manager appealed the sentence to the 9th District Federal Court and got a reversal, so your guys are back in prison."

"Yes, but the trial itself was a mockery of justice. The judge kept rushing it because he had to finish the case before he could retire. He gave the prosecutor six days to present and review their evidence. He gave our lawyer one day and prevented the testimonies and evidence that would have exonerated my husband and son. The court staff literally ushered us out the doors and brought in the cake to celebrate the judge's retirement."

Five

"What do you mean, you don't have a car available? Here's my reservation and confirmation number."

Amy's upbeat attitude dissolved.

"I'm so sorry, ma'am. We had a bad storm through here yesterday and lost a quarter of our fleet to hail damage. We're moving cars in from other locations, but they aren't here yet."

While upset, Amy couldn't get mad at them for something so out of their control. Yet, she didn't know how to proceed.

"So, do you have any suggestions?" She told him which hotel she had booked and where Richard's apartment was in Arlington.

A look of relief covered the rental agent's face and she smiled. "Well, you're in luck. That hotel offers a shuttle to and from the airport and we have a rental location less than a mile from there. *They* have vehicles available. I can have a car delivered to you at the hotel in an hour, hour and a half at the longest."

Amy felt the agent's relief flood across the counter to her.

"Thank you. Thank you so much. I'm here to surprise my fiancé and that will be perfect." She looked around trying to locate where to go for the shuttle.

The agent must have read her mind. "The shuttle is that direction . . ." She pointed to Amy's left. ". . . just outside the terminal. They run every twenty minutes this time of day. Oh, and you'll be able to turn the car back in here if you wish. Or at the other location and then use the hotel shuttle to get to the airport." She leaned toward Amy and lowered her voice. "If it was me, I'd choose the latter. Much easier and less time consuming."

Amy smiled. "Thanks." She grabbed her bags and papers and headed toward the shuttles.

Forty minutes later, Amy walked into the hotel, registered, and found her room. No sooner had she freshened up, the room's phone rang.

"Ms. Gibbs, a car rental agency is here with a car for you."

"Thanks. Be right down."

She pumped her fist once in the air. "Yes." She couldn't have timed it any better. She had asked God to prepare her path and open the doors she needed to walk through. He seemed to have answered that prayer.

Armed with her purse and her phone—containing Richard's address and Google Maps for GPS directions—she took charge of the car and headed into early evening Arlington traffic. After a couple of confusing instructions that had her turn the wrong way, she found the street where Richard's apartment was located. She slowed down to scrutinize the addresses.

Almost there, she thought. *Won't he be surprised?*

From the street numbers she calculated ahead to see which building it might be. As soon as she spotted it, she saw Richard on the front sidewalk talking with a woman. She couldn't see her face, but her hair was perfectly coiffed and her tailored suit spoke "money." Within seconds, both climbed into a Mercedes SUV and the woman, who was driving, pulled into the traffic lane right in front of Amy as if she hadn't seen her at all.

What the . . .? thought Amy. She decided to follow them and surprise Richard wherever they stopped.

After several minutes, it became obvious they were heading north. They meandered through an area marked North Arlington, slowing down but not stopping. They continued north and Amy saw signs for McLean.

McLean? Has Richard been recruited by the C.I.A.? She chuckled at the thought but then realized he'd be a perfect candidate. He'd already gone undercover to take down a human trafficker and rescue her.

Of course, he, and his escort, would have a lot to learn to become spooks. She had been on their tail for almost 30 minutes and they seemed to have no inkling they were being followed. She debated pulling up close and honking to catch his attention and get them to pull over, but her curiosity won out. They certainly seemed focused on residential areas. What was he up to?

Soon the homes they passed looked like those in St. Louis' more exclusive neighborhoods, like Ladue where Lynch had been a detective. Lynch would have noticed her car trailing him had he been that SUV's driver.

The lots increased in size commensurate with the homes sitting on them. They turned off onto a side street where the lots appeared to be one to two acres in size. The SUV pulled into the drive of a beautiful Georgian style home with a four-car garage and expert landscaping. The place had to be worth at least a million dollars. What was he doing here?

She decided to pull up short of the house and watch. Richard and the woman climbed out of the car and the woman began to point here and there. They hadn't gone ten feet from the SUV when someone down the street caught their attention. The woman waved back.

Amy's mouth dropped open. It was *her*. That drop-dead gorgeous, redheaded reporter who had been used in an attempt to ensnare Richard in a blackmail scheme against them both. The alleged proof—photos of some fictitious sexual affair between the two—had been the products of a Photoshop expert, but that didn't blot them from Amy's memory.

After a brief conversation, the redhead left the other two and the first woman escorted Richard into the house. Amy sat there, stunned. What was going on here? She had no suspicions of Richard cheating on her, but then, the spouse—or in her case, fiancée—was always the last to know. No. That simply wasn't Richard. He wouldn't cheat. He'd break things off if he was interested in the redhead now. Still. What was he doing in a house just doors away from that woman's apparent home? Was the first woman a work associate and all of this simply coincidence?

What was it her father always said? For a Christian, there is no such thing as coincidence.

Richard stood outside his apartment building awaiting the real estate agent. Maggie Walther had called saying she had the "deal of the decade" for him in upscale McLean. That would have been convenient to work, had he worked at the C.I.A. However, she assured him that even in rush hour—barring the unforeseeable accident—he was no more than 45 minutes away from the American Party's Arlington offices. With a little flexibility in his work hours, he could cut that time almost in half.

As she pulled to the curb, she exited her SUV looking excited.

"Ms. Walther, good evening. Thanks again for being flexible with your time."

They shook hands.

"Please, call me Maggie. I have a place you're going to love. Perfect for a family, a bargain in today's market, and an investment guaranteed to give you a great return when the nest is empty, and it's time to downsize. Ready?"

Richard nodded and climbed into the passenger's seat. She pulled away in a hurry and almost got hit by a car driving up the street.

"You said this place is in McLean. I've been thinking that I'm really looking for something with more of that urban-suburban feel. I was doing a little research, and North Arlington seems to be on the rise. I've driven around there a little, and I like the vibe there."

She nodded. "It certainly is one of the trendy spots to be these days. I'll drive through some of the nicer areas there, if you like. But I really want you to see this place in McLean. When I say it's the deal of the decade, I mean it."

"Well, from what I've read, isn't McLean out of my league? It's like the second most expensive zip code in northern Virginia."

"True, but North Arlington has moved into number five on that list. Trust me on this one."

They drove through several streets of nice, but older and smaller, homes. Many were being updated. He flinched at some of the price tags. *Three-quarters of a million for that?* he thought on more than one occasion.

As they left North Arlington, heading north, he used his phone to do some more research. She was right. The average home price in North Arlington was only $100,000 less than that of McLean. Now she had his interest.

They talked about real estate and current trends, the flavor of different neighborhoods, and more. He had been absorbed in their conversation when she suddenly pulled into a driveway. The home made his eyes bug out. It was magnificent. Needed a little maintenance and appeared as if no one currently lived there. The place had to be well out of his price range. But . . . she had said to trust her.

Outside the car, she began to point out aspects of the home's exterior and landscaping.

"Maggie! Richard! Hi there!"

Richard saw Maggie wave before he could turn toward the voice, a voice that seemed vaguely familiar. He blanched when he turned and saw who approached them. *Whoa. Good thing Amy's not with me,* he thought. *That would not go over well.*

"S-Summer," he said as she approached. "I didn't expect to see you here." That was an understatement.

"What? Maggie didn't mention I lived out here?"

Could she sense how uncomfortable this meeting made him?

"My house is three doors down, but I'm rarely there. Actually, I was supposed to be in Atlanta now, but that story got cancelled. I'm off to Detroit tomorrow for a story on the water conditions in Flint."

They chatted for a few minutes—a few too long in Richard's opinion. By the time she left, he had decided this would indeed have to be the deal of the decade, no, deal of the century, to make him buy a home so close to her. He wasn't comfortable with the idea and he knew Amy would want nothing—nada, zilch, zero—to do with a house near her.

"Come on. Let me show you the house."

Maggie ushered him into the home and his first impression was WOW. Now he knew he couldn't afford this place. Two-story entry foyer with a chandelier that probably cost more than his car. Living and dining rooms with raised ceilings and ornate crown moldings. A kitchen worthy of a Food Network celebrity. Private study. Wood paneled library. Fully built-out basement with game room, bar, media room, and more. Four bedrooms, each with separate bath.

Yes, this was way out of his league. What was Maggie thinking? Or smoking?

They returned to the foyer and Maggie turned to him in excitement.

"The bank, just this afternoon, dropped the price to, guess what?"

He stepped back and took a deep breath. "Gosh, I don't know. A million two."

Her eyes gleamed as she shook her head. "My friend at the bank has given me a two-day exclusive on this place before announcing the new price to the whole market. If you don't take it, I'll have it sold tomorrow morning. Guaranteed."

"A million even."

She laughed. "Maybe you should sit down on the steps." She waited as if expecting him to comply.

"Nine hundred fifty."

She shook her head again and used her thumb to indicate lower.

"Um, I haven't the foggiest idea." He realized, however, that her excitement was becoming contagious. Even at nine-hundred thousand, this place was a steal. And he'd have to take to stealing to afford it.

"It went on the market after foreclosure three years ago at a million nine. They dropped the price to a million five after twelve months. A year later, they went to a million one. Now, they're desperate to get this property off their books, so today they finally decided to drop it to what the previous owner still owed." She took a deep breath and looked as if she expected a drum roll. "Four hundred thousand." She clapped her hands and squirmed in excitement.

Richard thought he'd heard her say "Four hundred thousand." That couldn't be close.

"Four hundred-K? Is that what you said?"

Two thoughts rushed through his head. *What's wrong*

with it? And . . . for that price, I could live three doors down from Summer Stanton. She's never home anyway.

He sat down on a step. "What's wrong with it? Termites? I know the plumbing still works. Does the basement flood? What?"

"The house is in perfect order. Um, what you see is what you get."

There was more. He could see it in her eyes and hear it in her voice. There was something she wasn't disclosing.

"What's wrong with it? Why would a house like this sit empty for three years? What am I getting that I don't see?"

Her mouth twitched. He could see an intense mental battle underway.

"Well, I'm not required by law to disclose this, but does the name Eric Pearce mean anything to you?"

Of course the name Eric Pearce meant something to him. He was a high-ranking official with the Democratic National Committee. In charge of voter registration and their mailing lists. He'd also been rumored to have had information about a certain former first lady and Secretary of State. Before his suicide—alleged suicide—that is.

His alleged suicide . . .

Richard's gaze turned back and above him to the top of the beautiful, cherry wood curving staircase. He pointed to the top. Maggie nodded.

"Yes, I'm afraid this is, was, his house, where he, you know, met his demise. He was found hanging right here in the foyer."

"That's all? This place hasn't sold because of superstition?"

Maggie nodded. "But like I said, I have only one day before it goes on the multi-listing service with this price. If I don't sell it before noon tomorrow, it'll be sold by someone by dinner."

Richard's worldview held no room for ghosts or hauntings or superstitions about a home where a death occurred—suicide, murder, or otherwise. For a home this magnificent, at less than a quarter of its market value, he'd be a fool not to take it.

He debated about calling Amy to tell her about this deal. Yet, she was so practical-minded, she'd insist on wanting to see the place before making a decision. He saw little chance at convincing her over the phone. And the place would be sold before she could ever get here to see it.

No, he'd figure out a way to soothe over Amy about both the house and Summer Stanton living on the same street. If she absolutely refused, he could always flip it after living there awhile.

"Sold."

Richard and Maggie shook hands on the deal.

"Why don't we head back to my office and we can start on the paperwork?"

Richard nodded and followed her out the door. He practically skipped down the front walk, thinking of the great deal that had fallen into his lap. Amy was going to be impressed, minus, well, the part about a certain neighbor.

They talked as they walked toward her SUV. After they

turned a curve and passed by some tall shrubs, he saw her leaning against the SUV. His face went pale.

"May I help you?" asked Maggie.

"A-Amy. I-I wasn't expecting you. Um, wow, this is great." Then he wondered how. "How in the world did you find us here?"

She did not look pleased. Tears began to flow and they weren't of happiness.

"I could hear you talking as you came down the walk. You've agreed to buy this place, haven't you?"

"Amy, wait. When you hear about what a deal this place is, you'll understand why. And you'll love the house. It'll be great for our family. Let us show it to you."

She shook her head. "No, Richard, I won't live here."

He had never seen her so angry. Even the frustration he'd heard in her voice each time he'd told her he couldn't make it back to St. Louis for a visit didn't match what he heard now. Raw anger. Had she seen Summer Stanton? She must have. The only way she could have found him was to have followed them there.

"Did you see Summer Stanton? Is that it? I had no idea she lived on this street. Honest."

He noticed Maggie looking lost, but nodding her head in agreement to that statement.

"Yes, I saw her. But that isn't the problem."

He saw her beginning to tug at her engagement ring. No. Not that. Had he misjudged his plan all along?

"Richard, you won't even agree on a wedding date.

You know I don't want to leave my family behind in St. Louis. Yet, I was beginning to rethink that. But now? You're buying a house here without even discussing it with me? Don't you think I should be part of a major purchase like that? A new car? That's a nice surprise. A house in a town where I don't want to live? I-I . . ." She shook her head. "Richard, this isn't going to work."

He stood there, helpless, as she tossed her ring at him, turned, and ran for her car.

Six

After a tour of the ranch and additional discussions, Graham and Lynch expressed their thanks for the Edmonds' hospitality and headed towards town. With the high mountains to their west, sunset came early and the light quickly waned as they drove north.

Lynch leaned toward the driver. "Tony, head straight to the airport. I'll call ahead as soon as we have cell service again and have the pilots prepare the jet."

He felt a hand on his shoulder and turned to see his boss shaking his head.

"Find us rooms at one of the motels instead. I want to stay one more day and go out to this protest that's started at the refuge headquarters."

That was the last thing Lynch wanted to hear. And yet, it was so in character with his boss, he should have expected it and arranged for the rooms from the beginning . . . along with rooms for the Secret Service detachment they'd been able to ditch for this impromptu meeting with the Edmonds. His counterparts in the service were going to throw a tantrum when they learned of Graham's overnight plan to stay in an unsecured motel and then go to an even less secure protest in the middle of nowhere.

"Sir, I understand your desire, but is this really wise this close to the election?"

Graham looked thoughtful. "Wise in whose eyes? My campaign manager's or God's?"

Lynch knew he'd already lost this debate.

"The Secret Service is—"

"I know. They're already having conniptions over this trip. It was and remains the right thing to do. Washington is so out of touch with the people that they probably don't even know about this protest." Graham looked out the window for a second. "Take that back. They, somebody, probably knows. They don't care. Somebody has to show the people that we care."

Lynch took a deep breath and sighed.

Graham chuckled. "I heard that. On the way into town from the airport, I saw a little place. All American Inn, or something like that. Looked clean and easy enough to secure. Let's check there first. Once we have rooms, you can notify the Secret Service of the change."

"You just like to make sure I earn every dollar of my paycheck, don't you, sir?"

"Every penny."

Lynch saw Tony smile at that comment and faced their driver. "No comments from the peanut gallery."

Tony laughed and shook his head. "Not a peep out of me. No sir, Sir Lynch. Maybe we should call Sir Mack and get him out here, too."

Okay, now Lynch really needed to change the subject. He'd had enough teasing about being knighted by the new King of England. Even their boss would get in on that if he let it continue.

"So, what's your take on what's happened to the Edmonds, sir?"

"Well, *Sir* Lynch . . ." Mischief gleamed in Graham's eyes. ". . . The injustice done to this family is egregious at best. It demonstrates the worst behavior of a bureaucracy—one that becomes vindictive and reaches way beyond its authority. But it also shows the worst of our government in many ways not obvious."

Lynch furrowed his brow. He had done some research on the area. He had to in order to understand the lay of the land for security purposes. However, he hadn't really checked into the history of the area or other problems lying beneath the surface.

"How so?"

"Before 1870, when the white settlers began moving in, this whole region, almost a million and a half acres, was the unceded land of the Northern Paiute Indians. The tribes used the Malheur Lake area as a seasonal hunting range. In 1872, the government created an Indian reservation there, but the white settlers wanted more and more land, and the government kept reducing the size of the reservation to comply with those demands. In 1878, the Paiutes joined with the Bannock people and fought the U.S. military over the land. They lost. Remaining tribal members were interned on the Yakima Indian Reservation in Washington territory and the reservation was dissolved in 1879."

Lynch checked to see if he had cell service yet. His boss continued.

"For some reason, something political, in 1908

Teddy Roosevelt created a new Indian reservation around the lake. It was comprised of just over 80,000 acres. He also designated it as a natural habitat for wild birds, which now flocked to the area because of the irrigation system created by the whites. No Indians ever lived there. In time, the government took back the land and made it the wildlife refuge we see today. They've re-written the history a little, too. The official story now is that Roosevelt created the Malheur National Wildlife Refuge with no reference to it being listed as an Indian reservation in 1908." He paused. "Oh. And now, as they continue to buy up land from the whites, the refuge is over 180,000 acres."

Lynch thought about that for a moment, but it was Eric, sitting next to the boss, who spoke up.

"So, the land belonged to the Indians, but the government drove them off the land to give it to the whites. Then they gave some of the land back to the Indians, only to fight them and take it back. Then they gave some of it back again, but in name only. And they took that back, too. And now they keep taking it from the whites whose families have lived here since the government first gave it to them. No wonder folks around here have no love for the government."

Lynch nodded. "That's the story of the west. I read that the federal government now owns almost 30% of the nation's land, almost all of it focused in the states including and west of the Rockies. Something like 85% of Nevada is owned by the Feds. Over 50% of this state is, too."

"And that's why I want to go to this protest tomorrow. The guy heading it came from Nevada, where his own family had been involved in a big protest and battle with the Bureau of Land Management. I want to hear his, and the others', perspective on all of this."

Lynch understood his boss's desire and knew his heart for the people. But, this was not a good idea. Graham's Secret Service detail, men Lynch had personally vetted as well, was hundreds of miles away, angry at them, and Lynch had himself and three other men to protect their boss. Three *good* men, but still only three. How many protesters were there? Or, of greater concern, how many federal agents with ties to The Assembly were already there? He wondered how quickly they could get the team he trusted to join them . . . and whether or not he could convince Bradley Graham to wait for them.

Seven

Amy arrived home late that next morning, emotionally exhausted. True, she hadn't slept much that night, but the physical fatigue paled in comparison. Her mind had developed a looping replay of the events of the previous evening—pulling up to that home, watching Richard greet that redheaded reporter, waiting, overhearing Richard agree to buy the place, their argument, and her throwing the ring back to him.

Repeat.

Repeat again.

Still, something else bothered her. She had purchased a more expensive airline ticket that allowed her to change her flight at no additional cost. She never did that. Why? Had she subconsciously suspected something like this would happen?

Throw. The. Ring. Back.

Repeat.

Another why. Why had she thrown the ring at him? That was so out-of-character for her. Had her frustration with Richard grown to such a level that she vented by being melodramatic?

She needed a distraction. She had promised to let her

father know when she'd returned but knew that would not be the distraction she needed. She hesitated calling him because she didn't want to do yet one more replay. She also didn't want to turn her phone back on. She had turned it off as she climbed back into the rental car following the confrontation. Easier to avoid Richard than to prolong the discord on the phone.

She powered on her phone and watched as notification piled upon notification. Seven. Ten. Twelve missed calls. Six voice mail messages. All from Richard. She cleared her call log but decided to keep the messages. Perhaps after some time to filter and digest what happened, she would listen to them.

But would she call him back?

She dialed her father, hoping to get his voicemail.

"Hi there. How's D.C.?"

"Dad, I'm home. Told you I'd call when I got back."

An uncustomary silence replied. After several seconds, he said, "Ookaayy. Do I need to come over so we can talk about what happened?"

He knew her so well. In reflection, her father had been her closest friend and confidant throughout her life. It seemed strange for a daughter to say that her *father* was her confidant. Yet, ever since her mother died, he had been there for her. Through college and the occasional boyfriend. When she and Lynch had started to get serious, only for him to drop out of her life. And then when Lynch returned, only to disappear again, presumed dead. Richard's coming into her life. Her father hadn't hesitated in volunteering to help Richard rescue her when she'd been kidnapped by that human trafficker, Darko Komarčić. Guns blazing, if need be.

Yes, he knew her well. And she had grown to trust his advice. Maybe that was one of the reasons she found it so hard to leave St. Louis. He had already lost a son to the wars in the Middle East. She didn't want him ever to feel he had lost her, too.

"No, Dad. You don't need to come over." She went on to explain what had happened. Another replay, but one that somehow seemed cathartic. When she finished, she asked, "Dad, is it wrong for me to want to stay close to family?"

His answer wasn't immediate. In her mind she could see that contemplative look on his face that she'd seen so many times.

"Amy, I might not be the right one to answer that question. Is it *wrong*? Of course not. But in my day, a woman followed her husband wherever his job took him. Times are different. The man isn't the sole breadwinner anymore. So the real question you need to ask yourself isn't about family. It seems to me that you really need to decide how you feel about Richard."

As usual, he went to the crux of the matter. Was Richard the right one for her? Her father had told her numerous times that love wasn't an emotion. Love was an action. She had to *choose* to love. And if she was going to make that commitment, her actions would have to follow. Was Richard someone she could make that pledge to? Even if it meant leaving family behind?

At one time she had thought so. Now? Could she make that obligation to someone who wasn't willing to make it to her?

"You're right, Dad. As usual. I've got some real soul

searching to do and a decision to make."

"Look, sweetie, I know it's hard. And right now I'm afraid I need to muddy the waters even more. Richard's a great guy and I'm convinced he has your best interests at heart, that he loves you. He probably sees this house in two ways—as a great home for the family he wants and as a good investment. From what you overheard, it sounds like a fantastic deal. And yet, you're right, too. This was not a decision he should have made on his own. But here is where I'm really going to stir things up. I don't think you're over Lynch yet."

"What do you mean you're calling in sick? You can't call in sick. Even if you're dead we need you here."

Richard wasn't in the mood for his boss's humor. "You sound like a Democrat registering voters, Ben." He paced around his apartment floor. "Look, I can work from home, but I'm not up to coming in."

Ben Manning had been asked to become the new chairman of the American Party after an explosion at the party's St. Louis headquarters had killed Dominick Standish, his predecessor, and others. However, he had opted to become the party's communications director, a job Dominick had attempted to fill as well, before the party had grown to its present size and status. Whereas Dom had given his employees more leeway on work schedules and placed great value on family matters, Ben was stricter and more demanding of his employees' time. To Ben's credit, they were in that part of the political season that demanded their full attention. The vote was just weeks away and Bradley Graham was the first third-party candidate to have a serious chance at winning.

Richard knew there was no way he could go to St. Louis at that moment, so his hope was pinned to working from home. Unlike at the office, at home he could focus on contacting Amy. If only they could talk, he knew he could convince her that he'd been thinking of *them* when he decided to house hunt. He admitted to himself that he'd blown it in how he'd communicated his plans to her. And yes, she was right. Buying a house should have been a joint effort and decision.

Still, that house in McLean was a deal he wasn't going to pass up. He could rent it out, should Amy not like it and agree to live there. He'd already signed the papers, arranged the financing, and made plans to move in at the end of the month.

"Just come in late. But come in."

"Ben. I'll be there tomorrow and I'll monitor things from here today, just like I do in the evenings."

He heard Ben's frustration through the phone. The man knew Richard's skills were in demand and that he'd received offers elsewhere at a considerable pay increase. Richard didn't intend to hold that leverage over Ben's head. He believed in what the party was trying to accomplish and in its platform. He liked his work.

However, dragging into work after a sleepless night would do him—and them—no good. If he hoped to make it through the day, he needed the calmer environment of home to do so. And if he hoped to make it through the weekend without emotionally crashing, he needed to talk with Amy.

Sooner, not later.

"Okay, okay. If I need something urgent, I'll call."

"Sure, Ben," Richard answered while thinking, *You'll get my voicemail if I'm on the phone with Amy.*

Richard checked his watch. Of course, he had to assume she'd left for home. He'd called every major hotel in the area and no one had her registered as a guest. There was a remote chance she was still in northern Virginia in a motel he might have missed. *Yeah, as remote as my voting for either major party candidate in November,* he thought. So, he had taken the next step and had already checked all airline schedules with flights to St. Louis. There was a great chance she was in the air right now. But maybe not.

He dialed and the call went straight to her voicemail. Again. That was his twelfth call since he'd parted with Maggie Walther the previous evening.

"Amy, please call me back. We need to talk this over. I've already said I'm sorry in several previous messages. Please. Call me."

Amy declined her father's invitation to lunch, and to dinner, and to breakfast the next morning. She had always admired his persistence. Not so much this time, as she had to cut him off before he suggested the next day's lunch.

She wanted to be alone, to think and to pray. She needed that. She also turned her phone off again, after alerting her father that she was planning to do so. She didn't want him to worry. For that alone time, she turned to a place she had used many times before, the August A. Busch Conservation Area, just fifteen minutes from her home.

The nearly 7,000-acre area held over two dozen small lakes for fishing, trails for hiking through grasslands or its 3,000 acres of forest, and areas for hunting or simply viewing the wildlife there. She had first visited Busch Wildlife, as locals called it, while visiting St. Louis with her family. They had hunted butterflies and explored the shores of a few lakes. When her father left the Army and settled in St. Louis, she would come "home" from college and often find herself walking a trail, picnicking with friends, or fishing one of the lakes with a wannabe boyfriend. With their renovated facilities, she now used the shooting range to keep up her pistol skills, particularly after her home had been invaded.

Stepping out of her car, the smell of autumn greeted her amid the glory of rust, gold, and crimson leaves. The seasonal color had reached its peak and bright sunshine promised to accentuate those hues. Unusually warm weather would make this day outdoors even more pleasant.

The Busch Hiking Trail meandered for three miles through grassland and forest. She often walked the trail at a pace meant for exercise. Today, she wanted to savor the forest and its autumn beauty. She wanted to quiet her mind and let the still, small voice of God come through. The rustle of fallen leaves as she walked blended with that of the breeze easing through the treetops and of squirrels scampering across the ground. She stopped to watch several furry-tailed rodents as they searched for food and chased each other. She was in no rush.

As she resumed her hike, she turned her face toward the sky, and said, "Lord, I'm at a total loss on how to proceed. I really need your guidance." She thought about what her father had said. Was it Richard? Was he not the man she had hoped he'd be? Or did she have unresolved feelings for Lynch that now kept her from moving forward with her life? "Lord, you know my heart, my thoughts, my needs. I'm asking for clarity. I—"

Absorbed by her thoughts, she had stepped into a spot where a service road crossed the trail and was almost run down by a young, black man carrying a large backpack. He pushed her aside as he passed.

She turned toward him. "I'm sorry. I didn't . . ."

The man hurried away, ignoring her. He gave no sign of acknowledging her.

She shook her head and watched him rush along the trail. She had planned on going that way, but now had reservations about doing so. Yet, to continue on her current path would lead to meeting up with him again since the trail at this point formed a loop. She had the choice of meeting him head-on or following him. The former option held a 100% chance of their passing again, while the latter held a near zero percent chance, unless he doubled back.

She decided to go with her original plan and wandered down the path in the direction of following the guy, hoping not to run into him again. Soon, she was once more lost in thought.

This portion of the trail followed a ridge overlooking the area's largest lake, designated Lake 33.

She only caught glimpses of the water, though, as the trees had yet to drop enough leaves to open up that view.

On her right, she passed several of the old ammunition bunkers. In preparation for World War II, the U.S. Department of the Army had purchased over 17,000 acres of land here and contracted the production of trinitrotoluene, or TNT, to the Atlas Powder Company. One hundred storage bunkers had been built into the hillsides, along with roads and buildings. All of those bunkers remained within the conservation area, with most having had their massive steel doors welded shut.

Bunker 65 was one of her favorite "thinking" spots, as its concrete loading dock looked out over the lake. She could sit there and ponder her situation for hours without being disturbed. Today, she found that she had an open view of the lake from that perch, and she watched several fishermen working its waters as she again tried to gain insight into her current dilemma. She silently prayed once more for guidance.

However, it didn't take long for her reverie to be disturbed again. Voices. Two, maybe three, men arguing further along the trail. Another bunker, number 64, sat in that direction. Yet, what caught her attention was that the argument was not in English, nor in Spanish, which she also understood. Mostly. It sounded like . . . what? Not Arabic. Not Slavic. She admitted to herself that she was no expert in foreign languages.

The sound level waned but did not disappear completely. A few minutes later, the volume returned. The last time Amy had been to Bunker 64, it appeared to be used for storage. Two large fuel oil tanks stood outside with lines running into the concrete face of the bunker. The door had been secured with a lock but was not among those that had been welded to keep people out.

She sat overlooking the lake and tried to return her focus to Richard . . . and Lynch. Her effort was unsuccessful and curiosity won out.

She scooted off the edge of the loading dock and began to ease her way toward the next bunker. She remained vigilant. The last thing she wanted was to be surprised by someone jumping out of the bushes at her. She also put her hand into her back pocket and pressed the power button on her phone. Once the tones that signaled her phone was active ended, she moved more confidently toward the sound of the voices.

As she neared Bunker 64, she saw them. Two men. She disliked the idea of racial profiling, yet she couldn't deny that they looked African. Not African-American, African. They suddenly stopped talking and looked about. Had they seen or heard her? A minute later, the argument resumed.

Amy pulled her phone from her pocket and called up the digital recorder app. On MedAir calls she had frequently used the app to record quick notes on her patients. Now, she used it to record the argument. The phone's video recorder would have been a better choice, but she couldn't get a clear shot of the duo without risking exposing her presence to them.

Movement near the bunker caught her attention. A third man was shimmying out of a rectangular opening below and to the left of the main door. She had forgotten about this opening. In the past it had been covered with plywood. Now it acted as an open window into the lower part of the bunker.

The man stood up and brushed himself off. She couldn't see his face, but by his clothing, she knew it was the guy who had nearly knocked her over on the path earlier. He wore the same gray jacket with a thin maroon stripe running across both shoulders and down both arms. She desperately wanted to get clear pictures of this trio but saw no vantage point where she could do so and remain hidden. As the man turned, she realized he had no backpack.

The man calmed down the other two who seemed to recognize him as a leader. As one of the two men began to speak, a single word from the third shut him up. Yes. He clearly appeared to be the leader.

The three men rushed off down the trail away from her, and she sighed in relief that they had chosen that direction. Having looked about, she realized she would have had no place to hide had they come her way.

No longer able to see or hear the men, she eased her way toward the front of Bunker 64. The man's backpack was nowhere to be seen. That meant one thing. He had left it behind . . . inside. Did she dare?

She walked over to the rectangular opening and squatted in front of it. She could see nothing but scrap heating ducts and pipes. She stepped back and looked in the direction the men had taken. No sign of movement. No voices.

She quickly moved to the opening and worked her way inside. Using the flashlight on her phone, she found her way between old ductwork and into the main room of the bunker. She'd been in a couple of these bunkers as a teen.

After all, what teen could resist? This one was no different than she recalled. The arched ceiling peaked at what looked to be twelve to fifteen feet high and the room was roughly twenty feet wide. The bunkers extended thirty to forty feet into the hillside. This one seemed on the shorter side.

As she scanned the room with her light, she saw sheet metal ductwork. She worked her way past one pile of such and then she saw it. The man's backpack. But not just one backpack. There were at least a dozen.

She opened the closest sack, the one she had seen the man carrying earlier. Inside were dozens of cheap cell phones. A second pack contained the same. The third pack, however, caused her heart to accelerate.

Rectangular packs of a doughy-looking material wrapped in heavy plastic. A faint almond odor reached her nostrils. Explosives?

She prepared to open a fourth bag when she heard voices. The men were back.

She closed the bags she had opened, hoping they would appear as they had been when she found them. She looked about, frantic. The voices were louder. One or more of the men was about to climb through the opening. She had no way to get out.

She ran to the nearest pile of ductwork. On the bottom was a large duct, big enough to accommodate her and long enough to hide her five-foot, eleven-inch frame. She cringed at the sight of dense spider webs near the opening. The thought, *brown recluse spider heaven,* went through her mind as she turned out her light and slid into the duct as silently as she knew how.

Eight

"Sir, we need to wait for more men. There are just four of us to watch you and we don't know what we'll be facing at that refuge."

Lynch tried to keep the tone of his voice neutral, but heard a tint of pleading color his statement.

"Lynch, I understand your concern, but we need to do this and get back to the campaign." Brad Graham took another sip of coffee and glanced toward the window of the motel room. "You know you snore, don't you? Remind me not to bunk with you again." He laughed.

Lynch shook his head. "Then we make quite the chorus, boss. You can rattle the windows, too." He eased back the curtain of the window and saw Tony standing dutifully outside. "Besides, we had no choice. They only had two rooms. And you're changing the subject."

"Let's get breakfast and head south to the refuge."

Lynch knew this was Brad's way of avoiding confrontation when his mind was set. He decided to give it one more stab anyway.

"I talked with your Secret Service team leader while you were in the shower. They can be here this afternoon if we send the jet back for them. Then we can still head to the refuge before dark and fly on to Dallas to meet up with the campaign this evening. It really won't be much of a delay."

Brad took another sip. Was he actually considering Lynch's request?

"That won't work. I'm supposed to attend a dinner with two Texas congressmen. That means wheels up and in the air right after lunch. I can only do that if we go to the refuge this morning." He grinned at Lynch. "Stop worrying. These folks know I'm on their side. Nothing's going to happen."

Lynch wished he felt reassured, but he didn't.

"Oh, and call Michael to see if he can get to Dallas in time to meet the congressmen if we can't."

That definitely didn't bolster Lynch's assurance. Michael Goodwell, their vice-presidential candidate, was a good man—a man whom Lynch personally felt could step into Graham's shoes if unforeseeable tragedy should occur. He was in New Orleans and could get to Dallas without difficulty. Lynch hoped that would not be necessary and that his boss's statement would hold true.

Brad stood up and set his mug on the table under the window. "C'mon. Roust the troops and let's go."

Their meals consisted of fast-food breakfast fare en route to the wildlife refuge. Lynch had that déjà vu feeling as they again traveled the route they had taken the day before. This time there was no roadblock by the sheriff. However, half an hour north of the Edmond Ranch, at the turnoff to the wildlife refuge headquarters, they encountered an army of reporters, remote transmission news vans, and twice that number of law enforcement officers.

Tony pulled the SUV to the side of the road behind a news van out of Portland. Lynch and his three men exited the car and surveyed the area. So far, so good.

"Okay, boss," said Lynch through the remaining open door.

Graham left the car and the group moved no more than twenty feet toward the police barricade before he was recognized. A murmur of recognition ran through the crowd and a dozen reporters swept across the grass to surround them.

"Mr. Graham—"

"Mr. Graham, what—"

"Tell us why you're—"

The cacophony of voices persisted despite Graham's attempt to quiet them with raised hands. "I have—" His voice became part of the collective noise, unable to rise over that of the reporters.

Lynch felt his heart accelerate. He saw his men scrutinizing those closest to their boss, as well as others within shooting distance. He, too, looked beyond the cameras and voice recorders for telltale signs of a weapon. All he saw were tools of the media trade. When he noticed Graham trying to respond without success, he put two fingers to his mouth and released a loud, shrill whistle. The noise abated.

"Thanks, Lynch." Graham looked toward the mass of journalists blocking his route. "Folks, I have nothing to say at the moment. We just got here. But, if you'll bear with me, I'll speak after I've talked with the protesters. It's my desire to help end this standoff." He tried to step ahead, but his men could not move. "Folks, please, let us through."

A handful of reporters stepped aside, and Lynch and his men moved forward with their charge. They stopped at the police barricade where he saw the sheriff off to their right. The man hadn't seen them yet. A man in an FBI jacket walked up to them.

"Sorry, fellas, but no one is allowed through."

Graham stepped up. "Who's the agent in charge here? Would you please let him know Bradley Graham is here and wishes to talk with the protest leaders? If possible. Thanks."

The agent reached toward Graham, and Lynch reacted by stepping between them until he realized the man simply wished to shake hands.

"A pleasure to meet you, Mr. Graham. You've got my vote." He said the last part in a near whisper.

Graham responded by shaking the man's hand. "Thanks. Hope you guys aren't running into trouble here."

The man shook his head. "Not so far. I'll find Special Agent Tanner."

Lynch watched the agent move off and followed his progress. He stopped about a hundred feet away at a cluster of other men and one woman, all wearing FBI jackets. The man pointed their way, and Lynch watched one man look to the sky and shake his head. That would be Tanner. No doubt their presence here had just "made his day." Lynch understood the sentiment. He'd been in the man's position more than once, back when he'd been a police officer.

Tanner put one hand on the back of his neck,

rubbing it, while lifting a cell phone to his ear with the other. Just who was he calling? Higher ups for instruction on how to handle a prominent politician wanting to butt his head into the mess here? The thought that he might be contacting a handler within The Assembly crossed his mind, but unless every agent within that cluster was in cahoots with them, that wouldn't be the case. Still, Lynch made a mental note to put his "spidey sense" on high alert.

Tanner lowered the phone and walked toward them. He extended a hand in greeting.

"Mr. Graham, I'm Special-Agent-in-Charge Art Tanner. I understand you'd like to talk with protest leaders, but we aren't allowing anyone into the compound."

"Special Agent Tanner, I understand. I'm hoping to help defuse this situation, maybe even help bring the protest to an end. I'm not here to add to the trouble. How can I help you?"

Lynch gave a subtle nod. He hadn't expected that angle from his boss and yet recognized that it was so in character with the man. Obviously, that approach caught the agent by surprise, too. His face reflected some serious consideration.

"Sir, I appreciate your offer, but we definitely won't allow someone in there without an invitation from inside. Someone just walking down the road might find himself surprised, and not in a good way."

At that moment, another agent—the woman from the cluster Lynch had observed—walked up to Tanner and handed him a note. He read it and looked up at Graham. Then he read the note again and gave a subtle shake of his head.

"Well, guess you got the right connections. You just got

that invitation."

Lynch felt as if they were leading actors in a TV show. Only on TV did DNA results come back within hours, facial recognition receive a hit within minutes, or the right connection come at the right time. But then he realized that for Christians, all things were possible through Christ. God was directing this show.

Lynch glanced down the road to the refuge and spotted an older sedan coming their way. If that was their transportation, they were right on cue.

Two younger men climbed out of the car. The passenger stood next to his door with some kind of rifle in hand. Lynch couldn't make out what it was but guessed it to be some type of hunting rifle with a larger bore than an AR-15-style rifle. The driver walked to the back of the car, leaned his butt against the trunk, and folded his arms across his chest. An agent walked toward him but stopped about ten yards from the man. A few words were said, but they were too far away for Lynch to make out the conversation. The agent started to walk toward them, pointing to Graham and nodding.

"Looks like your ride is here, Mr. Graham," said Special Agent Tanner.

The agent who had talked with the driver came up to them.

"Mr. Graham, you're welcome to meet with the people holed up in there and you can take one man with you. Just one."

"No way," protested Lynch. "My whole team goes."

The agent gave him a look of understanding. "I already made it clear that you would not be comfortable with that, but they insisted. Their terms, or go home, was the gist of their answer."

Graham put his hand on Lynch's shoulder. "We'll be fine, Lynch. You and me, let's go."

Lynch scanned the faces of his team. To a man, they remained calm, professional. But Lynch knew their minds. FBI, local law enforcement, even National Guard, would not keep them out should things go sour.

"My weapon?" asked Lynch.

"They didn't say you had to go in unarmed."

Lynch made sure his handgun was in reach, but concealed.

"I don't like this, but let's get this over with, boss."

Graham took the first step toward the car and a minute later, they stood next to the driver. The man looked at Lynch.

"Armed?"

Lynch nodded and pointed to his gun, although it remained hidden under jacket.

"Okay. We're trusting you as a sign of good faith. But you will be watched . . . closely. Climb in."

Lynch and Graham sat in the back seat and the driver took to the wheel. Two minutes later, the car pulled up to the front of the refuge's headquarters building. No one stood there to greet them. Their escorts led them to the front door and opened it for them. Inside, Lynch noted four men of which one half-stood, half-sat on the edge of a desk. The man looked upset as he watched them enter. Lynch recognized that man as the leader of the protest, Simon Slattery.

"Who are you? What are you doing here?" The three

men with him stood, and the tension in the man's voice emanated across the room, putting Lynch on edge.

"Mr. Slattery, I'm Bradley Graham. This is my security chief, Lynch Cully." Graham extended his hand, but the gesture was not returned.

"Yeah, I recognize you now. How'd you get in here?"

Lynch scanned the room. One short hallway, two closed doors. Four men inside, two immediately outside—that he knew of. He could feel the adrenalin take command of his body. He did not like this turn of events. It became obvious that they had not been invited after all.

"I was asked by Lacy Edmond to visit and talk with her, which I did yesterday. While I was here I hoped to talk with you as well. The FBI wouldn't let us in at first, but then someone sent out an invitation and car for us."

Slattery looked about at the other men. "Any of you know anything about this?" They all shook their heads, denying involvement.

Lynch eased closer to Graham. "Boss, I don't like this. We need to go."

Slattery must have overheard because he raised his hand and said, "Please stay. I don't know who set this in motion, but if you came to talk, let's talk. Fellas, give Mr. Graham a chair. Sam, you and Jim go see if you can find out who sent that invitation out to the Feds. Thanks." As these men left the building, he looked directly at Lynch. "I'd offer you a chair, too, but I know you won't sit. Make yourself at home, best you can."

Lynch found a spot where he could watch every

door and the hallway, and leaned against the wall. Nope. He did not like the scenario they'd fallen into at all, but so far there had been no sign of danger. He watched carefully as Slattery grabbed a carafe of coffee and poured two mugs. He handed one to Graham and offered one to Lynch. The other remaining man already had coffee.

"Thanks, but I'm good."

Slattery lifted the mug to his lips and took a drink. Lynch could see that it was meant as a way of assuring Lynch no one had slipped poison into the drink. Not that such a move had been of concern to Lynch. The brew smelled good and he would have liked a mug, but he needed to keep his hands free.

Slattery pointed to the remaining man with him. "This here's Rory Grayson. He's from southern Idaho and he's had his share of problems with the BLM, too."

Grayson extended his hand to Graham. "An honor, sir. Love the way your campaign has shaken up the elites in Washington."

The men sat down while Lynch remained on guard. He glanced outside the windows but saw no activity. That was the hardest part about anticipating the unexpected . . . it was, by definition, unexpected.

The men talked, Graham asked pointed questions, and to Lynch, the discussion was pretty much a rehash of what he'd heard at the Edmond Ranch. Grayson's story added a new touch. He'd been granted logging rights to section within a national forest and had hired men and leased equipment to do the work, only to have the rights taken away at the last minute. A handful of environmental types had protested that a certain owl had not been seen in that section of forest in five years and that logging would disturb its habitat. Lynch shook his head at that one. If the bird hadn't been in that area for at least five years, how would logging *now* disturb its habitat? Either something else had already disturbed it or the owl didn't want to inhabit there to begin with. Typical ass-backward Washington logic.

After nearly an hour of discussion and three mugs of coffee, Graham stood up and stretched. "Simon, where would I find a bathroom? All that coffee has worked its way south."

Slattery smiled. "Normally, I'd say any tree outdoors would work, but we do have ladies present in our ragtag company. There's a latrine outside and to the left. Nothing in the building here."

Graham nodded. Lynch took point, heading out the door first. He waved for his boss to follow and together they made their way toward the latrine building.

"You about finished here, boss?"

"I think so, Lynch. Another enlightening discussion about our government's war, you might call it, against its own citizens. It's easy to see why so many people in the western states resent Washington."

"Yes, sir. I'm seeing that, too."

Lynch checked out the small building with its two stalls. There was electric heat, but it was still just a glorified outhouse. No one inside. The immediate area was empty.

"I'm going to make use of the facility, too, sir."

"Meet you back outside." Graham said before entering one stall.

Lynch attempted to empty his bladder quickly, to beat Graham outside, but he heard the other stall door open and close before he finished. *He had three cups of coffee*, he thought. *How could he finish so fast?* He zipped, adjusted his clothing, and rushed out. He didn't like that Graham was outside unaccompanied.

As he went through the door, he saw no one there. Where was Graham? Then, as the door closed, he saw him. The door had blocked his view. Graham was limp, being dragged off by two men toward a pickup truck. As he reached for his gun, he felt the barbs enter his skin and the electric jolt of the Taser® pulse through his body. He fell to the ground, his mind alert and his eyes watching his charge being carted away, but his muscles would not—could not—respond to his brain.

The Director began to fidget in his chair. Everyone assumed he was the "most powerful man on earth," but he had gained that title in truth only upon assuming the directorship of the world's shadow government, The Assembly. Still, power or not, he sat through another security briefing as his mind wandered to events playing out in Oregon. He wanted more details, a play-by-play description of what he envisioned to be happening there. Yet, he wasn't getting that.

The Assembly had the most advanced communications and intelligence array in the world—much of it piggybacking off the intelligence communities of every government. His predecessor had instant access to that information. As the new director, he did not . . . and would not until he left his very public position the following January, after the inauguration of his own predecessor. She would make sure his legacy—The Assembly's legacy—would continue in bringing down the U.S. and in making it an average player on a leveled global field. No more superpowers—other than The Assembly itself.

However, one Bradley Graham, the unexpected superstar of the conservative movement, had become increasingly troublesome. The progressive Republican candidate now languished like some third-party candidate of old. The American Party rose from the ashes of obscurity like a political Phoenix because of the message of Christian conservatism being promoted by their candidate Graham. The mainstream press continued to push the Democratic candidate as the heir apparent in Washington, but revelations about her past now tarnished the brass ring they thought was so easily within her grasp. Instead, every revolution of the election merry-go-round brought Graham's brightly painted horse closer to letting him grab that prize.

Until now. The Fates, those white-robed incarnations of destiny, had smiled upon them. Graham had taken the bait to talk with those thugs in Oregon. If all went as planned, he would, in time, meet his demise there and the protesters would be blamed—the proverbial killing of two birds with one stone.

But right now, the "most powerful man on earth" couldn't get the latest details on the implementation of that plan. He had no clue as to what was happening on the other side of the country.

Nine

As Richard paced his small apartment, his thoughts wandered from Amy to his job and back to her, over and over. As far as work was concerned, the campaign's social media numbers continued to climb and he'd had no fires to put out, so his boss left him alone and stopped calling to entice him into the office.

His hourly attempts to reach her by phone all went straight to voicemail. That meant she had her phone turned off. Why wouldn't she talk with him? It wasn't like her to simply skirt an issue, or to avoid him. She had never backed away when he called to tell her he couldn't come to St. Louis as planned, which he now realized was more often than not. All he could conclude was that she was really mad—truly, unarguably, genuinely angry with him . . . and that she meant what she said, that it was over.

He just didn't want to accept the finality of that.

His phone rang on the table. *Amy?*

He rushed across the room to pick it up. His hope deflated as he recognized the local number.

"Hi, Maggie. What's up? I didn't expect to hear from you so soon."

This call was unexpected. He had signed the bid papers and completed the loan application the night before, but

Maggie would not have been able to offer them to the bank until that morning when the bank opened, maybe four hours ago at the earliest.

"Richard, good afternoon. And it *is* a good one. For you anyway."

That sounded uplifting.

"It is?"

"Yes, it is. I don't know who you know who could pull the strings you've managed to pull, but not only was your bid accepted, your loan was approved. I don't think I've ever had this happen in only three hours. You must have some influential friends."

Richard looked askance. He had no friends here at all, much less influential ones. Did Ben Manning know people who would have stepped to the plate for him? Richard made a mental note to ask.

"None that I can think of. You know I just moved here several months ago."

"Well, sometimes political winds bring good sailing. Whatever. You just sailed into one heck of a great deal. In fact, they've already sent me paperwork for you by courier. Once you sign off, we can close and you have yourself one beautiful home. Since it's empty, you could move in by the end of the week if you wanted to."

He realized his days of apartment living were about to end and he glanced about the room. This *was* a good day. If only he could talk with Amy, smooth things over with her. Then it would become a *great* day.

"Well, I have you to thank, Maggie. You gave me favor when you brought that house to my attention.

You could have offered it to other clients."

He sensed hesitation on the other end of the line. Maybe she *had* offered it to others. If so, why did they turn it down? Simple superstition?

"Richard, you happened to be at the right place at the right time. We were scheduled to look at houses and that price change came through shortly before I picked you up."

"Still, you didn't have to show it to me first."

Hesitation again. There was something she wasn't saying, but he decided to ignore it. He would soon own a fabulous home in a prestigious neighborhood.

They settled on a time for him to sign the paperwork and said goodbye. His first instinct was to call Amy and tell her the good news. That, on second thought, was not a good idea. Yet, he dialed her number one more time. And went to voicemail immediately one more time. He chose not to leave a message.

Amy lay as still as she could inside that dirty, rusty, and web-filled duct. Her thoughts went to Edgar Allen Poe's story, *The Telltale Heart*. Was the thumping of her heart audible, amplified by being cramped into that enclosure and the sheet metal acting as a speaker? The man was sure to hear it, and if not that, her breathing.

Aaargh! What had she been thinking? Why had she let her curiosity win out? Were these men terrorists? They had to be. Cell phones and plastic explosives. Who else would make use of those two items?

And if they discovered her, what then? Would they kill her and stuff her body back into this duct, never to be found until someone decided to clean out the bunker?

She felt a sense of panic. Was she far enough into the duct to be hidden? She used her feet to push forward a few more inches, but her hands now felt squeezed into a smaller space. The duct ahead of her had narrowed. She could go no further. This would have to do.

She closed her eyes and focused on her breathing. Normal, easy breaths. She tried to calm herself. *Happy thoughts, think happy thoughts.*

From the noise, she determined that two of the men were climbing up from the lower level to where she hid. Her heart raced. They talked in a language she did not understand. Could they hear her?

One or both seemed to walk past the duct toward their cache. From the sounds penetrating her hiding place, someone was rustling through one of the backpacks. A moment later, she heard the jingle of keys and a chuckle from one of the men.

Was that all? The guy had left his keys in the backpack? His car keys perhaps. She resisted letting out a sigh of relief, but a sense of calm engulfed her as the men worked their way out of the bunker. A few minutes later she could no longer hear them talking outside.

Had they noticed her? They gave no sign of such, but she couldn't understand a word that they'd said. Maybe they had and were simply waiting outside for her to come out. She decided to wait awhile longer. She couldn't retrieve her phone from her pocket, so she began to count seconds and minutes.

After an estimated five minutes, she decided it was

safe to move. She knew she couldn't move forward because some kind of reducer that took the duct to a smaller-sized pipe, one she had no hope of fitting through. She tried to ease backward. What? She couldn't move. She couldn't flex her elbows to use her arms. Her arms were wedged into the reducer. Without them to push her body backward, would she be able to get out?

She tried to use her toes to pull herself back. She pointed them away from her body, pushed them into the wall of the duct, and pulled them back toward her body. Did she move? She couldn't tell in the dark. She tried to bend her wrists and push with her hands. She hadn't enough leverage or strength there to help. She tried using her hands and feet together. Nothing. From the position of her hands, she could tell she hadn't moved. She was stuck.

The work day drew to a close and Richard still hadn't reached Amy. Just that persistent voicemail. *She must* really *be upset,* he thought. He had never known her to leave her phone off for such a long period. With that thought he began to worry that something had happened to her.

He tried to focus on his last task of the day, but that worry wouldn't leave him. After fifteen minutes, he decided to call her father. He answered on the second ring.

"Colonel, it's Richard."

"Hi, Richard. Must say I didn't expect a call from you."

"Oh. I guess she's talked with you about yesterday." He paused. "Of course she talked with you. Why should I think otherwise? I really blew it."

"Yes, you did."

Richard wasn't surprised at the reply, but the tone of the man's voice that caught his attention. Maybe sorting things out with Amy was going to be more difficult than he'd imagined.

"Look, she isn't there with you by any chance, is she?"

"No."

Richard heard an audible sigh from the man.

"Look, Richard, I'm not going to get in the middle of this. You two need to work it out, or not."

"Sir, I'm not calling to ask that of you. I've been trying to reach her all day. I've called like 15 times without success. I thought she might be there. Now, I'm worried. She's never left her phone off this long."

No immediate reply came.

"When did you last call?"

"Just minutes ago, and half an hour before that. I can understand her being mad and not answering my calls, but my calls go straight to voicemail. Her phone is turned off."

After a moment more of silence, Amy's father responded. "I know she wanted to be alone, but you have a point. In fact, I was expecting a call from her before now. Let me check into it. I can't say she'll call you, but I will pass on your concern about her. Thanks."

Richard knew her father would track her down. After that, he could only wait for her to call him back. If she would.

Richard placed one last call to his office. All was well there. He considered driving out to the house to look around, but dusk approached. He was to meet

Maggie at her office in the morning, before heading into work. He had the evening before him . . . and it seemed so empty, so lonely. He and Amy talked almost every evening, even if only a brief conversation about each other's day. Tonight, he knew that wouldn't happen.

He changed from his fleece workout gear to clothes more suitable for dining out; grabbed his wallet, keys and coat; and headed for the door. At the front door to his building, he was shocked to see Summer Stanton outside, pressing the intercom button to his apartment. He didn't know whether to turn around and hide, go out the back door, or just say 'hi' and move on.

At that moment, she turned and saw him. She waved. Now he had no choice. He opened the door, but not to let her in.

"Surprise, neighbor!" She held up a bottle of wine.

"Yes, this is a surprise." He tried to sound as matter-of-fact as he could.

"Maggie called and told me you got the house. Congratulations." She glanced toward her feet. It was a coy look that did not go unnoticed by Richard. "Look. I know you're engaged and I'm not here to mess that up for you."

Richard felt surprise that Maggie hadn't told her about the fight with Amy. Or had she?

"But I was in this area and I simply wanted to welcome you both as new neighbors. So, here." She extended the bottle toward him. "For you guys to share."

He hesitated in taking the gift and needed to change the subject before she asked where Amy was. "Thanks. I thought you were supposed to go to Detroit today." He had recalled that fact from their brief conversation outside the house the previous night. That made him even more curious about why she was at his doorstep.

"I was, but the local station did a piece that my producer liked. He decided to save money by using their work and not sending me there. I'm now scheduled to stay in town for at least a week to highlight some charities. Then I'm tentatively scheduled to resume my coverage of your candidate's campaign. In southern California, I think."

"Sounds about right. Well, thanks for the wine. I'll pass on your greetings to Amy." He lied. A greeting from Summer would be the last thing he'd share with Amy, even if they were on good terms right now. He turned back into the building, but Summer caught the door.

"Hey, look. I know we haven't been on the best terms, professionally. And, again, I know you're engaged. I value that. But, we've never really sat down and discussed what happened to us in Kansas City. The way you and Bradley Graham treated me there, with respect and honor, touched me. Considering how I had reported on him . . . I didn't deserve that, but you still did it. I'd likc to get to know you better, and learn more about what makes Graham tick."

She had a point. Maybe they did need to iron out some differences and come to a better understanding about why they had been selected for blackmail. He had his ideas. Maybe she had some insight from a woman's perspective. And he felt good that they had made an impact on her. He had perceived a difference in the tone of her reporting about the Graham campaign. Maybe he could gently nudge her to "their side."

Still, warning sirens sounded their clarion call in Richard's brain. So his next words surprised even him.

"Well, I was just heading out for dinner, and Amy had to head home. Would you like to join me?"

Ten

❧ ◆ ❧

"Cully? What the . . ."

Lynch remained disoriented as Slattery gently shook him. The man swore at the discovery of the Taser® barbs and wires extending from Lynch's back. Lynch surmised the man was astute enough to recognize the implications of that discovery.

"Fellas, pick 'im up and make him comfortable inside."

Lynch felt two sets of arms lift him from the ground. He tried to talk but couldn't form an intelligible word. His neck, however, had recovered to where he was able to turn his head and watch Slattery check the latrine and its surrounding area, muttering profanities throughout the search.

By the time they ended up inside, Lynch was moving and functional, although sore. In his police training, he had always had the "advantage" of knowing the shock was coming. Getting hit out of the blue proved more bewildering, but the sudden, massive, total body muscle cramp was just as he recalled.

Slattery reentered the building.

"Cully, what happened?"

Lynch explained what he knew. "Graham looked

incapacitated as they dragged him off, so he must have been hit with a stun gun, not a Taser®. They juiced me twice to make sure I couldn't react."

"Maybe they drugged him," said one of the men who had carried Lynch.

Lynch shook his head. "Not enough time. Only in Hollywood does a drug work instantly. Plus, someone being grabbed for an injection or chloroform puts up a struggle first. I didn't hear any scuffle in the short time between hearing his stall door close and my following him."

Slattery nodded. "Yeah. Stun gun sounds more likely. The right one can put you down for five, ten minutes." His face turned somber. "Cully, trust me. We had nothin' to do with this. We're here peacefully. Don't want any trouble like this, believe you me."

Lynch did believe him. Whoever did this wanted Graham out of the election and saw an opportunity to accomplish that and blame it on these people. He had a good idea who that "whoever" was. Based on the growing body of emails leaked to and released by WikiLeaks, the Democratic National Committee held no qualms about such dirty tricks. However, Lynch felt sure that they received their marching orders from higher up. He had no idea who had assumed leadership of The Assembly after the bogus suicide of Karolus Karling, but this had The Assembly's fingerprints all over it.

Lynch looked up at Slattery. "You realize what this means, right?" The man's face looked defeated as he nodded.

"Fellas, tell folks to round up their gear and start to ease outta here. Don't need no caravan calling attention to us, but don't waste time either. Use the service roads to get to the back county roads and give wide berth to Hines and Burns. This place is about to be crawling with Feds."

The men didn't need to be told twice. They hurried out the door.

"How many people and cars do you have in here? You might just need a caravan to get them all out. I can't sit here and wait on them to *ease* out of here, as you put it. I need to inform the FBI down the road right now. Every minute lets these jokers get farther away with Graham." Lynch stood, prepared to fight his way out.

Slattery didn't stop him. "I'll go with you. I need to tell people we're innocent."

Lynch stood at the door and looked back at the man. "I'll support you on that one, but I have to move on this."

He opened the door and watched a pickup truck pull away with a generator, followed by two older cars. People rushed between buildings and cars. No doubt the threat of an invasion of Feds stimulated the protesters into the action. Slattery was going to get a caravan exodus whether he liked it or not.

Slattery pointed to a dark blue SUV right outside the building. "That's mine. Climb in."

Before the protest leader could start the vehicle, Lynch was on the phone to his men at the cordon, preparing them. He then placed a call to their Secret Service team leader, himself prepared for a verbal barrage that would put Slattery's earlier tirade to shame.

As they approached the FBI police line, Lynch

looked for Special Agent Tanner. The man leaned against a car, sipping something hot. Lynch could see wisps of steam rise from the cup.

"There's Tanner." He pointed toward the agent and Slattery steered that direction.

In an instant, a small army of FBI agents formed a defensive line as if they expected the car to career into their leader. Slattery stopped well away from them, and Lynch jumped out. He ran toward Tanner and a lone male agent began to run toward him. The agent seemed intent on tackling Lynch, but the special agent called him off.

"Let him through, Carlton!" Lynch could see concern spread across Tanner's face as he tossed the foam cup aside and ran to meet Lynch.

"Graham's been kidnapped. You need to mobilize your agents and the locals, now!"

The gravity of the situation took a moment to sink in with Tanner, but then anger filled his face. A major presidential candidate had just gone missing on his watch . . . and he would blame Lynch.

To his credit, Special Agent Tanner didn't stop to berate Lynch. Instead, he began to bark orders to his agents and called over the county sheriff, ordering him about as well. Lynch figured that wouldn't sit well with the sheriff, but who cared?

A government SUV pulled up next to Tanner. "Cully! With me!"

As Lynch moved toward the vehicle, he motioned toward Tony with his head to follow them. Tony nodded.

Lynch pointed to an area away from the scene of the abduction. "Park over there."

The agent who drove Tanner's vehicle complied, and every truck, car, and SUV following them pulled in behind. Lynch led Tanner to the main door and stopped. He noticed that not one protester could be seen and the dozen or more cars that had filled the area were gone. He mentally wished them all luck getting out of the area without being picked up.

"Around the corner, outside the latrine building. That's where it happened. Follow me."

He gave the crime scene a wide berth and then pointed out where the truck that had taken Graham had been parked. Two agents who had followed them took charge of the others and they began to set up the scene.

"Okay, Cully, what happened? I told you not to trust these people." Tanner's composure had settled down, but his displeasure still emanated from the tone in his voice. "Speaking of which, where are the protesters?" He glanced about, much as Lynch had done a moment ago.

Lynch debriefed with the special agent, who took notes and asked questions sparingly during Lynch's recounting. Lynch noted that the man's anger toward him dissolved as the story unfolded. Clearly, Lynch had not failed. He had been outgunned.

The lead agent who had taken charge of the area where the truck had been parked walked up to them. "Sir, we're getting casts of the tire treads, but there's not much else there . . . except this." He handed the special agent a paper evidence bag.

"What's in it? I'm not gloved."

The agent, who was gloved, opened the sack and

pulled out a jacket. "We found this in the grass where the truck had been. Must have fallen out of the truck."

Lynch saw anger return to the special agent's face, but Lynch said nothing. No doubt Tanner was having difficulty digesting his own words. Who were they supposed to trust when the jacket was one of their own—official FBI gear?

Brad felt at ease with Simon Slattery. The man, described by the press as an angry cowboy intent on using public lands for his personal gain, was far from that portrayal. His earlier run-in with the federal government, at his own ranch in Nevada, was not so much about his loss of grazing rights—as with the Edmonds—but about a federal government that opposed its own people.

For over a century, ranchers throughout the west had used public lands for grazing their large herds. Those herds fed the country's desire for beef. Those ranchers knew better than most how to conserve the land, to preserve the heritage of that land. Their livelihoods depended upon it. But the government's appetite for land had become insatiable. Every year they bought out farms and ranches that had been in families for generations, for the sole reason of "conservation." Some mouse here, or owl there, became a *cause célèbre* for environmentalists intent on taking all of the land back to its "pristine nature." But the ranchers knew that the government had no concern over a mouse. They wanted control over the natural resources buried beneath that land—the oil, the minerals, the natural gas.

Simon Slattery was one of the first to finally stand up against the government. He did so, not because of personal gain, but because someone had to draw attention to the corruption of the federal government. The masses of people in the east, where the government owned less than 15% of the land, had no idea what was happening west of the Mississippi River.

Yes, Brad felt at ease with this man. They shared a common goal. People first, not government. The United States and its Christian morality first, not a humanist global agenda where a small group of people controlled events, the economy, and all aspects of people's lives to satisfy their personal love of power and wealth.

Brad stepped out of the headquarters building feeling he had fulfilled his reason for being there. He was ready to head back to the campaign trail, where he could vocally support movements like Slattery's that put people first. He needed a pit stop before leaving.

Brad knew that Lynch was still inside the latrine as he left the small building. He felt no concern in exiting the building first. Lynch seemed overprotective much of the time. Who would harm them there?

The electric jolt of the stun gun felt like a thousand bees stinging him all at once. Confused and disoriented, his muscles would not respond to his brain. The willpower of a hundred men could not get his legs to support him, to help him flee these attackers. He fell to the ground, and in an instant, the arms of two strong men pulled him up and dragged him toward a pickup truck. He watched as Lynch, too, was attacked by a third man. Immobile, Brad couldn't even yell for help.

The men bound his wrists behind him with a zip tie, followed by the binding of his ankles in like manner.

Duct tape covered his mouth. He was tossed into the bed of the pickup truck, covered with a tarp, and soon felt every bump and turn in the roads they used to take him wherever they intended to go. How many movies had he seen, and books had he read, where the kidnapped, blindfolded protagonist counted every right and left turn, listened for telltale sound clues, and counted the seconds between turns in order to know exactly where he was. Now that he was in this predicament, he had no concept of where to begin. And sounds? All he could hear was the rattle of the truck on a rough road.

After a period of time, their speed slowed to a crawl on an uneven road. That much he could determine from the way the truck slowly rolled one way and then another. The movement of the truck reminded him of a fishing trip he had taken to the Rockies where they used a four-wheel-drive jeep to climb to 9,000 feet along an old logging road. There they had slowly eased up over boulders and dipped down into ruts to work their way up the mountain. The rock and roll of the pickup had the same feel—without the comfort of sitting in a bucket seat. He bounced back and forth between the walls of the bed.

Through the tarp he sensed that the sun was high in the sky. He had gone to the latrine about eleven a.m., so perhaps the time had closed in on noon. In his current position he had no way to glance at his watch or pull out his cell phone.

His cell phone! Lynch had installed a GPS tracker app on the phone. They'd be able to find him through that. Maybe. He couldn't tell whether his phone was still in his pocket or not. He knew better than to get his hopes up. Someone sophisticated enough to stage this attack and take him would know to get rid of a phone or at least take the battery out.

The rest of the trip lasted only fifteen minutes. Maybe thirty. He couldn't really say, but the truck stopped and he heard two men talking as they opened the doors and exited the cab. The bright sun stunned his eyes as one man yanked the tarp off of him. He squinted and his eyes adjusted to the midday light. The other man lowered the tailgate of the truck and began to pull him toward the back.

"At this point we're not carrying you. You should be able to move just fine, so I'm going to clip the tie binding your ankles."

Brad sat up and gazed about. The "road" they had most recently traveled looked more like a creek bed. With his hands bound behind his back, he had little chance of getting away. He would need his hands for balance and to work his way along the rocks. Besides, he had no idea which way to go. Or whether he'd get shot in the attempt.

He scooted to the tailgate and dropped to the ground after the man cut the zip tie. He turned and looked past the truck. He rotated his head in all directions. Whichever way he looked, it all looked the same.

"That way."

As the man pointed, Brad started to walk. "Who are you and why have you taken me?"

The older of the two replied, "Who we are is unimportant. As for your second question, someone wants you out of the way for the election and this is how they decided to do that."

Brad saw the machinations behind that action. By going to meet with the protesters at the refuge, he had walked right into a perfect trap. Take him out and blame the protesters. He shook his head in disgust that someone, or some group, could stoop so low and be so threatened by him as to have him kidnapped.

The men led him in a zigzag path with enough changes in direction that he had no clue which way they headed, except that it was uphill 90% of the time. He guessed they had walked half an hour, maybe 45 minutes, when he glanced up the slope they now climbed to see a cabin tucked into a small canyon, above which a mountain seemed to rise forever into the sky. As a stranger to the region, he knew only that mountains existed on all sides of the broad valley in which the wildlife refuge sat. He could be in any of them.

As he approached the cabin, he noticed the building had seen better days, but that the roof seemed intact. Moss grew on some of the wood siding. He walked up three steps to a narrow front porch, which was barren of any chairs that once might have been there. His younger captor opened the door and allowed him to enter first. To call the spare furnishings rustic was an overstatement. Fifty years ago they would have been rustic. Yet, several new cots and sleeping bags sat in one corner, and bags of groceries filled the counter next to an ancient sink, as well as a scarred butcher block table. Several boxes on the floor contained gallon water jugs. They looked prepared to keep him until the election.

"So, what if I decide to walk out that door? Are you also under orders to kill me if I try to escape?"

Neither man answered, but the look on the older man's face reflected a distaste for that idea. The younger man, however, seemed agreeable to it. Brad made a mental note of that and decided to test him further.

"Do you have names, or do I call you Tweedledee and Tweedledum?" He used his head to point first at the older and then the younger as he mentioned the names. He emphasized the 'dum' in the second name.

The younger man seemed to bristle at that. *Yes, he's the one I need to be careful with*, thought Brad.

The elder spoke up. "Call me Homer and him Virgil. And yes, you're likely to die if you try to escape. Not necessarily by our hands." Homer did not elaborate.

"Homer and Virgil. Your real names?"

"What do you think? First thing that came into my mind."

"Thank you, Lord," said Brad under his breath. To him, those names were a sign. He had never doubted that God's angels surrounded and protected him. Now, he knew that God's own hand covered him, too. The main themes of Homer's *Iliad* and *Odyssey* were those of glory and homecoming; while Virgil's *Aeneid* was the epic tale of the founding of Rome and the Roman Empire. Like the heroic Aeneas, Brad considered himself devoted and loyal to his country, and set on restoring its prominence, not on his personal gain.

"Turn around," said Homer.

Brad complied and felt his hands gain freedom as the man cut that zip tie as well.

"No monkey business. We'll both be watching you.

There's food in the sacks over there. Help yourself. We're not fixing anything for you."

At the mention of food, Brad recognized the hollow sensation in his gut. He walked to the grocery bags and made a show of rummaging through them. As he did so, he made a clandestine check for his phone. It wasn't in his pocket.

"You won't find it. We ditched it just outside the refuge," said Virgil.

"Find what?"

"Your phone. We scanned you for GPS tags, too. You're clean."

Brad acted as nonchalant as possible, but that told him two things. His phone wouldn't bring the cavalry charging . . . and they were close observers, very close. Trained, most likely. Under other circumstances, he would know to be very careful with his actions, but as it was, he had nothing else to hide, no reason to guard his movements.

All he could do now was trust in the Lord and wait to be found.

Eleven

Amy had no idea what time it was. The outside light never penetrated the darkness of the bunker and she could not retrieve her cell phone. Her arms remained at her side, barely able to move, much less flex into a position to get her phone or otherwise assist her.

She had failed so many times to back out of the duct that she had given up. How had she become so wedged into that metal pipe? Why had she sought concealment in it in the first place? Maybe she could have hidden *behind* the pile, if she had only taken 30 seconds more to search. But a delay might have also led to her discovery.

Yet, now she longed for discovery.

Her mind wandered to concerns about not being found. Her car would be noticed by the rangers. However, it might be another day—after seeing it unmoved—before they get suspicious. Would they mount a search? Would they focus on the wooded areas? Would they check the bunkers in that search? Would they search them in time? Worry about becoming dehydrated and passing out washed over her. If she was unresponsive when they came into the bunker, they might never find her within the duct.

"Help! Anybody out there?"

Could they hear her if they were? More problematic was that the echo within the duct made her ears ring every time she yelled. She needed her hearing intact if someone was searching for her and calling her name.

She again stretched out her toes and curled them toward her in an effort to move herself backwards. Repeat. And again. Had she moved? It didn't feel like it.

She heard a noise. Little feet. Scurrying along the floor not far from her.

Then something poked her left shoe.

"Hey!"

She wiggled back and forth, rocking the duct. She kicked her feet. More scurrying feet. But it was a distinctive "Squeee" that set her heart racing. Rats!

"Are you sure no one will see us here?"

Richard looked about at the lively bistro where Summer had suggested they go for dinner. Millennials, mostly. A few middle-aged men trying to hit on the younger women. One older couple who reminded him of his parents—willing to try the trendy new eateries even if they did stand out in the crowd.

"I'm sure someone *will* see us here. But they'll likely recognize just me, and who I go out to eat with isn't exactly material for the tabloids or news portals. Relax." Summer picked up the menu, scanned it, and set it down.

Richard watched her. "That was fast."

"I've been here before. I know what I want."

He continued to peruse the menu, which consisted of *tapas,* appetizers, and wine flights. *Small plates*, he thought. *I might need two of them. Maybe three.* He acknowledged his hunger.

Summer waved to someone across the room. Richard wanted to lift the menu to hide his face. Sometimes being six-foot-three and built like Thor had its disadvantages. Being seen at dinner with Summer was the last thing he needed, for work or for his relationship with Amy. Regarding the latter, all it would take would be a photo of him and Summer there at the bistro to be the final nail in the coffin.

"Richard, relax."

"Sorry, maybe this wasn't a good idea."

She shook her head. "Nonsense. Again, no one knows who you are. You're a behind-the-scenes player with Graham."

"Yeah, but his conservatism doesn't play well with the crowd currently surrounding us. If someone finds out who I work for—"

The waitress interrupted and briefed them on the daily specials. They gave their order and their drinks arrived within minutes.

"So, tell me more about *his* conservatism, as you put it."

Richard thought for a moment. "To start, his positions are very much based upon Biblical teachings. Take borders; the Bible says that God established the borders of each people, or nation, just as He established the border between land and sea. The Bible also shows that God expects people to respect those borders, just as He commanded Moses not to cross certain borders during those years wandering the wilderness. Graham believes in strong borders, because without borders a nation ceases to exist. The Democratic frontrunner wants open borders and no restraints on who enters the country."

He went on to explain other positions of the American Party platform, and Summer seemed to soak it all in. She asked pointed questions, but never confronted his viewpoint. He appreciated her skill at listening.

The meal was delicious and Richard savored each bite. After three drinks, he finally relaxed, while also committing himself to no more. He needed to drive home and he had enough presence of mind to understand that a DUI stop would not sit well with his boss. And a DUI stop with Summer in the car would *really* not benefit him.

Summer smiled and he realized that her smile was dazzling.

"See. I told you nothing would come of our having dinner together. I'm glad to see you're relaxing a bit now." She reached across the table and stroked the back of his hand with a finger. "You know, I think you and I could get along really well. I think I'm going to like having you as a neighbor."

Richard blushed. No, this was not what he had intended. Yes, Summer was gorgeous . . . and intelligent . . . and socially well-placed. But he had Amy. Or did he? Maybe their relationship truly was over. He wouldn't know until he talked with her again. Of course, if she continued to refuse his calls, wasn't that a clear signal in itself?

With the stroke of a fingertip Summer Stanton had shown that his half-hour discourse on conservative values had gone in one ear and out the other. She was interested in *him*.

Andrew Gibbs looked at his watch. Only five minutes had passed since his last glance. Richard's call had disturbed him. Not because it was Richard, or that Richard and Amy were not on great terms at the moment—that was something he would only involve himself in if asked. No, the call concerned him because Richard was correct. Amy was not one to leave her phone off for hours. She also wouldn't ignore the two messages he had left on her voicemail over the past 35 minutes, requests for her to call him.

He paced the floor of his study. In an hour it would be dusk, and full darkness would not delay waiting on her.

When she had been in college, stressing over some wannabe boyfriend or career choices, she had made a habit of walking the trails and roads in the Busch wildlife area. He had discovered that she had one trail that she favored over the others because it formed a loop. He couldn't recall if it had a name, but if he had a map of the conservation area, he could pinpoint it.

He moved to his computer and searched for "Busch wildlife." The Missouri Department of Conservation's page topped the list and he clicked on the link.

There. A map.

He clicked on the PDF file at the bottom of the page and pulled up the map. There were fewer actual trails than he had recalled, but the one he looked for was obvious. The Busch Hiking/Biking Trail.

Duh. How could I forget that one?

He found one other piece of information on the page—the area's phone number. He grabbed his phone and dialed.

"Busch Memorial Conservation Area. How can I help you?"

"Hi. My name's Andrew Gibbs . . ." He went on to explain his concern.

"So, you don't know for sure that she's even here?"

"No, ma'am, I don't. I'm hoping someone could check to see if her car is anywhere near the Busch hiking trail."

The woman hesitated. "I, uh . . . Sir, the rangers are awfully busy with the archery deer season." She paused again. "Tell you what, let me see if anyone is in the vicinity of the trail. If so, maybe they could swing by and check. What kind of car would they look for?"

He gave her the make, model, color, and license tag of the vehicle. He then gave her his cell phone number.

"I can't promise anything. Especially since you don't know for sure that she's here, but I'll call you back, one way or the other."

"Thank you."

He had a feeling the search would be up to him. With God's grace, he'd get a call from Amy as he drove toward the area. Or a ranger would call to inform him that her car was not found near the trail's usual access points. Of course, that didn't mean she wasn't somewhere else in the conservation area.

But what if they called back to say they spotted her car? What then?

He grabbed a coat and his large flashlight and rushed to his car. Busch Wildlife was a 40-minute drive away. He would have but minutes before the sun set and searching the trail in the dark would be a challenge.

Richard returned home and collapsed on the couch in his main room. Summer's subtle advances were not what he had anticipated. Such flirting was not foreign to him. He had learned to deal with such in college where some of the women had made much more obvious overtures. Those lessons had served him well in his employ by Darko Komarčić, the human trafficker whose business Richard had infiltrated for the FBI. Even then, surrounded by beautiful women whom Darko encouraged to compromise Richard, he had been able to focus on one woman and one woman only, Amy.

But tonight?

Something was different.

Andrew had memorized the map, so that as he entered the wildlife area he knew exactly where to turn. He turned left at the first intersection, but then he had a choice. The first right would take him to the north end of the trail. The second right would take him to lakes 19 and 20, with access to the southern end of the loop.

The gravel road became a washboard and forced him to slow down. The sun had moved to the western horizon. He needed to speed up, not slow down. Yet breaking an axle would be worse, so he accepted the slower speed.

As he came to the first turn, he had a decision to make. Go north or south.

His phone rang.

"Mr. Gibbs, this is Maureen, at Busch Memorial. We found her car at Lake 19."

He sighed in relief. At least he knew she was there.

"Thank you. I'm actually almost there. I was about to turn toward the north loop."

"Ranger Marie Duckett is on her way now. She'll meet you there."

Andrew continued to the second right turn and a minute after turning, pulled into the lot at Lake 19. Amy's car was there, as reported. Andrew exited his car and walked to his daughter's. Locked. Everything looked in order. As he walked about the area, a pickup truck with the Department of Conservation logo on it appeared. A middle-aged woman, of average height and weight, climbed out of the cab.

Andrew approached her. "Ranger Duckett?"

She extended her hand. "I am. You must be Mr. Gibbs. This your daughter's car?"

"Yes. It looks in order. I think she came out here just after lunch. I can't reach her. Either her phone is turned off, or . . ." He didn't want to think about the alternative.

"Okay. Well, I've got one of the other workers heading this way, one with an ATV that has lights. We'll be able to search the trail with it, but if she's gone off-trail and something happened to her, we'll need more people and better light. Sorry. That's the best we're gonna do this late in the day. On the positive side, the temperature is only supposed to go to about 50 tonight, so hypothermia won't be as big a risk."

Andrew looked at the sky. They had maybe 20 more minutes of light, although it would be fading.

"Look, to save time, I'm gonna head to the north loop. I've got a bright flashlight to help."

The ranger shook her head. "Sir, I don't know . . . We don't want you getting lost in the dark, too."

"I never get lost. I'm a retired Army aviator. I can navigate by the stars if I have to. If you folks start here, I'll start up north. We don't have much light left."

The ranger still didn't look convinced about his plan.

"Sir, I can't stop you. You still have your cell phone, right?"

"I do and it's fully charged."

She gave him a cell number.

"That's direct to me. Keep in touch."

He nodded and ran back to his car. Five minutes later, at a 90-degree bend in the road to the north loop, he pulled into an area for parking. He grabbed his light, and a new decision faced him. To his left, a service road acted as the southern part of the north loop. If he went that way, he would end up back at his car where the trail emerged from the forest to his right. Or, he could start to his right and hike the loop in reverse. If Amy had come to this part of the hiking trail she would have come into it from the south, so he chose to head left first.

He hiked more slowly than he liked, but he needed

to search the area. With the canopy of colorful leaves, dusk became dark as soon as he entered the forest. He used the light to scan the trail, as well as the immediate areas right and left of the trail. He moved twenty feet forward and repeated the process.

This is going to take forever, he thought.

"Amy!" No response.

He continued his pattern of searching, and yelled her name every fifty feet or so. About two hundred yards along the trail, he came to the first of several bunkers. He inspected it to find the door welded closed, but again he yelled her name. Nothing.

An hour later, he guessed he had searched about half of the trail's northern loop, along with four bunkers. The result at each bunker was the same as the first. Night had firmly established its grip on the area, but the dark would not deter him.

His phone rang.

"Mr. Gibbs, it's Ranger Duckett. We've searched one arm of the southern loop and we're heading back along the other. How are you doing? Can I send some volunteers your way?"

"Ranger, that would be greatly appreciated. I think I'm about halfway around this loop. I started on the service road that heads west from the parking area and have turned north. I can get a glimpse of a large lake through the trees."

"Okay, that would be Lake 33 and that means you're better than half way."

"Tell me something, I've come across several of the old ammo bunkers, but the doors are welded. Are there any that someone could gain access to?"

"Don't think so. All but one are welded shut. Bunker 64 has some old building materials stored inside, but it's solidly locked. At least it was last time someone checked. There's nothing of value so we don't check them often."

"Thanks. I'm going to keep going. I'll keep an eye out for those volunteers."

Andrew pursued his course and kept to his routine. A short while later, he came to bunker 65. Secure, as he expected it to be.

"Amy!" Again, the still of the night was his only answer.

Bunker 64 would be coming up next. He planned to inspect that one a bit more closely.

Amy's gut growled and she was thirsty. Her bladder screamed for relief, but she resisted releasing it. Being wet would increase her risk of hypothermia. At first, she wondered about the overnight weather forecast. Then, she realized that inside the bunker the temperature was unlikely to change. The place was a man-made cave.

The scurrying feet had continued, and several more times she had kicked away a curious rodent that decided to check her out from that end. Twice she sensed activity in the duct ahead of her. The last thing she could handle was a rat coming for her head. She used her entire body to move and rattle the duct when that appeared to be a possibility. So far that had worked. As she weakened, however, how long would she be able to continue that?

Surely it was dark outside by now, but the area didn't officially close until 10 p.m. Did the rangers make a sweep of the roads to look for stragglers before closing? If it was dark, would her car even be noticed?

What was that? She was hearing things. Her blood sugar was no doubt low. She thought she heard her name.

She listened for it. She stilled her breathing, but the activity of her "neighbors" seemed to echo within the bunker.

"Quiet!" Her ears rang for a moment from the reverberation, but the "neighbors" must have understood. The nearby activity became silent.

She focused on her hearing. Nothing. Yes, she was hallucinating. Her "neighbors" began to party again and she resumed that game that Lynch favored, 'what-if.' She recalled that the last time she'd played that game with herself, she hadn't liked the scenarios that came to mind. This time her choices were worse. She resolved never to play this game alone again.

Lynch. Now, why had he come to mind and not Richard? She didn't want to think about Richard. That mental replay had worn itself thin. What was Lynch doing at that moment? He was probably having a nice dinner, at some first-class hotel, while Bradley Graham sat safely tucked away in an adjacent room.

She started at a new noise. Someone was outside the opening. Were the terrorists back?

"Amy!"

The terrorists knew her name?

Wait a minute. That sounded like her father.

"Dad! Dad, is that you? Help!" She rattled the duct with her body.

"Amy! I'm coming."

The catharsis of being rescued brought a flood of tears. "Thank you, Lord," she said in a quiet voice.

She heard her father work his way into the upper chamber. She could see a light scanning the room.

"Amy? Where are you?"

"In here. I'm stuck." She used her feet to kick the sheet metal of the duct.

"You're stuck? In an old duct? What in the world . . ." He started to laugh.

"It's not funny! Help me out of here. You need to pull me out by my feet."

She felt his strong hands grab hold of her ankles and begin to pull. At first, she moved just an inch or two.

"Sorry. You're pretty wedged in there. I have to get in behind you to pull."

She felt him scoot backward and then pull again. This time she moved several inches. That process repeated.

"Okay. I'm outside the duct and can reach you. Ready?"

"Of course I'm ready." She didn't like the levity she heard in his voice.

Suddenly, she was free of the pipe. She stood up and gave him a bear hug. Then she grabbed his light.

"Stand right there. Don't go anywhere."

She exited the bunker as fast as she could, found a spot behind a bush, and her bladder thanked her a minute later. She adjusted her clothing and returned to the bunker. Her father was just as she left him.

"Sorry. I couldn't wait."

He started to laugh again. "Okay, there has got to be a good story behind this one. How did you end up stuck in that old duct? You're filthy, by the way."

"Yeah, goes with the territory." She ran through the story of the man nearly knocking her down and then her encounter with him and his friends. "Something was fishy, so I decided to check it out."

"Why am I not surprised?"

She gave him a look. She then resumed her story about the men returning and her hiding in the duct. "Dad, I think they would have killed me if they'd found me in here. C'mere. Look!"

With that she led him to the back of the bunker and its stash of backpacks. She opened the first one, as she had earlier and shone the light on the dozens of cell phones.

"They would kill you about some cell phones? I don't think so."

"Not that. Check this one out." She opened the next pack and illuminated its contents.

Her dad let out a low whistle.

Twelve

The Director ascended to his private family quarters after a long day of policy meetings. Since the passage of his signature healthcare bill, hundreds of additional pages of regulations had been issued. His staff now estimated they had written over 20,000 pages of healthcare laws and regulations.

And more good news came today. Three more major health insurers announced they would be leaving the health insurance exchanges. Critics were gloating at the impending implosion of his program. Yet, that was part of the plan all along—making healthcare insurance so complicated and expensive to provide that no sensible businessman would consider offering it.

Few today recognized the Hegelian Dialectic—much less its offshoot, the Marxist Dialectic—as used by The Assembly within governments around the globe. In simple modern terms that three-phase system of reasoning might be described as "Problem-Reaction-Solution." In the practical sense, it was best stated as the government creating a problem, and allowing the people to react to the problem, while expecting them to call upon the government to provide a solution to the problem. As the son of a Marxist mother and raised by

Marxist grandparents, he understood this process and logic better than anyone else.

Still, his legislation was but the final leg of a three-pronged attack against the U.S. healthcare industry, which they saw as the final obstacle to real global control. Marxism, now known as Progressivism, saw any affluent, intelligent, and independent group as a threat to its march to global power. The first prong had been the development of strict controls over the pharmaceutical industry, while intermingling industry leaders with government bureaucrats to perform the oversight of the industry. The resulting collusion guaranteed their cooperation.

The second had been removing the physician "class" as independent professionals by making them employees of large health conglomerates. Employees could be controlled. With private practice all but destroyed, where could a doctor turn if threatened with termination by his employer?

And now, as more insurance companies abandoned the industry, the government would be set to take over all of healthcare—the single-payer system as pundits called it. The final solution to the "healthcare crisis" they created. Controlling healthcare would enable them to control the people.

He looked about the family quarters and saw no sign of his wife and children. Perfect. He now had a moment to catch up on other matters. He pulled out a special cell phone that had been cleared for his use. The NSA monitors, who would otherwise alert security to any unauthorized cell phone activity within the building, knew to ignore calls on this phone. The Assembly had made sure to guarantee that by manipulating the personnel now assigned to that task.

"*Oui, monsieur.* This is François. How may I be of service?"

"Good evening, François. I'm ready for my evening briefing."

"Yes, yes. Please, give me a moment to get to the study. I was not expecting your call until later."

The Director could hear the man's padded footsteps as he walked.

"Sir, again let me thank you for allowing me to stay in the penthouse. It has been much, much easier than having to relocate our communications equipment. Ah. Here we are."

After the "retirement" of Director Karling, the decision had been made to keep François in his current position and to maintain the New York City penthouse. Upon leaving public service in January, the Director was at the top of the list to fill the opening of the vacated office of the U.N.'s Secretary General. There he could keep their agenda moving forward, working in unison with the new president when she assumed office in January.

"Shall I start with the Chinese, sir?"

"That would be fine."

The man briefed the Director on new developments in the South China Sea, and then moved to new tensions between Pakistan and India over Kashmir, movements of ISIS along the Syrian-Israeli border, more ramifications related to BREXIT, and finally to events surrounding the U.S. elections. *Saving the best for last*, thought the Director.

"You will be happy to know that Bradley Graham

has been removed and his disappearance is to be blamed on the protesters at the wildlife refuge. Fortunately, all of the protesters except Simon Slattery vanished as well. This will make it easier to blame them for Graham's abduction. I have been informed the FBI will not waste resources looking for them, while they put on the appearance of looking for Graham."

"Reasonable. We must make it look like no expense will be spared looking for our kidnapped candidate. And the news media? How are they reporting this?"

"Until now, the FBI contingent at the wildlife refuge has managed to keep the press there in the dark. The press only knows that the FBI moved in on the refuge headquarters. Evidently, Monsieur Graham made a comment to the press that he hoped to help end the protest and standoff. They are reporting that it appears as if he succeeded."

The Director did not like that.

"No, no. We cannot make him appear a hero. We need to focus on getting the story out that he's been kidnapped by the protesters."

"*Oui, monsieur.* I have already positioned our people to play up that information within the press. We are guaranteed that it will be the lead story on the late night news and leading into tomorrow's news cycle."

As always, François anticipated the needs of The Assembly. The Director appreciated the man's talent and dedication. Had the previous director treated the man more as the operative he truly was and less a servant, he might still be alive today.

"So, François, give me your educated estimate. Will cutting off the head of the American Party eliminate the threat they pose to our plans?"

The man hesitated, and that concerned the Director. François' intelligence was another trait he admired. So, his delay in answering meant one of two things—he was formulating a detailed answer . . . or he had an answer the Director would not like.

"Sir, I do not think so. True, they have no other viable candidate in the wings, but there is a slow swell of nationalism building in this country. The death of Graham would make him a martyr, and that risks turning the swell into a tsunami. His disappearance will only slow the rise of this trend. I believe The Assembly risks much by moving too quickly. I once advised Director Karling of this, but he ignored and belittled me."

The Director reflected upon this statement for a moment. "Thank you, François. I will certainly take your comment under consideration."

He did not wish to stymie François' efforts, but the man did not have the full picture. However, he agreed with the man's assessment about turning Graham into a martyr. As such, he would get word to his operatives not to harm the candidate, only keep him from the campaign trail. With the media's control of election news and their relentless, negative public portrayal of Bradley Graham, they only needed to slow him down. The polls continued to show their Democratic candidate in the lead. The Director's legacy would be secure.

"Thank you, sir. To that end, I took a step that I hope you will approve and that I think will give us an advantage."

The Director perked up. François' role until now had been an analytical one, along with carrying out the Director's orders. For him to move autonomously was new and, for someone within The Assembly's middle ranks, bold. Despite his admiration for the man's abilities, perhaps he still underestimated François.

"And that is . . ."

"Sir, I have stepped in to offer assistance to Maggie Walther and Summer Stanton. I believe we can manipulate Richard Nichols to provide inside information from their party. I need to direct them as to what information would be useful. To that end, I arranged approval for Nichols to purchase the Pearce home in McLean. With your permission, I wish to become Walther's handler."

"Please give me more details." His subordinate complied.

"What about the house itself?"

"*Oui, monsieur.* Following Pearce's unfortunate death, Ms. Stanton used her access to the house to clear it for us. The home was cleansed for the general market."

"So, we have no means for monitoring inside the house?"

"That is correct, sir. And we'll have no means to do so. I am confident his employer will sweep the house for such things. If we feel it necessary, we can access the home and add what we need later."

The Director smiled. He had indeed underestimated François. Information from inside the party would be invaluable. Giving him the real estate deal of a lifetime would ingratiate him to Walther. Having him living near the temptation of Summer Stanton? Well, that was one well-played move.

"Excellent, François. Very good indeed. Yes, become her direct handler. Do we still have our other resources in the neighborhood, if Nichols become a problem like Pearce?"

"*Oui, monsieur*. We will have Nichols fully contained."

Thirteen

Lynch fumed as he and his men were escorted off the grounds of the wildlife refuge. Bradley Graham was his, *their* responsibility, and he had insisted on working with the FBI in searching for him. Yet, his arguments had fallen on deaf ears. No, Tanner had countered, this was now the jurisdiction of the FBI until the Secret Service arrived to take the lead. At that time, *his* agents would assist, not Cully's team. He had gone on to explicitly blame Cully for having left the Secret Service behind in the first place, as if that had been Lynch's decision.

This turf war could have gone badly—for Lynch. Good thing Tony saw what Lynch was about to do and stopped him from landing the first punch. The results of that move, had Lynch succeeded, would have left the team in worse shape, with Lynch on his way to jail and his photo splashed across newspapers and news portals all over the world.

Never had Lynch been so angry. Not just with Special Agent Tanner's excluding them, but with himself. He should have *insisted* on waiting for their Secret Service detail. He had been lulled into a sense of complacency by the remoteness of the location and his boss's confidence that all would be well.

"Stop the car!"

They had just pulled onto the main road back to Burns, leaving behind a government SUV that blocked their return to the refuge.

"Why?" asked Eric, who now drove the vehicle.

"I need time to think. And I don't want to get too far away while I do it."

Lynch left the car and began to pace along the shoulder of the road. What were his options at this time? If he tried anything on his own, or even attempted to assist the Feds, they might slap him with an interference charge. Besides, he had no knowledge of the region. He knew no one local who could help him.

Yet, he had to do something. He no longer trusted the federal agencies, not after the discovery of an FBI jacket at the crime scene. He knew the protesters had not taken Graham. So, who would benefit? The answer to that was obvious—a certain Democratic candidate whose flagging poll numbers gave Graham a good shot at winning this election. That same candidate had left a trail of bodies behind her throughout her dubious public career. Would Graham become another notch on her gun? Lynch pondered that for a moment and decided that, no, they couldn't afford to kill Graham and make him a martyr. That realization gave him hope.

Lynch noticed Tony approaching him, holding up his cell phone to display the map app.

"Lynch, look. You have two choices of direction here. North and back to town, or south to who knows where. They won't let us back near the refuge headquarters and that road is the only one going east from here. There are no roads heading west. If we're going to do anything, we need to learn the lay of the land and plan our next moves, not park here by the side of the road. Let's go back into town, buy a map, sit down, and eat while we brainstorm."

Lynch saw on the phone that Tony was correct. They had three options to get east of the refuge, where their only clues might be found. One option was a road halfway to town. The next was a road just south of town, and the third was through the town itself. It had been hours since breakfast. Maybe they would think more clearly with full bellies.

Half an hour later, Eric pulled into the lot of a mom-and-pop restaurant that appeared popular with the locals, based on the number of cars there.

"You guys go on in. Order me a burger, fries, and iced tea. I'm going across the street to that store to look for a map and get some other supplies. We might be on the road for awhile."

Lynch left his team and crossed the road. As he approached the store entrance, a man—clearly Native American, hunched over, and in tattered clothing—teetered toward him. The guy looked homeless and in need of a bath and some basic grooming, but he didn't look malnourished.

"You want picture with real Indian? Ten dollars. Or teach you real Indian dance. Fifteen dollars."

The man's leathery red skin spoke to days spent outdoors. His speech, however, spoke to watching too many grade B westerns. He half expected the man to raise his hand, with his palm facing Lynch, and say, "How!" Did the guy really earn money using that antiquated, racial stereotype on tourists? Sad.

"Not today. Thanks." Lynch tried to brush past him. He had no time to waste.

"Hmm. Indian have ear to ground . . . and finger in wind. Maybe help you find something?"

This time Lynch stopped and turned back to the man.

"Or someone?"

The man definitely had his attention now.

"What—"

The man straightened up, adding a good three inches to his height, and pulled a smartphone from the cargo pocket of his torn pants.

"The sheriff put out a BOLO for a pickup truck with two guys in the cab. Possibly heading north from Malheur. Stop and inspect. I made a couple of calls and found out a man's been kidnapped. I also learned that local authorities were not to assist that man's security team, that the FBI was taking the lead. As I said, I have my ear to the ground, so it didn't take much to deduce that the man must be Bradley Graham. No one else around here has a security team. It also doesn't take a rocket scientist to recognize that when I see four serious-looking men in suits jump out of a SUV with Portland plates, not government plates, they are probably that security team. You *are* Graham's security team, right?"

The man's stilted dialect and shifty gaze had disappeared. Who was this guy?

Lynch nodded and extended his hand. "I'm Lynch Cully, and you are?"

"Leonard Coby, formerly of the Burns Paiute

Indian Reservation police." He shook Lynch's hand.

"Formerly?"

Coby's head waggled back and forth a bit. "Yeah, long story, but let me just say that Special Agent Tanner and I go waaay back, and there's nothing I'd like more than to, well, stuff his face into a fresh buffalo pie and rub it in real good. And I figure helping you might just give me that opportunity. Figuratively speaking, of course."

Lynch chuckled. "We might be on the same wavelength there. What do you go by? Len? Leo? Coby?"

The man's grin appeared partially toothless, but then Lynch saw that the gaps were simply teeth blackened with the putty that makes them look absent. This guy was good when it came to the homeless vagrant role.

"Coby works for me. Folks around town call me Ol' Chief when I play this game. We get a kick out of recording tourists' reactions. Lots of new folks in town because of the protest. In fact, Betsy there was probably recording you when I approached."

He waved to a young woman standing at the window inside the store. She waved back, turned, and returned to her checkout lane.

"Believe it or not, I can make a hundred dollars or more in an afternoon from these suckers. The people from the East Coast are the easiest hits. So gullible." He laughed.

"So, how can you help? That is, if you want to."

"You go by Cully, or Lynch?"

"Either."

"Well, Cully works for me. Coby and Cully. Now, that sounds like a team. Anyway, I know this region better than anyone. I can track anything that moves. I believe I can help you find Graham."

Lynch's gut, despite growling from hunger, told him that Coby was the man they needed. More than that, though, he saw this man as his unlikely answer to prayer.

"Okay, and what do you want in return?"

Coby looked surprised at the question. "Me? Ha. Showin' up Tanner is good enough for me."

"Can we at least pay you for your time?"

The man shook his head. "Thanks, but I don't need anybody's money. You guys going to eat over there?"

Lynch nodded.

"You'll like it. Best food in town. Tell you what. Tell 'em Ol' Chief wants his favorite and I'll join you in fifteen minutes. Got to get cleaned up first."

"Okay, I need some things from the store. I'll—"

"Don't worry 'bout supplies. Got you covered." With that, Coby disappeared behind the building.

Amy's father assisted her through the opening to exit the bunker. Once outside and standing on the path, Amy pulled her cell phone out to discover the battery had died. Her father put his hand over the phone.

"I've got this. I have the number for the ranger, who along with several workers, is out looking for you, too."

He hit redial on his phone. The call apparently went right through. "Ranger Duckett, I found her. Bunker 64 . . . Yes, she's okay. Hungry and thirsty, that's all . . . Yes, we'll wait for you here, but you'd better call for some help. She stumbled onto something you're gonna find hard to believe . . . You'll see when you get here. In the meantime, you might want to call the State Patrol and a bomb squad."

Amy couldn't hear the ranger's side of the conversation until her father mentioned bomb squad. *That* caught the woman's attention.

"She'll be here in a few minutes."

Amy nodded, and moved to sit on the bunker's concrete loading platform, only to have second thoughts about doing so. Actually, she preferred moving as far away from Bunker 64 as possible.

True to her word, Ranger Duckett appeared on a 4-wheeler in under five minutes. She appeared to be a friendly, blonde woman whose face reflected the concern she had about what Amy's father had told her. Her father made the introductions.

"Ms. Gibbs, would you tell me what happened to you and what you found?"

As with her father, Amy repeated her story for the ranger. She focused on every detail she could recall and realized this would not be the last time she told this story tonight. At that point in her tale when she recorded the conversation, she started to replay it for the ranger but remembered her phone had died.

"Sorry, I'll need to recharge the phone before I can play it for anyone."

By that time, she heard several vehicles converging on them and pickup trucks bearing the Conservation Department logo arrived from both directions, lighting up the area in front of the bunker with their headlights.

Uniformed rangers emerged from both vehicles

"Ms. Gibbs, Colonel Gibbs, this is Ranger Sneed and Ranger Wolfson. Ranger Sneed is our chief ranger. Harry, I can fill you in on what happened, but she was just about to tell me what she discovered in the bunker."

Amy could see on the man's face that he wanted the full story.

"Sir, in a nutshell, I had an encounter with a man carrying a backpack on the trail. I later heard him with two other men talking in a language I didn't know, and I noticed he'd left the backpack in the bunker. It was suspicious so I decided to check it out. While I was in there, they came back and I had to hide. I got stuck in my hiding place until my dad found me a short while ago. Anyway, inside are at least two backpacks filled with cheap cell phones and another pack filled with what I believe are bricks of plastic explosives. I only opened those three packs, but I counted at least six more. There could be others."

"I'll check it out," said Wolfson, as he moved toward the opening in the bunker.

Sneed stopped him. "Leave it for the bomb squad. I don't want anyone getting hurt." The chief ranger looked at Ranger Duckett. "Why don't you take the Gibbs back to the parking area? The State Patrol will want to interview them. The nearest trooper was ten minutes away from the area, so he should be here soon."

As the man walked back toward his truck, Amy could hear him on his phone calling the county's

Bureau of Special Enforcement, which included the bomb disposal unit. As Ranger Duckett's ATV began to take them away, she heard him tell the other ranger that the squad would be there in 30 minutes and to back up his truck.

It looked as if they were going to have a long night ahead of them.

Fourteen

Richard awoke with the rising of the sun. The previous day's emotional whirlpool had slowed to a mild eddy and he felt rested after a much-needed night's sleep. After no sleep the night before, falling asleep hadn't been difficult, despite his emotional stress.

He quickly shaved, showered, and dressed. He was to meet Maggie to sign the final papers at eight-thirty, but he wanted time to try to reach Amy.

As he worked on a bowl of instant oatmeal, his phone rang. Amy? Was she finally returning his call?

With mild disappointment, he saw that it was Maggie again. Had something soured their deal?

"Richard, it's Maggie."

"Morning. Something wrong? I thought we were supposed to meet at your office in an hour."

"Oh, good. I'm glad I caught you. Yes, that was the plan, but I had a big customer call and ask for some early showings. Your place was on the way, so it ends up I'm just a block away and I have the papers with me. Can I stop by?"

"Sure."

"See you in a minute."

That minute stretched to three, but his intercom buzzed announcing that she was at the front door to the building. He confirmed that it was her and buzzed her through the door. He met her at the door to his apartment.

"C'mon in."

She entered the apartment and he noticed her glancing around, giving his modest abode a realtor's appraisal.

"Quaint."

He laughed. "That must be realtor-speak for shabby and unkempt."

She offered a subtle nod.

"Well, you're trading up, that's for sure. Looks like you'll need a lot more furniture. I can give you some names of places to shop. Give them my name and they'll work with you."

"Thanks. I agree it's time to move beyond hand-me-downs from my parents and others." He paused. *Yes, definitely time to move up,* he thought. "So, what do you have for me?"

They went through the final papers, which he signed. Then she handed him a ring with a dozen keys on it.

"The locks were all changed after the last owner, so you needn't worry about that. Aaannd . . . it's all yours. You are officially a homeowner. If it weren't seven-thirty in the morning, I'd offer a bottle of champagne and a toast. Tell you what, let me know when you've moved in, and I'll stop by with a bottle for that celebration." She grinned and he noticed once again that she had the whitest, most perfect smile that money could buy, as shown on her billboards, which almost seemed to backlight her smile. He chuckled inside at the thought that should the spotlights on the signs ever fail, she'd look like the Cheshire Cat.

Curiously, he thought of Summer. Of the people he knew, only she had a smile that could compete.

"Thanks. So, when can I move in?"

"You have the keys to your castle. You can move in whenever you want to."

He smiled and looked around. The sooner the better in his opinion. She handed him a business card.

"Here's the card for a moving company I use a lot. From what I see here, they could have you moved in by tomorrow afternoon. Up to you." She gathered up her copies of the papers and her things. "Have to run. Congrats once again . . . and don't forget to let me know when you've moved in. I *will* bring a bottle of champagne."

He watched her leave and looked at the key ring as he twirled it around his finger. He had planned on renting a truck and moving himself, but maybe a moving company would be the faster option. He'd call for a quote *after* trying to reach Amy.

He warmed up his coffee in the microwave and sat down at the table. He dialed Amy and once again, the call went straight to her voicemail. He debated calling her father again. They were in the Central Time Zone, an hour behind him, and he didn't want to call and wake up the Colonel. *No*, he thought, *I'm gonna call and if I wake him, I wake him.*

Colonel Gibbs answered on the first ring. But, instead of the usual greeting, Richard heard, "Richard, now's not a good time. We've been up all night and right now, she's being interviewed by the ATF. Call later." Click.

What? The ATF?

Richard started to call his boss to see about getting time off, but the phone rang before he could hit the speed dial. It was his boss.

"Nichols, I don't care if you're dying, get in here pronto. Graham's been kidnapped. I need every man at his battle station."

Amy sat in the conservation area's headquarters building nursing her sixth cup of coffee for the night. Upon arrival at the building, she had been offered a drink—cup #1.

Her interview with the State Patrol had been delayed until nearly midnight as they waited for the correct investigator to arrive—cup #2.

That interview took more than an hour, but she had been able to recharge her phone and provide the man with a copy of her recording—cup #3.

She received notice that the bomb disposal unit had removed eight backpacks full of C4. Enough explosives to create a new lake where the hillside now sat, according to Ranger Duckett who had passed that information on to her on the sly. Now the head of the bomb squad wanted to talk with her—cup #4.

Next came word that the ATF had arrived on the scene and their agents wished to interview her . . . but not until after they had investigated the scene—cup #5.

Her hand shook as she sat there with the ATF agents, but she wasn't nervous about her testimony. Caffeine?

Maybe she really didn't need that sixth cup. In fact, her bladder seemed intent on telling her to lay off. She needed to use the ladies room. ASAP.

One of the two agents eased his chair away from the table. Was this his signal that they might be finished and ready to let her go home . . . via the rest room?

"Well, Ms. Gibbs, our state, perhaps our nation owes you a debt of gratitude. We can't go into details, but you may have stumbled upon a major terror plot. It's certainly the largest cache of explosives this state has ever seen. However, we ask that you not talk with anyone about this. It's important that we keep this discovery secret."

She nodded. "I know how to keep secrets, and I fully understand the need for discretion in a case that's still under investigation. I won't say anything. However, I ask that this go both ways. I don't want my name mentioned either. Let me just say, I've had encounters with some unsavory types in the past and I don't wish to invite trouble."

Both agents gave her an inquisitive look. She refused to elaborate.

"Can I go home now? I'm exhausted."

The lead agent answered, "Yes. Thank you for your cooperation. I know it's been a long night. Here's my card, if anything should come up."

She accepted the business card and made a beeline for the ladies room. Feeling relieved, she headed toward the building's main door where her father awaited.

"Want me to follow you home?" he asked as he

stood to greet her.

"No, that's okay. It's out of the way for you and I'm only fifteen minutes from home. I'll be fine."

"Okay. Well, go home and get some sleep. I'm going to do the same, but if you need me, call."

She smiled and gave him a hug. "I will, Dad. Thanks. You're always here for me. Love you."

He smiled. "Always. Love you, too."

She watched as he walked out the door and then went to find Ranger Duckett, who had promised her a ride back to her car. As she passed the two ATF agents, she overheard one commenting to the other.

"You aren't gonna believe this. I've got a friend from our academy days who was assigned as liaison to the FBI at that protest in Oregon, the one at the wildlife refuge. He texted me that everything there has gone to hell in a hand basket, but not in any way we'd expect. Bradley Graham's been kidnapped."

The other agent swore under his breath, and continued, ". . . gonna hit the fan when that gets out. That's sure going to shake up this election."

Amy gasped. Whatever mental fog from fatigue she had begun to feel vanished. She turned to the men. "What? I-I'm sorry. I didn't mean to eavesdrop, but . . . Do you know if anyone's been hurt? In Oregon."

The first agent looked at her with a curious demeanor. He said no more.

"Again, I'm sorry. I know Bradley Graham and my, uh, . . ." She caught herself short. She was about to say boyfriend. ". . . a good friend is his security chief. Are they okay?"

Boyfriend? Seriously? Was she about to call Lynch her

boyfriend? What was with that?

The man's look softened. "Sorry, all I know is what you heard."

"Th-thanks." She rushed away to find Ranger Duckett. She needed to get home.

She found the Ranger in her office, asleep in her chair.

"Ranger Duckett?"

The woman awoke with a start. She glanced around and then toward the door. As she saw Amy, she smiled and then gave Amy a look.

"Sorry. Been a long night for all of us. Honey, you okay? You look like you ate something awful."

Amy took a deep breath. She didn't feel at liberty to repeat what she'd heard.

"Just exhausted. Can I get that ride to my car now?"

"Sure thing."

The woman rose from her chair and led Amy to a back door. Her truck sat parked just outside. Six minutes later, they pulled into the parking area where Amy had parked her car. The place looked like a military operation post. Every agency involved in the situation had vehicles there.

"They set up the command center here for everyone. I hope we can get your car out." The ranger glanced about. "There it is. Looks like it'll take a little maneuvering, but you should be able to get out. I'll help you."

They parked along the access road and headed toward Amy's car. Ranger Duckett stopped short and shook her head.

"Well, that's no good. Not good at all." She pointed to Amy's car.

Amy looked and saw nothing wrong, at first. Then she noted both back tires were flat.

"What the . . ." She wanted to cry. The emotions of the past 20 hours had caught up with her. She felt the Ranger's arm wrap around her shoulders to comfort her.

"Honey, don't you worry. Tell me where you want it to go, and I'll personally make sure it gets towed there. You can leave a key with me."

Amy wanted to call her father but realized he'd be halfway home already. Plus, with two tires flat, there was little he could do. She pulled a card from her purse and made a call. Hoods Automotive & Towing. Joe always took good care of her and his shop's mechanics were the only ones she trusted, besides her father.

She returned to the ranger's side. "Ranger Duckett, I've made arrangements for Hoods Automotive to come get the car. Here's the key. I told them you'd have it. It'll be at least an hour, maybe more, before they can come."

The woman nodded. "Got it. I'll make sure they get it. But how're you going to get home?"

Amy thought about that for a moment. She didn't want to disturb her father. Macy. She'd call Macy.

"I'll call a friend. She should be getting off work about now. Can we go back to the headquarters?"

The woman nodded, and Amy gathered up the few things she wanted from her car, leaving it unlocked for the mechanics. She took up pursuit of the ranger heading toward her truck and had almost caught up to her when she saw something unexpected—a taxi.

The orange and black County Taxi pulled into the crowded lot, and she watched two ATF agents exit. She thought that unusual until she realized that the ATF had so many cars on scene already, they didn't need to tie up additional vehicles. Why use more assets when the men would have no trouble finding transportation back to the office? Wherever the ATF had its offices.

"Ranger Duckett!" The woman stopped walking and turned toward her. Amy pointed to the taxi. "I'm going to see if he's open for a fare."

The woman nodded. "I'll wait!"

Amy ran up to the taxi driver's window and tapped on the glass. He lowered the window.

"Are you available? I need a ride home. St. Peters. It's not far from here."

The man looked her up and down. "Yes, I take you. I take cash or credit card. No check, no debit card."

The man's accent seemed oddly familiar. So did his slim, dark face.

"Great. Thank you." She climbed into the back seat and gave him her address. Within a minute they had turned around and started out. Amy waved at Ranger Duckett as they passed her.

"A taxi was the last thing I expected to see at the conservation area. I bet you don't get many calls to go there, do you?" She wanted to talk to stay awake.

"Is my first time here, but I have friends who also drive taxi, they have been here."

She tried to see his face in the mirror, but all she saw were his eyes—eyes that stared at her as much as they watched the road. His skin was the color of a rich, dark chocolate and his features were sharp.

"So, I notice you have an accent. Were you born here in the U.S. or did you immigrate into the country?"

The man's eyes narrowed and his brow furrowed as if he did not like the question. After a moment he answered.

"I am from Somalia, as is my family. We have lived in U.S. for fifteen years. My brothers, uncles, and cousins all drive taxi."

"Do you miss Somalia?"

His face remained serious. "Would you miss starvation, bad water, warlords, and fighting?"

"Good point. Sorry if I seem naïve. I don't know much about Somalia."

She was tired, and her mind wasn't firing on all cylinders. She needed to stop talking and focus on other things. She worried about Lynch, but her thoughts turned to Richard. Their getting back together was unlikely, and she owed him that discussion. After a rest, she would call him.

"We are here. That will be $27.50."

Amy blinked. Did she hear him correctly? $27.50 for that short ride?

She pulled out her wallet to find only $18 in cash. She handed him her credit card and watched carefully that he didn't pull anything "funny" on her. He handled her card in full view, so she was satisfied.

"Thank you, lady. Have a nice day."

As she said goodbye she thought again about the accent and the familiarity of his thin, dark features. And then she saw it. On the front passenger seat sat a gray jacket with a thin maroon stripe running across the shoulder and down the sleeve.

Fifteen

Richard walked into the American Party offices and thought the world had gone to war. Everybody had been called in. Makeshift desks filled corners. Phones rang continually. Several large-screen televisions filled the main conference room. Aluminum easels holding flipchart paper and markers filled voids around the room as well.

" 'Bout time you got here, Nichols!"

Ben Manning appeared unshaven, unkempt, and unhinged. He had clearly been here for hours.

"You only called 20 minutes ago. Have you been here all night?"

"Pretty much. I got the call last night from the main office in St. Louis, which got the word directly from Brad's security team yesterday afternoon. Don't know why they sat on it so long. The press had been shut out at that point, but rumblings of something wrong began working through Twitter about an hour after the call. When I got a call from the Washington Post just after midnight, I knew we were gonna be barraged by morning. I came in and prepared for it."

"You could have called sooner. I could have helped."

In truth, Richard was glad the man hadn't called earlier. In the mood he'd been in, he didn't know whether he actually would have been helpful or would have been looking for another job by morning.

"Yeah. To be honest, I wasn't thinking straight. My mind has been racing a thousand different directions since I got the news."

Ben proceeded to fill in Richard with the details as he knew them—the meeting with Simon Slattery, the attack outside the building with Cully being Tasered®, Graham being dumped in the back of a pickup truck and hauled away, and the FBI jacket found at the scene. Richard's thoughts focused on that jacket.

"Any ransom notes or manifestos?" he asked.

Ben shook his head. "None. The FBI's now stating he was taken by the protesters, who all vanished by the time the FBI came onto the scene. They have Slattery, who is denying any involvement, but the Feds won't give the press access to him. Cully backs Slattery, but he's been told to keep his mouth shut or else."

Richard half smiled. "Yeah, like Cully is one to back down. What's he planning to do?"

Ben shrugged his shoulders. "You know him better than I do. What do you think? I tried to reach him earlier, but he seems to have gone off the grid."

"That sounds like Lynch Cully."

Lynch had never had a problem with getting up at dawn. Yet, to be honest, his current job with its late night schedules of fundraising dinners, meetings with backers, and late evening travel to get to the next city had knocked the 'early riser' attribute from his character. The previous evening, when Coby told him to be ready to move by first light, Lynch balked at the idea.

Now, however, as the first hints of dawn began to tint the sky with a broad palette of oranges, yellows, and pinks, he was ready. Though his body had been supine all night, his mind processed and re-processed the events of the previous day, as well as the scant evidence they had. On a positive note, Tony had managed to take a photo of the tire tread casting made by the FBI forensics team. Lynch had viewed that image so many times, the tire's tread design could only have been impressed more upon his brain by having run over his head directly.

Dressed in hastily purchased "ranch wear," he looked like an East Coast tenderfoot at a dude ranch for the first time. The jeans were stiff, but the boots were stiffer and seemed a sure bet for creating blisters the size of tumbleweeds. But what choice did he have? He couldn't wear his suit. Nor did he have time to ship in comfortable clothes from home.

He tasked his team with trying to learn what they could from the FBI and to offer themselves in assisting the Secret Service team deployed to the search, with as much smoothing of ruffled feathers as they could achieve after ditching the team to come to Oregon. "Blame it all on Graham," he had told them. That's what the boss would have instructed. The buck stopped with him.

Lynch stood outside the restaurant where they'd

eaten the day before. Coby's assessment that it was the best place in town had lived up to his word. Where was he?

He was surprised when the door opened behind him.

"C'mon in."

Coby stood with the door open, despite the sign stating clearly that the place didn't open for another 30 minutes.

Lynch entered the restaurant and watched the man relock the door.

"I didn't think they were open yet."

"They aren't, but for me they're open anytime."

Lynch gazed at the man. His skin was seven shades lighter and the long, disheveled, coal black hair was now a dark brown, short and tame. The wrinkles from working outdoors hadn't disappeared, but now they gave him a distinguished appearance, not the haggard look of Ol' Chief. His clothing was much like that which Lynch now wore, but used, washed, and comfortable.

Coby led Lynch to a booth near the back where coffee filled two mugs and a carafe on the table. Coby pointed to one side and sat on the other.

"Got eggs, bacon, hash browns, juice, and coffee on order. Hope that's okay with you."

Lynch nodded, as he scrutinized his "host." There was more to this Coby fellow than met the eye.

"Guess I look a bit different today, eh?"

"You're a mind reader, too?"

The man chuckled. "Yeah, something like that. I get this reaction from folks who meet me first as Ol' Chief. That's all a bit of fun—the theatrical makeup, wig. I only took time to change clothes yesterday before eating with you."

"I get that. What about this place? You own it, don't

you?"

"What gave me away?"

"The key ring, when you locked the door. Too many keys for some ranch hand, laborer, or even an ex-policeman. You handled it with familiarity. Picked out just the right key from what, fifteen, sixteen on that ring? You must own other properties, too."

Coby nodded. "Very observant . . . and astute. That's good, 'cause you'll need those abilities today. We should get along just fine." He took a long sip of coffee, which Lynch copied.

"Umm, that's great coffee." He took another sip.

"My own brewing technique. You learn a lot cooking outdoors, surviving a winter hunt, or staking out a poacher."

The door to the back opened and the cook brought out large platters of scrambled eggs and hash browns, followed by a rasher of bacon and pitcher of orange juice. Coby stood up and walked to a service counter where he picked up two plates, glasses, and silverware. He placed a set for each of them on the table.

"Help yourself. Jed can cook up more if you're still hungry."

Lynch tucked into the food and filled his plate.

"Eighteen, by the way."

Lynch looked up with a mouth full of eggs. "Huh?" he mumbled.

"Eighteen keys, you were off by two. Not bad for a five-second glance."

They talked more about each other. Coby owned the grocery store where they first met, along with a gas station, mechanics shop, and convenience store. On top of that, he had a 15-thousand-acre ranch north of town, part of which was in the Paiute reservation. No wonder he had no need to be paid. For him, this hunt was for fun, a diversion to get him back outdoors, his first love. Lynch, in turn, shared about his physician father, college professor mother, and life as a detective. Coby wanted to know how he ended up as security chief for a political candidate and Lynch answered with the fifty-word short version. Coby understood.

As they finished eating, Coby asked, "So, where would you go if you were the kidnapper?"

Lynch thought about that as he chewed. After swallowing, he started into his answer. "First, I want to agree with your using the term kidnapper. I'm convinced Graham is still alive because they can't afford to kill him. Talk about civil unrest. The protesters after Ferguson, Baltimore, and the like had to be paid to get them on the streets. Taking out Graham would have conservative patriots, all legally armed, on the streets in droves, voluntarily. No, he was taken to keep him from speaking out, to make people question his candidacy. Besides, if they wanted him dead, they've had ample opportunities."

Coby nodded in agreement. "Yup. And many from the military and police forces would support those protests. Mainstream media wouldn't have a chance against social media. But back to my question, where would you go?"

Lynch finished up what was on his plate and pushed it aside. "I've been thinking about that. If it was me, I'd want a hiding place secluded and hard to reach, so I could keep him in check without having to keep him restrained. He's still a major candidate for president, so mistreating him could cause another set of problems once he's released. Plus, unless I was a local, I'd need seclusion because folks around here seem a bit nervous about strangers. You know who belongs here and who doesn't. I wouldn't want to be noticed as out of place." He stopped for a sip of coffee.

"Okay. I can see the logic there. Still doesn't answer my question."

"I'm getting there. So, I spent a lot of time on Google maps last night. We know they headed east from the refuge headquarters. Going west would have put them right into the FBI's lap. Also, going west offers few, if any, options for hiding. Mostly arid grassland and few structures. They could have turned north once they hit the next highway, but that route takes them into town. With Graham in the pickup bed, that would risk discovery. It wasn't a crew cab pickup, so they couldn't have moved him into the cab with them and still kept him under control. That leaves heading east or south."

Coby nodded as he drank more coffee. "So far, I can agree with that. Could have changed vehicles, though."

Lynch ignored that last statement. That thought opened up too many cans of way too many worms. "Could have put him in a light plane and flown him to Mexico, too. Look, all I can do is focus on the immediate area. If we start thinking about more complicated scenarios, then I'm out of chances. We'll have to depend on the Feds."

"Changing vehicles could still keep him in the immediate area."

Lynch saw a mischievous grin cross Coby's face. Was the man messing with him?

"Okay. I accept that, but that doesn't really change what kind of place they'd want. Where do *you* think they'd go? You're the guy who tells me you know this region better than anyone else."

Coby set down his mug and leaned toward Lynch. "Like I said, I agree that east or south are most likely. Going west offers nothing, like you said. They could find the seclusion needed going north, but they'd have to go through town to get there and the sheriff's BOLO had folks there on high alert before they could have driven there from the refuge. Even changing vehicles wouldn't have helped. Everyone was getting stopped." He sat back and took another gulp of coffee.

"Look, I'm trying to get a feel for two things from you. Your deductive reasoning is good. I think I can trust you to make good decisions. But, we're looking to head into some rough country and I need to know you can operate on your own if we get separated."

Lynch didn't know what to think. At home he had been highly sought and respected for his abilities. He hadn't had those abilities critically appraised, much less questioned, since his rookie days. And yet, he had to admit to himself that he was on foreign soil. He could hold his own in any city. But, in a wilderness? Maybe all this questioning was a good thing.

Coby reached into a bag on the seat behind him and pulled out two paper maps of the area.

"Here. One for each of us. Now, looking at *this* map, *show* me where you think you, as a kidnapper, might have gone. You've said east or south, but not *where* in either direction. Show me you know how to use a *paper* map."

Lynch opened up and stared at the map. The man was right. He'd have no access to Google or any other resource other than what sat before him now. And this map wasn't as much like Google maps as he would have liked.

"Okay. I get it." He began to point to places on the map. "There are a couple of places they could reach quickly heading east, secluded mountains that could offer cover, but they're relatively small areas that wouldn't take long for the authorities to cover. Further east, they move into Idaho where the Sawtooth Mountains would be ideal cover, but if it was me, I wouldn't take a chance moving Graham in the back of a truck for the four hours it would take to get there. So, to me, *this* is where I'd head." He pointed to a place called Steens Mountain.

Coby smiled and let out a deep breath. "Finally. Why didn't you say that 15 minutes ago instead of all this gobbledygook? We can get on the road now." He began to ease out of the booth.

"What? That's all you wanted? The name of a place?"

"Yup. Out here you just need to start somewhere. You start doing all these 'what-if' games and pretty soon all you're doing is sitting here drinking coffee. There's too much territory to cover for that. It's feet on the ground that counts."

Coby grabbed a Thermos from his pack and emptied the coffee carafe into it, before grabbing a second Thermos and taking them both to fill to the top at the coffee maker. Lynch grabbed his things and followed. He was a master at 'what-if games,' as the man had put it. In fact, he loved playing 'what-if.' But out here? He had a feeling he was about to experience something new and unfamiliar.

"Follow me." Coby led him through the kitchen and out the back door.

Lynch stopped in his tracks. Before him sat a new Ford F-250 with a fancy trailer hitched to the back. But not just any trailer—a four-horse trailer holding three large horses.

Horses?

For Richard, the real firestorm on Twitter and Facebook erupted about an hour after he arrived at the office. The story about Graham being kidnapped started with one tweet by a reporter on the scene at the wildlife refuge, a tweet posted as a question: *Have the protesters kidnapped Bradley Graham? #2016election #BradGraham*

That tweet had gone out in the middle of the night, as Ben had informed him. Now, as the East Coast moved into full gear for the day, that single tweet found over 1,000 retweets and the avalanche became unstoppable. By the third iteration, it was no longer a question, but a statement of "fact." And yet, Richard and his team saw familiar handles among the giant snowslide as it headed downhill—people well known to them not as *reporters* of the news but as the shapers and creators of news. They cared little about facts and wished only to mold public opinion and advance an agenda being promoted by the elites in Washington.

Richard made a point of forcing each person in his group to take a break and grab some lunch. But by early afternoon, his team looked weary. More than once he witnessed each member stop typing to work the stiffness out of his or her fingers. He was no exception.

"Richard, we can't keep up." Jared, one of his nimble-fingered staff members, looked up from his laptop, shaking his head. "We can't contain this story. I think we need to stop the direct rebuttals and try to reshape the story."

Richard had already moved in that direction. He had direct quotes from Simon Slattery, Tony, and Eric of the protection detail, and at least one anonymous FBI agent who had alerted them to the agency's plans to stall any real investigation. That latter communication had now been validated by two more anonymous agents. He had also pulled together a list of quotes from Graham himself, to keep that message going.

"Already on it. Here." He began to pass out the list of statements they could use. "Get these out to our own channels and let's see if we can turn the narrative around." He stood up from his workstation. "Back in a few minutes. I have to talk with Ben."

He walked to his boss's office to find the man with a phone at each ear. Ben motioned for him to sit down. Over the next two minutes he finished one, then the other conversation.

"Sorry. This is an absolute nightmare. We had the momentum in our favor with this election and now? What a move. This is a new low for derailing a campaign."

Richard nodded. "Yeah, but watch, it'll come back to bite them. Big time."

Ben shrugged. He appeared unconvinced. "So, what do you need? I have to call Stan in St. Louis in about an hour and I need to finish some things before that call."

"About the statements from the FBI agents . . ." Richard and Ben discussed the statements and risks taken by these men. "I don't want to use these unless our backs are against the wall. These men could lose everything if their identities are discovered. I mean everything . . . their livelihoods, their homes—even their lives."

Ben looked contemplative. "Okay. We can consider these our nuclear option."

Richard started to get up, but Ben stopped him. "Hey, so what gives? I know you weren't sick or nothing when you called in yesterday. Everything okay?"

Richard hadn't expected this. Ben had never been the type to ask about anything other than the work you performed. This seemed out of character, and as such, Richard wondered just what he should divulge. He decided against saying anything about Amy. He hoped to resurrect their relationship, so he saw no sense in bringing up a problem that might be solved in the near future. Instead, he decided to use the house as his response.

"Everything's great actually. I fell into a real sweetheart deal for a house in McLean. Signed the final papers and got the keys this morning, in fact. Right before you called." He went on to detail what happened, minus the fact that the house had been the scene of a well-known suicide. "I was going to ask you for a day off to move, but then all this happened."

Richard expected a reaction to his comment about needing time off, but the man stared at him with a mix of concern and questioning on his face.

"You know, Richard, have you really looked into this Maggie Walther lady? I mean, falling into a deal on the price could happen. By itself, I'd say that makes you lucky. But then you add in the facts that the price was accepted without a hassle and the loan went through in less than a day, and I'd say there's too much *coincidence* here. Think about it, you saw this house what, two days ago? It's a fantastic house and now you already have the keys? Really? Nothing about this stinks to you?"

Richard didn't know what to say. The man was right. What was it Amy's father would always say about coincidence? That there's no such thing as coincidence for a Christian. To close on a house like that within two days ranked right up there with the parting of the Red Sea. Either there was something major wrong with the place that Maggie hadn't disclosed, or . . .

Richard didn't consider himself much of a Christian these days. According to Amy, his priorities were misplaced. She said that Biblical priorities held God first, family second, and a job last. He had to admit he had them in reverse. He wasn't spending time with other believers or going to church. Those were habits he'd "given up" while helping to take down a human trafficker, and he'd not made much effort to move back to doing them. Actually, he'd made *no* effort to find a church or make Christian friends who could keep him accountable.

But now, it was as if he had sprouted a pair of

spiritual antennae. And they were tingling like he'd been hit with the ice bucket challenge on a hot summer day. But was that God? Amy had also said that God would meet him where he was, that he didn't have to get his act together to find God. Was this God meeting him there, in the office? Part of him wanted to believe that. Yet, part of him was convinced he'd just gotten really lucky with the house.

Sixteen

About an hour later, after driving through arid scrub brush-filled land, Coby turned onto a little-used road just east of a place called Voltage. From what Lynch could see on the map, this road aimed straight west from the main drag, which dipped southwest before turning north again to where these two roads would meet again. Yet, as he gazed about, the flat, dry land offered no place to hide.

"Isn't Steens Mountain still to our south?"

"Yup, but we need to see if we can pick up a trail somewhere. I'm hoping to get as close to the refuge headquarters as possible from this side, to see if we find anything that points us in a direction. Like I said, there's a lot of territory to cover. Helps to have a place to start."

"So, just name a place. Isn't that what you said back at the restaurant?" He smirked.

Coby looked at him as if about to give a serious retort, but then seemed to realize that Lynch was messing with *him* this time. He gave a brief nod.

"Okay. Got me on that one. We got two choices. Well, three. As you see on the map, there's two main roads that pass by Steens—one to the east and one to the west. And a bunch of smaller roads that crisscross the ranches and refuge land in between. Then there's a place called Diamond almost in the middle. If we start there, we might as well flip a coin about which direction to head."

Lynch perused his map as Coby spoke, following his comments.

"So, if we find which way they went, it'll help somehow?" Lynch knew the answer, but wanted one more dig at Coby.

Coby's look this time seemed to be one of surprise. "Sure. If they took certain roads, that might point to them headin' to the western half of the mountain. Other roads would take 'em east."

"Soooo . . . You're playing that 'what-if' game after all."

The red man actually reddened, and smiled. "Okay. Got me again. Guess I need to put my cards on the table. When you were in the bathroom at the restaurant last night, your guys told me about your love of playing 'what-if.' Thought I could have a little fun with that, but here we are only an hour or so into the search and you've already caught me at it."

Lynch sensed there was more to that story.

"What else did they tell you?"

"That you're really pretty down-to-earth for being a royal knight and all." He grinned. "*Sir* Lynch."

Lynch rolled his eyes and laughed. "I promise not to make you genuflect."

"Genu-what?"

"Genuflect. That's—"

Coby laughed. "I know what it means. And I don't kiss no rings either."

As Coby pulled to the side of the road, Lynch added, "You do realize that was a double negative."

Coby shook his head. "Yup, but you don't wear any rings." He pointed to the door. "Get outta the truck . . . and start lookin' around. We need to make it fast."

They were at an intersection with what looked like a service road to the north.

"This road heads the wrong way."

Coby nodded. "It's the east service road into the refuge compound. From what you said, they should've exited this way. I'm hoping to confirm that."

The man moved to the eastern edge where the two roads met and began studying the area. Lynch walked about thirty feet north along the service path and did the same. After a minute, he saw a familiar pattern.

"Coby, over here."

Coby approached and compared the tread mark Lynch had found to that on the photo on his phone. "You got it. Good." He started to follow that mark along the road. As he reached the road, he moved off the edge into the dirt. "Yup. They were in a hurry and went off the road a bit as they turned. But they headed east, as we suspected. Back in the truck."

As Lynch straightened up and began to walk back to the pickup, a glint of sunlight reflecting off something on the ground caught his eye. He stepped to the side of the road to check it out.

A phone! And not just any phone, but his boss's phone.

"Coby! It's Graham's phone."

The ex-lawman didn't say anything until Lynch

began to bend down to retrieve it.

"Leave it."

Lynch wanted to protest, but stopped short. Instead, he treated the spot like a crime scene. He used his phone to take a video of the area in general—narrating as to where they stood, the date and time, and who was with him—and then zoomed in on the phone, giving its details and identifying the phone as that belonging to Bradley Graham. He replayed it and was satisfied with the result.

As he climbed back into the truck, Coby said, "Good move."

"Good call on leaving it there. We wouldn't want to be caught with any evidence."

"Yup, but finding it there has me wondering."

"What?" Lynch wasn't sure where he was heading with this.

"It's been what, 20 hours since you notified the Feds of the abduction? They've had a whole day and no one's bothered to investigate the most likely escape route?" He sounded incredulous.

Lynch heard a bunch more questions implied by that last comment. As Coby maneuvered his rig to turn around with the trailer, Lynch pondered the situation. Had he been in charge of the investigation, he would have had a team checking each route out of the compound immediately. That was pretty basic. And while true that he hadn't noticed the phone until the light caught it, he hadn't been looking for it or for clues other than the tread marks to confirm that the truck had passed that way. Anyone searching for clues or evidence would have spotted the phone. A Cub Scout out hiking would have spotted it.

"So, what do you make of the fact that it seems the FBI hasn't bothered to look around here?" asked Lynch.

"Exactly what I was wondering. First thing came to my mind was that they're obviously not looking very hard. And that gets me wondering about why."

Graham sat up on the cot and eased his legs over the side, the hard edge of the portable bed pushing into the backs of his thighs. Maybe tonight he'd try sleeping on the floor. That couldn't be less comfortable. Of course, he'd have to clean it first.

His captors still lay on their cots. If only the one cot wasn't placed directly across the door, he'd consider simply walking out. The two grimy windows, he had noted the day before, were nailed shut, although that might have been simply to keep them from falling out. But then, he wouldn't consider climbing out a window anyway, and even if the one cot didn't block his way, would he really contemplate leaving? He remembered Homer's comment about being likely to die, and not by their hands. Maybe he could get the man to explain that.

He walked to the small coffee maker, emptied the old grounds from last night, added water from a gallon container, plus a new filter and grounds, and placed it on the portable camp stove after lighting it. Within minutes the aroma of brewing coffee filled the cabin. Homer and Virgil began to stir.

A moment later, Homer sat up and looked around. He clasped his hands and breathed on them. "Aren't you cold? It's freezing in here."

Brad poured coffee into his cup and tested its temperature. "Hadn't noticed," he lied. He, too, was cold, but if it made these guys sleep longer, that gave him more time to consider his options without interruptions. Plus, he had no intention of making it comfortable for them . . . just as they refused to cater to him.

Homer lit a portable propane heater and cranked it up. He then went to the wood stove and checked it. He muttered to himself about Virgil letting the fire go out as he worked to build a new one. As the logs began to catch and burn, he held his hands in front of the opening.

"There. That should get things warmed up soon."

A short while later, he turned off the propane heater and then kicked Virgil's cot.

"C'mon. Get up."

Virgil rolled over to face the other way. "Why? So we can all sit here and watch each other breathe?"

Brad remained unperturbed. He had decided the day before that it was better to offer a poker face to these guys rather than give them any clue as to how or what he was feeling. At the moment, he was seeing a split forming between these two. Maybe he'd be able to use it to his advantage.

Brad set about to fix himself some breakfast. First, he figured out a way to toast some bread on the wood stove. The method was a bit clumsy, but it worked. With toast made and buttered, he scrambled two eggs and cooked them over the small stove.

"That smells good," said Virgil, who now sat up looking at him.

Brad said nothing, but sat down and ate his food. He

resisted making sounds of satisfaction just to get at Virgil, who he'd discovered the previous night couldn't even "cook" baked beans from a can.

"I'll fix us some." Homer seemed intent on keeping his partner content.

Brad finished up eating, and then tossed his paper plate into the wood stove before rinsing and washing his utensils. They were the sturdy plastic kind made for camping, and he'd marked his. The last thing he wanted was to share a fork with Virgil, whom he couldn't trust to wash it well.

"Any good books here?"

Homer shook his head.

"The place clearly doesn't have Wi-Fi or cable."

Homer gave him a look. "Yeah, funny guy. You just need the password."

"Seems we *both* need to stick to our day jobs. No stand-up comedy in our futures."

Homer seemed to calm down. "There's a deck of cards over there."

"So, just what *are* your day jobs?" asked Brad, knowing the question posed a long shot.

Both men remained silent. Still, there was a way about them. The way they stood. The way they assigned tasks among themselves. The way they talked when they didn't think he could hear them. These guys weren't career criminals. They were ex-military or ex-police. Maybe current police. Or Feds? Brad mulled that over. He could see them as trained federal agents working under orders from higher up.

Brad killed time playing solitaire for a while, until

his body told him he needed to relieve himself soon, not later. He had already been told he could step outside the door and pee from the small porch. That's not what he needed.

"I need to go to the bathroom, and I don't mean just take a leak."

Homer nodded. "Latrine's behind the cabin. Feel free to go."

Curious, thought Brad. *They really aren't concerned about my leaving.*

He walked out the door, and sure enough, they didn't even bother following him. It was cold outside, and he wasn't equipped for such weather. Maybe they figured that alone would dissuade him from trying to hike out.

Upon returning to the cabin, he found Homer outside, throwing food scraps to a small murder of crows. He had done the same the evening before. Homer followed him inside. Brad decided to take the opportunity to ask them outright. "Okay, I really want to know something. Last night you said if I left I'd probably die and not by your hands. Today, you gave me free rein to go in and out. What would happen if I left?"

The two men looked at each other as if unsure about what to do or how much information to share.

Homer turned toward him, and said, "As we said, you'd probably die. Behind the cabin, this canyon goes another half mile or so, I'm told, all pretty much uphill. When you get to the top, all you'll find is a sheer drop to the desert below. Almost a *mile* below. Should you go the other way, downhill, odds are you'll get lost. There are no landmarks to guide you. You'll go in circles trying to find your way out. And it's rugged country so you'd be lucky to put four, five miles behind you each day. Since it's also desert country, with a good fifty miles to the nearest water source, you'd become dehydrated long before you could find help."

Virgil seemed to gloat as Homer passed on this information. "I see you looking at the water jugs. You have no backpack or way of hauling supplies with you. How many of those jugs you think you could carry in your hands? Hands you'll need to climb and maneuver and balance yourself as you try to find your way out. And Homer didn't mention the temperatures. This mountain is over 9,000 feet high. We're sitting at over 7,000 feet. The nighttime temperature is below freezing this time of year. So, take your pick. Hypothermia. Dehydration. Falling to your death from one wrong step. What do you think your odds are?"

Seventeen

Richard stared at Ben in disbelief. The office was working in catastrophe mode. Their candidate had been abducted. Ben had called him back to his office in midafternoon and wanted to chat. Chat? Now?

"So, tell me more about the house."

"I thought you still needed to call Stan." Richard felt cornered. Plus, he had work to do.

"I do. But it can wait another five minutes if it has to." The man stood up, turned to look out the window for a moment, and then turned back to Richard. "Something about this house is fishy. Hey, I'm glad you got such a deal, but a little voice inside me says, *Look out.* I don't mean what I'm gonna say next to belittle you or diss you in any way. Okay?" He paused and waited on Richard to respond.

"Okay. I guess." Richard wasn't sure he wanted to hear what was coming next. He already felt a little vulnerable with everything going south between him and Amy.

"Good. You know me. I'm just gonna say it. There's a reason you were picked for that stuff that happened in Kansas City with Summer Stanton. We don't know what it was, or if things have changed in the minds of those who concocted that scheme, but what if they still see you as a source of information, as someone who can be swayed?"

Richard's immediate reaction was to protest that the person who "concocted that scheme" jumped over an upper floor railing in the atrium of the hotel and died. Yet, maybe she wasn't the one who called those shots, even if she was the one pulling the strings. Richard had assumed that Karolus Karling had been in charge, and he was dead, too. However, if The Assembly's plan had deeper roots and others involved, maybe he *was* still a target.

And then there was Summer Stanton. It did seem convenient that she lived three doors away from this new house. Had she somehow been involved with Eric Pearce, too? The answer to that question could prove quite enlightening. Another thought hit him about her. What if she wasn't as innocent in the Kansas City affair as she had proclaimed? What if her role in that blackmail attempt had been staged all along?

Suddenly, Ben's concerns became real to Richard. He still couldn't quite accept Ben's suspicions—particularly after having had dinner with Summer—but he could understand the need to be cautious.

"You know, Richard, one of the things I like about you is you're a decent guy. You're true to your word. You're a Boy Scout kind of guy—the type who helps little old ladies cross streets or rescues kittens from trees. But . . . you also want to see only the best in people. You find it hard to believe someone might be setting you up or using you."

Richard didn't want to accept that. He thought himself a good judge of character and of people's motives. Yet, his old buddy Clive had once told him the same thing when he had helped Richard move into an apartment in the upper floors of an old house in St. Louis, the home of an elderly widow who needed the extra income. Clive had even used the term 'Boy Scout.'

Ben sat down behind his desk, and again said, "So, what can you tell me about this house?"

Richard sighed. He now saw this house from a new perspective. "Do you want the realtor version . . . or the bottom line of what you're looking for?"

Ben gave him a look.

"It's a great house. Sits on a full acre that's beautifully landscaped. It has five bedrooms and—"

"Cut to the meat of your answer."

"Summer Stanton lives three doors away and Eric Pearce committed suicide in it."

Ben's jaw dropped. He didn't respond for two full minutes.

"And *that* didn't make you suspicious?"

Now Richard felt embarrassed. "Well, the suicide thing doesn't bother me. In fact, it explained why the house was available so cheap. And when I learned that Summer lived close by, I wasn't happy about it. But why would I suspect that Maggie Walther and Summer were in on it together?"

"Summer? You're calling her by her first name?"

"Well, yeah. I got to know her a little bit in Kansas City, and . . ."

He stopped short as he realized he was about to divulge more information than he desired. Ben, however, caught his mistake.

"And what? Have you seen her here?"

Now Richard felt convicted—a step beyond

embarrassment. He resisted answering.

"Have you?" Ben had no anger in his voice, but his concern was palpable.

Richard took a deep breath. "Well, I saw her for a minute or two when Mag- . . . Ms. Walther showed me the house. That's when I learned she lived down the street." He stumbled over his next words. "And we had dinner together last night."

"Dinner together?" Ben sounded incredulous, but still no anger reflected in his tone. "And your fiancée wouldn't have any trouble with that?"

Richard had dug the hole he found himself in. Now he felt as if he was pulling the dirt back in . . . on top . . . to bury him there.

"I, uh, I have no fiancée at the moment. Amy came to town to surprise me and ended up following me to the house two nights ago. She overheard me agreeing to buy it and got upset that I had chosen to do that without her."

Ben stood again and paced behind his desk. He stopped and gazed at Richard for a moment and resumed his pacing. Richard wanted to know what thoughts were going through the man's mind, but also did not want to ask. His concern grew as Ben began rubbing his hands together and mumbling to himself. He had seen that behavior before and it hadn't fared well.

After five minutes, Ben sat down, stared at Richard, and smiled. He'd seen that smile before, too. Was it too late to leave the room?

"You've been undercover before, right?"

Richard looked for the door and tried to think up an excuse for an emergency exit.

"I think we can use this to *our* advantage, and to *your* advantage. Kill two birds with one stone as they say. If you do this, I'll tell Amy that I put you up to it, to buying the house. I'll tell her that we wanted to gain Summer Stanton's trust to be able to feed her false information because we suspected her of working for The Assembly and DNC. Maggie Walther, too."

At first, that idea appealed to Richard. It could certainly help get him out of the doghouse. But the appeal eroded like a beach in a hurricane. He had promised Amy he'd never lie to her. Should she uncover this ruse after they were married, well, *hasta la vista*, Richard.

"Sorry, I won't lie to Amy. However, I don't like getting duped. So, if we can prove somehow that these two women are trying to get to me for nefarious reasons, I'm willing to become that double agent."

"Nefarious. Good word. I like that word."

He appeared to write it down. Richard had no doubt it would end up in some speech or social media campaign soon. Ben looked back at him.

"All right then. Let's get you moved in. I've got contacts. Tomorrow."

Eighteen

Never before had Lynch spent so much time looking at dirt. After confirming that the pickup truck of the abductors had left the refuge compound via the east service road, Coby had backtracked to the next closest road heading south. Within minutes, they found the tread marks they hoped to see, and Lynch felt they were on a roll. More than that, he felt their discovery was a God-given sign pointing them in the right direction.

The next intersection of roads didn't provide such providential results. Or the next. Or the following one. Lynch took the wheel of the rig while Coby walked the road looking for anything to confirm they were still on the right path. Twenty yards down the road at the second intersection. A quarter mile later after the third. Eventually, he would find what he needed, although just what that was eluded Lynch.

Four hours after that first confirmation and the discovery of Graham's phone, Lynch was convinced of Coby's tracking abilities. The man had found the trail on the hardscrabble surfaces they traveled. Lynch would have given up three hours earlier.

Coby motioned for Lynch to move to the passenger

seat and then climbed into his driver's seat.

"Man, that's the toughest trail I've ever pursued, but I think I can safely say they're headed back out to Frenchglen Highway. From there, they'll head south, but we run into a few problems. Beyond Frenchglen is a small airport at Roaring Springs. We should cover that base and make sure no small planes took off yesterday. Then we have a choice. The Steens Mountain Loop heads into the wilderness area at Frenchglen, and comes back to Route 205 north of the airport. Steens Mountain Road is the southern end of the loop and would get us onto the mountain itself faster, but Fish Lake Road on the northern part of the loop offers more access to places where they could hole up. There used to be dozens of old hunting cabins scattered through the area. Most are gone or in various states of being reclaimed by nature. A handful have been maintained by the BLM as emergency shelters."

"Hey, you're the guy who said he knows this region better than anyone. I have to trust your instincts and knowledge of the area." Lynch now recognized that this hunt was not going to be easy . . . or over in a day or two.

"Well then, glad you said that 'cause I have a plan."

Lynch wanted to grimace but held back. The tone of the man's voice suggested that this idea might not be to Lynch's liking. And he still wondered why they were hauling horses.

"We'll check the airport first and then head up Steens Mountain Road toward the summit. There's a campground called Jackman Park near the top. We'll set up base there."

"Set up base? You mean, like tents?"

"Well, there's no Hilton there. And we've too much ground to cover to commute in from Burns each day. So, yeah, tents. You never been camping?"

"Sure. Been awhile, but I'm good with that. Just want to know what I should expect."

Coby nodded. "Good. Then tomorrow we set out on horseback with my secret weapon, weather permitting." He grinned.

"Horses and a secret weapon. Sounds like a trip I'll never forget."

"What? Don't tell me the city boy's never been on a horse."

"Sure. I've been on a horse." Lynch would never admit that his only times on a horse were as a kid at a handful of festivals that had rides and a petting zoo. His first time on a horse had been at the age of six. He could say he'd ridden a camel, too, for that matter. He hadn't lied about camping either, but he didn't have to admit that his camping experience consisted of Boy Scout camp one summer.

Nineteen

Amy's first actions upon arriving home that morning were to shed her clothing right into her washing machine, take a shower, and go to bed. She was glad she had gotten time off from work and wouldn't have to explain her inability to go to work to her boss. Her fellow employees had already voted that she should have her own reality show. She didn't need them broadcasting a new episode.

Her fatigue had numbed her mind and the shower hadn't helped her think. The warm water had, however, relaxed her tense muscles and facilitated her falling asleep.

Now, six hours later, she bolted awake. The jacket!

She also recalled the taxi driver's features and accent. He wasn't the man from the bunker, but she had little doubt they were of the same nationality. Yet, the jacket disturbed her. She couldn't reconcile that coincidence in her mind.

She dressed quickly and grabbed a light snack from the kitchen before settling into her favorite chair with her laptop. First, Somalia. She delved into its culture and discovered that it was 99.8% Muslim with a majority being Sunnis. There was also a strong presence of Sufism, a mystic dimension of Islam known for its asceticism. She scanned through information on its economy, education, and more.

She wanted to know more about its pirates. Their

actions against ships off the Horn of Africa had become well-known after the Tom Hanks movie, *Captain Phillips.* She found the information she wanted but realized that had nothing to do with what she had discovered. Did the country have any known terror groups?

Her eyes widened as she saw the results of her search. The Harakat Shabaab al-Mujahidin, known more commonly as Al-Shabaab. A violent, jihadist terror group of Wahhabist roots that was not only at odds with the Sufis in Somalia but was a willing exporter of terror. They had been listed on the U.S. terror watch list since 2008. What had she stumbled upon?

She sat back in her chair and reflected on her discovery. What was it the driver had said? All of his male relatives drove taxis. Were some of them linked to Al-Shabaab and through it, Al-Qaeda? Had she upset some plan of theirs against St. Louis? Maybe the whole Midwest?

She dashed into the kitchen and found her bag. She rummaged through it but could not find the business card she looked for. She dumped the bag's contents onto her table. Nothing. What was the agent's name? Maybe she could track him down through the local ATF office.

Then a thought came. She rushed into her laundry area and pulled her clothing from the washing machine. She checked the pockets of her jeans. There it was.

Back in her chair, she began to dial the number but stopped. She'd forgotten a strategic piece of information. Using her laptop, she pulled up the website for the cab company. Maybe they had a staff photo. If so, maybe she could point out the man, or men, from Busch Wildlife.

She surfed from page to page but found no group photos or individual photos of anyone who worked there. She was about to exit the site when she saw a link to a page for interested drivers to apply for a job. She saw it as a long shot but she'd visited every other page on the site. As soon as the page loaded she saw it. The jacket was company apparel provided to all of the drivers.

A minute later, she had the ATF agent on the phone.

"Agent Tiffin, this is Amy Gibbs."

"Good afternoon, Ms. Gibbs. I want to thank you again for—"

"I think I have something more for you. Have you translated the recording I gave you?"

"I'm sorry, but at this point, I really can't discuss anything further with you. I hope you understand."

"It's Somali. The men were Somali and I think one or more work for County Taxi."

She went on to explain how she had discovered that. The agent, in turn, asked a few questions but did not divulge any information that would satisfy her curiosity. Where was Lynch when he could be helpful? He'd always had ties to the various agencies. He could find out what they had learned.

"Thank you, Ms. Gibbs. Once again you've been very helpful. We won't forget this."

As Amy hung up she didn't think about the conversation. She again wondered why Lynch had come to mind. She shook her head. She needed to clear the cobwebs. That relationship was long over,—pre-Richard—and her engagement to Richard was now over, too.

She took no time to dwell on those losses. She called her dad.

"Hope I didn't wake you."

"No, sweetie. I set my alarm and gave myself four hours. Otherwise, I won't sleep tonight. What's up?"

She proceeded to tell him of her discoveries.

"Wow. I'm sure that'll help the Feds. Do you want me to come over? Or would you rather stay here?"

Amy puzzled over his questions.

"I-I don't think so. Why do you ask?"

"Make sure you stay armed then."

Now he scared her.

"Dad, don't joke."

"I'm not. You just told me the guy, maybe all three guys, from Busch Wildlife might work for the taxi company. In fact, you said they all might be related. That means they might also be related to the driver this morning—a driver who now has your home address and name."

Amy closed her eyes and shook her head. Her reality show episode had now become Part 1—To Be Continued . . .

"Scat. Leave. Go home. Grab some empty boxes from the storeroom and start packing. We'll be at your apartment at eight a.m. to move you. Go!"

Ben pushed Richard toward the door.

"We're too busy. I've got to keep on top of what we're doing. I think we're making a dent in the public misperception of what's happened to Graham."

"We got it covered. Besides, until we hear more from the security team, we have nothing new to say. Scram. You have a long night ahead of you."

Richard shook his head, but ambled toward the storeroom.

"I'll help you carry some of those to your car."

Ben grabbed four empty boxes and consolidated them to make them easier to carry.

"What is with you, Ben? You're usually all about getting our work done and being more productive, not less."

"I see an opportunity calling." He smiled.

"Yeah. Next thing, you'll be suggesting I call Summer Stanton to help me pack."

Ben stopped and his face brightened.

"Would you? That's a great idea. Talk about working you into her graces while she's trying to work into yours. That would be perfect."

Richard shook his head. "Not gonna do it." He picked up several boxes and resumed walking toward the door but stopped and turned to his boss. "Besides, you're making an assumption about her. This could all be your imagination. Maybe I really *did* just get lucky on this house."

"Sure. And Her Royal Candidate would be a kinder, more beneficent, and more altruistic leader than Brad. And the Republican's billionaire would be less black and white, softer in his rhetoric. Now *that* would be using one's imagination. Look, Richard, I've lived and worked in this town for twenty years. Unless you're a bright-eyed idealist, you learn quickly to expect the worst and mistrust most. My gut tells me I'm right on with this one. But, you know something . . . let me make you a deal. You prove me wrong, and I'll buy you both the best meal at the priciest restaurant in town, along with front row, behind-the-plate seats at a Nationals game of your choice."

Richard snorted. "Great. Now you're setting me up for a date with her *and* wanting me to cheer on the Nationals. I'll be a Brewers fan forever."

Ben chuckled. "We'll see."

Richard thought about Ben's comments as he drove home. Maybe Amy was right about how living in the D.C. area changed people. Still, he'd met a number of great people, kindred spirits of sorts, since moving there. No one he'd call a true friend yet, but given time, maybe.

He made a couple of trips to gather everything from his car and carry things to his apartment. After a snack, he rediscovered the roll of packing tape left over from his move to Virginia and reassembled the two boxes that had been broken down to carry. Half of the boxes—the sturdier boxes that had held reams of paper—he carried to the kitchen, where he stared at his collection of mixed cookware, utensils, thrift store dishes, and cheap cutlery. Where to begin?

An hour later, with his dishes wrapped and packed in two boxes, and the cookware and cutlery in another, only the utensils and foodstuffs remained. He glanced at the clock and decided to call Amy. They needed to iron things out, and she should have had enough time to sleep since his call that morning. Plus, the ATF? What was that about?

He dialed and for the first time in two days, she answered—on the second ring.

"Hi, Richard. I was going to call a little later, after you got home from work."

"Are you okay? I called this morning and your dad said you were talking with the ATF. What's going on?"

"Sorry, but I'm not at liberty to say anything right now."

Richard noted the flat tone to her voice.

"I was worried about you."

"Thank you, Richard. I'm fine."

Her conversation was terse, not like their usual talks.

"Hey, look, about the house, I—"

"Richard, this just isn't going to work. Us. This relationship."

"Amy, please, let's sit down and talk about it. I'll fly you back here and we—"

"But you won't make the effort to come here. Is that it? Richard, it's not about the house. That was only the last straw. We were engaged for over a year, but you'd never commit to a wedding date. You'd make plans to come here and I'd make plans for your visit, only to have you back out at the last minute. That happened what, ten, twelve times? You could have kept up with your team from the party's main offices here, but you chose to stay there. I visited you twice in Virginia and spent most of my time sitting in the motel room after you got called back to work. We had tickets to the Kennedy Center and reservations for romantic dinners and they never got used."

She paused, and Richard wanted to rebut her comments, but he couldn't. The facts were on her side. Surely she knew that despite those facts, he loved her.

"But, Amy, I love you. I want us to have a life together."

She didn't answer right away. Had she stopped loving him?

"Richard, I love you, too. I do, and that's what makes this so hard. But over the past year you've shown me what that life together would look like and that's not the kind of life I want with my husband. Your priorities are backwards and you've shown no interest in changing. If anything, you seem more committed to things the way they are by buying that house when you knew . . . I'd explicitly told you . . . that was a decision to be made together. Maybe it's Washington that's changed you, or maybe I just didn't really know you like I thought I did, but I-I can't stay in this relationship. It has become toxic to me."

"Amy, I . . ." Tears welled up. He hadn't expected them to, but they did. "I can change."

"Can change and will change are two different animals, Richard. Everybody *can* change. You've shown no *will* to change. B-bye, Richard."

"Amy, please . . ." The line went dead.

He dropped his phone on the couch next to him as he fought the tears. His world, his hopes, his . . . He felt emptied of everything he had planned for, the life he had dreamed of. He knew there was life after this election cycle. Things would change. He would change. He would be able to parlay his current job into one with a high six-figure income. With the sweet deal of a house he'd gotten, they wouldn't be house-poor, would be able to live well on that income, and could raise their kids in a lifestyle he'd never had growing up. But not now. The woman of his dreams had become just that, a dream.

Amy didn't know whether to be mad or glad that her father had pointed out what she should have seen. She could understand not recognizing the danger while in the taxi. She hadn't seen the jacket and made the connection until it was too late. Yet, she should have understood her risk before talking to Agent Tiffin. He might have been able to assuage her concern, make her feel comfortable that she was not going to become a target for some crazed terrorist group bent on revenge for ruining their plans.

She wanted to ease her worry by thinking the bad guys had no way of knowing she was the one who had stumbled upon their cache. After all, how could they? By now, they had to know their hiding place had been found. The place had been teaming with Feds, which the taxi driver would have reported to them, whether he was actively involved or not. And *she* was the only one to have used a taxi to leave the area. They would expect her to know something. She was someone they could lash out against, not caring whether she was involved or not.

She wasn't making herself feel any better.

She busied herself around the house double-checking all doors and windows. She carried her Glock 17 nestled into the waist of her jeans at the small of her back.

When she found herself repeating the circuit to check the doors, she realized she was more worried about it than she'd admitted to herself. She needed a distraction.

And that distraction was her phone ringing in the other

room. She rushed to answer, only to stop in her tracks when she saw that it was Richard. She had planned on calling him, before her father's alert had taken her mind elsewhere. Was she ready for this?

She took a deep breath and answered.

"Hi, Richard. I was going to call a little . . ."

She fought her emotions and thought she had maintained a calm demeanor as she made her case . . . until he said he loved her. Then she started to choke up. She loved him still, but . . .

". . . You've shown no *will* to change. B-bye, Richard."

She quickly disconnected the call and began to sob. Her emotions roiled, not just because of Richard and the finality of the way she ended the call, but because of the events that now wrapped around her. She felt so alone. She had invested so much of herself into the relationship that its end created a void, a hole in her very soul. She, too, wanted a great life together with her spouse. She had wanted that life with Richard. It was not to be.

She lifted her head up toward the heavens. "Lord, you are my Comforter. I ask for your peace in all areas of my life." She would trust in him, no matter what happened.

Richard sat on the couch for what seemed like forever. The loneliness that engulfed him upon recognizing that his life was now empty of the hopes he'd nurtured for the past year knocked him down.

Maybe he could crawl into bed, go to sleep, and not wake up to what now seemed like a nightmare to him.

He needed to call Ben and cancel the move. He needed to let him know that he wouldn't be into the office for a few days while he sorted out his life. He needed . . . he needed. Amy had been correct. He thought only of *his* needs. He hadn't really considered hers. He had screwed up his life royally.

He stood and walked into the kitchen, where he unpacked a glass, added a few cubes of ice, and two fingers of scotch. He returned to the couch and downed the spirit faster than he had intended. He resisted the urge to refill the glass. Going on a bender wouldn't solve anything.

He picked up the phone and dialed Ben.

"Hey, all packed yet?"

Richard sighed. "No. Don't think I'm going to get it done tonight. Could your guys postpone the move by a day?"

Richard heard a huff of exasperation on the other end.

"No chance. They start an out-of-state move that day and won't be back for at least a week. Maybe longer if the company can contract a move from that area. They don't make money running empty. For my guys, it's tomorrow or wait a while."

"Well, maybe I need to wait a while then. This just isn't—"

"Okay, buddy, what's up? I can hear it in your voice."

Richard didn't like spilling his life's problems on his boss, but if he was going to ask for time off to nurse his wound, he'd have to tell Ben more than "I'm not up to it." Besides, Ben was one of those good people he'd encountered in Washington, a man he was developing a friendship with, boss or not.

"I called and talked with Amy. It's really over. She said our relationship had become toxic to her."

"Ouch. Sorry. If you really want to wait, I can set that up. But you might find moving and setting up your new place just the distraction you need."

Richard thought about that. The activity would help, but so would the activity of being at work. He looked around at the apartment. Did he really want to stay here for another week or two when he had that beautiful home waiting for him?

"Okay. I'll get back to packing."

"Good lad. I'll see you in the morning. Oh, and don't forget to call Summer Stanton. You know, just to give her a heads up that you're moving in tomorrow."

Richard heard a sense of mischief in Ben's voice.

"I don't think that would be wise. I'm not in the mood."

"Mood-smood. You're going undercover, remember."

Richard preferred to forget. The last thing he wanted at that moment was another entanglement with Summer Stanton.

"I'll think about it. I don't even know if she's home. She could be away on assignment."

"Look, if they want her to get to you, she'll be home. They'll keep giving her local assignments to make sure she's around."

Richard thought about that. There was some logic to Ben's comment. He now wished to find her out of town covering the oil pipeline protests, or riots somewhere, or the war in Afghanistan. He still didn't want to believe she was part of some plot to use him for information on the American Party and Bradley Graham.

"Okay. Then just to prove you wrong I'll give her a call."

"Have I been wrong yet? See you in the morning."

Richard decided he needed that second drink now and saw to it. With half of it gone, and feeling bolder, he called Summer.

"Summer Stanton. I'm not available at the moment, so please leave me a message at the tone."

Richard felt some relief. She was likely on assignment somewhere.

"Hi, Summer, it's Richard Nichols. I—"

He heard her connect on her end.

"Richard, hi. I didn't recognize your number and let it go to voicemail. I guess I should add your number to my contact list, now that you're going to be a neighbor."

"Just thought I'd let you know I'm moving in tomorrow, so you wouldn't be concerned if you saw people at the house."

"That's fast. And fantastic. If you need some help, I'd be happy to come over. I'll be in town for a while."

The Director glanced at his watch. The day had become a blur of activity, and the evening, too, had slipped past him. With his wife reading a new novel and their children in bed, he stole away to his private study. He'd heard murmuring from Homeland Security about a serendipitous discovery of explosives outside of St. Louis. Their formal briefing was scheduled for the morning, following completion of the initial investigations by the FBI and ATF.

Right now, he wanted the behind-the-scenes story. He had a gut feeling that this uncovering of a terror cell's cache was not going to be to his liking.

"This is François. I've been expecting your call, sir."

"Yes, well, what do you have for me?"

"Yes, sir. Starting in the Middle East, the Iranians are again testing the resolve of the U.S. Navy. Their—"

"Yes, yes, François. I am aware of that. I am more interested in Operation New Year."

Operation New Year was The Assembly's backup plan should the conservatives somehow steal this election—the long shot that such an occurrence was. Scheduled for launch on New Year's Eve, over a dozen venues were to be the targets of a coordinated attack designed to inflict casualties and provoke the public into demanding protection. That protection would come in the form of Martial Law, which would allow them to stay in power.

"Yes, sir. Operation New Year. I'm afraid that plan has suffered a serious setback. The Somali cell in St. Louis had nearly completed its collection of C4 and was about to distribute to other cities, when someone stumbled upon the hidden collection. The ATF and FBI are investigating, but we have none of our agents there. They were moved to the protest in Oregon to deal with Bradley Graham."

The Director wanted to throw the phone against the wall. He began to pace. St. Louis, again. Events and people from St. Louis had led to the downfall of Karolus Karling, the previous director. The American Party nuisance was based in St. Louis. Bradley Graham was from St. Louis. What was it about St. Louis?

"Haven't we learned, François? Why was St. Louis used for this when we have had such trouble from people in that city?"

"Sir, we had little choice. Its central location in the country was deemed critical to the plan. In addition, its large immigrant community is useful. The Somalis guaranteed they could get the C4 without raising suspicions and that's where they are."

That did little to lessen the Director's ire. They had been slowly collecting the explosives to avoid raising an alert. To replenish the entire stock in time would bring them to the attention of local police authorities where The Assembly held much less sway.

"Do we know how it was found?"

"Purely coincidental. A young woman hiking in the area came across three of the Somalis and thought they looked suspicious. She got curious and found the cache."

The Director shook his head. Even their luck ran bad in St. Louis.

"I guess whoever she is makes no real difference. Just a bad turn of events for us."

"Well, uh, sir. It might. Her name is Amy Gibbs. She's a nurse with a medical helicopter company."

The Director caught his words, "It might."

"You say her identity *might* make a difference. How?"

"Sir, Amy Gibbs is Richard Nichols' fiancée."

"The Richard Nichols at the American Party? The one we have Maggie Walther working on? That Nichols?"

"*Oui, monsieur.*"

The Director sat at his desk. This was an interesting turn of events. Maybe their luck hadn't gone bad after all. He pondered how he might use this information.

"And how is that project going?"

"Quite well, sir. We expedited his loan approval and Madam Walther gave him the keys to the house this morning. He can move in whenever he wishes."

"Good, good. And our people across the street, from when Pearce lived there, still have eyes on the place?"

"*Oui, monsieur.* And Summer Stanton lives three doors away. We have him covered."

Twenty

Lynch awoke to the smell of brewing coffee. Coby had wakened before him, but that didn't surprise him. Despite sleeping in small individual tents, the man's snoring had kept Lynch awake until the point where his fatigue overwhelmed him. Lynch had lain there imagining the man's tent fluttering with every snore. He wondered if the noise also kept the bears and mountain lions at bay—if there were bears and mountain lions in the area. He'd have to ask about that. He didn't want to be startled by seeing such an animal emerge on the trail in front of them.

He had stripped off his outer clothes to sleep but had kept them inside the sleeping bag with him to keep them warm. As they got dirtier, or if they got wet, he wouldn't have that "luxury." Nothing like donning ice-cold jeans in the morning. Brrrr.

As he reflected on the previous day, he realized that they had progressed several steps forward. They had found the trail leading to the Steens Mountain area, even if they hadn't been able to track it all the way to wherever Brad was being held. They had been able to write the Roaring Springs airport off their list. No planes had used the facility for over a week. They had also cleared a couple of mountain roads from their search plans. The gates had been closed and locked to keep vehicles out for the upcoming winter. Their focus now turned to the Steen's Mountain Wilderness and some adjacent areas.

He dressed quickly and joined Coby by the camp stove.

"Mornin'. Coffee?"

"Sure. Thanks. Black is good."

"Glad to hear it. That's all we got." Coby grinned.

"Aren't you allowed to build campfires here? Seems we could warm up faster around a nice fire."

Coby took a sip of his coffee and nodded.

"That it would, and yes, we can have fires in designated areas."

Lynch looked around. "So, this isn't one of those areas?"

"Yup, it is."

Coby took another sip of coffee, and Lynch wondered why there wasn't a fire.

"I didn't build one 'cause we won't be here long enough to mess with it."

"Oh." Lynch looked around again and saw that the horses were out of the trailer and tied to a line stretched between two pines. A small pile of hay sat before each, as well as a bucket of water. He wasn't sure how this day would pan out.

"Now that you're up, I'll fix us some breakfast. Normally, I'd cook up some bacon and then scramble eggs, but doin' bacon right will take too much time. So, hope hash browns and eggs'll work for you."

Lynch nodded. "Sure. Sounds good. What can I do to help?"

He watched Coby place a chunk of butter in a frying pan and place it on the stove. As it melted, he opened a bag of frozen hash browns, now mostly thawed, and dumped it into the simmering butter.

"Can you cook up these potatoes? I'll get the eggs from the cooler. How many you want?"

Lynch took the spatula and said, "Two's fine."

Coby returned and took over the cooking. "Found some green peppers, too. And a few spices. Okay with you if I just cook it all together, or you one of those folks who don't like their foods to touch each other on the plate." He grinned again.

"Your way sounds great." Lynch looked out over the horizon. The sun seemed brighter at that altitude, or maybe it was simply the lack of air pollution. He again relished the freshness of the clean mountain air. "Hey, do you think we can get cell reception here? I'd like to call my team and check in."

Coby nodded. "Cully, up here you can probably pick up the cell towers in Portland."

Lynch laughed. He knew that to be an exaggeration, but he had no idea how far they were from the nearest towers. He retrieved his phone from the tent and discovered he had five bars of reception. He dialed Tony.

"Hey, Lynch. Good to hear your voice. Where are you?"

"On top of Steen's Mountain. We tracked the truck most of the way here."

"You tracked the truck? On gravel roads?"

"I think Coby could track a flea from dog to dog if he chose to."

"FBI is saying they headed north, not south."

"No way, Tony. I saw the treads myself. What are they saying about Graham's phone?"

"They haven't been able to ping it."

"What? Why ping it when they could trip over it? I found it yesterday morning and left it in place for them. It's right where the east service road meets; just a minute . . ." He walked closer to Coby. "Hey, Coby, what's the name of the road where we found the cell phone?"

"Narrows-Princeton Road."

He gave the man a thumb up as he returned to the call. ". . . Tony, the northeast corner of the intersection of the refuge service road and Narrows-Princeton Road. It's in the grass and easily seen from the road."

"Whoa. The Feds are saying they took the other service road north over the canal or ditch or whatever they call it, and fled that way."

"One second . . ." Lynch asked Coby about that route and got his answer. "Coby says no way. That just leads to a bunch of service roads that weave around and through the refuge. There are two access points to those roads on Route 205, but the gates are kept chained and locked. I bet you can check those gates to see if they've been tampered with. My bet is they haven't been opened in months."

"Will do, boss. I'll let you know. But I have to say this whole investigation is sounding off base to me now. I mean, they didn't even find Graham's cell phone? Incredible."

Lynch nodded as he concurred. "They aren't doing anything. Someone has given them orders to stall. In addition to checking the gates, go find Graham's phone. Let's see if they even bothered looking over there. But hey, document every move you make. Get it all on video and handle the phone like any evidence at a crime scene. Gloves, bag it, the whole works. Okay?"

"Got it. Oh. I've been getting calls from headquarters. What do you want me to tell them?"

"Check the gates and phone first. If we're right, let Stan know what's going on. He can decide how to handle the information and what to tell the press. And have him reassure Mrs. Graham that we're on the trail. We'll find her husband."

Lynch returned to Coby to find half of breakfast already gone. Coby pointed to the remainder.

"That's yours. Eat up while it's still warm. I'll saddle the horses and get the packs ready."

"Sorry. That took longer than expected." He related the details of the conversation to Coby. "What do you think?"

"Sounds to me like somebody doesn't want Graham found any time soon and Tanner's going along with it. Yup, looks like we're gonna find that fresh buffalo pie and rub his sorry face in it after all. Let's go find your candidate."

Lynch wolfed down the food. "Hey, this is good!" he yelled toward Coby who was with the horses now.

Coby yelled back, "Of course it is. Best restaurant in town didn't start without a good cook at the helm."

Lynch finished his food and began to pack up the camp stove. He then washed their dishes and utensils, using their water as sparingly as possible, and packed them. By the time he carried them to Coby, the tents were down and the horses were packed except for the cooking gear. Lynch saw that two horses were saddled for riding, while the third carried most of their gear. One of the riding horses also carried a plastic duffel of sorts behind the saddle. Coby added the cooking gear to that horse's load. The other horse had a smaller duffel and a square, hard-shell package that looked like it held electronics of some sort. Lynch wondered what was in it.

"Your secret weapon?" he asked as he pointed to the container.

Coby nodded. "Yup. You're gonna love it. Saddle up."

Coby moved toward the horse carrying the secret weapon. Lynch stood in place like his feet were anchored.

"C'mon, Charlie there won't bite. Oh. Sorry. Forgot to make the introductions. That's Charlie, this is Ed, and that's Sally Mae."

Lynch rolled his eyes. "Really? Charlie, as in Charlie Horse? That's the best you could do?"

Coby shrugged. "What can I say? I let my kids name them as colts."

"And Ed? Like in the old TV show, *Mr. Ed*?"

Coby nodded. "Yup. The kids loved that show, but watch this." He walked toward the horse's head and stood in front of it. "Hey, Ed, do you think we'll find Mr. Graham today?" The horse's lips started to move just like the horse on TV, but no voice came out. Coby looked at Lynch. "Guess the soundtrack is off today." He started to laugh. "I trained him to do that and my kids would make up their own scripts. We've got some old VCR tapes of them talking with Ed. They're hilarious."

Coby patted Ed on the nose and gave him some sort of treat. Lynch couldn't see what it was.

"And Sally Mae? Did the kids name her, too?"

"Yes and no. My daughter named her Sally. Not sure why. Later on, I added the Mae 'cause there's days she *may* let you ride her and others she *may* not. She has a cantankerous streak as wide as that big gorge we stopped to see, but she seems more content to carry a load than to carry a man. She'll be fine with our gear."

"Okay, mount up."

Lynch walked to the right side of the horse and lifted his leg to get to the stirrup. Charlie stepped away. Lynch tried again. The horse stepped away. He looked to Coby for help, but Coby stood there staring at him.

"I thought you said you'd ridden a horse before. You always mount from the left side." The man shook his head. "Just where did you learn to ride?"

Lynch moved to Charlie's left side. He tried to ignore the question.

"No. Really. Where?"

He put his foot in the left stirrup and pushed up. But Charlie moved again and he landed back on the ground. Lynch felt his face flush.

"Well, uh, I . . . I didn't say I *learned* to ride, just that I'd ridden a horse before. I was six, and they had horses to ride, in a circle, at the Apple Butter Festival in a little town south of St. Louis. I rode a camel, too."

It took Lynch a second attempt, but he made it into the saddle. He turned to see Coby in the saddle staring at him.

"Great. A greenhorn." He patted Ed on the neck. "Ed, this is gonna be a long day. Charlie and us, we've got some serious ITS training to do."

Lynch gave him a questioning look. "ITS training?"

"In the saddle, greenhorn. Hope you're a quick study, 'cause we've got some serious riding to do."

Brad stirred with the light of dawn and the creaking of his cot as he moved. The first thing he noticed was how much colder it was in the cabin this morning. The previous night had seen the fire in the wood stove maintained until after midnight by his captors. Had they ignored that need last night?

He sat up and looked toward Homer's cot . . . that is, where it had been yesterday morning. There was no cot. There was no Homer. He glanced toward the door. Virgil was gone as well.

"Well, that's great," he said to the empty room. He rose from the cot and walked to the nearly cold wood stove. *First things first*, he thought. He relit the fire and waited to make sure it had caught, warming his hands at the same time. He added one more log and then turned to the food supply. The men had left everything behind.

He walked to the front door, opened it, and peered outside. Not a sign of them.

I guess they were serious when they said I might not make it if I venture out on my own. Then he wondered if that had been their plan all along.

He grabbed a glass of water along with his bowl. He filled the bowl with dry cereal and debated making up some powdered milk to use on it. That sounded so unappetizing that he ate it dry and then made toast on the wood stove. He took inventory of what Homer and Virgil had left behind and calculated he had food for up to two weeks if he ate modestly. With what they'd stocked up, he'd more likely eat sparingly. The boxes held the delights of a junk food junkie. Yet, he also realized that if he got hungry enough, he'd eat even the worst food scientists could come up with.

The cabin had warmed up, and the sun now filled the cabin's east window. He looked about for something to do after cleaning up from breakfast. Cards . . . clearly only good for solitaire. Three paperback novels, two of which he'd read before. He found a spiral notebook of lined paper and a handful of pens. He grabbed one and tested it. He couldn't get the ink to flow, but the second one he tried wrote well. He killed the next hour journaling about his experience so far, along with detailed descriptions of both men and the truck, which had no license plates when he looked.

"Bladder calls," he said to break the silence. In thinking about whether he would start talking to himself, he decided not to. He noticed that one of the men had left behind a heavier jacket than the one he'd been wearing when they took him. It hung on a peg near the back northwest corner of the cabin. When he went to retrieve the item, he saw a note pinned to it.

We stayed for a day to make sure you could handle things for yourself. You definitely are capable. We'll be back when our boss says to come get you.

Or not, he thought. Did he really want to wait for them? As he'd been writing, he realized that all he had was their word that he couldn't get out alive on his own.

He donned the jacket and made his way to the latrine. With nature's call answered, he decided to test what they had told him. He continued to climb the canyon behind the cabin. Homer had said it ended up at a cliff that dropped off nearly a mile to the desert below.

Brad had no idea how long he'd been climbing. The terrain was the most rugged he'd ever encountered and his shoes didn't help. The leather soles of the dress shoes he'd been wearing when kidnapped gave him no traction and the leather uppers proved inflexible for climbing over boulders. He had slipped and fallen numerous times and the knees of his slacks were close to tearing. And he could feel the bruises on his fleshy knees—and shins and elbows—with every movement. He hoped Homer had left some type of anti-inflammatory medicine with the foodstuffs.

He continued the climb. He was not about to give up. For all he knew, there could be a road at the top. He was thirsty now. He recalled a physical trainer from his past saying that people didn't realize how much moisture they lost with the heavy breathing of exercise and that staying hydrated was critical. At home, that had never been an issue. Now, he understood.

He fantasized a search helicopter flying overhead, but heard nothing except the wind rustling through the treetops. Those treetops were thinning out, however.

He noted the increasing level of sunlight around him. He had to be nearing the top.

He pushed ahead, and within a brief period—by his best guess since he had no watch or cell phone to check the time—he came to a narrow grassy area. The trees had given way to scrub brush. Ahead was a short rise, but above that was sky. He had reached a horizon. On top of that rise he expected to find out whether Homer had told the truth or not.

Buoyed by the fact that he'd made it to the top, he climbed the small hill and staggered backward to avoid the vertigo that hit him as he saw the entire mountain fall away in front of him. Homer had not lied. Although not a sheer cliff, the jagged stair steps he witnessed below were tens, if not hundreds, of feet in height as they dropped to the bottom.

Brad sat down to rest. As he did so, he noted that the sun appeared to be high in the sky. The time had to be around noon, meaning he had spent hours climbing that canyon. How did he have the strength and endurance to accomplish that? He also marveled at the majesty of God's creation all around him. He acknowledged the incredible view, even as he realized he would now have to descend the canyon and hope that Homer's other admonition was wrong—that he'd get lost. He said a quiet prayer for guidance and began the arduous return trip.

Twenty-one

Eight a.m. rolled around much too early for Richard. He'd continued packing until almost two a.m., but despite being tired enough to sleep standing up, he hadn't been able to sleep much. He'd fall asleep only to dream about gasping for air in a cloud of toxic gas and awaken, struggle back to sleep and dream about choking on toxic berries, then awaken, and repeat with new scenarios. At six a.m., he gave up on sleep, but all he could think about was Amy's comment.

The front door buzzer sounded at 8:10. Richard downed his coffee, rinsed and dried the mug, and repacked it into a box before answering. He pressed the intercom button.

"Hello."

"Hey, wake up, Sleeping Beauty. The gang's all here."

Was his fatigue that evident in just saying "hello?"

He pressed the button to release the door lock. Within seconds he could hear footsteps clomping up the stairwell, and he opened the door to see Ben holding out a Starbucks Quad Espresso Macchiato and four men standing behind him.

"Here. Figured you could use something stronger

than your usual coffeemaker home brew."

Richard took the cup. "Thanks. And you're right. Not much sleep last night, so I hope I can keep up with you guys." He took a sip. The temperature was perfect. If the extra dose of caffeine didn't keep him awake, his bladder screaming for relief in an hour would.

"So, did you call her?"

"Yes."

"And?"

"Told her I was moving in today."

"And?"

"That's it. I told her."

Ben shook his head. "C'mon, I can tell you're holding out on me. I'll cut you some slack and blame the lack of sleep."

Richard really didn't want to tell Ben all of it. That would give credence to his theory that Summer was in on some conspiracy to use him against the American Party. He took another sip of espresso and watched the movers assess his belongings. He overheard them talk about what to take first, and saw two of them begin with the couch.

"She's in town for a while, isn't she?"

Richard wouldn't lie. He nodded.

"She offered to help, too, right?"

Richard sighed. "Yes. But that still doesn't mean she's some Mata Hari or Anna Chapman bent on infiltrating the party."

Ben, sipping his drink, raised his brow as if to say, 'Oh yeah.' When he finished, he said, "We'll see, won't we? My deal is still on about that dinner and ball tickets."

The two men joined the others and began to carry

items down the stairs to the truck, where they left them for the men to arrange within the truck. Between the caffeine fix, activity, and conversation, Richard felt a second wind lift him up both physically and emotionally.

Two hours later, Richard stared at the empty apartment. It had served him well as a place to crash after long hours at work. He had never seen the space as being semi-permanent in his life. Cozy was the description of the rental agent. Cramped was the reality. He'd be back later to finish cleaning and turn in the keys. There was no rush since his rent carried him for two more weeks.

He led the way to McLean and the house, with the truck behind him and Ben pulling up the rear. Once there, he pulled up to the garage and jumped out to unlock the place. The truck stopped on the street with the rear at the driveway. This put them fairly close to the walkway leading to the front door, where they would unload the great majority of his things. The driver had refused Richard's offer to back into the driveway itself, and now that they had arrived, Richard was glad that the man had done so. Between the curve of the drive and the adjacent landscaping, there was a greater than 50-50 chance the truck would have damaged something.

As two men opened the gate of the truck and prepared to unload, Richard watched one of the others join Ben and walk up to the house. The guy held equipment Richard had only seen in movies.

"What's this?"

"We're gonna sweep your house," said the man who went by John.

"Huh?"

"For electronics," said Ben. "Listening devices. Video cameras. That kind of sweep. We need to do it before Anna Chapman's twin walks over to help you. Hopefully."

Richard shook his head in disbelief. "Is that really necessary? You think they'd bug my house?"

"Maybe we should ask Eric Pearce his opinion on that. Oh yeah. We can't 'cause he hung himself from that railing right there." Ben pointed to the top of the main stair railing. "I'm assuming that's where it happened."

Richard nodded. As much as he hoped Ben was wrong, Richard couldn't argue with the action. A man thinks his home is secure, untouchable—his private realm. What better place to catch him off-guard?

Within twenty minutes, Richard could only follow them around awed and dumbstruck. While he intermittently directed the three men carrying boxes and furnishings to the appropriate rooms, Ben and John found six video cameras and a dozen audio transmitters. The last room to be scanned was the library. Richard found them there.

Ben looked at him as he entered the room. "Nice room. It'll be a great study, or a pool table could go there."

"Or I could just use it as a library. That'd be a novel idea." Richard used his best sarcastic tone.

Ben smiled. "I see what you did there. Ha. *Novel* idea. I didn't see one box of books in what we loaded into the truck, but I see they left you all sorts of reading material." He pointed to three rows of leather-bound books partially filling one wall's shelves.

He nodded toward them and John swept his wand across each row. About two-thirds of the way down the bottom row, the equipment emitted a solid tone. Ben walked to the spot and began to inspect the books. "Looks legit enough, but they're fixed in place, like they're all one unit." He came to a book that came off the shelf easily. He leafed through it. "Leon Uris. I remember him. Good suspense."

He set the book back in place and went to the next, and the next. When he reached the second book from the end, it didn't slide out. As he played with it, it tilted out as if hinged at the bottom of the spine. As it did so, the unit of books lifted up to reveal more electronics.

"Aha. The mother lode. We didn't find any kind of recording equipment or longer range transmitter in the rest of the house, and the other devices were all short range. I wondered if we just hadn't found it, or whether it had been removed. Guess we found it."

"Aren't you going to get rid of all this? I don't particularly want to live in a house that records my every move and conversation. This isn't some reality show."

Ben looked at him with the most serious face Richard had ever seen on the man.

"Nope, this is real reality, not some semi-scripted tripe for entertainment. Eric Pearce lost his life because of this." Ben paused and nodded for John to leave. Once they were alone, he continued. "Look, I had this place figured wrong. I thought maybe they—the DNC, The Assembly, whoever—had bugged this place to get the goods on Pearce. But this is all recording equipment and it's basically in plain sight. By that, I mean it's in the house, not linked to a transmitter. And it's a bit stereotyped, at that. I mean really, the library? Hasn't that been overdone by Hollywood?" He paused.

"I guess."

"So, think about it. If you were an outsider wanting to bug the place to get evidence on the owner, would you put it in the library? There's a good chance Pearce collected these books. Would you risk his noticing someone had tampered with them? Not me, I'd hide the transmitter in the attic or in the eaves. Someplace the owner is unlikely to find it.

"But it's right here, and it's a recorder, not a transmitter. That makes me think the owner had it installed. Maybe to monitor meetings here in the house. He could turn it on and off at his pleasure. I don't think this is the work of the DNC or The Assembly."

Ben pushed the eject button on the recorder, but nothing happened. No power. He started to inspect other books.

"What are you looking for?"

"I'll know it when I find it. A DVD or two would be nice."

Richard began to help. Together they had examined a dozen books when a female voice echoed through the house.

"Richard? It's Summer. Where are you?"

Ben pushed the trigger book back into place and the collection of books moved back into place, hiding the gear. He raised his brow as he looked at Richard.

Amy paced in the hallway between the front rooms and her bedroom. The hike had started in the living room and spread to the dining area. When that circuit became too short, she moved to the hall. Her pacing reflected both her anxiety and her desire to stay awake after a mostly sleepless night.

At one point while she struggled to fall asleep, she had felt that a little light reading might help her relax. She had grabbed her book from the front room and headed back to her bedroom. But in passing the room she used as a study, she glanced out the front window to see a taxi drive by. Any chance of falling asleep vanished at that moment. She ran to the window to check it and saw that it was a different cab company. Still, the sudden surge of adrenalin had fully wakened her—again.

Now, as she paced, she debated calling her father for moral support, but decided she bugged him often enough. He needed time to recuperate from their all-nighter, too. She honestly didn't know what she would do without his encouragement, sage advice, and spiritual discernment. He'd been there for her in every aspect of her life—good and bad. Yet, she didn't want to be a burden to him again during her emotional tumble from breaking off her engagement. She felt determined to push through this situation without falling back onto his shoulders to catch her tears.

She rubbed her shoulders. The muscle tension had continued to build all of the previous day. Some people felt stress in their guts, causing stomach upset, nausea, and dyspepsia. She felt stress in her shoulders and upper back. She walked into the kitchen to grab some naproxen. As she filled a glass with water to take the pill, she decided she needed something more to ease the discomfort, something to help her relax as well.

A float! Yes, she needed to float.

She had learned of Float STL from Erica, a police officer friend, after they opened their second location in Maryland Heights, a northwest suburb. The place still wasn't *close* to work or home, but it was worth the drive. Just the thought of entering a pod filled with warm water and enough Epsom salt to recreate the Great Salt Lake made her muscle strain ease. The salt enabled you to float without effort. The pod isolated you from all sound and light. You could sleep and not drown. Her 90-minute floats relaxed her more than a massage, and didn't require her to lie naked, save a sheet, in front of someone else.

As she looked for the owner's business card, she thought about the facility itself. The serene spa-like lobby, or transition area as they called it, was bright and light-filled. No one could get in or out without being intercepted by the owner or employees. The computer-controlled water system was tamper-proof by anyone unfamiliar with the software. She could also lock her room before entering the sleek pod. Yes, not only would she relax physically, but her mind would be at ease that no one—Somali or otherwise— could get to her while there.

She dialed.

"Float STL, this is Kevin."

"Hi, Kevin, it's Amy Gibbs. I need an emergency float. Is there any way, any way at all, I could get into one of the pods? I *really* need it."

"Hi, Amy. Hey, I wish I could help, but I have zero openings for the next three weeks. We have another pod on order, but it won't be installed for at least a month. I can put you on a waiting list for today or tomorrow, and call if someone cancels."

Amy wouldn't let the disappointment eat at her. She had known her chances of getting right in were slim. The place had become that popular.

"Would you, please? I am under such stress you would not believe."

"Got you covered. You're number six on the list."

Number six?

"You mean there are five people ahead of me? How many cancellations do you get?"

"Last one was a month ago, so not many. Sorry. It's the best I can do. Lots of folks feeling stressed with this election."

Now the disappointment was getting to her. She understood all of the angst about the election, but those people hadn't just broken off their engagement to marry, spent a day trapped in a musty bunker filled with rats, and upset a Somali terror cell. What did a presidential election have to compare with that? She needed a float!

"I . . . I . . . I really need a float. Um, thanks, Kevin. Maybe I'll get lucky. Hope to hear from you soon."

She looked skyward. "Lord, I could really use your peace right now."

She used her phone to Google floating in St. Louis. A large number of canoe and raft liveries dominated the search results. She added the word 'pod' to her parameters. That was better. Float STL hit the top of the list. In fact, different pages on their website claimed the top four results of the search. But there at number five was a different company, The Dead Sea Experience, and it was right there in her community, five minutes from her house.

Yes! She pumped the air with her fist, and then tried not to get her hopes up. They might be just as busy. She wondered why she hadn't heard of this company yet. She dialed.

"Dead Sea Experience, join us for a relaxing float in salt water like that of the Dead Sea. This is Carol."

"Hi, Carol. My name's Amy. I was wondering if you could tell me more about your company."

The woman's description seemed to match that of Float STL. However, they had opened only three weeks earlier and had just two pods.

"I'd like to try it. Do you have an opening today?"

"Why, yes. Someone just canceled for six o'clock. That's currently our last float of the day."

"I'll take that one."

Twenty-two

Brad found his downhill trek more demanding than his climb to the top. He tried to gauge in his head how long he'd been moving, but that had proven dispiriting. He couldn't track the sun, despite the sparse foliage, and the small canyon twisted and turned to the point he lost his bearings on the sun. Although he could rule out heading south, he no longer knew if he was moving west, north, or east.

He came to a large boulder and used an adjacent stone to climb on top. He sat down to rest and gazed about him. As he caught his breath, he realized something was off. This ravine seemed different from the one around the cabin. The surrounding rock walls were steeper, the valley narrower. There appeared to be no dry creek bed anywhere within sight, and yet he thought he had followed one for part of the way up.

Homer had been correct on a second count. He was lost. He had no food, no water. The sun would set behind the mountain earlier than the official sunset time and the chill he had noted before would be even colder without the protection of the cabin.

He thought about his predicament. He hadn't been smart. On his climb to the top he had only focused on getting to the top and had paid no attention to the surroundings. Clearly, if he had, he would have noticed other small canyons diverging from the one he currently called 'home.' He must have strayed into one of those.

He had but one choice. He had to climb up again and find where this draw met another.

Charlie followed Sally Mae who followed Ed nose to tail through most of the day. In that sense, Lynch's ride seemed no different than the one he'd had at age six. What became glaringly different was how much his butt began to hurt. His five-minute ride in a circle at the Apple Butter Festival had been exciting, something new for a child raised in the suburbs. Now, three hours turned to four, and saddle sore took on a whole new meaning for Lynch.

The day had been glorious so far. Bright sun, fresh air, no hint of a pending storm that might chase them to take cover, and the remnants of what must have been incredible autumn color. The views, too, had been something he had never experienced. Breathtaking was the word that came to mind as they came to Kiger Gorge for the first time.

The one thing that surprised him, however, was the open barrenness of the area. They rode above the tree line amid sagebrush and scrub. The Rocky Mountains at this elevation seemed like lush rain forests in comparison. The difference lay in the arid climate of the region. Only those valleys that hosted creeks in the spring and early summer held enough moisture for trees in their lower altitudes.

"Another gorge is coming up to our north," said Coby.

For such a garrulous man at the two meals they'd

shared, he'd been nearly silent for most of the ride. And yet, that suited both of them and allowed them to focus on the task at hand.

"You know, Coby, we've not seen a single hiker or anyone else on horseback. I had hoped for some help."

Coby nodded but kept facing forward. "Yup. Always helps to have more eyes and ears on a search." He rode a bit farther before adding, "If we're still batting zero by end of tomorrow, I have some friends I can call on to help."

That made no sense to Lynch. Why not get all the help they could from the start?

"Why wait?"

" 'Cause the more people who know we're here searching, the more likely the Feds will find out. And if the Feds find out, the more likely someone will come after us . . . or kill Graham."

"But if you trust your friends to be discreet, why not call on them?"

This time Coby stopped his horse and turned to look at Lynch. "It's not them. It's other folks who'll get curious when half a dozen horse trailers head through town and go south at the same time. There's only so many ways to get here and folks along the way could get curious, too."

Lynch pondered his statement for a moment, and then said, "I figured people here would be used to seeing horse trailers being towed. Plus, isn't it hunting season? Wouldn't horse trailers be a common sight?"

Coby shook his head. "Bowhunting season ended a couple of weeks ago. It's whitetail deer season in the

Cascades and coastal areas, but not here. Elk hunting doesn't start till mid-November. A hunter could be after black bear or cougar right now, but not many folks are into that and they're not common here. Too dry. We're outside the usual tourist season, too. Nope, a caravan of trailers heading this way will have folks thinking there's a search goin' on for a lost hiker or someone. They'll call the sheriff's office to ask questions or volunteer to help, and that'll get to the Feds. Trust me."

The man resumed riding and Charlie joined in the procession without Lynch's urging. Lynch thought Coby was being too paranoid, but Lynch couldn't claim to know how the local people thought or reacted. Coby understood them. As Lynch thought about it, the last thing they needed was to have the wrong people find out they were searching for Graham on Steens Mountain. If indeed he was here somewhere, they'd have time to respond. Even if killing Graham wasn't part of the picture, they could move him. Then nobody, Coby included, would be able to track them because they'd have no starting point.

"We're here." Coby stopped Ed and climbed down from the saddle.

Lynch looked around and saw nothing different. "Here where? I don't see anything."

But then, he'd seen little to distinguish their last three stops. At those stops, Coby had left Lynch to mind the horses while he headed into the trees, only to return twenty or thirty minutes later to report he'd found nothing.

"You want me to watch the horses again?" he asked as he dismounted. His derriere welcomed the change.

Coby led Ed and Sally Mae to a nearby tree and lashed

their reins around a low branch. "Nope. Tie Charlie to something secure and follow me—quietly."

Lynch complied and caught up with Coby at the top of a downhill slope. To Lynch it looked more like a cliff. He struggled to follow Coby through the rocks and underbrush without triggering a rock slide or sounding like two freight trains colliding. About 100 yards down, Coby motioned for Lynch to join him behind a large boulder.

Coby whispered, "Another 100 yards or so is one of those cabins I told you about. I haven't been here in a good five years, so I don't know what kind of condition it's in. But if there's someone there, I figured both of us should be here. You are armed, right?"

Lynch looked at him like he'd asked a stupid question. Which it was. "Of course I'm armed. Don't leave home without it."

Coby nodded, and using military hand signals, he motioned for Lynch to move left while he went down the right side. Lynch worked his way to the left side of the small gorge—small in comparison to Kiger Gorge—but stayed in view of Coby, particularly as they descended below the tree line. Several minutes later, Coby pointed to something further on. As Lynch passed some rocks, he saw the cabin. Coby must have gotten a full glimpse as well because he walked into the open and toward Lynch.

The cabin's roof had caved in, and what remained hosted moss and lichen. The few windows had been broken out a long time ago, and Lynch could see holes in the walls, too. On closer inspection, he saw that the front porch had rotted and rocks the size of bowling balls sat on the decaying floor inside. The rocks and the holes in the walls appeared to match in size. Someone had had "fun" helping nature reclaim the structure.

"Well, clearly this isn't the place," said Coby. "We have another twenty-minute ride to the next one . . . unless you're up to moving at a faster pace."

Lynch thought about that for a moment. His spirit was willing, but his flesh was weak, mainly his backside. Still, he would improve, and the sooner they found Brad, the sooner he could start that recovery process.

"I'm willing to give it a try."

Coby gave him that now familiar mischievous grin. "You sure? It won't be like the Apple Sauce Fair, or whatever you called it."

Lynch regretted having fessed up to that. He might never live it down.

The climb back to the horses took a bit longer than their initial descent, but soon enough they were back in the saddle and following the crest of the ridge between two large gorges, each carrying a creek. The creeks, responsible for carrying snow melt, were mostly dry at this time of year. Lynch had learned that the tree line here was lower than in many parts of the west because of the desert conditions. The dry sagebrush they rode through offered scenic vistas at almost every turn, but became monotonous.

"So, tell me again, why we aren't simply following the road and looking for signs of a turnoff."

"Following the loop, we'd have 52 miles of road to follow and we'd have to walk a lot of that to see any evidence of a vehicle leaving it. It would be slow and tedious.

And even if we lucked out and found the tread marks we're looking for, the usable cabins would be far up those valleys. We'd have to walk that, too, 'cause I don't have the right kind of vehicle to attempt it. Up here, we have about half that distance to cover, we're closer to the cabins, and we have the advantage of high ground . . . and my secret weapon."

Lynch had yet to see this thing, this device, unveiled.

"Not much use inside its box."

"Yup."

Coby urged Ed into a trot, and Sally Mae and Charlie took up the pace. Lynch thought he'd landed on a perpetual motion washboard, but was amazed at how easy it was to stay in the saddle. Still, he wished he had an ice pack to sit on at the end of the day.

After a dozen minutes, the pace slowed again to a walk.

"We're at the next checkpoint."

Coby found a spot to keep the horses and they dismounted once again.

"There's a bit of grass here. Tie Charlie low enough to let him get to the grass."

Lynch watched Coby tie off the other two horses and mimicked his action.

"So, same drill here? We head down to check out the cabin?"

Coby shook his head and then smiled. "Nope. Secret weapon time."

The smile morphed into a wide grin as he removed the square pack from Ed's back. As he opened the case,

Lynch saw Coby's special toy: a six-propeller drone with hi-def camera. Coby lifted it out of the case and placed it on bare ground nearby. He flipped on its switch. He then took the drone's remote control from the case and turned it on. Within seconds, the two devices had synced, and Coby used the controller to lift it ten feet off the ground.

"Full battery. Winds are acceptable. We're good to go."

Lynch laughed. "My friend Amy'd say something about a boy and his toys at this point."

"And she'd be right. This thing has been invaluable on cattle roundups. This thing has been invaluable on cattle roundups. I bought it to look for strays. Faster than a man on horseback and cheaper than a helicopter. Figured it'd be just the thing for rounding up a different kind of stray. But this baby has one feature few have and I paid dearly for it."

Lynch gave him a curious look. "Oh?"

"Basically a more portable version of FLIR."

"FLIR on a drone, why not? I've only seen that on helicopters, but mounting it on a drone makes sense."

Forward Looking InfraRed thermal imaging technology had been around for over forty years, and advances in technology had reduced the size of such units dramatically. Lynch had heard first responder friends talk about wanting it on a drone, but they had implied it wasn't available yet. Obviously, it was now.

"Helicopter Search and Rescue. That's what gave me the idea, and when I started checking into the idea, well, I found a company right here in Oregon making them. Shoot, they've been around since 1978 and lead the world in this technology. Just south of Portland. Can't beat that with a stick. This baby is top of the line; 640 by 512 resolution and a full hour of flight time on a battery pack. I've only got five backup batteries, so I gotta be selective in using it."

Lynch understood. An hour's time was measured in ideal conditions. The slightest headwind or change in those conditions would reduce that time.

"So, I picked this canyon to test it. There's a cabin about a mile away. Seems like a lot, but it's 12 miles from the other end. The terrain between here and there is rough, so that mile would mean an hour-plus, on foot, to get there and longer coming back. This baby can fly up to 30 miles per hour and climb 30 feet per second. And with the infrared capability, we can get a heat signature from the air. Bad guys won't even know we're spying on them."

Lynch nodded with admiration. "I'm impressed. So, can I do anything?"

"Sure can. I'll focus on flying her, if you'll focus on the infrared camera. Something as hot as a body should show up orange to red in color. Something really hot, like a campfire, will be white. If you see something, let me know and I can hover over it and switch to visual camera."

"Got it. Let's fly."

Lynch watched as Coby guided the drone to a perfect liftoff and stared after it as the aircraft headed down the valley at an altitude about 100 feet above the sage and then above the trees below the tree line. After ten minutes of flight, Lynch still saw no heat signatures large enough to point to a man.

"I'm switching it to visual," said Coby. He set the controls to keep the drone in a hover and gazed at the screen. "I think I'm below the cabin, so let's watch as I bring it back."

A minute later, Lynch saw the cabin. "There it is. Slow down." Lynch scrutinized the video. Nothing. No signs of life.

Brad sat on the ground chastising himself. Why had he thought he could safely explore the wilderness he'd been taken to? He had no gear, inappropriate clothing, and no outdoor skills to speak of. He was a city boy whose outdoor experience consisted of rafting, hiking, and trail excursions all guided by experts who provided the equipment and knew their surroundings well. He hadn't even taken a supply of water with him and he was parched now.

Yet, he knew his mistake would not be a fatal one. Just as Abraham was willing to sacrifice Isaac because he knew God would raise him from the dead to fulfill His promise through the boy, Brad had faith that God had told him he was to be used in a mighty way for his country. That hadn't happened yet.

He took a deep breath and stood up. He was once again near the crest of the ridge, but not where he had originally emerged from the sage to see the precipice to the desert below. He had found no footprints from that first arrival to the top. He needed to be smarter, to place markers where he'd been so he could avoid moving in circles and repeating mistakes.

He collected rocks and built a small pyramidal tower in the most open spot he could find. From there, he would venture 30 strides, about 100 feet, in one direction along the ridge in hopes of finding his original footprints. If unsuccessful, he would backtrack to the rock tower and try the other direction. He felt confident that he would find that first spot somewhere within that 200-foot span. He simply couldn't be that far off. If he could find his original tracks, maybe he could follow them back to the correct gorge and ultimately the cabin.

He started off and observed the ground closely with each step. His progress was slow, but he could not afford to miss any sign that he'd been there earlier. He came to an area with taller scrub and searched for a way through the dense foliage. As he began to push through, a bird darted up and startled him. Wondering where it came from, he looked closely through the bushes and discovered he was on the edge of a sheer 20-foot drop. Had he pushed through he would have fallen.

"Thank you, Lord!" he said looking to the sky.

Clearly he had not been that way before. He backtracked to an open spot and found more rocks. These he laid out in a circle about three feet in diameter with a line through the middle. His own "Do Not Enter" sign.

He then followed his own prints back to the rock pyramid. From there, he headed in the opposite direction, scrutinizing the surrounding ground with each step. About 15 strides into his search, he saw them. From the scuff marks and prints he saw in the dirt, he had been there before. This time he built a pillar of rock and then broke off a branch from a nearby shrub, which he placed upright in the stones like a flag.

His confidence increasing, he carefully followed his

original footprints back down the slope. Roughly a hundred yards along, however, the dusty ground began to turn rocky. His tracks were harder to see. After a few more yards, he could see them no longer.

He scanned his surroundings and saw a large rock, about shoulder high and broad, not far from his trail. He moved to it and began to toss rocks on top. If he could climb onto it, he would build another rock pyramid to mark the location. After amassing a suitable collection of stone, he circled the rock looking for an easy spot to climb it. A quarter of the way around, he found an indention suitable for a toehold and managed to get on top.

He built his marker and then took time to gaze around him. From that higher vantage, he saw that the valley split in two not far down the slope. A smaller rift started to his left, while the main draw continued before him. He didn't think that smaller ravine was the one he'd found himself in earlier. It sat in the wrong direction. But was it the valley that held the cabin? It appeared big enough.

To him, it made sense that the cabin would sit in the larger valley. That just seemed right.

He hopped down from the rock and began to descend toward the bigger draw. It fell away before him. As he worked his way down the rocks, he stopped and looked back up the hill. He had climbed it earlier that day and it seemed familiar, as he would expect, and yet, at the same time, not. His mind was hazy. Maybe he hadn't climbed it and just wanted it be recognizable.

He turned back downhill and descended another dozen feet. Off to his left, the smaller ravine dropped towards its mouth at the base of the mountain. He continued another

100 feet down the main depression and a noise caught his attention.

Crows. He stopped and looked about. Above him, a dozen or so large black birds cawed, talking among themselves as they flew toward him. But instead of flying over him and down the larger valley, they veered to the smaller rift and flew out of sight. He could hear their raucous calls for another minute before the sound faded to silence.

His confidence in the direction he now headed faded with the birds' calls. He couldn't afford another mistake. The sun was already behind the mountain and the temperature had dropped noticeably. His gut grumbled for food and that reminded him that Homer would have been feeding scraps to the birds again about this time of day. The birds were looking for their next meal. If he wanted a next meal, maybe he should follow them. As if in confirmation, his mind recalled the Old Testament story of Elijah being fed by the ravens.

Despite growing weak, he hastened back up to the point where the two ravines diverged and began to descend the smaller one. He soon saw that its appearance at the top was deceiving. The valley broadened and the trees became denser. In this dry country, that meant water. Several hundred feet farther down, he saw the beginnings of a dry creek bed. *That* looked familiar.

As he approached the rocky plot, he saw a stone that appeared overturned. *Yes!* he thought. He recalled stepping on that stone and its turning under his weight. He had thought he had twisted his ankle, but was relieved to find it stable and uninjured for walking.

He quickened his pace, driven by the thought that food and water were not far off. Soon he heard the crows again. Their chatter increased in volume as he progressed toward his goal. Tonight, they, too, would have a feast. As he passed a thick grove of pines, he saw it. The cabin. He was almost there.

Twenty-three

Six o'clock could not roll around fast enough for Amy. Her shoulders ached and her mind raced. The news had picked up on Bradley Graham's disappearance and speculation ran wild. In addition to her own worries, she now added concern for Lynch to that list. She had debated calling him, as a concerned friend she told herself, but did not want to disturb him. He was no doubt up to his neck in problems.

She pulled into the small strip mall where an elegant sign announced the location of The Dead Sea Experience. So far, so good.

The experience did not begin in the lobby, however. The small lobby, with its eight-foot ceiling and institutional white walls, did not say "Welcome to our spa." Quite the opposite—the claustrophobic would flee out the front door. The front desk appeared as something purchased from a used business furniture store. The single plush couch seemed comfy enough, but the chairs looked like they came from IKEA and were assembled by three-year-olds. In one corner, a standard, office water cooler sat with its paper cup dispenser. This was a far cry from the lofty open space of the Float STL transition area or their offering of iced water or hot tea in cute ceramic mugs.

"Hi, you must be Amy. I'm Carol. Welcome. Is this your first time floating?"

Amy recognized the young woman's voice from their earlier conversation. Carol appeared to be mid-twenties, with shoulder-length, light brown hair and a clothing style that spoke hipster. Actually, her clothes looked like Miley Cyrus cast-offs.

"Hi, Carol. This is my first time here and I'm looking forward to floating."

Amy completed her registration paperwork—on paper, not electronically on a tablet as at the other place—and handed the young woman her Discover card to make payment.

"Amy, I'm sorry, but we only take VISA and MasterCard at the moment. We should be able to accept Discover by the end of the month though. I'm sorry."

Amy whipped out her VISA and paid.

"Thank you. I'm sorry for the inconvenience. Please have a seat. There's cold water over there, or I have hot tea in the back. Sorry about the way the lobby looks right now. We had a major flood while installing our second pod. It happened the same day we moved the furniture in and ruined most of it. The new stuff is on order."

Amy settled for cold water, sat on the couch, and tried to relax. An older man, about her father's age, arrived and went through the same routine. Again, Amy heard Carol apologize for the things she had no control over. The man's name, she soon learned, was Emmet and his wife thought he was too tense. She had purchased this float as a hint that he needed to relax, or maybe she was simply trying to get him out of the house. By the time it was their turn for an orientation to the facilities, she had learned all about the man's wife and two kids, how long he'd been married and where he'd proposed to his wife . . . and on . . . and on. She expected details of his tax returns to be shared next.

The orientation took place in room one, where Emmet would be floating. As with her previous floats, Amy—and Emmet—were expected to shower and use the supplied organic body wash before entering the pod. Ear plugs were provided, as well as towels. The pods appeared new, as expected, although they were not as sleek in appearance as at Float STL. These clamshell-shaped pods had chrome rails at the front of both the top and bottom halves of the shell. Amy had had no trouble accessing or exiting the pods at Float STL without the handles, but maybe these would be easier.

"Now, to get into the pod, simply lift the upper shell using this chrome hand bar. There's a hand-hold inside to close it once you're in there. Of course, from the inside, just push up to open the top. To enter the pod, we recommend supporting yourself with the chrome hand bar on the lower shell and then stepping into the pod. Once inside, close the pod, lie down . . . aannnd . . . float. The magnesium salts will allow you to float effortlessly. You can even go to sleep safely. There's . . ."

Carol continued with her briefing, covering the lights and music, which continued for ten minutes to help you relax and would resume in the last ten minutes of the float to alert you to your time ending. They left Emmet in room one, and Carol led Amy to room two.

"And here's your pod, Amy. Any questions?"

"None. Thanks. You were quite thorough."

"Very good," replied Carol in a crisp, business-like tone. "Enjoy your float."

Amy dropped her bag on the chair and moved to lock her door. She pushed the button on the knob, but it wouldn't stay depressed. She tried again. Same result. She opened the door and tried again. Same thing and the door would not lock. She walked to the front.

"Carol, the door won't lock on my room."

The woman looked sheepish. She sighed, as if she went through this with everyone using room two.

"I'm sorry. I forgot to mention that. One of our earliest floaters got claustrophobic in the pod after the lights went out, struggled to get out and find the door. She broke the lock in the process. The owner hasn't gotten around to replacing it." She sighed again. "It's just you, me, and Emmet. No one can get to the back without coming through here. You'll be fine."

Amy debated asking for a refund. How could she relax knowing she wasn't fully secure? But as she thought about it, she'd gotten only good vibes from Emmet. He seemed a bit harried by his wife, but came across as a good guy, innocent. And she *needed* to float, to relax and clear her mind. Plus, she came prepared.

She returned to the room, closed the door, and proceeded to undress and shower. Before entering the pod, however, she returned to her bag. Uncertain about what to expect, she had brought a swim suit. The float might not be as relaxing as wearing only her birthday suit, but her peace of mind would compensate for the difference.

She entered the pod, closed the lid, and lay back into the water. With the lights out, almost immediately the warmth of the liquid began to ease the strain in her shoulders and upper back. The music helped quiet her worries and as it ended, the state of relaxation she had hoped to achieve had arrived. She drifted off, oblivious to the passing of time.

She had been in a half-sleep state for an unknown period when her mind suddenly snapped to attention. What had disturbed her? Was someone in her room? Even with the earplugs in place and her ears just underwater, she thought she heard something. There it was again.

She sat up and pressed the button to turn on the inner light. Nothing.

"Is someone out there?"

Suddenly the water jets at the back of the pod began to eject turbulent, cold water. She sensed the pod quickly filling with water and hurried to push open the lid and climb out. The lid wouldn't budge. She was trapped inside.

Twenty-four

"Don't worry, Director. She's with him as we speak."

The Director cut short a meeting with the Labor Department Secretary in order to slip away to the residence and make some secure calls. Between briefings from the FBI, the ATF, and Homeland Security, the situation surrounding Bradley Graham, as well as that around the young woman in St. Louis, were not going as planned. He needed to learn what was happening behind the official scenes.

"Ms. Walther, I cannot stress enough the importance of getting someone on the inside of the Bradley Graham campaign. As you've no doubt heard, he was kidnapped by anti-government protesters in Oregon, and I want to know what they know, the American Party leaders."

The Director had heard rumor that the Graham campaign's security chief had not been seen since the abduction, despite being told by the lead FBI agent on the scene to stay clear or face federal charges. That security chief was well-known to The Assembly, but the Executive Council had made it clear, he was not to meet an unexpected demise. The Director had heard whispers that the man and his allies had amassed information on individuals within the council, thanks to lapses in security by Karolus Karling. That would change once their candidate was elected to the presidency, allowing him to focus on such issues. However, right now, he wanted to know what the party was doing.

"Mr. Pr—, um, excuse me, Director, we're working on it. You can't just flip a switch on someone to get them to trust you and open up to you, much less ask them to turn on their employer. Perhaps you should have thought of that before your so-called protesters took Graham."

"Careful, Ms. Walther." His tone was clear.

The woman clearly had her own sources of information. She, too, had the full protection of the Executive Council, but the Director understood her value within Washington, D.C., social circles and would not protest that decision.

"Sir, all due respect, we are working as quickly as possible here. The man is no longer engaged and will be on the rebound. He is vulnerable and we will take every advantage of that. He suspects nothing."

No longer engaged? How had that tidbit of information escaped his briefings?

"Just keep François in the loop. He remains your handler. You will not hear from me directly again." He disconnected the call.

He dialed François.

"*Oui, monsieur*? Your call is early."

"I wanted to inform you that I called Maggie Walther directly. I still have complete faith in your ability to handle her. I simply wanted to add a little pressure for her to complete her task. I do not plan to call her again."

"*Oui, monsieur.* I understand the importance of her task. The email scandal for our candidate has not been good for the election."

The Director took a deep breath. He personally saw no issues with this alleged scandal, and his people at the Justice Department and FBI had their marching orders. As did the media. And yet, there were now concerns within the Council about this.

"I did not mention that to Ms. Walther, only the abduction. Any updates?"

"There is still nothing solid about Lynch Cully's activities. However, while he may think he's gone off the grid, we have people monitoring for cell phone activity. His phone turned on briefly and was triangulated to the motel where his team is staying. He made and received no calls during those ten minutes, but it would appear he remains at the motel commanding his team."

"No, François. That simply says his phone is at the motel. If no one has seen him there, we cannot trust that he is there."

He was surprised that François would fall into the trap of believing that the security chief remained out of sight at their motel simply because his phone became active for ten minutes. Had any calls taken place and his voice been confirmed by recognition software at the NSA or FBI, then such an assumption might hold credence.

"I agree, sir. I did say it would *appear* as such, not that I believed it. We have a team watching the motel at all times. They do report that food is being taken into one of their rooms as if someone is there."

A clever ruse, thought the Director. No, he did not trust

this Cully.

"Ms. Walther told me something I hadn't heard from you, François. She said that Nichols and this Gibbs woman in St. Louis are no longer engaged."

"*Oui, monsieur.* I said nothing until I had full verification. That came through this afternoon."

"Then it is unlikely she will be useful as leverage against him. What is the latest on her status?"

"I've been told that the Somalis feel dishonored to have been defeated by a woman. They are not willing to stand down as we requested. I have sent a different liaison to them to convince them that it remains in their best interest not to go against us."

The Director thought about that. If the woman would no longer be useful to them, he had little reason to keep her alive.

"No, François. Call off your man. If we cannot use her to persuade Richard Nichols to work with us, then we have no need for her. Let the Somalis have their honor."

"Sir, do you wish to assist them? The Somalis have not been known for their thoroughness. They tend to be clumsy, to believe they will always succeed with even the worst plan."

"No, François. We do not need to waste our resources helping them. If they fail the first time, they can try again. It is not our concern."

Richard finished unpacking and organizing his bedroom and walked into the kitchen to find Summer unloading the last box marked "Kitchen." He watched wistfully as she placed the utensils on a counter. The task was something he had envisioned Amy performing, but now a stranger helped. She was a beautiful and well-educated woman, but still a stranger . . . and one whose real motives were yet to be tested.

"Summer, thank you. You really didn't have to help, but I appreciate your taking the time and your willingness to do so." He paused. "You know, I'm still not sure *why* you're willing. Our past encounters haven't exactly been friendly ones. Still, I thank you."

She laid down the bowl she had in her hands and approached him. She came a little too close for Richard's liking, but he did not move. He had been tasked with discovering her true purpose for befriending him.

"Richard, you and Bradley Graham treated me with dignity in Kansas City when you could have simply let me fight my own battle. Or worse, you could have thrown me to the dogs. But you didn't. You made me part of the team and respected my opinions. In fact, you gave me veto power over anything you planned. For me, that was unexpected. So, when I heard from Maggie that you were moving into the neighborhood, I wanted to return the favor. Besides, I believe in being a good neighbor."

Richard looked into her eyes, trying to read the thoughts behind her statement. All he saw were deep, crystalline green eyes set in a flaw-free, alabaster, Irish complexion that could beguile a man faster than a leprechaun's enchantment. He turned away in confusion. He would not "cheat" on Amy, even with his eyes, and yet, that relationship had ended and its restoration seemed out of reach. He might be a "free man" once again, but this was much too soon.

He walked to the counter where she had been working and began to open cabinets and drawers.

"Since you put everything away, I'm going to have to learn my way around my own kitchen, not that I use it much myself."

She moved in close to him and leaned forward toward the cabinets, exposing more than a bit of cleavage. "Well, I *do* use my kitchen, when I'm home, so I put things into order in a way that I considered logical. Dishes, glasses, and cutlery closest to the dishwasher. Those horrible things you call pots and pans are near the cooktop. Trashcan is under the sink. I don't think you'll have trouble getting used to it." She slid closer, until her hip touched his. "You know, I-I could come over and cook you dinner sometime. I'm told I'm pretty good at it."

He stepped back and walked to another counter where he began looking into the surrounding cabinetry. Yes. Too soon.

"I'm sorry, Richard. That must have seemed awfully forward of me. I did just mean it in a neighborly way. Plus, when I'm home and not on assignment, I get tired of eating alone, which, believe it or not, is most nights."

Richard didn't know how to respond to her and tried to focus on what was in which cabinet. A few of these cabinets held food, but most were empty. He checked the refrigerator. He found a handful of condiments, some lunch meat, and a 12-pack of beer—

New Glarus Spotted Cow—his Wisconsin home favorite.

He closed the door and turned to face her. "I was going to offer you a glass of wine, but it looks like I don't have any. Looks like I need to make a major grocery run, in fact."

He hoped she would take the hint and excuse herself to head home, but she didn't. He didn't want to be rude and ask her to leave, especially after all her work in helping him, but he felt uncomfortable around her. Tackling Ben's undercover assignment would prove to be tougher than he'd imagined.

"I'll take a beer, if that's okay. A girl can't grow up in a half-Irish home without learning to appreciate a pint of Guinness, as well as others." She smiled.

"Sure." He reopened the fridge and took out two Spotted Cows. "I'm from Wisconsin and this is a home state favorite. You can't buy it outside the state." He checked one drawer. "Um, you might need to direct me to my bottle opener."

She looked flustered. "Uhhh, right. Let me think." She found it in the third drawer she opened.

He opened both bottles and handed one to her. Then, with beer in hand, he guided her out of the kitchen toward the room he planned to use as a den. "Would you like the full tour?"

"N-not necessary. I-I've been here before . . . with the, um . . . when, uh . . ."

"When Mr. Pearce lived here? You don't have to avoid that, uh, history of the house. Maggie told me all about it."

She took a sip from her bottle. "Okay, but I don't think she told you all of the story."

Richard raised his brow. "Oh?"

"Yeah. I'm the one who found him. I still don't like coming through the front door. It brings back that horrible memory. You'll probably find me knocking on the back kitchen door when I come to visit."

Richard's first thought was, *It must have been awful to discover the man hanging there*, but then two other thoughts took his attention. She had said "*when* I come to visit," not if. That implied a certainty that she'd be back. More importantly, her use of the back door meant she could come to his house without ever being seen from the street. Was such a clandestine approach planned for reasons other than not liking the entry foyer? Maybe he needed to investigate her story about being the one to find Eric Pearce.

They retired to his den where he made a point of sitting in his sole chair and not on the couch where she might decide to get friendly again. She told him of her childhood growing up outside of Boston with an Irish mother and English father, and, yes, Summer Stanton was her given name. She had worked for Ted Kennedy briefly before his death and was a lifelong, blue-blood Democrat who had entertained no other ideology until her encounter with Bradley Graham and Richard in Kansas City. In that encounter, the conservative ogre suddenly had a compassionate face. She laughed.

Richard shared little, other than the fact that he'd grown up in Wisconsin, on a dairy farm, and yes, he was a conservative cheese head. He shared nothing about Afghanistan, the events that led to his nickname of Thor, or his activities in St. Louis that had led to meeting Amy. He pictured her pink version of his

Hammer of Thor and tried to submerge that memory.

After a second beer for both, Summer stood and said, "Well, I think I've overstayed my welcome. I should head home."

Richard stood, collected her empty bottle, and followed her to the kitchen. "Summer, thank you again for all your help. It will still take me a month to figure out where everything is." He laughed.

She nodded. "You're welcome. And if you want to move things around, trust me, you won't offend me."

She surprised Richard when she leaned up onto her toes and gave him a quick kiss on the cheek. Before he could respond, she turned and headed out the back door. As she closed the door, she waved and said, "Bye."

Richard watched her walk away until that point where she disappeared behind some shrubs. He took a deep breath and sighed. The past hour's conversation had been pleasant. He found Summer easy to talk with, but his mind wandered often to thoughts of Amy.

B.A.—before Amy—he would have found Summer's obvious attraction to him flattering and enticing. Now, he could only wonder. She knew he was engaged to Amy, but did she somehow learn that their engagement was off? Had Maggie Walther told her? He hadn't. He hadn't mentioned it to anyone other than Ben, but Maggie was there at the time. So, if she thought he was still engaged to Amy, why the obvious come-ons? Was she the competitive type who liked to make a play for someone she couldn't have? Maybe. She certainly worked in a competitive industry. More likely, though, was that Ben was correct. She was playing on his emotions—and lust—to gain leverage on him.

He would have to be on guard at all times.

He started to grab another beer but thought better of it. He filled a glass with cold, filtered water and walked to the library. After securing the blinds, he flipped on the light and moved to the bookcase. The whole thing of a hidden surveillance system seemed surreal. The old phrase, *If walls could talk*, entered his mind. *That's for sure*, he thought. These walls *could* talk.

He found the book that opened the hidden compartment. He stared at the equipment that was now revealed. A nine-inch, high-def touchscreen that allowed him to toggle between the cameras they'd found. A small speaker would allow him to listen in on the audio transmitters, which included the video cameras. And it was all recordable on a DVD recorder. There was even an 'away' setting. He wondered if it was sound or motion activated, or both, when set for 'away.'

While inspecting the gear, he found a switch on the wall behind it. He flipped it and the system came alive, offering only the slightest hum. He played with the toggles and checked the video cameras. *Amazing quality*, he thought.

He pressed the 'Eject' button on the DVD player and was surprised when the tray slid out and presented a disk on it. He lifted up the disk and looked at it. Something had been recorded on it.

He stood up straight and pondered his finding. If this system was installed and operated by Eric Pearce, and no one else knew of it, then this disk had been there since before his death. If the system had been on at the time, it might even show his death. On the other hand, if others knew of the system, then the police would have claimed this disk along with other evidence in the house. But if the system *was* known, why hadn't Maggie Walther told him of it?

He took the disk with him to the den where his laptop sat next to the couch. He would take a look at it, but first he wanted to see about something. He knew where the cameras and audio bugs were because their sweep had revealed them. And they swept the house only because of Ben's innate suspicions. What if someone, say the police, had no reason to expect a surveillance system of that magnitude? The house had its intruder alarm system, too. The police would have expected that in a house of this caliber in a neighborhood of this type. But if they had no reason to expect something more sophisticated, would they have found the system?

Richard scrutinized each area where they'd found a device. He knew where to look and still couldn't pinpoint them. These were expertly hidden. So, if the police never looked for them, they'd never have spotted them serendipitously. That meant that there was a good chance the police knew nothing about this surveillance setup.

But the opposite possibility was the one that concerned him. What if this equipment was installed by people who wanted to watch Pearce? What if Ben was wrong about the DNC and The Assembly? Perhaps they staged his death. No one really believed he committed suicide. If this was true, then they could watch *him*. Maybe the recording gear was a ruse. Maybe there was a transmitter somewhere on the premises after all. But then, why put the gear here with the risk that he'd find it? Richard was confused.

There was only one way to know. He returned to the disk and his laptop.

He opened the video files on the disk. The recordings were dated and time stamped. As the first video began, Richard couldn't believe what he watched. All six video cameras had recorded in their own area, now displayed in picture-in-picture mode. He could select which camera to highlight and bring to the foreground. In multiple screens, police were scouring the home. But the action that caught his attention was that captured by the foyer camera. Amid the crime scene discussions and detectives examining evidence, medical technicians wheeled out a full body bag on their gurney. He was watching the crime scene investigation of Eric Pearce's death itself, but curiously, from a point well into the inquiry.

The second recording was dated the following day and showed a clean-up crew cleaning the front foyer under the watchful eye of a policeman. The next dozen or so recordings were intermittent and brief, but showed Maggie Walther showing the property to prospective customers, including himself. And that was it. Curiously, it didn't show him moving in.

Two questions formed in his mind. If the system was active, *why* hadn't it caught the activity of his moving in? More importantly, however, was the big question that his mind now focused upon. If Pearce was dead, *who* had changed the disk?

Twenty-five

Lynch and Coby rode along the ridge, and Coby passed by areas that dropped off into space with a nonchalance that amazed Lynch. He, on the other hand, kept trying to urge Charlie away from the edge, well away. One misstep of the hoof and they'd tumble to a bone-crushing death. Or so it seemed. Charlie sauntered along behind Sally Mae with the same could-care-less air as Coby.

"You know, Coby, I've climbed a utility tower to talk down a suicidal man and sat with my feet dangling outside police helicopters. I've never had a fear of heights. But I have to admit, I'm a bit unnerved riding on the edge of these cliffs. Are you sure these horses won't—"

"Not on your life. Their steps are as sure on this trail as yours would be on a concrete sidewalk." He paused. " 'Course, for a greenhorn like you, there could always be a first."

Lynch could detect the smirk on the man's face despite seeing only the back of his cowboy hat and neck.

"Get used to 'em, Lynch. Tomorrow we take a trail that goes over the edge, down into one canyon, and back up to a different ridge. You're gonna get a taste of what riding in the Grand Canyon is like. Folks pay for that experience."

Oh boy. Lynch couldn't wait.

"The ridge widens again in about 50 feet and we'll be away from the edge. About a quarter mile farther and we come to another canyon that used to have a cabin. Not much of a place, and I'm not expecting to find anyone there, but can't just assume that. We'll check it out."

Lynch tried closing his eyes and focusing on the rhythm of the horse's walk. It didn't help. When he opened his eyes he saw that he had a white-knuckle grip on the saddle horn with both hands. Fortunately, the reins were buried in there somewhere, too. The situation reminded him of flying with Amy the time she had decided to show off her aerobatic skills. She still reminded him that her father had yet to repair the damage Lynch had done to the seat with his death grip.

He sighed in relief as the trail widened and left the narrows for broader space.

Coby brought Ed to a stop and the horses following halted as well. It had been that way all day, and Lynch still wondered how Sally Mae and Charlie stopped in time to avoid running into the horse in front of them. Did they have telepathic stoplights?

"Time to give the horses a rest."

Lynch dismounted and watched as Coby offered water to their mounts. He glanced at his phone and saw that he had five bars. If Coby wasn't pulling his leg about the next day, and they'd be descending into a canyon, he wouldn't have that kind of reception for hours. He took the opportunity to call Tony.

"Hey, boss. How're you holding out?"

"I'm fine. No problems."

"Oh."

Tony sounded disappointed. Lynch had his suspicions as to why.

"So, you guys must have another bet going on. What'd you lose?"

"Was it *that* obvious? That's why I won't play poker with you anymore."

Lynch laughed. Tony wouldn't play poker with anyone on the team. Everyone else won because he was such an easy read. The man had tells anyone could spot from across any room.

"Well, if it helps, my butt feels like it's been sledgehammered and I'm pretty sure I'll be walking bowlegged for days."

He heard Tony place his hand over his phone and yell to others with him, "Hey, I won. Told you he'd be sore within six hours."

Lynch shook his head.

"So, how's the burn phone working, Lynch? You sound good on this end."

"And you sound great on this end. We're heading into territory where I won't have cell service, so I thought I'd better call while I could."

"Gotcha. We've been turning your phone on and off, and bringing food into the room, but we're still being watched 24/7. The guys aren't even trying to hide the fact that they're there. I thought maybe I'd go offer 'em a beer later." Tony laughed.

"Go ahead and call the main office and use the digital recordings I made. Stan should be expecting the call and have the script by now."

"Okay, but I'm not sure that'll convince them you're here behaving yourself."

"Maybe not, but it'll keep them off-balance. And I figure you'll be under surveillance, no matter what. I still haven't figured out what the game is here, other than trying to pin something on the protesters."

"Well, that part is being played up big time in the media. And both main party candidates are painting Graham as naïve and unfit to be president because he put himself in harm's way and should have known better than to sit down and talk with the protesters."

Lynch hadn't thought of that line of reasoning, but it didn't surprise him. He hardened his resolve to find Graham quickly . . . even if that meant trusting his horse to walk down a cliff.

"Well, nothing from this end so far. We have one more place to check today, but Coby doesn't expect much. We have three more cabins to inspect tomorrow." He went on to explain how they saved time using Coby's "secret weapon." He made a point to call it a toy in a voice loud enough for Coby to hear. The man grinned.

"I'll call again late tomorrow if we get back into range for cell service."

"Yes, sir. Be safe."

He returned to where Coby had the horses.

"Mount up, greenhorn. We have a short ride ahead of us, and I want to use my *toy* again."

"Oh, hi, Richard. Ben says you snagged a beautiful

home. He's in the other room. I'll get him."

Ben's wife, Clare, was quite the catch herself. Beauty pageants had led her to the crown of Miss Kansas, but the scholarship that came with the title had taken her to Harvard Law. Beauty and brains. That made him think of Amy.

"Hey, buddy, what's up? Lonely in that big ol' house already?"

"You need to come over, ASAP."

Richard couldn't get the questions out of his head. He now understood how paranoia began. Yes, Ben had stated that Pearce was most likely the one who installed the monitoring system. Yes, Ben's rationale was logical. But. Why hadn't the system recorded his moving in when it had recorded Maggie showing him the house days earlier? Where was the rest of the police investigation, the first part? Who switched the disks? Who turned the system off? What if The Assembly *was* behind this? Maybe they knew how to piggyback onto the system even though Pearce had installed it. Maybe they were watching him now.

Richard couldn't settle down. How in the world would he be able to sleep there?

"What? I was there most of the day with you. Clare and I were just about to head out on a nice dinner date—something we've not had much time for lately and might not have again before the election. Plus, you're a good 45 minutes away."

"Sorry. You still need to come over. I need your help."

"Well, tell you what, Richard, that's not at all what we had in mind for the evening. If you catch my drift."

Richard wasn't sure how to say what he needed to say.

He no longer trusted both the monitoring system in his house or his phone. Someone else might be listening to his words at that very moment.

"Well, you know me, Ben, Mr. Discreet. Don't want to sink any ships with loose lips and all that." He was babbling. He needed to take a different tack. "So, Summer Stanton left about half an hour ago and I was, you know, exploring my new place, trying to figure out where to put the *DVD player* and entertainment center in my *library*. I was moving things and I think I slipped a *disk*. It just sorta *popped out* unexpectedly and I need some help figuring out how to deal with it. You're the guy I figured would know what to do."

There was a moment of silence on the other end.

"I thought we put the enter—"

Ben sounded more confused than Richard felt.

"Oh man, are you able to move at all? Can you make it to the kitchen to get some ice? Oh wait, we didn't connect the ice maker, did we. Um, yeah, let me grab Clare and we'll get you some ice and ibuprofen on our way. Sit still, buddy."

From the sudden change in tone, Richard figured he'd gotten his point across. Now, all he could do was wait.

The summit of Steen's Mountain rose over a thousand feet above them and the sun was already beginning to slip behind it. Although sunset was still some time away, their light would fade much sooner. That didn't hamper the FLIR system on Coby's drone, but it would affect his ability to fly it through and over the rough terrain.

"No heat signatures?"

Lynch shook his head. "Nothing. No lions or tigers or bears either."

Coby nodded and flipped the camera to normal vision, much as they had done on the previous two flights. He attempted to fly a pattern across the canyon, but the light now dimmed faster than he liked.

"Do you see any cabin?" he asked.

Lynch shook his head and replied, "Not yet."

"Not good. I really don't want to come back here in the morning for another search, but we can't call the search conclusive if we haven't confirmed the location of the cabin. Let me go a little further down the canyon."

"You sure? It seems to be getting dark fast." Lynch valued Coby's "toy" as much as the man did.

"Yup. We're good. If we don't see anything, I'll take her high enough to clear any potential obstacle and we can use the FLIR to spot us and home in here."

Lynch thought that sounded reasonable and returned his focus to the monitor. Five minutes later, he thought he saw a structure.

"There, to the left. Is that it?"

Coby changed the direction of the drone and flew it over the area that Lynch pointed out.

"I don't think so. Let's check the infrared."

Lynch watched the image on the screen change. No heat signatures.

"Nothing."

The video returned to normal vision and Coby

continued his search.

"Ten more minutes and I need to come back. The battery won't give us any more time in the air."

Lynch knew they needed to conserve the batteries. Coby had the ability to recharge the batteries back at his truck and trailer, but that would take hours and take them away from the search. He had hoped to have four batteries remaining at the end of this day. Wind conditions and the terrain had forced them to use one battery on each of the three flights they'd made so far. That left three to go.

"Okay, got to head back. If my toy goes down from battery failure, it could take days to find it."

Lynch watched the course change on the screen. Coby focused on the opposite side of the canyon on the way back.

"Would you switch it to FLIR? Getting hard to see on the normal setting."

The screen changed again.

"Hey, up ahead. Straight ahead on the course you're taking. There's a yellow heat signature."

Coby nodded. "Tell me when we're on it."

Less than a minute later, Lynch tapped him on the shoulder. "It's below the drone."

Coby descended and followed the heat.

"You're on it, you're on it. Switch to visual."

Lynch saw the source of the heat.

"We found the cabin. All that's left is the ruins of a rock fireplace and chimney."

Coby immediately took the drone up and directed it toward them.

"Makes sense. The sun today heated up the rock and you spotted the result."

The drone controller began a slow beep. Coby took a deep breath and issued a mild profanity under his breath.

"C'mon, baby, come to papa."

"What's that beep? Battery?"

"Yup. C'mon, baby." The man focused on keeping the drone on as straight a course to them as he could.

Lynch gazed in the direction of the sound he now heard. Soon he saw it.

"There it is. You're almost here. Bring it right a bit. Right as you're flying it, not as we see it."

The beeping on the controller quickened its frequency. The drone came close enough that Lynch could see that only three rotors were in use. Either Coby or the computer had cut down the battery consumption by cutting out half of the motors.

"Maybe 100, 200 feet away. You're almost here."

Lynch knew that Coby would have to descend soon, but that would make it hard to see. At the moment, the device was easy to spot against the brighter sky. Dropping into the shadows that now engulfed them might render the drone invisible to them.

The tone became a solid bee-eeeeeeeep and the drone dropped.

"Quick, Lynch. I dropped it before losing everything and flipped on its small landing light. It'll last maybe five minutes before the battery dies completely."

Both men jumped to their feet and ran in the direction where they had last seen the small aircraft. Even with the light, they would have to be nearly on top of it to see the light within the scrub brush. The two men worked together, searching ten feet apart as they moved away from the horses and their gear. Twenty feet away. Fifty feet away.

"I see it!" yelled Coby.

Lynch felt a surge of relief flood through him. That was too close.

Richard began watching his driveway about 40 minutes after his call to Ben. True to his word, at precisely 45 minutes his friend's BMW pulled into the drive and stopped at the front walk. He watched on his home intruder alarm system as Ben and Clare exited the car and Ben grabbed a bag of ice from the trunk. He had gone all out for the appearance of helping an injured friend.

Richard had limped to the front and unlocked the door. He returned to the den and waited for them. He understood the ruse being played by Ben outside. He played the game on the inside. If he was being observed, he could not appear to be healthy in answering the door or in walking normally inside.

The bell rang, followed by several knocks. Richard texted Ben that the door was unlocked. He knew Ben would play the part. There were more knocks and Richard heard them testing the door, finding it unlocked.

"Richard?"

"On the couch in the den!"

He saw Ben and Clare as they joined him in the

den. He feigned several attempts to sit up.

"Here, let me help," said Ben. As he bent over to assist, he whispered, "Is this act really necessary?" He helped Richard sit up. "Let's get you to the bedroom."

Ben and Clare each took a side and hoisted him to his feet. Supporting each shoulder, the three walked to Richard's bedroom, while he held on to his laptop. Once inside the room, they separated and Richard closed the door.

Richard looked at his friend and the man's spouse. "To answer your question, I don't know, but I don't want to follow Eric Pearce. You're sure this room is clear?"

Ben nodded. "We found nothing in this room, or the other bedrooms." He looked at his wife. "Honey, just to keep this charade going a bit longer, could you get the ice from the den, take it to the kitchen, and make an ice pack for this grade B actor. That was the phoniest limp and back pain performance I've ever seen, by the way."

"So, don't nominate me for a People's Choice Award."

Once Clare had left the room, Richard said, "Are you sure you want to involve your wife in this?"

Ben shrugged. "She already is and won't say no for an answer. She's the one who insisted we actually get ice and play along. She's also got one of the sharpest analytical minds I know."

"Okay. I'll wait till she's back, and I'll fill you both in."

A few minutes later, as the ice pack melted in a sink of the master bathroom, he explained what had transpired with Summer and how he'd gone into the library after she'd left. He then played the first recording on the disk.

"That . . . that's Eric Pearce's body being wheeled out.

This is the police investigation."

Richard nodded and waited for the implication of that to sink in. Clare was the first to voice it.

"If that's the police investigation, it starts with it already in progress. So, who switched the disks? Who put this one into that recorder you told me about?"

Richard raised his brow and looked at Ben. "She knows?"

"Everything, buddy. I told you she's one of the best."

Richard had nothing to say. He wasn't sure that if he was in Ben's shoes that he would have involved his wife. At this point, it was water under the bridge.

Ben looked as if light had dawned. "Right. Which means at least one other person knows about this system."

Richard nodded. "Yeah. And that means there might be a hidden transmitter and that someone is watching and listening to everything we do and say."

Ben shook his head. "No way. My guy would have found it. Period. He's one of the best in the business."

"You're sure?"

"Absolutely."

Richard took a deep breath. "So, you think I'm overreacting."

Ben started to answer, but Clare cut him off. "No. I think that was a perfectly sensible reaction. Much better to play it safe. As Joseph Heller said, 'Just because you're paranoid doesn't mean they aren't after you.' "

From the look on Ben's face, he wasn't thinking in the same terms. Richard laughed.

"And you were going to agree that I'm overreacting, weren't you?"

Ben looked sheepish as he offered a subtle shrug and single nod of his head. "Definitely over*acting*, but she's right. Better to be safe."

Richard began to appreciate Clare more and more. If she could keep Ben in check, she was definitely someone you wanted on your side.

"That still doesn't give us a clue who this person is," said Clare. "Do you know anything about Pearce that wasn't in the papers? That's really all I know about him."

Richard only knew the name and suspicious circumstances around his death. He hadn't had time to research him online. He shook his head.

Ben said, "I know what you know, honey."

"Then this is where I might be able to help. I'm on great terms with our law firm's lead investigator. If anyone knows the dirt on a guy like Pearce, he should. And if he doesn't, he'll get it for me."

Twenty-six

Amy used every bit of strength to push up against the pod's upper shell. She couldn't move it. She pounded on the inside.

"Help! Someone help!" She hammered away at the inner shell as water continued to fill the pod. "Help! I'm trapped in here! Help me!"

She noticed that water had begun to spray out of the pod through the thin gap between the two halves, but it was not enough to match the volume of cold water coming in. The pod continued to fill.

Kneeling inside, she managed to keep her head in the air pocket at the top.

"Help! Someone help!"

Where was Carol? Where was Emmet? She felt dismay that someone might have killed them to get to her.

Her efforts at making noise diminished as the water deadened any sound she produced. The water also provided resistance against moving her arms, so her pounding was not as forceful. Considering the loss of force and the muffling effect of the water, she gave up on hitting the pod to make noise. Instead, she found herself focusing on finding air.

"Help! Help me!" Her screams seemed to echo within the pod, but could they be heard outside?

Although air remained trapped in the top of the pod, the turbulence of the water worked to diminish that pocket of vital gas. Soon, she had to tilt her head to keep her face above water.

"Hellll...lllp! Someone help! I need help in here!"

The water seemed to suppress her screams.

She realized she now faced a new threat. Clearly water from pipes within the building had been depleted and water cooled by the ground outside now flowed into her pod. And while temperatures were currently seasonal, a mid-October cold spell had frozen the ground's surface for a few days. The effect of that was evident. The temperature of the water surrounding her was frigid.

"H-help! I need h-h-help!"

She began to shiver. She tried to think. A body in water cooled 25 times faster than one in air. She had seen a chart once about survival times in cold water. She tried to recall it. In water above 70 degrees a person could survive for hours. Her oxygen might run out first. But ground temperatures were usually in the fifties and this water was being chilled by the ground. Below 50 degrees and her survival time dropped fast. Thirty minutes. Maybe an hour. Would she succumb to a lack of oxygen or hypothermia first? With both, she would simply drift off into unconsciousness and ultimately drown.

"Help! Help! Help!"

She worked her arms in an attempt to warm up, but she noticed that doing so reduced the size of her air bubble. She decided to keep her arms active by trying to help water escape the pod. That wasn't working.

"Help! Someone help!"

"O . . . m . . ."

It sounded like someone was in the room, but if so, the speech was garbled and distorted by the water.

Someone pounded on her pod.

"Yes! I'm in here! Help!" She pounded back.

"Jus . . . a . . . min . . . wor . . . o . . . it." The muffled speech came again.

Why didn't the pod open? She was now face up in the top of the pod and shivering more.

Suddenly the pod burst open, and the water flooded out into the room. Amy gasped for a deep breath. She wiped away the salty water from around her eyes and opened them.

Emmet stood there in all his natural glory, bathed by the rays of the emergency lights. She shut her eyes again.

"Sorry. Sorry. My towel came loose as I worked to cut the belt. Sorry. Okay. I'm good now."

Amy re-opened her eyes to gaze upon her blushing savior.

Tears of relief added to the flooded room. Shaking, she held onto the edge of the pod and stepped out. Towel or no towel, she reached out and hugged the man. Oh, and he felt soooo warm, too.

"Are you okay?" He reached over to the nearby chair, grabbed her towel, and wrapped it around her shoulders.

"I-I am, n-now. Thank you, Emmet. Y-you saved my life."

He smiled. "All I can say is it's a good thing I noticed a change in the water in my pod. It wasn't much, but it caught my attention. Then I tried to turn on my light and nothing happened. I climbed out of the pod and discovered the floor was flooded, but not from my pod. That's when the emergency lights snapped on. I peeked out the door and saw water pouring out from under the door of your room."

He bent down, careful to keep his towel in place with one hand, and picked up a wide leather belt. He extended it to her.

"This was wrapped around and tightened onto the handles of your pod. I couldn't get it loose, so I had to get my pocket knife to cut it. I don't know who you are, young lady, but you sure must have pissed off someone. Ex-husband or boyfriend? Jealous mistress? Who would have done this?"

Jealous mistress? Emmet watches too much TV. "Long story, Emmet. But where's Carol?"

Amy grabbed her top and covered up. She grabbed a second towel from the supply table and rushed to the lobby. She found Carol lying behind the reception desk. A large hematoma bulged from her left temple. Her pulse was strong and her breathing seemed okay. Amy wished she had her trauma bag with her.

She stood up and saw Emmet emerge from the back. He had on pants and his shirt.

"Do you have your cell phone? Mine is on the chair in the room."

He shook his head. "Sorry. Not anymore. It got knocked off into the water. Dropped mine in the water, too." He began to search the desk.

Amy joined the search and checked Carol's clothes for

the young woman's phone. Nothing. She extended her search to the rest of the room and spotted a phone under the couch. It had to belong to Carol or the business. She most likely lost it in whatever struggle she endured.

Amy retrieved the phone and dialed.

"9-1-1, what's your emergency?"

"We need police and EMS to The Dead Sea Experience, STAT." She proceeded to give the operator her name and an explanation of the problem.

By the time she hung up, she could hear sirens. Barnes-St. Peters Hospital was less than a mile away. The ambulance crew based there could be on-site in two minutes, provided they weren't tied up on another call. And the business district where the spa was located had heavy police coverage. She didn't know which would respond first.

She tended to Carol as she waited. The woman seemed to be coming to, but Amy restricted her movement. The woman could have a serious neck injury and needed immobilization before being moved.

Amy saw the ambulance pull into the lot first. A paramedic, carrying his response bag, rushed into the lobby.

"Amy? What the . . .?"

"Oh, JJ, I'm so glad it's a crew I know." She had worked accident scenes with this crew before. Carol would be in good hands.

Amy told JJ a condensed version of what had happened as he placed a collar around Carol's neck and checked her vital signs. She heard a rattle at the door, and saw the other paramedic trying to work the gurney through the door. She jumped up to hold the door.

"Amy? What are you doing here?" Candy, the other paramedic, looked as surprised as JJ had been at seeing her.

"Long story. I'll let your partner fill you in. I need to get my clothes on."

She left the team to do their jobs and returned to the room. Cold water continued to pour into and out of the pod. In the dim light, she could see that her bag had been knocked off the hook she had hung it on and now sat on the floor. Its contents were soaked. At least her clothes remained on the hook. She grabbed them, hurried to the woman's bathroom, and changed. The dry clothing felt so good. She began to warm up more quickly now, despite the adrenaline rush wearing off.

She left the bathroom and started to turn back toward the room. Should she grab her bag or not? Would it be considered part of a crime scene? Probably. Plus, retrieving it now wouldn't change anything. She turned toward the lobby.

"Mssss. Gibbs." A man's voice slurred her greeting as he let out a long sigh to accompany it. "Why should I not be surprised to find you here?"

Amy noticed an unmarked police car next to her car outside, its grill lights flashing. JJ and Candy both gave her a look and rolled their eyes as they started to wheel a now-conscious Carol out to their rig. They moved past the plainclothes officer who had spoken her name and Amy got a good look at him for the first time. Her heart sank.

"Detective Hoskins . . . We, um, meet again."

Why did it have to be this guy? He had been the

detective who responded to her home invasion a year or so earlier, right before she'd been kidnapped by a human trafficker. Then earlier this year, he had responded to the call about a shootout in her driveway between a deranged social worker and depressed father. At that time, he was the one who had arrested her for harboring a fugitive. She now forced herself to drive the speed limit within the city limits, partly out of fear that he'd be the one to pull her over.

"Why don't you have a seat over there while I check out the back?"

"Yes, sir. The, uh, water is still pouring out back there. Someone needs to turn it off."

He just pointed to the couch and sloshed his way to the back rooms. A few minutes later, Amy heard the sound of running water end. Shortly after that, the detective returned to the lobby, his shoes soaked, and carrying her bag. He handed it toward her.

"Here. I'm guessing this is yours. I don't think we'll need anything in it as evidence, so it's all yours. Unless, of course, you find something of interest in it, or something missing. Oh, and I dropped your phone in there. You might need to put it in rice for a few days." He turned to look at Emmet. "Mr. Emerson, let me get your statement first. Ms. Gibbs and I don't want to hold you up."

Emmet looked at Amy as if she had been featured on *America's Most Wanted* and moved across the room to talk with the detective. Amy sat and fidgeted. Her phone was useless. She hadn't brought a book. She stared out the window at the evening traffic passing by.

That managed to command her attention for all of a minute. She noticed Emmet glancing her way occasionally as he spoke with the detective.

She turned her focus onto her bag. She pulled out her phone first. Wet? Yes. Fortunately, for reasons called Richard, she had turned it off prior to floating. Her pocket calendar was drenched. She opened it and laid it out on the nearest arm of the couch. Her traveler's pack of tissues was DOA. Her makeup pouch was waterproof, so she set it aside and didn't bother to open it. Her car keys. Was the fob doomed to fail? She would let it dry before testing it. She placed it on the arm of the couch as well.

Soon she had a pile of throwaways on the floor in front of her and everything else sat scattered across the couch to dry. Well, to start drying anyway. She hoped she wouldn't be there long enough for all those things to dry completely. She arose, collected the pile of disposable items, and carried them to a nearby trash can. As she sat down, she noticed the *tête-à-tête* between Detective Hoskins and Emmet winding down.

Emmet gave a slight wave good-bye as he left the building. Detective Hoskins towered over Amy for a moment and then gingerly sat down in one of the rickety chairs.

"Yes. So we meet again." He keyed up his digital recorder and added his introductory comments—names, date, time, location. "Well Ms. Gibbs, where should we start? You've done this before, so . . . Go for it. Tell me what happened."

His mood seemed to have softened. Surely he understood that she was the victim—one of the victims— here. She began with her entering the establishment and continued with her signing in, getting the orientation, the broken lock, and so on. She ended with finding Carol and calling 9-1-1.

The officer said nothing as she finished. After a moment, he said, "Okay, I won't ask if you have any enemies out to get you. That list might be too long."

She gave him an "are-you-kidding-me" look.

"So, who do you think did this?"

"Somali terrorists."

Now he gave *her* a look. "Be serious, Ms. Gibbs. This is a formal police investigation. Someone assaulted the receptionist and tried to kill you. It's not a time to make jokes. Who do you think did this?"

"Somali terrorists."

She went on to explain. His look of petty dislike for her began to morph into one of respect.

"I'd heard rumors of what happened at Busch Wildlife. The Feds are keeping a tighter-than-usual lid on it. Wow."

"Yeah. You might not want to spread that all around. You know, a need-to-know basis. I figured you needed to know."

He nodded. "I'd better consult my chief on how to pursue this one. We'll have to let the Feds know what happened here, too. You might want to consider the witness protection program."

She didn't know if he was serious or jesting.

"You know, you might want to consider moving. Me and the guys at the station will donate to the cause. Your leaving our fair community would reduce our caseload by, I don't know, maybe ten percent. And sounds like it's a win-win situation for all of us. We reduce our cases and those terrorists won't know where you live." He opened his wallet and handed her a ten. "Seriously, will you at least consider it?"

Is this guy serious? She was about to throw the bill back at him when he broke into a grin. That was the only time she had ever seen him smile.

"Just for that, I'm keeping this." She shoved the ten into her pocket.

"Keep it. Your discovery of those explosives has probably saved hundreds if not thousands of lives." He stood up. "But if you decide to move, we all *will* chip in."

Amy stood and gathered her things back into her bag.

"I've got reinforcements joining me, and I need to get ahold of the owner. You okay to head home by yourself? I can get one of the patrol guys to escort you and check out the house."

She shook her head. "I should be fine. Remember? I have a home security system built by Glock."

He sighed. "Yeah, I recall. Please don't use it tonight."

She grabbed her keys. "Oh, I need to see if my key fob still works. It was in my bag."

She pressed the button and waited to see her lights flash from across the parking lot. She was rewarded by the blinding flash of her car exploding, taking the detective's sedan with it. Alarms sounded on a dozen nearby cars.

She stood there in shock, her mouth wide open. Witness protection suddenly seemed like a good idea. The detective ran from the building and from one end of the plaza to the next. Amy knew that the surrounding businesses had closed for the day, but her medical instincts kicked in. She followed after him, to give aid to anyone in need.

"Nobody else around," said the officer as he returned to her. She took a step closer to the cars and he restrained her. "We need to get back inside. Gas tank in my car didn't blow like yours did. It could go at any time."

Sirens flooded the air all around her. She allowed him to escort her back into the soggy spa, where moments later they watched the fire department work to extinguish the flames. Foam soon filled that end of the parking lot. He stood there shaking his head slowly. Disbelief filled his countenance. He turned to face her, pulled out his wallet, and took every bit of cash from it. He said, "Please move," and handed her the cash.

Twenty-seven

Richard stirred in his bed. Something had wakened him. He opened one eye and saw daylight meandering into his room around the blinds. His radio alarm clock still reported the time when he'd unplugged it the previous day. He'd forgotten to plug it in and reset it, which reminded him that he'd also been neglectful in replacing its backup battery.

He debated climbing out of bed to find and check his watch. One of the advantages of being head of his section was that he controlled the schedule. Sunday was his day off. Yet, to be fair, he gave every member of his team one of the weekend days off and he was on call every day. But not today. This was his weekend to move and he didn't want to get out of bed. Ben and Clare hadn't left until one a.m., after which he still had to reassemble his bed, find his linens, and make the bed. He'd managed the reassembling step before collapsing on top of it fully clothed.

He heard pounding from somewhere in the house. Was that what woke him? The noise stopped, but he climbed out of bed, answered nature's call, and checked his appearance in the mirror. To say he looked a bit rough was an understatement.

The pounding resumed.

As he neared the den, he noted that the noise sounded

"

like someone knocking on a door. He stopped by the archway to the foyer and listened. Not there. Plus, someone at the front door could use the doorbell. Then it dawned on him. The person seeking his attention had to be at the back kitchen door, which meant it was likely to be a certain redheaded neighbor who didn't like walking into his foyer.

He sighed. He had no idea what time it was, but it couldn't be more than fourteen, fifteen hours since she'd left. He walked into the kitchen and confirmed his suspicion. Summer stood outside the back door.

"Hey, good morning. Did I, um, wake you?"

"What time is it?"

She shrugged. "I'm not sure. I think it's about eight."

Eight? She's up and at it by eight on a Sunday morning? This undercover task could take its toll on him in more ways than he'd expected. But then he realized that Amy was usually up early and getting ready for church. He wondered what was going on with her. No doubt she was enjoying a cup of coffee, getting ready for her day at a leisurely pace. Maybe he would try again to call her, although her 'toxic' statement still rang in his ears.

Summer extended a white pastry box toward him. "Here. I hope you like cinnamon rolls. There's this great little bakery not far from here, and I'm convinced they have the best ones I've ever tasted."

I guess she's expecting to be invited in, too, he thought. That thought, however, brought his groggy mind to full alert. Had he closed up the compartment in the library? What if she wanted to nose around, ask to help him get settled further?

"Um, yes, you woke me up. I was up late. And, yes, I love cinnamon rolls, but I've had some awesome ones over the years, so the competition's pretty stiff. I'll see if these match up."

She gave him a coquettish look. "Sorry. I noticed you still had on the same clothes as when I left."

Richard sighed. Only a woman would notice that.

"Hey, I can make us some coffee. I know where it is, since I put it away for you yesterday."

"Uh, sure. I'll go get cleaned up and be right back." *Cleaned up, as in making sure the library's secure*, he thought.

It was, so he hurried to his bedroom, changed into fresh clothing, washed his face, and combed his hair. He expected that to refresh him somewhat, but it didn't. Coffee was now mandatory.

By the time he reached the kitchen, the aroma of brewing coffee wafted through the house, carried by the heating system. Summer already had pastries on two plates, as well as a fork and napkin for each of them.

"I didn't know if you used a fork or not, so I got you one anyway."

"Thanks. I'll probably just pick it up, unless it's super sticky." He carried the items to his small kitchen table.

"They're still warm, but I can zap it a bit in the microwave if you like."

Summer had taken over his kitchen, and he wasn't sure how he felt about that. He did appreciate her seeming willingness to introduce him to the best of the area, starting with her choice for best bakery. The cinnamon rolls looked amazing and the scent of brewing coffee now perked him up in anticipation.

They sat down and began to eat. He took a bite of the cinnamon roll and savored the spice, one of his favorites. He wondered if she somehow knew that.

"This is good, but the jury's still out about it being the best I've ever had. Have you ever been to St. Louis?"

"Sure. A number of times."

"If you go again, there's a French bistro and bakery called La Bonne Bouchée in one of the western suburbs. Try it and see how their cinnamon rolls rate." He remembered being introduced to the place by Amy. She loved the restaurant and their almond croissants. The thought of never again going there with her made him morose. He needed to fight that feeling.

"I might have to have another one . . . you know, to accurately rank it."

She smiled. "I knew you'd love them. Yes, there are two more, for you. One always fills me up."

She took her last bite, and followed it with coffee. "So, can I help you with anything today?" She stood and began to wander into the den.

My laptop. Where did I leave my laptop? Had it ended up in the den or was it still in the library? He felt confident that the DVD remained in it and wouldn't be spotted, but . . . he had to make sure. He jumped up and moved ahead of her. His computer was not in the den.

"So, what'd you work on after I left? This room looks the same."

"Um, I reassembled my bed, unpacked some clothes, and moved boxes into the library. The guys left them in the wrong room."

She glanced toward the hall that led to the library. "I love that library. The floor to ceiling bookcase and rich woodwork. The big bay lined with windows. If only it had a fireplace, too. I could sit in a room like that all day, reading in front of a fire." She sounded wistful.

Richard saw her head into the hall and rushed to head her off. She beat him to the room, but he was relieved to see that his laptop sat closed on top of his old desk, the disk nowhere to be seen. That relief was short-lived, however, as she turned her attention to the bookcase.

"That's weird." She seemed confused. "Those books."

Richard tried to change her focus.

"What? Books on a bookcase is weird?"

She rolled her eyes. "No, silly. Aren't those Eric's books? I mean, he used to have this bookcase filled with books. Mostly nonfiction, but these shelves were his fiction collection, all leather bound. I don't understand why these would still be here. You probably haven't had time to look any of them over, but a lot of these are first editions. Some are even signed. They have to be worth something."

She walked over to the case and reached for a book. Richard felt his heart rate increase. If she pulled on the wrong book . . .

He worked on remaining nonchalant, and walked over to join her. He stood between her at the "wrong" book. Make that books. What would she think if she pulled on the fake books that made up the hidden compartment?

She ran her finger across several titles and settled on one, which she freed from the dusty shelf.

"Leon Uris, one of my mother's favorites, wrote

historical novels based on years of research, if I remember correctly. *Exodus* was his biggest bestseller, but this one, *The Haj,* was one she liked. It's a story about a Palestinian Arab family in the early Israeli state before, during, and just after World War II. I think there's a copy of *Exodus* here, too."

She began to look for it, and Richard followed suit, scanning titles as quickly as he could to keep her from getting close to the "wrong" book.

"Here it is."

Richard felt relief to see her pull the book from the first position on that end of the shelf. She began to leaf through it.

"Richard, could I borrow *The Haj* for a few days? I'd be curious to read his perspective on the Israeli-Palestinian conflict from that era. That could be fascinating in light of the conflicts today." She laid the book on the shelf in front of her and began to thumb through *Exodus.*

He was about to say 'Yes' to her request when she stopped and a puzzled look crossed her face.

"That's curious. Here, on the front leaf, is a series of numbers. Wonder what that's all about. Some secret code?" She laughed at the idea.

Amy awoke to a noise coming from her kitchen. She grabbed her gun and cautiously inched her way in that direction. She was surprised to find her father drinking a glass of juice, part of his morning ritual prior to any coffee. The previous evening he had rushed to the spa to take her home as soon as she'd called him on Detective Hoskins' phone. He had been his usual reserved self at that scene as he surveyed her destroyed car and the flooded building. Now, however, he appeared more upset than she'd ever seen him.

"Dad? What are you doing here? I thought you went home."

She had, in fact, insisted that he go home after escorting her into her house and making sure all was secure. She had her Glock . . . and hadn't made any promises to Detective Hoskins about not using it. Her father's search of the home with *his* Glock in hand should have been her first clue that he was serious about her security and unlikely to leave her alone.

"Yeah, well, I was about halfway there and turned around. I let myself in and slept, sort of, on the couch."

"Dad, you don't—"

"Yes, I do!"

His anger boiled to the surface. Still, she knew his fury was not aimed at her, but at those trying to hurt her.

"You can be so bullheaded at times. Are you in denial? You almost died. These . . . these *animals* . . ."

She could see him struggle to control his tongue. The military, like the police, were accustomed to stronger language, Christian or not. Yet, she had heard him utter profanity only three times in her life.

". . . tried to kill you last night. Seriously. They even had a backup plan. You can't take this glibly."

Amy didn't think she was taking it too lightly. She was armed. She paid attention to her surroundings, now more than ever. Yet, she also knew she couldn't keep a guard around her home and car 24/7.

Of course, now she needed a new car. For a moment, her mind drifted to how she would get to work the next day. She began to brew a carafe of coffee.

"I, I'm not taking it lightly, and I'm not in denial. I *will not* let them control my life. I can protect myself. I refuse to go into hiding and I don't need a bodyguard."

"Yes. You. Do. Until these men are found, you need someone with you. *I* need someone with you."

Amy's emotions broke through her dam of stoicism as she saw tears well up in her father's eyes. She had seen him cry only twice—at her mother's and brother's funerals. The well of her emotions began to bubble up through her eyes as well.

"Amy, I've buried your mother and Chad, to cancer and war. Death is a potential outcome of both and something you can accept, as hard as the loss is. But this? Losing another child at the hands of murderers is not something I ever want to have to accept. I . . . I . . ."

Amy walked up to and embraced him. She had been so concerned about how she would handle losing *him*, that she never thought about how he would feel to lose *her*. It seemed almost cliché to say that the hardest thing a parent can do is bury a child, but she had seen it firsthand from the moment her family flew to Washington, D.C., to meet Chad's remains at Dover Air Force Base to the final graveside service. Her father hadn't eaten those four days. He had barely taken in enough fluid to avoid dehydration. She had been there for him. Who would be there for him if *she* died?

"Okay, Dad. You can be my bodyguard."

Twenty-eight

Lynch hadn't slept this soundly since taking the job as Graham's security chief. In itself that amazed him. His boss had been kidnapped. He hadn't expected to sleep much at all, but the fresh air and exercise had overridden his concerns. He found himself awake and preparing coffee, camp style, as he had been taught by Coby the day before. The warmth of the camp stove felt good. A nice campfire would have been better, but they were in an area where open fires were not allowed and Coby had already expressed his desire to get an early start. Dealing with a fire, if permitted, would cost them time and water to make sure it was extinguished.

"Well, can't call you greenhorn anymore."

Lynch turned to see Coby approaching from his tent. The man looked intent on getting packed and mounted.

"So, I've been promoted, eh?" Lynch grinned.

"Yup. Not only did you keep up yesterday, but now you beat me to makin' coffee. You might have the gumption to become an outdoorsman after all."

Lynch poured and handed Coby his filled mug. The man took a sip and nodded.

"Yup, taught you to make a good cup of joe, too. Can you fix breakfast while I pack the horses?"

Lynch nodded. Breakfast was one meal where he could hold his own in the kitchen. As Coby walked away to tend to the horses, Lynch yelled after him, "So, what's my new rank?"

The man stopped and turned back. After a sip of coffee, he said, "How 'bout rookie?"

Lynch shook his head. "No way. Means the same thing as greenhorn."

Coby looked down and rubbed his chin in contemplation. He looked up and smiled. "Probie, like those agents on *N.C.I.S.*" He turned back toward the horses before Lynch could respond.

Lynch chuckled. As long as Coby didn't start slapping him across the back of the head, he could live with that.

Less than an hour later, they were mounted and riding east along the top of the crest. Their camp had been in an area of tall brush, which had provided something of a windbreak for them. Now out in the open again, Lynch noticed a stiff breeze and a change in the smell of the air. Nothing unpleasant, just different. The sun in the east was unopposed by clouds, but this wind came from their backs. Lynch turned to face backward and saw the summit. The side facing them reflected the bright sun, but behind the mountain a bank of gray, ominous clouds collected, as if held back by an unseen force.

Charlie stopped abruptly in his tracks, catching Lynch's attention and causing him to face forward again. He looked back at the summit and then at the gorge in front of them. He didn't like the prospects either one offered.

"Over there. That's where we need to go," said

Coby as he pointed to a different ridge in the distance.

Lynch experienced a wave of vertigo as he looked down, and he clutched the saddle horn as he had the day before. The bottom of the gorge sat at least a thousand feet below them. As the imbalance departed, he saw the hint of a trail beginning its descent to that bottom.

"And you want to get there how?" He suspected he knew Coby's answer. He wanted to hear it spoken aloud.

"Well, probie, we've got two choices. We backtrack and work our way to the far end of that ridge, or we ride down, across, and up. The first option will take us a day, minimum, to get back to where these two ridges join up and another day to work our way to that end over there." He continued to point to a spot in the distance. "Then, we'll have to backtrack that ride to continue the search if we haven't found your boss by then. Going my way will get us there by early afternoon. We might even have time to search one or two more side canyons today."

Lynch understood the logic. He also valued the time they could save, but . . .

"Let me throw in one more wrinkle," said Coby. "I saw you looking back at the mountain. Those gray clouds hold what is likely to be the first snowfall of the season. Thermals around the summit are keeping them at bay. But at some point, that heat is going to dissipate enough that those warm updrafts aren't going to amount to much and that front will come storming across the mountain. Might be blizzard conditions, might be a gentle snowfall. Might be today, tonight, or tomorrow night. No one can really predict with accuracy when that's going to happen or how severely."

Lynch took a deep breath. Snow? Blizzard? He'd been in

blizzard conditions before. He preferred the Dairy Queen version. Maybe he could close his eyes on the way down. Yeah, right. Maybe he could walk behind the horses, make the descent on his own. Again, it wasn't the height that bothered him so much. Could he trust the horse?

He shook his head at the conundrum. He pointed to the distant ridge and said, "Let's go." He paused. Had he really said that? He added, "Before I change my mind."

When Charlie took that first step down, Lynch held his breath. By the time they hit the trail's first switchback 15 minutes later, Lynch realized that Charlie didn't want to fall down that hill any more than he did. At the second switchback 22 minutes later, Lynch's confidence in the horse had grown. When one hoof slipped, the other three held secure. There had been two points where Charlie held fast to the trail, but Lynch knew for sure he would have gone sliding butt-first on a long tumble. The comparison to vehicles became clear. Lynch was a two-wheel-drive sports car compared to Charlie's four-wheel, independent suspension, all-terrain sport vehicle.

The slope of the terrain decreased as they hit the tree line, but the trees made it difficult to see their destination on the other ridge. In addition, that autumn's leaf fall made it hard to see the trail. This was designated wilderness, not a groomed trail maintained by volunteers as in the east. Lynch knew they'd reached the nadir when they came to a stream. There was little water to be seen—an occasional pool dotted the streambed here and there—but Lynch could tell from the trees that water roared through this area at some time during the year.

At a small clearing on the other side, Coby stopped and dismounted. "Let's take advantage of this water for the horses and take a break for us, too. You did a good job, probie. We made good time. The climb up won't seem as nerve-racking, but it'll take longer."

Lynch took Charlie to get a drink. As the horse took his fill, Lynch checked his cell phone. No signal. He had expected as much, being so far down within the canyon.

True to Coby's word, the ride up took about an hour longer than the ride down, but focusing on the trail as it weaved up the canyon wall proved far less disconcerting than seeing how far you could fall as you descended. Also true, they arrived at the top before two p.m. Coby didn't stop, however.

Lynch did. He looked back at the gorge in wonder. He couldn't say exactly where they'd left the other ridge for their descent, but he marveled that he'd ridden a horse from there to here. He had always been something of a hot-shot detective back home, a maverick. Here, he'd been totally out of his element, but he had come a long way. Maybe Coby would promote him again. He chuckled at the thought.

"C'mon, probie! Catch up or get lost," yelled Coby from somewhere ahead of him.

And then again, maybe that promotion was a long way off.

Brad's day started late. He'd been exhausted by his trek

and slept longer than his usual seven hours. Three hours longer, to be precise. He couldn't recall the last time he'd spent that much time in dreamland.

This morning he started the small propane heater his captors had left behind. He would *not* rely on it. He didn't know what kind of carbon monoxide risk he took by using it. Plus, he had but one small tank of the gas that he could use for it, plus a second for the camp stove. If he used too much too fast, he risked both becoming useless. Right now, it was helpful in taking the morning chill out of the cabin before the wood stove fulfilled that task.

He went through the routine he'd set up for the previous two mornings. By the time he finished breakfast, his "friends" had arrived.

Caw! Caw!

He glanced out the dirty front window to see twice as many crows as the evening before sitting on the low branches of nearby trees. They must have informed their cousins and neighbors of the free smorgasbord at the canyon gulag.

He opened the door and the volume doubled. Several birds fluttered down, unafraid, to the deck of the small porch just feet away from him.

"Aren't you the brave ones? I thought you were supposed to bring me food, not the other way around." But then, he wasn't in need like Elijah. Although if the Democrats were behind his kidnapping, the same Jezebel spirit might be active behind the scenes. Her Royal Candidate certainly reminded him of Jezebel in the Bible.

He broke up several Pop-Tarts® and tossed the pieces onto the porch and ground right in front of it. A flurry of black wings settled onto the food. Almost as quickly, the murder departed.

Brad returned to the cabin and picked up the spiral notebook. He made notes on his experience of the day before and began a crude map based on his recall of his journey *back* to the cabin—when he'd made a point of paying attention to details.

Then he created and packed a sandwich, using a sheet of the notebook paper as wrapping. He took the empty gallon jug—that had held the water he had consumed over the previous days—and filled it about a quarter of the way from a freshly opened container. That would reduce its weight for carrying. He gathered some other snack food, too, and looked for something in which he could carry the sandwich and snacks.

He had no intention of sitting still, twiddling his thumbs, and playing solitaire, until Homer returned, if he had such intentions to begin with. He would make smart use of stone trail markers that he'd create as he went downhill. He would take his notebook and develop his map as he walked.

Still, how was he going to carry all that he wanted to take?

He looked about and had an idea. He would be wearing the heavier coat left behind for him. Maybe he could fashion a backpack of sorts from his lighter jacket, tie the sleeves together to form a sling he could slip over his head. He could then zip it up, forming a pocket that held his food, water, and notebook.

He went to work on it, but could find nothing to use to close the neck opening and form a closed pouch. A shoestring would work, but he had only the ties on his shoes. He needed those right where they were. He searched and searched for a substitute, but found nothing. Without securing the neck opening, even the gallon jug could slip out.

Frustrated, he sat down on the cot and scrutinized what he had sitting before him. *Some MacGyver I am*, he thought. Richard Dean Anderson's character could probably use items on hand to fashion a hot air balloon or some other device to carry him out of there.

The cardboard boxes of food caught his attention. As is, he could use one, but it would require both hands to carry and that would be awkward and inconvenient. There were places along the trail to the cabin where he and his captors required both hands to maneuver. But . . . what if?

What if. The term reminded him of Lynch. He had no doubt that Lynch was working 24/7 with authorities to find him.

Yes. What if. He grabbed the smallest box, emptied it, and studied it. He grabbed one of the plastic knives he'd been allowed to use and labored with the dull utensil to cut the box down along the corner folds. The narrow sides of the rectangle he folded outward. The longer sides he folded down, but then back on themselves. When he brought the two flaps together, they met up. He marked and cut matching handholds in both. Now when they came together, he had a handle. The shorter sides he now folded back over the longer sides. He cut some excess cardboard away, followed by two slits in each. With these, he stabilized the cardboard handle.

All done. He lifted his creation up with ease. It was like an oversized lunchbox—and sturdy. It would hold more weight than he expected to carry. More importantly, he could carry it with one hand. He could work with that at those spots where he might need two hands. MacGyver would be proud.

He had to lay the water bottle on its side to make it fit. He double-checked the lid. The last thing he needed was to lose his water. Besides not having it to drink, it would soak and weaken the cardboard. He tested it again with all of his supplies. Success. It wasn't as ideal as a backpack or shoulder pouch, but it would work.

He set off from the cabin and headed downhill. As he had noticed three days earlier, the trees and terrain looked the same no matter which way he looked. He set up his first stone pillar at the point where he could first see the cabin. He worked his way along and at each point where he lost sight of a pillar, he backtracked until he could see it again. There he'd build another pillar.

However, about an hour into his journey he reached an area of flatter ground. He no longer had "downhill" as a source of orientation. He ventured on, mapping his way, building his pillars. He came to a point where he was about to build another pillar, when he realized he now saw his two previous rock markers, not just one. He had gone in a circle.

Dismayed, he sat down, ate his food, and drank about half of his water. He tried to determine where he'd gone astray. With everything looking the same and no landmarks to guide him, he couldn't figure it out.

He walked back to his previous marker, enhanced it to make it unique, and set out in the opposite direction. Now he made each marker with its own look—different size, a distinct stone to top it. With three new pillars erected, he felt more confident. Then he walked ten feet farther and came across one of the stone structures he'd made before embarking on making them different. He'd simply gone in a bigger circle.

Once again Homer's comments had been validated. Without GPS, a compass, or something for orientation, he would find himself lost, with no food and no water. How far could he stumble before succumbing?

He recalled a rocky prominence about halfway around this latest circle. He wondered if that could place him high enough to see past the trees and gain some bearing. Using his markers, he retraced his steps and came to the right spot. He set down his box and struggled to get to the top of the rock thumb he saw sticking up from the hillside.

Sure enough, he was above enough of the trees to gain a panoramic view of his location. What he saw disheartened him more than wasting the day going in circles.

Looming before him was a broad gorge filled with trees and scrub. He could see a tall mountain ridge on the other end. And as he gazed down the length of the gorge, it stretched as far as he could see. Even if he could carry enough water and food for such a trip on foot, how many circles would he walk trying to make the trek?

Twenty-nine

Amy grabbed her Glock and eased toward the front door upon hearing a car turn into her driveway. She resisted glancing into the peep hole. She'd seen that disastrous trick on too many TV shows. She looked back to see her father, armed as well, work his way toward the window, where he peeked outside. She saw his shoulders release their tension as he lowered his gun and nodded his "Okay." She lowered her gun as well before opening the door as the bell rang.

"Ms. Gibbs, I, uh . . ." Detective Hoskins stared at her gun and she rushed to put it some place secure, but close by.

"Sorry, Detective. C'mon in."

He nodded and entered her home. He looked toward her father.

"Good morning, Colonel Gibbs. I'm glad to see she at least has someone with her. We couldn't talk her into moving to a safer place last night."

"Good morning, Detective. Coffee?"

"No, thank you, sir. I just wanted to make sure all was well and to pass on a few bits of information. I'll be brief."

Amy pointed to the couch. He shook his head.

"As I said, I'll be brief. First, we didn't find anything specific at the spa to point to the perpetrators. The belt they used was a common brand from Walmart. The water did a job on any other evidence. ATF, however, did match the explosives used on your car with those found at Busch Wildlife. By the way, I now have a piece-of-junk, old patrol car to use, thanks to those SOBs. It'll take months for the department to settle the insurance and get me a new SUV."

The detective's displeasure was obvious as he spoke.

"Anyway, Homeland Security is watching the cab company, but they don't have the manpower to keep tabs on three dozen taxis. They're focusing on learning more about the employees themselves."

"What about the spa company?" asked her father. "Don't they have some culpability here for the security of their clients?"

Hoskins shrugged. "Maybe, but I'm no lawyer. I was able to talk with the young woman there after she regained consciousness. She pointed us toward the taxi company, too. Said a cab pulled up outside and the driver came in saying he was supposed to have a fare waiting there. He hit her before she could even answer him. She never saw it coming, so she can't really be blamed. The safety issues regarding the design of that pod, well, that's another issue—one for the manufacturer. Any questions for me?"

Amy's father shook his head.

"I have none right now. If something comes up, I've put your phone number on my speed dial," replied Amy.

He appeared ready to be his sarcastic self, with some response about helping her move again, but then caught himself. "Anytime, but I hope I don't hear from you. I mean, just because nothing else happens, not, you know. Anyway, I was also asked to let you know that the ATF will be contacting you again."

"Thank you, Detective. I'll anticipate their call."

Amy watched and waved as Detective Hoskins pulled out of her driveway.

"Well, that confirms things." Her father looked up from his seat in her living room. "With the explosive used on your car matching the stuff you discovered, I guess we know who's behind the attempts on your life."

Amy nodded, although knowing that some nebulous group was after her didn't help her current situation.

"Dad, I guess you're also my chauffeur. I had planned on grocery shopping this afternoon. I also need a new car, but the dealers are closed today. So, that'll have to wait until after work this week." She sighed. "Sorry. I hate to inconvenience you."

He shook his head. "Never. It's never an inconvenience to help you, particularly now. We can hit the grocery stores whenever you want. As for a new car, I can make some calls. What are you looking for?"

"I liked my old Mazda 3, but I've been saving up and I think I'd like to upgrade. Like Macy did earlier this year. An Acura, or even a Lexus like Richard has. Used, of course. I could afford a one new, but I'd rather be sensible about it."

Her father had always encouraged her to consider late model, low mileage used cars over new since a new car loses so much value as soon as you drive it off the lot. She had gotten some great deals over the years, but it took a little time and perseverance to find them.

But, she also realized that her mention of Richard hadn't triggered a negative visceral response, as it had just two days earlier. She had no plans for reconciling their relationship, so maybe now she had moved on after all.

"Oh. I was thinking of something more along the lines of a used, military, armored Hummer." He smiled.

She huffed and feigned being insulted. "Great. Now you're talking like Detective Hoskins. Just what I need. Do you think I should move, too?" She smiled and laughed.

"Only if you move closer to me."

"Hah. You're retired. You could live anywhere. I have to work and your place is too far from MedAir. Maybe *you* should move closer to me."

He raised one brow. "Right now, I plan on moving *in*."

True, she thought. She needed to change the subject.

"So, why don't we go get groceries now and I'll get something for a nice dinner tonight. You up for salmon?"

"Sure. Let's go."

An hour later, having faced no threats other than a customer angry at the bakery personnel for misspelling a name on a birthday cake, they headed out of the store. Her father scrutinized the parking lot before moving away from the doors.

"Okay, I think it's safe to cross over."

Amy felt like a toddler with her parent looking out for her.

"Do I need to hold your hand while we cross the street, Daddy?"

He laughed. "No, but you can hold on to the cart."

Together they unloaded the grocery cart and put her bags into the trunk of his car. With every other bag, her father glanced about. She noticed the slight bulge in his jacket and knew that he'd be able to protect her long before she could retrieve her gun, if attacked. Fortunately, this chain of stores had abandoned its "gun-free" policy years earlier.

"I'll take care of the cart. Your door is unlocked if you want to get in. Back in a minute."

Amy saw no need to enter the car right away. She watched her father push the cart to the nearest holding pen about 20 yards away. She had his back just as much he had hers.

The sudden squeal of tires to her right caught her attention. An orange and black taxi raced around the corner and down the lane where they had parked. Her mind went blank. Her gun was in her handbag. Where was it? She realized she had placed it in the trunk with the groceries. She grabbed at the trunk's latch.

"Hey!" her father shouted.

She saw her father racing back, his hand latched onto his gun in its holster, ready to pull it in the blink of an eye.

The cab screeched to a stop next to her. The driver had already lowered his window, and through it, she saw a thin, black male behind the wheel. His face had a long scar down its left side and part of that ear was missing. His head appeared to be shaved, but the shadows within the cab made it difficult to confirm that.

"Yo missy. You dishonor us. Because of you we lose something of great value. You *will* pay. No one protect you. No place can hide you."

By then her father neared the back of the taxi and appeared to be pulling his weapon. The driver glanced into his rear view mirror.

"Remember this face, missy. I will defend our honor. Mark my word."

With that, he sped away just as her father pulled his gun.

Amy stood trembling at the outright aggression and threat of the taxi driver. She chastised herself for leaving her bag in the trunk. How had she been so stupid? Her father had encouraged her to get a hip holster. She hadn't felt a need for one. That would change ASAP.

"You okay?"

Her father ran to her and hugged her. Even with his gun drawn, her father might not have been able to stop the man from shooting her, had that been the man's intention. But the man was wrong about no one protecting her. If required, she could protect herself. She wouldn't make dumb mistakes again.

"I-I'm fine. He just threatened me. That's all."

"That's all? We need to call Detective Hoskins and let him know what just happened. I got a partial plate number."

She nodded. "But let's do that inside the car."

Once seated, she dialed the officer's number. She identified herself, told him where she was, and that the driver of a County Cab just threatened her.

"Be there in five minutes."

She sat back into her seat to wait and felt an unexpected peace surround her. *Lord?* she thought. She glanced at her father and saw that he was praying silently. Then she heard the words, "I am protecting you," as clearly as if her father had spoken them. And she realized that her Father had.

"Summer, thank you again for all your help here, but really, you don't have to go shopping with me. I can find the nearest grocery store and a Home Depot or Lowe's or something on my phone's map app."

He needed to stock his new kitchen and find a dozen or so items for the house, things he had noted as he moved in. He reflected upon two things. Ben wanted him to gain favor with Summer to be able to feed her false data. For Richard, that had been an effortless task. She seemed to want *his* favor more than the reverse.

It reminded him of the movie *How to Lose a Guy in Ten Days.* In that flick, Kate Hudson's character tried everything to make Matthew McConaughey's character ditch her, while he tried every move he knew to make her fall in love with him. The plot was predictable but funny. In Richard's current "comedy," he and Summer both were bending over backwards to gain the other's trust and friendship. It could only end in disaster.

At the same time, he also reflected on Amy. *She* was the one who should be shopping with him, helping him to organize the house, and putting her feminine touch on the home, not Summer. Sunday afternoon—she probably went out to lunch with friends after church. Maybe she was watching Mizzou football with those same friends. He had no doubts that her weekend had been more relaxing than his.

"Richard, I've enjoyed getting to know you and I'm

more than happy to help. I've said that before. Right now, I'd *love* to show you around McLean. You won't have to rely on your phone and I can show you the fun places the locals like, not just the big chain stores."

Richard had decided that he couldn't seem eager to be friends. He was supposed to be an engaged man, off the market. At least, he still thought of himself that way.

He hesitated. He wanted to hit the grocery store and a home improvement store in a direct hit-and-run approach, spend as little time as possible there, and get back home to explore that book Summer had found. The numbers intrigued him. To accept her invitation would lead to visiting several stores, maybe even tying them up until dinner, which would lead to having dinner together. Of course, that would satisfy Ben's goal.

"Okay, Summer. Thanks. But on one condition. You do realize that I'm an engaged man, right? I don't want this to mislead you in any way."

She looked as if she took affront to his statement. "Richard, really? Do you think I'm hitting on you?"

He wanted to nod but knew better.

"I-I'm sorry if I come across that way. I want to be a good neighbor and I'm grateful for what you did for me in Kansas City. I want to return the favor."

Something in her mannerism didn't jibe with her comment, but Richard couldn't really pinpoint what that difference was. Maybe she actually *was* hitting on him. He wasn't sure how to take that. Or maybe she was under "orders" like he was to become friends with "the enemy." There was something there. He'd figure it out in time.

Instead of a big chain home improvement store, she took him to McLean Hardware. In and out. Just as he had hoped. On the other hand, the trip to the grocery evolved into visits to the bakery, a boutique winery, a craft cheese store, an artisan olive oil shop, a specialty spice store, and Trader Joe's, along with a Safeway. Then came a side trip to a furniture store where every piece was custom made by the craftsmen who owned it.

As dinnertime rolled around, he found his budget blown. Besides enough groceries to feed everyone at his office, he now had a new dining room set, couch and matching chair, and a kitchen table with stools on order to be delivered at a time he had yet to determine.

And by the time they finished dinner at a contemporary Indian cuisine restaurant in downtown McLean, Richard's appreciation for Summer had grown. He had discovered that they shared similar tastes for food and furnishings. Maybe Ben's assignment wouldn't be so rough after all.

Thirty

Brad's trek back to the cabin took longer than he'd anticipated. The climb seemed steeper than it had appeared going downhill and twice he missed his markers, forcing him to backtrack or move laterally until he found himself on course. He felt that God had watched over him in both instances. He might have missed the markers altogether and become completely lost.

He had finished his water, too, and wished he'd taken more with him. Although his stomach growled in hunger, he could put up with that. Managing his thirst seemed more critical to survival.

He knew he was closing in on his home-away-from-home, when he heard his "friends" calling from a point uphill. He couldn't see them, or the cabin, yet he knew he was on track.

Within minutes he spotted the cabin. From this angle it looked different—taller, larger. He realized his perspective had changed. The previous day he had been uphill and the cabin seemed diminutive against the fall of the canyon. Now, it loomed overhead making it appear grander than he knew it to be.

One other feature stood out, and he stopped and

gazed at it—the chimney of the wood stove. He hadn't noticed it yesterday. Perhaps it had blended into the trees. Maybe he hadn't seen it because the approach to the cabin came from the opposite side.

Yet, he saw it now and it made him think. Smoke.

He was in the middle of a wilderness. Surely those who cared for the area watched for fires. He didn't know if they had watch towers, used planes, or had other avenues for detecting fires, but one thing had to be common for whatever method they used—they would watch for smoke. Where there's smoke, there's fire.

He rushed to the cabin. The crows had congregated for dinner, but they would have to wait a few moments longer. Inside, as he suspected, the fire he had built that morning had gone cold. He gathered some wood and a fat stick his captors had provided, and lit the fire. The fat stick flared and soon ignited the wood.

Satisfied that the fire would sustain itself, he grabbed some more Pop-Tarts® to feed his feathered visitors. Twice now, their presence had helped guide him back to the cabin and he desired to encourage their return. However, this time he threw the food off to the far side of the porch so that he could exit and enter the cabin without their interference and without scaring them away. The birds swooped down from their perches to grab pieces of the pseudo-pastry.

He descended the porch and walked to a spot where he could see the chimney. Looking up, he saw a curl of white smoke between the trees that dissolved into nothing visible against the sky. He would have to change that.

He ran back to the cabin and glanced about. He knew from backyard grilling and bonfires that petroleum produced darker smoke. He had no starter fluid or oil. He did, however, have a stack of foam bowls and plates. He grabbed a few, bowls first, and tossed three into the fire. He dashed back outside to see the effect.

Yes! He pumped his fist in self-congratulation. Dark smoke.

However, a minute later the effect had diminished to where he no longer saw the smoke. He calculated what he could do with the items on hand. With fewer than 50 each of the plates and bowls on hand, and knowing that burning three at one time had produced not more than two minutes of useful smoke, he reasoned that he had perhaps 20 minutes of useful smoke for each. Only with sheer luck would his smoke signal be spotted during such a short span. Maybe one plate at a time ...

Returning inside, he tossed one plate into the stove and rushed back out. He couldn't even see the smoke. One plate or bowl alone would not be enough. He needed something other than the dinnerware for a dense, sustained smoke.

He looked about. Green wood would produce smoke, but he had nothing but his bare hands to collect whatever he ended up using. And he had no idea what that smoke might look like.

The late afternoon shadows were already approaching the cabin. Dusk would be upon him in no time. He needed to experiment and to do so in short order.

*   *   *

Upon reaching the top of the ridge, Lynch had noted that Coby had turned left to head southwest, but that the ridge also extended northeast. Yet, he had also noticed that there was a trail winding along in the direction they now headed and none in the opposite direction. He reasoned those observations away. After all, Coby knew the area and probably had no reason to investigate the area to the northeast.

Having caught up with Ed and Sally Mae, Charlie fell into line and followed the leader. Lynch observed that this ridge seemed to grow broader as they traversed it. Although he suspected there were smaller canyons that descended both to their right and left, he had no idea where to expect them. He *had* to rely on Coby's knowledge of the mountain.

After about 20 minutes of riding along the ridge, Coby pulled Ed up to a stop and the other horses followed suit. Lynch still wondered how they didn't run into each other.

"There's a box canyon off to the right, over there ..." He pointed. "... and we need to check it out. It's fairly broad and used to hold two cabins. I think we have enough daylight left to cover it. I don't want to risk my drone by flying at dusk like we did last night."

Lynch dismounted and tied Charlie to some scrub. He assisted Coby with setting up the drone, and soon it soared over the valley as Lynch played spotter. They found the first cabin in short order, and it, too, had been left to decay for the mountain to reclaim it. The wind in this rift picked up as the search progressed and Coby fought to keep it flying in a suitable pattern. They found the second building. Its tin roof showed extensive rust but appeared intact. However, when Coby flew in for a closer inspection, the windows and door were gone and the far wall consisted of exposed studs.

"Well, no one's gonna be using that place," said Coby. He took the drone high and brought it back to their base.

"Hey, there's a heat signature! No—two, three, four. There're six altogether." Lynch's enthusiasm waned as he counted. He had seen only two men carry off his boss, not five. "Eh, probably animals, right?"

"Are they big?"

Lynch had no idea how to gauge their size from a camera at several hundred feet above the critters. "I have no idea from the image here."

"Probably Rocky Mountain elk. They'd be more likely in that area and more likely to run in a small herd. We've also got bighorn sheep. Those males can be up to 500 lbs, but they usually travel in larger herds and graze in the grassier areas."

"What about deer?"

Coby shook his head. "No deer to speak of on this mountain. There's pronghorn. They're about the size of a big dog and the fastest land animal in this country, if I 'member correctly."

Lynch figured the man was right about the elk.

"Well, I'm not gonna waste battery time going down for a look. My baby's almost here."

Lynch looked up and saw the drone as it neared. Coby brought it in for a perfect landing, and together they packed up.

Back in the saddle, the duo continued their journey along the ridge. Lynch found his thoughts going back to that unexplored end of the ridge. He looked back in the direction. Was that smoke? When he blinked, whatever he thought he'd seen was gone.

"So, Coby, why didn't we check out the end of the ridge? Back there, behind us."

Coby twisted in his saddle halfway to answer and shook his head. "No need. The ridge itself is real narrow. It turns back toward the Alvord Desert and that wall becomes a jagged drop of almost a mile to the desert below. The ridge itself ends in a sheer drop. Horses can't navigate it."

Lynch took a minute to orient himself. He wished he had a compass for that task. They'd made so many twists and turns, he knew only that their general direction now was to the southwest, back toward the summit and Coby's truck.

"What about the other side, to what, the north maybe? I'm turned around."

"Hey, that's pretty good. You're right. That'd be the north, with the desert to the south. Yup, so that north side has a few small box canyons. They're really steep and inaccessible by anything other than a 4-wheel ATV. Maybe a 4-wheeled pickup could get part of the way, but if they set up a camp in there, they would have had to carry your boss for quite a way."

"Or made him walk."

"Yup, or made him walk, but they would have to have freed his hands to climb. He could have turned on them."

Lynch thought about that. Not his boss. The guy had no fear and confidence was his middle name—one of many. But he also knew when to wait. He'd been stunned, maybe even drugged after that. He had no idea where he was or how to find help. He would comply with his kidnappers and then wait, analyze, and adapt. The man also had the faith of Abraham. He would allow God to work his hand while trying hard not to step ahead of God's plan. And God *always* had a plan.

"Besides, there's no cabin in any of those canyons. Like I said, I know this mountain like the back of my hand."

The Director had a decision to make. The press had exceeded his expectations of playing up the role of the Oregon protesters in the kidnapping of Bradley Graham, but public sentiment had not been swayed. Social media now blunted the message of the liberal media, and over a dozen members of that protest had used social media to denounce the claims that they had somehow been involved.

At the risk of facing federal charges, their stories came out. They embraced the Graham campaign and promoted it. They stated that Graham took seriously their concerns over a federal land grab in the west that used environmental concerns to hide the reality of politicians' desires to control the natural resources and award their big business cronies with generous mining contracts in the future. Their candor and willingness to go to jail for their roles in the protest had struck a nerve with many in the U.S.

The press struck back with stories about "fake news" and its role leading up to the election. Several stories, however, had raised the question as to what constituted such news. Many now looked at the sources of fake news as being CNN, MSNBC, the broadcast networks, the *New York Times*, and more. Even Fox News, the Director's personal nemesis, had been caught up in that dragnet.

And this shift in sentiment had brought the Director to the point of making a life and death decision—Bradley Graham's life or death.

"François, I'm available for my evening briefing."

"*Oui*, Director."

The Director's aide gave him a rundown of worldwide events with his usual behind-the-scenes information—information that his formal government intelligence briefings often missed. Compared to François' briefings, *all* public news became fake news. So much happened behind the scenes that the public would never know.

"As for our little project here in Washington, Maggie Walther says it is moving along *à la perfection*. She has Summer Stanton playing—how do they say it in basketball?—a full-court press. Ms. Stanton spent the entire day with Nichols, and I'm told it went very well."

The Director absorbed that info and added it to the variables he needed to process concerning Graham. The unexpected demise of Graham might make Nichols more wary and less inclined to cooperate. And while Graham's death would throw the party into disarray, it had grown to a size where it would not fade into the background upon one candidate's death. That death, in fact, might make Graham a martyr to the cause and lead to more growth of the party.

But, the martyrdom argument had been the one to win out in the beginning. That's why Graham was still alive.

"Any news from Oregon, François?"

"The status quo, sir. Our people are stalling the search and using social media to locate the protesters. Graham is still sequestered in the cabin and has food for another week. I have been told that the mountain might receive its first snowfall as early as tonight."

That bit of news made one aspect of his decision easier. Burning down a cabin in the dry season threatened to set the mountain on fire, and he respected the environment too much to take that responsibility. Burning down a cabin in the snow, however...

"Do we have our team in place with Michael Goodwell?"

"*Oui, monsieur.* You need only give the word and the vice-presidential candidate's vehicles will fail to protect him."

The Graham campaign had provided armored vehicles for both candidates. The Assembly had arranged for an identical SUV, minus the armor and possessing very poor brakes, to take its place at the Director's discretion. They were unable to do the same for Graham himself because of that same security chief he so wished would disappear. The man scrutinized every vehicle Graham utilized.

"Tell me something, François. I'd like your opinion, now, under current circumstances."

"I am honored, sir. Yes. How might I help?"

"I know I asked once before, but do you think killing Graham is wise or not?"

There was a pause on the other end of the call, but the Director knew that it was unlikely that François had no answer. Wanting to phrase his answer properly would be the more probable reason for a delay. And the Director appreciated that. Immediate answers were often rash ones. And rash answers often led to trouble.

"Sir, in mythology, cutting off the heads of the Hydra required two steps. I believe that killing Graham would be like cutting off a head, while killing Goodwell is like burning the wound. We won't see a new head grow back. But if I'm wrong, it will take the American Party years to recuperate and that gives us time to work our way inside."

The Director smiled. That was not a rash answer.

Thirty-one

Richard had spent the previous evening looking at the numbers Summer had discovered in Leon Uris' *Exodus*. Seven rows of four numbers each, except for the first line which held three numbers. The first column of the first line held a blank.

This morning, he brought the book with him. If he had time, he wanted to pass it by Ben, but at the moment, Ben had not yet arrived.

He grabbed a cup of coffee and proceeded to his desk. He had the last cinnamon roll in its bag and looked forward to savoring it. But first, he needed to boot up his computer and do his daily security scan to make sure no spyware had found its way onto his hard drive. At that point, he could enjoy his pastry while surfing the news portals for information on the election. Of course, he had his own inside tracks to the truth. He performed this routine to see what fake news the mainstream media pushed upon the people each day.

There was a knock at his door. He looked up to find Greg, one of his team members.

"Welcome back. How'd the move go?"

"Piece of cake. Any fires from the weekend I need

to put out?"

The young man shook his head. "All in all, considering our candidate was kidnapped and remains missing, we had an uneventful weekend." He rolled his eyes.

Richard nodded. "Yeah, other than that minor issue. Hey, thanks again for filling in for me so I could move and unpack."

Greg shrugged. "No prob. Didn't have anything going on, and the overtime will help." He started to turn away but stopped. "Oh. Ben said to tell you he'd be back around eleven. Something about checking into home security systems. And I should have the weekend stats for you shortly."

"Okay. Thanks."

Richard wondered just what that meant. Was his boss looking into the system they'd discovered at Richard's new home? Maybe he was concerned about his own home's security.

He scanned the news, purged his email inbox of unwanted messages, and reviewed their weekend posts on social media. As Greg had said, the weekend had been a routine one—if one ignored Bradley Graham's disappearance.

He glanced at the clock and saw that the morning approached the eleventh hour. He decided to grab another cup of coffee and see if Ben was in. His friend's office was empty, but as he walked back toward his own, he heard Ben's voice from the break room behind him. He turned and met Ben at the door to his office. He followed him inside and shut the door.

Ben looked at him askew. "What? I don't even get to

take off my coat and have my first sip of coffee?"

Richard put his own mug down on the corner of Ben's desk. "Sure. Take off your coat. But I know you've already had at least two sips of that coffee. You always take at least two drinks in the break room and top off your mug before coming to your office."

Ben grinned. "Busted." He removed his coat and tossed it to Richard who was closer to the coat hook on the back of the office door.

Richard sat down across the desk from Ben while fidgeting with the book in his hands. "Any news of Graham?" he asked.

"Nada, but . . . Nothing leaves this room."

Richard raised one brow and made a face to say, "Duh. That's a given."

"Cully and his team were ordered to stand down or face obstruction charges."

Richard had heard a rumor to that effect.

"Headquarters got confirmation that the guy is out on horseback looking for Graham. Can you imagine that? Taking to *horseback* to search for Graham? It's like going back to the wild, wild west or something."

Richard would not have predicted Cully taking this move, but he knew he'd do whatever he had to do to find Graham. Still, the idea of Cully playing cowboy struck him as funny.

"So, what's that? One of the books from your bookcase?" The last sentence came out as a whisper.

Richard nodded and went on to outline his previous day and how lucky he'd been that Summer hadn't stumbled upon the electronics in his library. He handed the book to Ben.

"Check out the inside front flap."

Richard watched Ben's brow furrow as he saw the numbers.

"This library of yours is getting curiouser and curiouser. Next thing you know, we'll find a hidden door or room or something."

"So, what do you make of it?"

Ben shook his head. "Got me. It's not latitude and longitude, or the Dewey Decimal System."

"Doesn't fit GPS coordinates and I didn't find any maps in the house."

There was a knock on the door. Both men looked up.

"C'mon in," said Ben.

"Oh, hey, sorry to disturb you." Greg held up a handful of computer printouts. "Here're the stats you wanted from the weekend. I left your copy on your desk, Richard." He walked over to hand the papers to Ben. "Wow, that's a neat book. You don't see many leather-bound editions anymore. May I?" He reached down to take the book.

Both men again looked at each other and Richard shrugged and nodded, with "Why not?" spoken in body language. Ben handed Greg the book and the young man turned right to the copyright leaf.

"Impressive. A first edition. Too bad it's not signed." His finger slipped off the page and it closed to reveal the inside cover leaf with its numbers. "Oh wow, cool. A book code."

Richard and Ben spoke in unison, "Book code?"

Greg nodded in enthusiasm. "Yeah. They're classic codes. They can have a few different formats. The common thread between the formats is that the numbers correspond to a page, paragraph, and word within the paragraph. Sometimes there's a number that points to the sentence within the paragraph and then the next number is the word within that sentence. The most intricate ones have an additional number to point to a specific letter within the word. That kind of code usually spells a single word. The hard part is figuring out where the next clue is hidden. Sometimes the code points to a different book for the next clue. Sometimes all the clues are in the same book."

Richard noticed Ben scrutinizing Greg as he spoke and then asked, "How in the world do you know this?"

"Oh, I'm a fan of mystery novels, good old-fashioned who-dun-its. It doesn't take reading too many of those before you run across a book code."

Ben then asked, "Okay, so what do you make of this one?"

"Well, since the first number is missing, my best guess is that the first clue is in this book." He thumbed through the book. "So, this would be the page. Here's the paragraph." He nodded his head as he counted the words. "And the word is 'Eric'."

Ben's eyes widened as he met Richard's own wondering look.

"So, 'Eric' could mean this is a list of people. It could be the first word in a phrase. Who knows?"

"How do we know if it's a list or something else?" asked Richard.

"I guess by figuring out the next few words." He flipped a few pages. "To me, the logical guess is that the first number means another book, because the next line makes no sense with this book. But you'd have to know where the book came from and how it fits into that collection. Sometimes the word you find points to the next clue. You know, like another book with the name 'Eric' in it, or by an author named 'Eric.' I keep saying another book because as I see it, if all the clues are in this book, whoever wrote this code would have needed only three numbers per line. Plus this book is several hundred pages and all of these first numbers are under 100. Again, just an educated guess on my part."

Richard looked at Ben and mouthed the words, "We need to go." It took Ben a moment to read his lips, but then he nodded.

"Greg, you and the others need to hold down the fort. Richard and I need to run an urgent errand. I hope we won't be long."

Thirty-two

Brad awoke to an eerie silence. The mute switch had been turned on for all of the noises he had become accustomed to over the previous days. Even the crows were silent. On the other hand, the light outside seemed brighter.

He arose from the cot and looked through the dirty window. Snow.

He blinked and looked again. There appeared to be several inches of the white stuff covering the ground. He shook his head. Nope, he definitely had not expected snow. That meant a major reconsideration of his plans. He did not have the clothing to cope with this change.

He moved to the door and opened it. He walked off the porch a couple of feet and estimated the precipitation depth to be at least six inches. *More than I thought.* That would make even the shortest hike dangerous for several reasons—from slippery rocks that his leather soles would glide across to the potential for frostbite as snow crept over the tops of his shoes and led to wet socks—*cold*, wet socks.

He returned to the cabin and added wood to the stove. Now he understood the chill in the cabin that had led to his waking several times through the night to keep the fire going. Fortunately, the cabin had been stocked well with firewood.

He ate some breakfast and waited to hear from his feathered neighbors, but their raucous calls did not arrive as he had expected. *I guess snow slows down traffic out here as well as in the cities,* he thought.

He set aside several Pop-Tarts® for the birds should they show up later, but then had second thoughts about doing so. He didn't much care for the engineered pastries, but he might need to conserve every bit of sustenance he had. He foresaw no shortage of water now, but his food stores might require tighter rationing. With snow, it might be a while longer before Homer and Virgil returned to check on him.

After eating, he sat in the wooden chair closest to the stove and warmed his hands and feet. He pondered his options. Foot travel, as he'd already decided, would be more treacherous, but there was less likelihood of his getting lost and unable to find his way back to the cabin. He'd have footprints in the snow to follow back.

That still didn't help, however. As he'd determined the day before, finding his way to civilization could take days, and now he not only lacked a means of carrying adequate supplies for such a journey, he did not have appropriate clothing. If this snow meant colder weather coming his way, and possibly more snow, he had a greater chance of freezing to death than making it to a road or home where he might find help.

No, his best option was to signal for help using smoke from the stove's fire. He had tested that idea the day before, with inadequate results. He needed a plentiful material for producing smoke because he might have to do that for several days before someone saw it and investigated, if at all.

If at all? He couldn't afford to think like that. He needed to act on his faith, not succumb to negative thoughts.

He had been disappointed to discover there were no pines among the trees around the cabin. In fact, he didn't recall seeing any pines or firs in his sojourns of the last two days. He had expected to collect some pine boughs with the hope the pine sap would produce a visible smoke.

He did, however, discover a small grove of junipers within easy walking distance of the cabin. He chastised himself for not collecting some of that the previous day. He would have to get some now, cold feet and all.

He glanced about the cabin. At least he had the two coats—the light one he'd been wearing when kidnapped and the heavier one left behind by Homer. He wanted something for his head and hands, but found nothing at all that might help keep them warm. He focused next on his feet. Within one of the food boxes he had stashed several plastic grocery bags. He emptied their contents into the box and nested two together, which he then placed over his shoes and tied around his lower leg. He repeated that process with two more on the other foot.

He stood and walked a few steps before realizing that he might make it ten yards before breaking holes into the bags, or shredding them altogether. Plus, they seemed more slippery than the leather soles alone. But he had an idea. He untied the bags, slid them off his shoes, and removed his shoes. He then placed the bags over his feet, tied them around his legs, and put his shoes back on over them. That would work. His feet and socks would remain dry—or at least drier—and the leather soles would take any damage from the terrain, as they had in his previous hikes.

He bundled up in the coats, folded the collars up over his neck, and emerged from the cabin. Now he simply needed to find those junipers again. Would the snow have hidden them or would the dark green stand out even more from a distance?

Lynch opened his eyes and wondered what time it was. He grabbed his cell phone and glanced at it. Seven-forty-three? *The sun should be up by now,* he thought.

As he slipped on his jeans inside the sleeping bag, his shoulder bumped the side of the tent. He heard the sound of something sliding off the nylon fabric and a bright spot appeared in the tent wall.

"Uh-oh," he whispered.

He used his hands to push on both sides of the tent and the same thing happened. Only one explanation ran through his mind. He unzipped the doorway and confirmed his suspicion. Snow.

He climbed out into the pristine landscape and hastened to don his coat and hat. He glanced toward Coby's tent to see a mound of snow where he expected to see blue nylon. He also heard snoring. Coby clearly was in no rush to get moving today.

Lynch turned toward the spot where they had cooked dinner and was surprised to find a tarpaulin lean-to protecting that spot of ground from the weather. Looking toward the horses, he saw that they, too, were now protected by a large tarp. Between the makeshift structures and half-foot of snow, their campsite looked totally different from when he'd turned in. Obviously Coby had been busy in the late hours of the previous evening. No wonder he still slept.

Lynch shuffled to the kitchen tarp and lit the camp stove. He prepared coffee and sat down on a log next to the fire. This was one morning when he longed for a roaring campfire, not their stove. He poured a cup of brew and gazed across the landscape. As beautiful as it was, he wondered what they'd be able to accomplish that day. Perhaps Coby had the right idea. Why rush into the day when a snug sleeping bag sounded so much more comfortable?

As he took another sip, his phone rang, and he fumbled to get to it in the inside pocket of his coat.

"Lynch, it's Mack."

Mack? What was he doing calling him?

"Hey Mack, how'd you get this number?" Lynch had no issue with Mack having the number, just with the possibility that someone else would learn of his possession of the burn phone and trace its location.

"Tony gave it to me, and don't worry, I know you're supposed to be sequestered in the motel there, and you don't want anyone knowing you're out looking for the boss. We've got you covered." He paused. "Hey, and if the Feds find out and hit you with some bogus charges, don't worry, I'll come visit you in jail. Bring you a cake with a file in it."

Lynch smiled. Mack would never change.

"So, what do I owe the honor of a call from knighthood?"

There was a pause on the other end.

"Lynch . . ."

Lynch noted the switch from "regular Mack" to "somber and serious Mack."

"I'm here in Dallas with the advance team, but I got wind of trouble in St. Louis, and you need to know about it."

Lynch wasn't sure he wanted another potential disaster to add to his plates. He was juggling enough of them at the moment.

"It's about Amy. Seamus O'Connor got hold of me when he couldn't get hold of you. One of your Fed buddies couldn't track you down and called O'Connor to let him know that she stumbled upon a cache of explosives and the ATF and FBI got involved. Feds think they belonged to Somali terrorists associated with Al-Shabaab, and evidently the bad guys found out about her. There were two attempts on her life on Saturday."

Lynch's mind went numb. Not Amy. Yes, he was on the outs with her. She was even engaged to another, but . . . he loved her. He couldn't bear the thought of something bad happening to her. The pressure to find Graham just rose logarithmically. He needed to find Graham, so he could be released to rush back to St. Louis.

"Mack, thanks. I, uh . . . Look, would you relay a message to O'Connor for me? Ask him to please watch over her in my absence. And ask him to get hold of Richard Nichols, her fiancé, and ask how he can help them."

"He's already on it and said he's doing what he can. He headed to her house yesterday to talk with her, but passed her with her father on the road. He caught up with them at a grocery store, but didn't want to approach her there, so he waited in the car. As they were loading the groceries into the car, a taxi approached her and stopped. He didn't think anything of it until he saw her dad racing toward the taxi with his hand ready to pull a concealed weapon. He tried but couldn't get to her, and then the taxi pulled away. At that point, he got called back to the city and couldn't follow up with her."

"Thank you, Seamus," whispered Lynch. He felt some relief at knowing that his friend was helping when he couldn't and that her father was with her. Her father would *never* let her down and he had the ability to be with her 24/7. Seamus O'Connor could never get that close. Amy simply wouldn't accept police protection. He knew that because he'd had that argument with her once before.

"He said something else, Lynch. She wasn't wearing a ring anymore."

No ring? She always wore Richard's ring. She never left home without it. No ring? Lynch had to get back to St. Louis.

Thirty-three

Richard disarmed his home's intruder alarm system and together with Ben entered his house. It still didn't seem like *home*, and Richard began to wonder if it ever would. He had planned on this house becoming his family's home, but family, too, now seemed a distant concept.

Ben headed straight to the library. Richard went to the kitchen and started a pot of coffee. Ben had told their staff that they'd be back in a couple of hours, but the fact was, they might be there all day. Richard felt thankful that he'd filled his larder the day before. The odds were that he'd be feeding Ben, too, before this was over.

He walked to the library with two mugs of coffee in hand and discovered Ben pacing in front of the bookcase. He had the book in his hands.

"Okay, so while you were in the kitchen, I went through the titles and authors and looked for any with 'Eric.' Nada. So that must mean the first number in the sequence points to a book here, if I understood Greg correctly."

Richard took a sip—still too hot. He set down the mug and approached the shelves. He pointed to the empty space at the end of one shelf.

"That's where Summer grabbed the book. Do you think we should consider it the reference point? You know, like book number one in the sequence?"

Ben nodded. "That seems logical." He opened the front of *Exodus* to reveal the code and laid the book, open, on the shelf at waist level. "The first number of the second line is 226."

Richard furrowed his brow. "226? How can that be? There are only 84 books here, and that's counting the fake books that make up the hidden compartment."

"Only 84? Are you sure?"

Richard nodded. "Yeah. Counted them twice, but feel free to confirm my count."

Ben began to count.

"Gee, thanks for the vote of confidence. I do know how to count, and I don't even have to use my fingers and toes."

Ben gave a subtle shake of his head. "Sorry, I do trust your count and that's not what I'm thinking. We don't know if these are all of the books involved. We have three shelves of books. These cabinets are, what? Looks like maybe 30 inches tall. Then the first shelf is empty, but the next three hold books. What if the upper three shelves had books, too? Or the first shelf here? Or all seven shelves?"

Richard had thought of that, but didn't want to dwell on the implications. If this was not the collection of books related to the code, or if it was but a subgroup, they had embarked on a literary snipe hunt. He watched as Ben resumed counting.

"42 on this shelf, which means 42 on that one as well. Annnddd . . . if you add a third row of 42, that would give us 126, not 226." He stepped back, crossed his arms over his chest, and stared at the bookcase. "Doesn't it strike you as odd that with books of different lengths, giving us books of different thicknesses, that there are 42 on each shelf?"

Richard replied, "It doesn't strike me as odd. It strikes me as planned."

Ben nodded. "It does, doesn't it? And if that was planned, then this must be the right collection of books."

Richard picked up the copy of *Exodus* and scrutinized the code. "Hey, these first numbers go as high as 340." He paused to calculate. "Even if all seven shelves had 42 books each, that's only 294."

He took the book and walked over to the window for better light. Now as he looked at the first number there appeared to be a small smudge between the first and second digit of the 226. That same smudge appeared between the first and second digits of each first number. He took a photo of the code with his cell phone, called up the image to view it, and expanded it to zoom in on the first numbers in each line. He smiled as he realized what he'd discovered.

"Ben. It's not a single number. Whoever wrote this put a small dot between the first and second digits and then smudged it to confuse things. He didn't want this to be too easy. That first number is really 2 dot 26. I think the first digit points to the shelf—either one, two, or three."

Ben's face brightened and he began to count along the second shelf. "Here. Book 26 on shelf two. What's the rest of the code?"

"One-twelve, three, sixteen. I don't see any smudges in any of the other numbers."

Richard approached Ben and watched over his

shoulder as he thumbed to page 112, moved to the third paragraph and counted to the sixteenth word.

"Huh?" Ben straightened his head and looked back at Richard. "Global? Eric global? That makes no sense."

Richard felt confident that his conjecture about row numbers was correct. Likewise with his assessment that the code writer didn't want to make things easy. He started at the other end of the shelf and counted to book 26. He flipped to page 112 and scanned it to the designated word.

"Was. Eric was."

"Eric was what? Gay? Someone's lover? A complete idiot? A whistleblower?"

Richard felt energized to move on. "I guess we'll find out. At least that makes more sense than Eric global."

He took the next number, 315, and counted from one end of the third shelf while Ben counted from the other. Ben worked faster than he did.

After finding the word, Ben said, "Break? Eric global break? Eric was break? Again, that means nothing."

Richard looked at his word and stood there, speechless and stunned.

Thirty-four

Amy and her father had taken turns sleeping. It had become evident that neither one could sleep if no one would be awake to watch over them and her home. Thoughts of worst-case scenarios filled Amy's head. Bullets from automatic weapons spraying through the walls. Molotov cocktails breaking through multiple windows at once—followed by sprays of bullets at their only escape routes. Grenade launchers. With thermobaric grenades that level the whole house.

Maybe she read too many thrillers. No. She'd never give up that addiction.

The thought that she was thinking through too many 'what ifs' made her think of Lynch. What would he say about her predicament? Maybe, once her phone dried completely, she would call him and ask. Then she wondered what Richard would say. He had changed since the Komarčić incident. Now, he would tell her to call the cops. She had done that and elevated it to the FBI. They hadn't been of much help so far. Lynch, on the other hand, would become pro-active, go hunting.

The two federal agents sitting in her office at MedAir reminded her more of Richard.

"Ms. Gibbs, if we were to get a sketch artist here, do you

think you could describe the man well enough to get us a picture?"

"As I already told you, I only saw the left side of his face. He didn't look directly at me. So, no, I don't think so." She cocked her head. "C'mon, the guy was in a County Taxi. We gave you a partial plate number. He's a thin black male, forties, with a long scar on his left face and part of his left ear missing. How hard can he be to locate?"

The two men looked at each other. The older, and clearly more senior, agent answered.

"Ms. Gibbs, we wish it was that easy. We have nothing to link them to the attacks on you. The man's actions in the parking lot yesterday, while unsettling, didn't break any laws, so we have nothing to use to get a warrant."

"The man verbally threatened me, a day after someone tried to kill me, twice!"

The younger man shook his head. "It seems easy to add two and two here, I know, but you have no witnesses and you didn't record it. We can't just go rousting up men at a prominent taxi company."

She sat there flummoxed. "You're not rousting up men, as you put it, you're looking for one man with a scar and damaged ear." She shook her head in disgust. "Look, the guy said I would pay and no one could protect me. In context of what happened the day before, that qualifies as a criminal threat, not free speech. I checked on that."

Then a thought hit her. She didn't want to sound racist or Islamophobic, because she wasn't. But the reality of current politically correct thought had now been laid at her doorstep.

"I get it now. You're afraid of going after a black man who is also very likely Muslim. He might even be an illegal alien. He'd win the Triple Crown with that combination. I have to become the next dead victim before you'll act. Is that it?"

The men looked sheepish, not angry or defiant. She had proven her point.

Tears welled up at the thought of becoming the next victim of liberal ideology. No wonder more and more of her friends now looked to the conservative Bradley Graham to bring the nation back to the rule of law and common sense.

"That's unfair," said the older agent.

She stood up. "Is it? Tell that to Kate Steinle's family, or the victims of the Boston Marathon bombing, or the business owners twenty miles from here in Ferguson who lost everything when rioters burned down their businesses over a lie. Good day, gentlemen."

Thirty-five

Lynch had trouble controlling his emotions. Mack's call had upset his world in ways the man would never know, and now he needed to act. They needed to find Graham and get back to civilization so Lynch could return to St. Louis. Amy needed help and he had told her he would always be there for her. He did not want that promise to even hint at being a hollow one.

Coby's snoring had stopped, but he hadn't seen any sign of movement inside his tent.

"C'mon, Ol' Chief, wake up over there! The day's not waiting for us!"

Lynch filled his cup with more coffee and proceeded to make breakfast. With or without Coby's direction, he would eat and then start to break camp. He'd watched Coby do it twice now. He might not be as practiced and efficient, but he'd manage.

Finally, a head emerged from the man's tent. "What's got up your craw, Probie? This snow's gonna slow us down no matter what we do."

"Yeah, so all the more reason to get moving. Here's breakfast and coffee. I'll go feed the horses."

It seemed strange to see the roles reversed— Lynch dealing with the horses and starting to break camp, while Coby ate. When Coby joined him to pack the horses, the man was grinning.

"Well, lookie at you. You *do* pay attention. Might just have to promote you again."

Lynch felt relieved that Coby wasn't angry at him. He also recognized that it took a lot to get under that red skin of his. He liked this guy more and more every day.

"Sorry for waking you up. I know you were up dealing with the snow while I slept."

The man shrugged. "No problem. You're right about getting moving. We can't waste time if something like a little snow comes along to slow us down."

They finished packing and mounted their steeds, but Ed, Sally Mae, and Charlie needed persuasion to start moving. Obviously, they didn't relish slogging through the snow either.

Coby pointed toward the summit as soon as it came into view. "At least we don't have to worry about more snow today. Clear skies ahead. Hope you brought sunglasses. You might need 'em."

Lynch noted the glare of the sun on the pure white snow. He couldn't recall ever seeing snow so white. City grime always seemed to turn it light gray.

"We have about an hour's ride before we come to another possible hiding spot."

Lynch wanted to enjoy the beauty around him, but Amy's threat positioned itself front and center in his mind. He had to force himself to calm down. He couldn't make the horses move any faster.

About ten minutes into the ride, he watched a flock of crows fly past them and head toward the end of the ridge behind them. He recalled that a flock of crows was called a 'murder' and wondered how it got that name. He twisted in his saddle to watch the birds until they disappeared from view.

As he started to face forward, something else in the periphery of his vision caught his attention. He took one foot out of its stirrup and twisted all the way around to see what it was.

Smoke! He hadn't imagined it the day before. There it was again, denser and darker than before.

He faced Coby. "Coby, are you sure we shouldn't check out the end of the ridge behind us?"

He watched the back of the man's head as he shook it.

"Told you yesterday. There's nothing back there to check."

"Well, you're the Indian. Do they still teach you smoke signals in Indian school?"

"What?"

Ed stopped as Coby pulled him up short and the parade stopped behind him. Coby turned to face Lynch.

"What kind of nonsense are you talking? Smoke signals. Have you been watching old westerns while you're out here?"

Lynch smiled and used his thumb, pumping it back and forth, to point behind them.

Coby's eyes widened before he replied, "Nope, they're talking a language I don't understand."

Thirty-six

"What? What's the word?" Ben looked eager to know Richard's word.

Richard took a deep breath. "Well, it's not break." He still couldn't believe the message that was forming from the book code. "Eric . . . was . . . you ready for it?"

"Get on with it. This isn't the Academy Awards."

"Eric was . . . murdered."

Ben's eyes widened. "W-we've always thought so, but . . ." He began to rub his chin with one hand. "Are you thinking what I'm thinking?"

Richard nodded. "Yeah. Probably. This code is going to tell us who killed the guy."

Ben nodded in unison. "That's exactly what I'm thinking." He returned to the open book and its code. "204."

Each man hastened to find the fourth book from each end of the second shelf. Ben then said, "412, 5, 4."

Richard found his word first. "Multinational."

Ben responded, "Cab."

Richard furrowed his brow. "What's that mean? Neither one makes sense. I was expecting a name or the word 'by.' "

Ben paced a few steps and turned back to him. "Clearly he wasn't run over by a taxi. Maybe this references a multinational conspiracy."

Richard knew they had to complete the puzzle. He checked the code. 340-62-1-12

Ben nodded. "Okay, since there are 42 books per shelf, that means it's the third book in from each side." He grabbed the third book from his end, while Richard claimed his. They both flipped to page 62 and counted to find the 12th word in the first paragraph.

"Mine is 'left,' " said Richard.

Ben frowned. "I got 'right.' " He shook his head. "This isn't making any sense. Right, left—they take us in opposite directions. How do we know which one it is?"

"Keep going," replied Richard. "Next line of numbers is 138-14-3-20."

Ben pointed. "Like the last one. Number 38 will be the fifth book from each end."

Richard discovered the word 'four,' while Ben found 'three.' The code was getting more confusing. The last line of code directed them to the 21st book of shelf two, which made them pull the two central books in that row. They were also the two books immediately left of the hidden compartment. Their words were the same: 'up.'

Both men shook their heads . . . again. Neither had anything to say.

Ben broke the ice. "Okay, whoever made this up didn't want it to be easy. That's well established now."

"Yeah, where's Cully when we need him?"

Ben gave him a quizzical look. "I think he's where he's needed most, trying to find Graham. Why did you mention him?"

"Because the guy can see patterns where no one

else does. He can put clues together in ways that few would ever think of, and yet when he outlines things for you, you want to slap your forehead and go 'duh!' "

Ben began rubbing his chin again. Richard could almost see the man's mental gears grinding.

"Patterns . . . patterns." Ben turned to stare at the bookcase. "Maybe you're on to something there."

Richard joined him in staring, but his mind worked no further than that. He'd never been a puzzle person. That game with the golf tees at Cracker Barrel? Forget it. He'd never won a single attempt. He gave up on jigsaw puzzles after the pieces exceeded 120. He still had a plastic money maze puzzle holding $50 that his grandparents had given him for his 12th birthday. If he ever got desperate enough, maybe he would finally have the nerve to take a hammer to it to claim the bill.

"So, are we in agreement that the first three clues are 'Eric was murdered'?"

Richard nodded once. "Yes. That much seems clear."

"Then, maybe those three words are the key to the pattern. The clue master would have to offer some kind of key, wouldn't he? Otherwise, he'd have to make the clues so simple the answer would be easy, and easy this isn't."

That made sense to Richard. He thought about the clues in order.

"Following that concept, the first clue was in book one over here." Richard pointed to the slot where *Exodus* had been sitting. "Then the next two clues were from books on this side of the shelves."

Ben smiled. "I think that's it. One over here, two over there. If that's true then the fourth clue comes from this side.

That's 'cab.' The next two are from that side—'left' and 'three.' And the last clue was 'up' and came from both sides."

"That gives us: Eric was murdered cab left three up." He paused and then added, "As you said, I think we can rule out a taxi for the cab clue."

Ben replied, "True. I hate to say this, but the first thing to come to my mind for 'cab' is it's short for cabernet sauvignon."

Richard brightened. "That might be it. Hey, I forgot to show you the wine cellar in this place, didn't I?"

Ben looked surprised. "Wine cellar? This place has a wine cellar? I'm getting more jealous every time I come here, and, no, you never even mentioned it, much less showed it to me."

"Well, you get to see it now. It came with about 50 bottles left behind. Think about it. Books were left behind here and for good reason, we now know. The wine must have been left over for good reason, too. Follow me."

Two minutes later, Richard opened a door at one end of the basement to reveal a wine cellar. Ben's mouth dropped at seeing the climate-controlled room with cooling units along one wall and open racks on the other. There were two sets of bistro tables and stools in the middle.

"Wow. Clare and I would be in heaven here. How many bottles can this place hold?"

"The realtor told me 2,000. Over here, I think." Richard led them to the open rack near the end of the room. He glanced at the rack. "Yeah, I did recall it right.

The plaque says cabernet."

He pulled out a bottle and confirmed that it was cabernet sauvignon. He showed it to Ben. He then glanced around. The majority of the bottles in the room were here. Either Eric Pearce loved cabernet, or these bottles were here for a reason.

Ben proceeded to work through the bottles. "Okay, it looks like there are five columns of cab, with six to eight rows. The clue said 'left' and 'three up'." He moved to the leftmost column and counted three rows up from the bottom. He pulled out the bottle and examined it.

"It's just a bottle of wine. There's nothing on it." He held it up to the light. "And nothing in it except liquid."

As Ben held the bottle, Richard stuck his hand into the slot on the rack. He felt something on the back side of the rack, just above the hole. Paper. Taped to the rack.

He gingerly used a finger to pry it loose and pulled it out. He slit the tape and opened up the paper. A note.

He read it aloud. "Not this cab, dummy!"

Ben looked dumbfounded. "What? What the . . ." He took the note and read it for himself. "Someone's messing with us now." He looked around the room. "You know, we never scanned this room. Are we sure we aren't being watched right now? Maybe we're being punked." He held up the bottle and showed it around the room. He raised his voice. "Just for that, I'm keeping this bottle. Whoever you are watching us."

Richard offered a half smile. "Ben, it's just us. No one is watching. We never saw the cellar on the video screen, remember?"

Ben looked at him. "Oh. Yeah. Okay."

He started to slide the bottle back into place, but Richard stopped him.

"That's okay, you can have it anyway."

Ben grinned. "Are you sure? This is an expensive wine."

"It's yours. For all the help you've been."

Ben admired the bottle as they walked back to the library. He set it down on a small table nearby.

"So, back to square one."

Richard disagreed. "I don't think so. It hit me on the way back here. Cab is also a computer abbreviation for cabinet, like they use for distribution files for Windows and such."

He walked back to the bookcase, but this time, he knelt down in front of the lower cabinets. There were three sets, each with double doors. The code had specifically stated 'left.' Richard reasoned that if the code had meant the third actual cabinet, its creator would have right one, not left three. Richard opened the third door from the left.

"Hey, that code was simpler than we gave it credit for," said Ben.

"What?" answered Richard, as he used his phone to light up the interior of the cabinet.

"Left three is the same door as right four. If you're in the right spot, either direction would have worked."

"I think the key words are 'right spot.' This cabinet is empty."

"Up. The last word was 'up' and it was given twice, maybe for emphasis."

Richard had already looked at the upper shelf of

the cabinet. There was only one other way something could be up inside. He used his hand to feel along the roof of the compartment. Maybe there was a hidden panel. Near the back, in the darkest corner, he felt something, but it wasn't a hidden panel.

He felt around the edges of the object until he found a loose spot. He slipped his finger into that gap and pried the item away from the wood top. It was a paper sleeve with one side sprayed with paint to match the color of the cabinet woodwork.

He stood up with his find and opened what was obviously a paper computer disk holder. Inside was a DVD disk similar in make as the one they'd found inside the DVD recorder. As he held it up, Ben gazed upon it almost reverently.

In that instant, both men bolted across the room to Richard's computer workstation where he had an old desktop system. He used his laptop most of the time, but had held onto this unit for times such as this—when he'd forgotten his laptop at the office. The SSD drive booted up within seconds and he started to place the disk into the optical drive. Ben stayed his hand.

"Nope. Disconnect Wi-Fi and cable and anything else that might tie this computer to the internet, even that printer there. Do you have spare disks so we can make copies?"

Satisfied that his computer was isolated, Richard placed the disk into the drive and they began to watch. Much of what they saw was mundane—until the time stamp showed them at two days before Pearce's death. Two men argued with Pearce in his foyer. Richard boosted the sound to just audible levels. The argument centered on Pearce's access to the Democratic National Committee's server. There had been some questionable activity, and it seemed to come from Pearce's account. Pearce's face was clear. The other men had their backs to the camera. The words got heated and one of the men began to push Pearce around. His face became clear to the camera.

"Hey, I know that guy," said Ben. "He's a cleaner for the DNC. A troubleshooter."

Pearce said something unintelligible to the microphone and the man stopped. The two men then stormed out through the front door.

The next time stamp was the morning of Pearce's death. Pearce now encountered several men. Again, heated words until one of the men hit Pearce with a stun gun. It was the DNC troubleshooter.

"Do you see where he tagged Pearce with the stun gun? Right in the neck where a rope could hide it."

Two of the other men picked up Pearce and carried him up the stairs, while a third carried a rope. As a noose was fashioned with the rope, Richard heard a familiar female voice. The noose was placed around Pearce's neck and the other end was secured.

"Drop him," said the woman's voice.

As Pearce's body dropped from the balcony, the woman stepped into view of the camera.

"That's Maggie Walther, my realtor," said Richard.

Ben sat there, silent. He started to retrieve the disk, but Richard stopped him.

"There's more. Wait."

The date remained the same, but the time had advanced to late afternoon. The police had arrived, as well as the medical examiner's team. They now viewed the first actions of the investigation, those that preceded what they had seen earlier on the other disk.

Ben again moved his hand to retrieve the disk, but again Richard stopped him. He had seen something in one of the other frames.

"Did you see that?"

"No, what?"

"Someone came in from the back of the house. We need to back up a few seconds." He reversed the play for thirty seconds and restarted it. "There. He paused the replay and selected that playback frame.

"He must have come in through the kitchen. That's the only way to get picked up by this camera. And it looks like he's heading for the library."

Richard agreed. "And that means that person has a key to my house and knows about the recording system." He stepped forward frame by frame until they had a better view of the individual.

"Ben, that hair. I know we don't see a face, or even enough of the body to be recognizable, but I know that hair. That's not a man. It's Summer Stanton."

Thirty-seven

Coby pulled up at a wide spot on the ridge. Well, wider than they'd been traveling for the past fifteen minutes. They had backtracked from last night's camp for a good 40 minutes before the ridge narrowed and the drop-off to the desert below heightened to the point that Lynch became uncomfortable. The smoke, in turn, had diminished and came in spurts now.

"Look here," said Coby. He pointed toward the ground. "Someone made a stone marker. Can't say who or how long ago, but I don't think hikers come this far. Too dangerous and there's no trail to anywhere."

To their left, Lynch saw another spurt of dark smoke. "There's the smoke again."

Coby shrugged. "Guess I need to get out more often. If there's a cabin down there somewhere, I've never seen it. Might be a tent camp. Let's fly."

With the horses secured, Coby and Lynch set up the drone, and Coby checked the battery.

"I have about 30 minutes on this battery and there's two left. The smoke gives me a direct target, so it shouldn't take but a few minutes to get there and check it out. Ready?"

Lynch nodded. He had a good feeling about this.

The drone's propellers accelerated and it rose without effort.

"We have lift-off," said Lynch. He watched the drone as it flew down the canyon. The smoke had stopped again, but they knew the general direction.

"Okay, Cully. Start watching the video. FLIR on."

"I see something already. Looks hot. You're heading in the right direction." A minute later, the outline of a structure became obvious. "We have a structure of some kind there and if I'm reading this right, the hottest spot is just above it, like with a stovepipe. Go ahead and switch it to visual."

Coby complied and took a look for himself. "I'll be. It is a cabin, and fairly new, too. Well, if you compare it to the ages of the others. It still looks decrepit. I wonder if the BLM knows about this. I'm going to navigate in by video and see if we can get up close and personal."

The drone was less than a hundred feet from the building when dark smoke reappeared.

"I see footprints in the snow, but it looks like just one set. Let me see if this place has a window . . . there, on the front wall near the door. What do you think? Do we knock or not? If it's not Graham, whoever is in there might not take kindly to our spying, particularly if it's a squatter with an illegal cabin."

Lynch doubted it was a squatter. "Would a squatter send up regular smoke signals? That's the action of someone wanting to be found."

"Good point, warrior."

Lynch looked at Coby and laughed. "Warrior?"

Coby shrugged. "Yeah, a field promotion. Let's see who's home."

Together they watched the video as Coby flew the drone right up and onto the front porch and to the window.

"Somebody needs to learn basic housekeeping," quipped Coby. "Those glass panes are filthy."

A second later, a hand appeared in the window and started wiping away the dirt. Then a set of eyes stared right at them through the grime. Coby backed off.

"Got their attention. Don't want to be too close if they come out swinging."

The cabin door flew open, and Lynch jumped into the air, pumping his fist. "YES!"

"It's Graham! Does this thing have voice communications? Can I talk to him, let him know it's us?"

Coby shook his head. "Nope. I could afford all the bells but not all the whistles. Let's see if I can point him our way."

Coby hovered the craft off to the side of the porch, flew it 20 feet up the hill, and then returned to a point near the porch. He repeated that action twice more. He pointed the camera back toward Graham. The man pointed to his right ankle and then limped back and forth along the porch.

"He's injured. I'm heading down to assist him."

Coby pointed to the packs on Sally Mae. "There's a length of rope in there. I noticed a really steep section of terrain about halfway there. If you tie off the rope at the top, you can use it to help yourselves back up. It's gonna be slippery."

"Good idea, Big Chief."

Coby smirked. "It's Ol' Chief."

"Not right now. There's nothing old about you here. Call it a field promotion."

Lynch ran to Sally Mae and retrieved the rope. He moved in the direction of the smoke.

"Careful. It's steep and slippery, even for the horses. Do you want me to guide you with the drone?"

Lynch shook his head. "I think I got this."

"Okay, I'm going to bring it back and change the battery. I noticed one other thing. This canyon splits in two about a third of the way down. Stay to the left, to the smaller canyon."

Lynch nodded and waved before he moved out of sight of Coby. It didn't take long before Lynch realized the man had understated the hazard. He slipped and fell on his butt three times within the distance of fifty feet. Despite being anxious to retrieve his boss, he slowed down to make sure he'd get there in one piece and be able to assist Graham up the canyon.

Time stretched to where it seemed like he'd been climbing down for hours when he came upon a split in the canyon. Coby had said that this division occurred about a third of the way. He hoped the man had miscalculated. He turned to the left.

Not much farther along, he came to a precipitous fall in the slope. *This must be the spot Coby mentioned about using the rope*, he thought. He found a sturdy tree along what appeared to be the best route and tied off the rope. He found it helpful in descending. Surely it was going to be helpful on the way up.

As he reached easier terrain again, he heard the buzz of

the drone. He looked up to find it homing in on him. It was carrying a small nylon bag. A minute later, the bag dropped and almost hit him on the head. Was he now target practice? The drone lifted higher into the sky.

He grabbed the bag and opened it. Inside he found two stun guns and a note:

> *2 heat signatures climbing toward the cabin from below. Thought you might want more than your gun.*

Thirty-eight

"See you tomorrow. My dad's outside to pick me up."

"Amy, we might have a vehicle you can borrow. I'm sure your father has other things to do besides being a chauffeur."

Amy's boss had been out of the office until after her visit from the FBI, so she had been spared having to tell him about her "fun" weekend . . . or her breaking off her engagement.

Craig Sheehan was a delight to work with, but he could be almost as bad as Detective Hoskins when it came to giving her grief. His reminders about the company's only two crashes occurring with her on board had diminished. She didn't want to give him fresh ammunition, and yet, something her father had said when he drove her to work stuck with her. She didn't want anyone at work to get hurt because of her. The terrorists had found her at the spa. There was a better than even chance they now knew where she worked, too.

"So, how's Richard? Did you guys have a great weekend?"

She stepped into his office and sat down. She held up her ring-free hand and explained that the engagement was off. She went on to inform him of her trip to Busch Wildlife to think and of what she stumbled upon. She told him that she had become a target of these terrorists and that he might want to beef up security for a little while. She did *not* tell him about the two attempts on her life.

"We can talk more later, but right now my dad's waiting."

She could see that he wanted to ask questions. She could see his concern as well.

Finally, he simply nodded, as if he expected nothing less, as if this was to be just another day in her life. His only comment was, "Look, if you need to move, I can find you a spot on any flight crew in any state we cover. Just let me know."

Great, she thought. *He and Hoskins can play tag-team now.*

She waved to her dad as she approached his car. He was outside the vehicle scanning the surroundings. He let her climb inside before doing so himself.

"Hi, sweetheart. Let's get home. I feel vulnerable out here."

They talked about cars for her. Her father had the line on a couple of great deals. Nothing more happened on the drive home.

Her father again insisted on "clearing" the house before letting her step foot inside from the garage. He helped her unpack her bags and then opened a beer for himself.

"You want one?" he asked, as he held it out to her.

"No thanks. I need to get busy. I promised you a salmon dinner the other day and we never got around to it."

"Can I help?"

"I don't think so." That didn't come out right. "Sorry. I don't mean you're not *capable* of helping, but I've got things covered." She turned to see him standing behind her in the doorway to the other room, and grinned. He saluted her with his beer.

She prepared the wild rice pilaf and started it on the stove. It would take the longest to cook. She then began to clean, trim, and cut up the head of broccoli to prepare it for steaming. Once that, too, was on the stove, she could prepare a cheese sauce for it, followed by broiling the salmon. She wasn't perfect on her timing, but everything would be cooked and ready about the same time.

"You handle that broccoli like your mom did."

His voice came from behind her.

"She's the one who taught me," she replied, still facing the sink as she cut and prepared it.

The knife slipped from her wet hands and fell to the floor. She bent over to get it.

CRACK! Shattered glass showered the back of her head and shoulders. She dropped to the floor with the realization that someone had just tried to shoot her through the window. And then dread filled her. *Dad? He was standing right behind me.*

Thirty-nine

Richard sat across the desk from Ben in the latter's office. He could see the anxiety in his friend's face, the same anxiety as he felt. They had discovered evidence of a crime committed by well-placed people, people with connections at the highest level of government. Those people had staged a murder to look like suicide. They would have no second thoughts at going after those who exposed them.

"Look, we can't let them get away with murder, literally," said Richard.

Ben gave him a dubious look, as if that was exactly what he wanted to do.

"Ben, they have to be held accountable."

Ben sighed. "Maybe we should wait to see who wins the election."

Richard slowly shook his head. "Seriously? What's happened to you? This could change the entire election. This corroborates things only hinted at in the emails released by WikiLeaks. This could destroy the progressives for a decade."

"Richard, we don't even have a candidate at the moment. If Graham and Her Royal Candidate are gone from the race, that only leaves the Republicans. Do you really trust having that braggadocio billionaire of theirs as the leader of the Free World?"

Richard shrugged. "Who knows? Still better than her. Besides, Graham's not out of the race yet. Cully will find him, alive, I'm sure. And if he's dead, we have no horse in the race anyway. Goodwell, as honest as he is, doesn't have the name recognition."

Ben still did not look convinced.

"Ben, the election is one week away. We can't afford having another president like this one. We need to change the course of things. Graham's disappearance has only strengthened her chances of winning, despite everything that's come out about their emails."

Ben stared at his desk for a long minute before looking up at Richard. "What do you propose?"

"We've made copies of the DVD. We, no, *I* will take it to the local police chief, the U.S. attorney, the district attorney, and the local media. I'll hold a press conference, and at the same time, we give it a *huge* social media blast."

"Why not send it anonymously?"

"Won't work. Who are they going to suspect first? Me. I just bought the place and moved in. Where else could the DVD have come from but a home security system? It's recorded from an angle that clearly couldn't have been someone's cell phone. So, I'm the logical one to expose it for the same reason: I just moved in and discovered it."

Ben mulled it over and said, "Okay, but I'll be at your side every step of the way."

Richard shook his head. "No way, buddy. Two reasons. Your position here would make it too political. The media would spin this as a political move. Yes, I work here, too, but

I'm the one who moved into the house. I can honestly say there was no way I could *not* come forward with evidence of a capital crime. The second reason is that I would never put Clare into danger. Or you. I understand. You know the risks and would be willing to face them, but I couldn't live with myself if something happened to your wife because you tied yourself to me in this."

"Clare's one smart cookie. You know that. She understands the risks. She'd be willing to face them."

"I know she is and I know she would. Write it off to being chivalrous, that Boy Scout in me that you always complain about. I don't want her anywhere near harm's way. I intend to make a big enough splash that I can't be targeted without drawing some serious attention. Plus, should they target me, I need someone to hold my insurance and go after them. I hope that would be you and Clare."

Was that a tear in Ben's eye? Had he struck a nerve in his hard-as-steel boss? The man quickly blinked it away.

Richard scribbled notes onto a sheet of paper, and following a brief rehearsal, recorded a 15-minute testimony detailing his discovery of the murder DVD. The men then arranged for next-day delivery of copies of the DVD and testimony to the individuals Richard had mentioned as well as their own party leaders. Each person would have it in hand by ten a.m. Ben called his press contacts to smooth the way for Richard to ask them for a press conference, which he wished to do at eleven a.m.

Richard finalized some tasks at the office and headed home. He had one more task for the day. But first, he tried one more time to call Amy. For the second time that day, his call went straight through to her voicemail. The finality of her leaving had now sunk in.

"Amy, I've come to accept and respect your decision, even if I don't like it. I love you and wish you only the best. God bless." He kept his message short and sweet.

He grabbed a bite to eat and summoned up the courage to walk over to Summer's house and confront her. It had become clear to him that not only had she known about the secret security system and changed the disks, she had hidden the evidential disk and written the clues. She also led him right to the book holding the clues, as if she had simply pulled the book at random. She had even questioned it being a secret code and laughed at the idea. The woman was quite the actress as well as an award-winning journalist.

But what really had him wondering was why? As a far-left-leaning mainstream journalist, why hadn't she simply buried the evidence that damned her favorite party and candidate? Why had she left that evidence for him? Had she also played a role in helping him get his sweetheart deal on the house? Was that deal even real? Did he actually own the house or was he somehow squatting now? He now wondered about that, too.

He finished cleaning up the kitchen and headed toward the coat closet next to the garage. As he donned his coat, he heard a familiar knock on the back door. He sighed. Her timing was impeccable. Maybe she had her own link to his surveillance system.

He removed his coat, hung it up, and walked to the back

door. As suspected, there stood Summer. He wanted to act nonchalant, as if nothing had changed, but he never had been a good liar.

"Come in, Summer. Here, let me grab your coat."

"Hi. I came over to invite you to dinner, but it smells like you've already been cooking. Am I too late?"

Her smile appeared radiant. At least *she* could act as if all was well.

"You are." He pointed toward the den. "Have a seat. Can I get you something to drink?"

"A glass of wine would be nice, if you have a bottle open. If not, one of those spotted beers you like would work. Thanks."

He did have a bottle of chardonnay in the fridge, so he poured a glass and carried it to her. He found her sitting in her usual place on his couch. He sat in his customary chair, at a distance, and pondered how he should approach her. He decided upon a frontal assault.

"Summer, I'd like it back, please."

She gave him a questioning look. "Um, like *what* back?"

"The key to my house. I'd prefer not having to change all my locks right away, although maybe I should anyway."

The questioning look persisted. "What key? What makes you think I have a key?"

"You said you were the one to discover Eric Pearce, but you weren't, were you? Did someone ask you to call it in and pretend like you'd found him? Did you have a key because you and Eric were more than friends?

Her questioning look morphed into one of concern,

as in concerned that he'd flipped his lid. She slowly put her glass on the side table and appeared as if she was about to stand and flee.

"Was Leon Uris really one of your mom's favorite authors? That code was quite clever, by the way. And you can quit acting."

She sat back down and took a deep breath. "Did you crack it?"

He nodded. "And I saw you on the surveillance disk. At least, I was pretty sure it was you. You just now confirmed that for me. You switched the disks and hid the one showing Eric's murder."

She nodded. "To answer your questions, I don't have a key, and changing your locks wouldn't keep me out if I wanted to come in. If you catch my drift. And no, he and I weren't lovers, just friendly neighbors. But you're wrong on your first statement. I did discover him, but I knew about the cameras. So I avoided coming into the house far enough to be seen on them."

"How did you know about the cameras?"

She didn't answer right away. Richard imagined he could hear the debate going on inside her head about what to tell him.

"Richard, can I assume you've taken that DVD to the authorities?"

He nodded.

"Can I trust you? I mean, really, really trust you, as in with my life?"

The Boy Scout streak in him stood front and center. He liked Summer as a person. Well, as the person she had presented herself to be. Time would tell if that was the real her. She had become quite the enigma to him.

"You can trust me, provided you've not committed a serious felony, or treason, or something like that. I won't hide you from the law."

"Fair enough. Please, come sit next to me."

It was his turn to mentally debate what to do. He decided to take a chance that she wasn't also an assassin for The Assembly. He rose and joined her on the couch. She took his hand in both of hers.

"Richard, first, I want you to know that I've truly grown to like you, and I do think I can trust you. But . . ."

Why was there always a 'but' to comments like that?

". . . you aren't in this house by accident."

"I've already figured as much. Do I actually own it?"

She smiled "Actually, you do. That's all legit. You got the real estate deal of a lifetime. For Maggie Walther, it was the price of doing business." She squeezed his hand. "Richard, what happened with us in Kansas City, well, I wasn't quite the innocent pawn in that situation as I pretended to be. After I saw on that DVD that Maggie Walther had Eric killed, I knew I had to find out more. I didn't know her before that, so I made a point of running into her at a party. We got to talking and I played along with what she said. Suddenly my career blossomed. I started getting assignments I had only dreamed of a year earlier. After about six months, Maggie let me know that she had mentioned me to friends in high places and asked if I was willing to risk a little more to gain a lot more.

"One assignment led to another. Then came Bradley Graham and the American Party. The people who control Maggie wanted inside that party. I still don't know who targeted you, but Maggie thought of me. She said if I was willing to risk national embarrassment, I would not only survive but thrive with her 'organization,' as she called it."

"The Assembly, and Karolus Karling. We exposed them in St. Louis and again in Kansas City."

"And Karling was removed, but the group still thrives."

Removed. Such a nice euphemism, thought Richard. His previous suspicions about Karling's death were now confirmed—another staged suicide.

"So why are you telling me this? Why did you lead me to the DVD? I never would have picked up that book, much less discovered the code inside."

"I led you to the DVD because Maggie Walther deserves justice. I knew you would do the right thing. As for telling you the rest of the story, well, I'll answer your other question first. I knew about the surveillance system because I'm the one who recommended that Eric have it installed, and I advised on who to install it, so that Maggie and The Assembly wouldn't know about it. They already had their suspicions about Eric."

"Do you mean the rumors that he was the one who leaked the DNC emails to WikiLeaks?"

She nodded. "He was killed because he *was* the one who leaked them."

"And you know that as fact when no one else can prove it?"

She nodded again. "Yes, I do . . . because I'm the one who recruited him to get them."

Forty

Coby's "present" was perfect. If the two people he saw climbing toward the cabin were simply individuals responding to the smoke, they'd have no trouble. On the other hand, if these were the kidnappers, he and Graham needed to be prepared. Killing the men would not help. Exposing them and the people behind the plot would be much more productive. For that, the stun guns would serve their purpose.

Still, he liked the reassurance his gun gave him. Should their intent be more malicious than checking up on Graham in the snow, he was prepared to defend his boss.

Lynch could smell wood smoke now. The cabin couldn't be too far off, although the air currents likely drew that smoke up the canyon before allowing it to drift skyward. The distance could be deceptive.

However, where was the duo? Was he on track to beat them to the cabin?

He passed an outcropping of rock and saw the cabin, flanked by an outhouse, maybe a hundred yards in the distance. He couldn't see the porch or front wall of the place from his perspective, so he would have to proceed with caution on the assumption that he hadn't gotten to Graham first.

He took two steps and slipped again. He slowed his pace, fighting the sense of urgency that had overtaken him since his call from Mack. Within a few minutes he passed the outhouse. As Coby had noted earlier, there appeared to be but one set of tracks to and from the structure.

He eased up against the outside wall of the cabin. He estimated the back wall to be 20, 25 feet long, with a metal stovepipe emerging from the top of it near one end before it angled up. On the FLIR, the heat source seemed above the building. He must have seen only that part of the pipe that extended above the roof line for proper drafting.

He peeked around the corner and saw no signs of activity. That wall appeared shorter, maybe 15 feet long before ending with a narrow front porch. The wood of the outer wall had been repaired in numerous spots, but the structure itself did not look to be new, as Coby had stated. He stood still and tried to listen for activity inside. There were no voices and only the occasional shuffle of someone walking on a wooden plank floor.

He slid along the wall toward the front. Upon reaching that corner he gazed beyond the building to see if anyone was approaching. So far, so good. As best he could tell, he had arrived there first. He stepped onto the porch, and the door flew open.

" 'Bout time you got here."

Lynch smiled. "Sorry, boss, we guessed wrong and checked the northern half of the state first."

Lynch entered the cabin and glanced around. Spartan was overstating the accommodations. "The 'tin roof inn' here looks mighty fancy. How're you going to rate your stay for the *Michelin Guide*?"

"I was thinking more along the lines of scratching 'Bradley Graham slept here' into one wall for after I become president. Let's get out of here. I have a campaign to get back to."

He started to don two coats. Lynch noted grocery bags wrapped around his feet and inside his shoes. Lynch smirked and pointed to Graham's feet.

"I see you've taken up fashion design, too. Very chic."

"Well, you have to look your best when you expect a knight to come to your rescue." He grinned. "I'm ready. Let's go."

Lynch shook his head. "Not so fast, I'm afraid. We have company coming up the hill. Coby spotted them with the drone as I worked my way down here. I suspect it's your kidnappers."

"Coby?"

"You'll meet him. Good man. I wouldn't have found you without him."

"How far away are they?"

"Don't know. But with your limp, they'd catch up with us in no time if we take off now. Besides, I think we need to know who these guys are."

Graham nodded. "Agreed. The older of the two gave their names as Homer and Virgil, which I found somewhat prophetic. They acted as if trained, either ex-military or police of some kind. Maybe federal agents. The younger guy, Virgil, seems the squirrelly one, the least predictable. They treated me decently and left me well-stocked with junk food. If they're coming back now, it means one of two things. They either want to make sure I'm okay in the snow, or whoever is behind this has decided I'm better off dead."

"Yeah, my thoughts exactly. Either way, we have a surprise for them." Lynch handed his boss a stun gun. "They shouldn't expect anyone else here. I followed your footsteps from the outhouse to the back of the cabin and stayed next to the building the rest of the way. They won't see a second set of prints in the snow. If you can tag one of the two, I'll deal with the other. But I need some place to hide."

Graham pointed to the corner behind the door. "We can lean the extra cots against the wall in the corner and you can stand behind them. When they close the door, you can get the man closest to you and I'll get the one closest to me."

Lynch offered a subtle shrug. "Guess that'll work." He grabbed one cot and leaned it against the corner. With the legs extending into the room, he had plenty of room behind it, but it wasn't quite wide enough to fully hide him.

The sound of the drone caught both men's attention. It buzzed outside the window for ten, fifteen seconds and bolted away.

"They must be getting close."

Lynch put the second cot next to the first and got behind them. That's when he realized he was too far away. He rushed to the window. He couldn't see anyone yet.

"That's not going to work. I'm too far away to tag the guy without alerting him. I'm going to have to wait outside. You take the first one in the door and I'll move in on the other guy outside."

They heard voices approaching. Two men were arguing, but the words were unintelligible. He looked outside and saw them just ten yards away. He had no time to slip out.

"Plan C," he whispered.

He quickly moved both cots so they were leaning against the front wall, but right behind the door. In fact, the door would hit the first cot if they flung it open far enough. He crouched down and hid behind them just as they heard footsteps on the porch.

The door opened and both men entered with guns drawn. They did not appear to be there to check on Graham's well-being.

"Ever hear of knocking?" Graham's air was nonplussed, but calm.

"Funny. Looks like you're heading somewhere," said the older man.

Lynch assumed him to be Homer. He wanted to get the man closest to him, the one blocking the door, but Graham was too far from Homer and risked getting shot.

"In fact, I was heading to the latrine." He took two steps toward the door, two steps closer to Homer, but still too far away.

"You won't need that. The powers that be have decided they don't want you returning to the campaign after all. But I hate to put a hole in my coat. Why don't you take it off and toss it over there?" He pointed toward the middle of the room with his gun.

Graham stood his ground. Lynch didn't know what he thought he could gain by resisting. He needed to get closer to Homer.

"Go ahead and shoot. Or try, anyway. Your guns

won't work in here."

Lynch heard the younger man snicker, and watched as he raised his gun directly toward Graham. Graham had told him the younger one, Virgil, was the one to watch out for.

"Yeah, right," said Homer.

"Yes, that's true. The God I serve has assured me that I will rise to the presidency, so nothing you attempt to do will stop that. Like Daniel in the lion's den, God will protect me."

Lynch's eyes widened as he watched his boss step up to Homer and lift the man's gun right to his chest. At first he wondered if the isolation had made his boss snap, but then he saw what was happening. Homer now blocked Virgil's shot and Homer would have to be a deranged psychopath to shoot a man 15 inches away from him, staring him straight in both eyes. If indeed the man was a trained law enforcement officer, that would be anathema. He wouldn't be able to pull the trigger.

Lynch's focus returned to Virgil. In horror, he saw the man's finger begin to squeeze his trigger. The man was willing to take out his partner in order to fulfill his mission. Lynch wouldn't be able to take him down in time.

CLICK! And nothing. The gun had jammed.

In that split second, Graham used one hand to knock a surprised Homer's gun to the side while hitting the man with a full charge from the stun gun in his other hand. Lynch lunged from hiding and took down a stunned Virgil. Both men hit the floor hard.

Lynch disarmed both and patted them down. He found zip ties in Virgil's pockets—enough for several men. Virgil appeared to question Homer's dedication to the task they were assigned to do and was prepared to deal with him as well as Graham. He also found a small container of lighter fluid and matches. The fate of the deceased—whether one body or two—seemed evident.

Graham hit both men with another jolt of electricity and watched as Lynch secured their wrists and ankles with the zip ties. Lynch then relieved their back pockets of their phones and wallets. He took their driver's licenses and tossed the wallets back onto the floor next to them. He flipped both men onto their backs and continued to search their clothing. In Homer's coat, in a zippered inside pocket, he felt something familiar. He pulled out a leather credentials folder.

"Well, look at that. Federal Bureau of Investigation. Special Agent Elliot Esperanza. Won't you make the director proud? And guess what, boss? The squirrelly one's name really is Virgil. Virgil Bass." He frisked the man again, but found no other ID. "I guess he was smart enough to leave his creds at home. Won't be hard to trace with his driver's license. And these phones should be a treasure trove of information."

Graham nodded. "Grab their keys, too."

Lynch complied and tucked everything away in his coat. He then took his own cell phone and made a video of the cabin, the kidnappers, and Graham—minus his chic footwear. In Graham's own words, he detailed what happened during and after his kidnapping and verified that the men they had in custody, via a "citizen's arrest," were his kidnappers. They would be left secured in the cabin to await law enforcement, which would receive the cabin's GPS coordinates shortly.

As Lynch prepared to leave, he saw Graham comparing his foot to those of each man. He smiled as he began to untie Virgil's boots.

"Looks like we wear the same size, Virgil. I'm going to need these to get out, but I'll leave mine behind for you."

Virgil appeared alert enough to try to spit on Graham, but succeeded only in dribbling on his own cheek.

"Then again, maybe I'll take mine with me." He patted Virgil on the dry cheek and the man's eyes flared with anger. "Yeah, I'll just take them with me."

Lynch stood there observing the exchange and slowly shaking his head.

"Boss, I always knew you were confident, but you've got bigger brass ones than I'd have ever guessed. You actually put the man's gun to your chest."

"Can't say as I've ever described my faith like that, but what I said wasn't for show, Lynch. One week from now I will be elected as the 45th president, against all odds and showing the pundits who mock God to be the fools of this world, to paraphrase the Word."

"I hope so," said Lynch. "Still, it's a good thing Virgil's gun jammed. He tried to shoot you both."

"Jammed?"

Graham took Virgil's gun from the table, stepped over next to its owner, placed it a foot from Virgil's face, and as horror filled the man's eyes, pulled the trigger. The bullet splintered the wood floor four inches from the side of Virgil's head.

Forty-one

Richard sat next to Summer, amazed at this turn of events. Her reputation as a mainstream journalist had been built on her support of the liberal agenda and castigation of all things conservative. Now he learned that she was the one behind the exposed emails of the DNC and its leaders, as well as the emails of their candidate's campaign leaders. Had he entered the *Twilight Zone*?

"Summer, I am totally confused and amazed at the same time. You? You're working with WikiLeaks? And why are you confiding in me about this?"

Summer took a deep breath. "Do you have more wine? This could take a while."

Richard complied with her request. In truth, he would have gone out to buy more wine, her favorite wine, if he had to. He didn't want to miss out on this story.

Summer took a long sip and savored it a moment before resuming.

"The story begins with my grandfather. You know the story of Chappaquiddick and Ted Kennedy, right?"

Richard shrugged. "Yeah. Kind of. I mean, that was a decade before I was born, and I don't know any details. A lot of people thought Kennedy got away with manslaughter following a tryst with the girl who died. It prevented him from running for president in the seventies."

"That's right, and my grandfather was one of those people. He was involved in the Grand Jury that was never allowed to see any of the real evidence or even the judge's findings in the death inquest. The Grand Jury was a sham and he threatened to go public with it. Instead, he found himself with a broken leg and a business that suddenly became insolvent. Anonymous reports of infidelity, ties to organized crime, and other malfeasance destroyed his reputation. He lost his home. Two of his four children wanted nothing to do with him. He left Cape Cod a ruined and bankrupt man, but at least my grandmother stuck with him. She knew the truth."

She took another drink and stared into space for a moment.

"My dad was the youngest child and stayed with his parents. His hopes of going to college were gone, and when he turned 21, he changed his name and went off on his own. He, too, knew the truth about his father and he tried to investigate who was behind his father's destruction. That's when he discovered a group of people, a shadow government that directed much of world affairs. And he realized they were moving beyond the inner circles of politics. Journalists before that prided themselves on their independence, but the world was becoming increasingly interconnected. Transportation, communications, politics, everything. They knew that they needed to control what people saw in the news and media, and to shape how people thought. They extended into education to gain control over what children learned. The explosion of computer technology and the development of the internet gave them their first real chance at global control.

"Names like the Illuminati, the Trilateral Commission, the Council on Foreign Affairs, the Bilderbergs, and others became the fodder of 'conspiracy theorists,' a term coined by the media to deride those who sought to expose them. My dad was one of *those* people, but he knew enough to stay under their radar. He had seen what happened to his father. Still, there were those who pounded away against these people, making use of the growing alternative media and books to expose their activities. Then, somewhere along the line, someone decided that the best way to get these conspiracy nuts off their backs would be to reinvent themselves. They became what we know today as The Assembly."

Richard scrutinized Summer's face as she talked. He witnessed sincerity, not deception.

"So, daddy's little girl sat on his lap, so to speak, listening, watching, and absorbing all of this."

She nodded. "I did. And I made a plan. In high school, I got a prestigious summer intern's slot at Senator Kennedy's office. To be fair, the man sincerely held his beliefs. How he came to, and who helped form, those beliefs might be questioned, but the senator worked tirelessly for what he thought right and for the people of his state. In my opinion, I think Chappaquiddick changed him. He knew he got away with something and he fought to make up for it. Anyway, in college I decided on communications as a major and my connections from that summer job helped me get established after graduation. Still, like so many, I had to earn my stripes. It was meeting Maggie that finally moved me to where I am today. All along, I've been amassing data, forming alliances inside and out of The Assembly, all to build an unbreakable case against these people whose only goal is power, money, and control. I want to finish what my father started."

Richard wanted to pinch himself to see if this was all some weird dream. He still couldn't see Summer Stanton in the role she now proclaimed to hold.

"So, I'll ask again, *why* are you telling *me* this? And why the complicated scheme to give me the DVD of Pearce's murder? You could have just told me, or handed me the disk."

"If I had, what would you have told the police? That I gave it to you? Then, I would have been charged with withholding evidence and obstruction. I needed you to expose Maggie with a plausible story. You just moved in. You found a book with a code and it led you to the DVD, but you have no idea who set it up. That is what you told the police, right?"

He nodded. "I've sent out copies of the DVD and a brief explanation of how I found it. I'm scheduled for a press conference tomorrow morning."

"Yes, I know. I was asked to cover it, but I haven't seen your recording."

He explained what he had said.

"Good. Thank you. For bringing justice to Maggie and not implicating me."

Summer released his hand and slid onto his lap. She caressed the back of his head with one hand. Richard felt his heart accelerate but couldn't tell if it was because he felt an attraction to her or because he was uncomfortable with her boldness.

With a softer voice, she continued, "So, why did I tell *you*? Two reasons, really. I already told you I felt Maggie deserves justice. As soon as she's exposed in Eric's death, The Assembly will take care of her. Some secrets just need to die with her. And with her gone, there's a good chance I can move up to fill her shoes."

Richard now recognized that his increasing heart rate was because he no longer felt comfortable with her. Something had changed in her demeanor.

"The second reason is that you deserved to know the truth, like Eric did, before you die."

Richard didn't see the thin, sharp blade she had pulled from her boot until it was too late. He felt it pierce his chest just below his sternum, pointing up and into his heart. She deftly slid the blade back and forth a few times before pulling it out. He knew it to be a fatal wound; he'd been taught it in the army. He felt his chest filling with blood, and his breathing became labored. His cell phone sat on the side table next to the chair where he'd been sitting. Part of him screamed to fight, to call for help, but he knew he had no chance. The exertion of moving for the phone would hasten his end. He'd never reach the table.

Summer stood, picked up her bag, and pulled out a DVD disk. "And as insurance, this disk is going into the recorder in the library. It's date and time stamped for this evening and shows Maggie Walther entering your front door."

She walked out of the room and returned moments later. She approached him as he began to slump over on the couch and kissed him on his forehead.

"I'm so sorry, Richard. I really have come to like you, but my secret must remain so. Taking Maggie's place is just the beginning."

He watched Summer calmly pick up her wine glass and head toward the kitchen. The last thing he heard was water running and Summer's soft humming of a sweet melody.

Forty-two

Amy stared at the television screen as Bradley Graham talked with the press about two rogue FBI agents who had kidnapped him at the wildlife refuge. The men had been picked up by Special Agent Tanner and a team of agents under his supervision. Tanner himself was under investigation for his role in the hunt for Graham after it had been revealed that his search had been so amateurish it missed finding Graham's cell phone just a few hundred yards away from the refuge headquarters building.

Amy had watched this press briefing several times over the past few days as she sat in the hospital at her father's bedside. Lynch would step up next to detail his search for Graham and how the FBI had failed. He would then introduce his guide, Leonard Coby, formerly of the Burns Paiute Indian Reservation police force and now a successful business entrepreneur. Amy felt as if she knew the presentation by heart now.

Graham's polling numbers had skyrocketed following his return to the campaign trail. Even the mainstream press, pushed by the increasingly popular Summer Stanton, speculated about just who was behind the kidnapping, with a 50-50 split pointing fingers at the Republicans and Democrats. A few far-left groups tried to accuse the American Party of staging the kidnapping as an election stunt to gain attention. They had failed to gain any traction with their clearly weak assertions.

The story's resurgence in the news this morning was the response to news that the two kidnappers had been killed, along with the two U.S. Marshals charged with their transportation, in a fiery crash while in route to a federal detention center. That brought the conspiracy theory crowd out of the woodwork with accusations.

Richard's unexpected murder hit her much harder than she could ever have imagined. She had replayed his last voicemail a dozen times, but the sheer emotional fatigue of the past days had overwhelmed her. She had no more tears. Her body operated on autopilot and the days and nights became a blur. She couldn't even recall whether she had slept.

Richard's had delivered a DVD showing two prominent Washingtonians—a realtor and a DNC operative—involved in what was now classified as the murder of Eric Pearce and a recording of what Richard believed to be the motive behind the man's killing. But the "coincidences" kept mounting as a new DVD found in Richard's home implicated the realtor as being involved in Richard's death. Hours later, she was found dead in her home from an alleged self-inflicted gunshot wound, while the man employed by the DNC had disappeared.

Amy knew she should feel bad for the families of the two marshals, but she couldn't find any emotion left inside. Everything she felt had been drained from her—even her anger at the federal agents who failed to find and detain the

Somalis she believed responsible for her father's murder.

"Amy, it's time to go. The limo is here." Her best friend, Macy, approached her and turned off the TV.

Amy nodded. She didn't think she had any tears left, but the reservoir broke loose. Macy took her gently by the elbow and led her to the door. Once outside, Macy locked up and assisted Amy to the limo where her two brothers and their wives waited. The ride to the cemetery was a silent one.

The pastor's words never registered in Amy's mind. As she watched her father's casket being lowered into the grave she knew she would see him again. They would share eternity together at the feet of their Lord, and yet, the pain of his loss was more than she could bear. Her mother's death. College. Nursing school. Moving to St. Louis. Lynch Cully. Darko Komarčić. Two helicopter accidents. Richard Nichols. He had been there for all of the highs and lows of her life. He was her best flying partner. He was her mentor, her handyman, her greatest cheerleader.

And now he was gone.

She realized she had resisted all thoughts of moving from St. Louis, simply because he was there. Had God called him home to get her attention, to get her to listen to her Heavenly Father? Tears flooded her cheeks at the thought that he might still be living . . . if only she had been more receptive to God.

A paraphrase from Psalm 56 came to her mind: *You record my wanderings; put my tears in your bottle. Are they not in your book?* Right now, the list of her wanderings would be short, but that bottle would be huge.

She wiped the tears from her face and turned toward the long line of vehicles. The word 'wanderings' stuck in her head.

Friends from over the years had flown into St. Louis to honor her father. Some were now generals and congressmen. Others were common laborers her father had befriended through church. He had shown no favoritism. Now it was time to thank them for coming. The crowd dispersed and her brothers walked with her on both flanks back to the limo, which would take them to the wake. She knew she needed to put on a brave front, but could she?

As she prepared to enter the limo, a familiar voice rose up from the other side.

"Amy . . . I am so sorry. I got here as soon as I could."

Lynch walked around the back of the vehicle and up to her. He held out his hand to her, but she simply gazed at him, unsure about taking it. Part of her wanted more than his hand. She wanted to embrace him and release the tension that had built up between them. Yet, she had chosen Richard and that choice had become a wall between them. She didn't know how to respond now that Richard, too, was gone from her life.

She finally accepted his hand. "Thank you, Lynch."

Her father had liked and respected Lynch. And he had seen something between the two of them even while she wore Richard's ring. One final piece of advice her father had offered was for her to look deeply inside about her feelings for Lynch. Maybe she would get to that place. In time.

She looked into his eyes and saw pain. She knew that he also loved and respected her dad. She gave him a wan smile and ducked into the door of the awaiting vehicle.

As the door closed, she heard him say, "I'm here for you, Amy."

"Amy, are you sure you want to do this? I really hate to see you go."

Craig Sheehan, her boss, stood behind his desk at the MedAir headquarters and walked around it to her.

She nodded. "I am. I-I need a break. I can't sleep in my own home. All I see is my dad lying on the kitchen floor. My brother is going to try to sell my place, as well as Dad's house, while I'm gone."

"But you don't need to quit here. I can find you a place somewhere else in the company—Texas, Oklahoma, you name it. We can help you relocate."

"Craig, I really, really appreciate that. I do. But I . . . well, I'm looking for more of a break than that. Thanks."

"Well, I'm not going to accept your resignation. I'll put you down on an extended leave of absence. I can do that for up to a year, like we do for military reservists."

"Thanks, boss. I won't know if a year is enough until it's almost over, but I'll keep that in mind. And if you have to fill the slot in the meantime, do so. I can't promise you I'll be back."

Craig sighed. "I'll hold it as long as I can. I want you back." He reached over and hugged her. "I mean that."

"Thanks." A tear formed in the corner of her eye. She hadn't expected him to make leaving so difficult.

She walked out the front door carrying one box of mementos. Macy waited for her in the car and popped the latch on the trunk as she approached. Amy placed her box there and climbed into the passenger seat.

"Girlfriend, I honestly didn't think you'd go through with it. Guess I need to take that to your storage unit, right?"

Amy nodded. "If you don't mind. That should be the last thing I need you to put there for me."

As they drove away, Amy's phone rang. She looked at the Caller ID. The number, while unlisted, had become familiar to her. She debated answering but did so before her voicemail intercepted the call.

"Ms. Gibbs, it's Agent Doerr. Have I caught you at a good time?"

"As good as any."

The man had called weekly since her father's death. Word had filtered down that she was a friend of President-elect Graham and to treat her well. Amy had little doubt that Lynch was behind that. While Lynch's duties had been assumed by full-time Secret Service agents, he had been asked to stay on the transition team. Amy now expected that he would work at the White House following the inauguration in January.

"I have good news. We caught the men responsible for the explosives you found and we believe one of them might have been involved in the shooting at your home."

She noted how he was careful not to say "the shooting of your father." Kid gloves. They definitely treated her with kid gloves now.

"And the man with the scar and missing ear?"

She heard a sigh of frustration on the other end.

"We think his name is Abdullah Said Abdi, a Somali warlord who disappeared from that country five years ago.

We weren't sure about that because, at first, we thought the scar you saw might be a tribal marking. But we learned that Abdi received such a scar and lost part of his ear during a confrontation with another tribal faction. Anyway, he's dropped out of sight here as well. Members of the Somali community won't talk, but an anonymous source says he's left the country. We're still working to confirm it."

Amy felt a sense of partial closure. Through the men they had in custody, they would soon find those who killed her father.

"Thank you, for the update. It's comforting to know you're finally making some headway."

"Yes. Yes, we are. And we all still owe you a debt of gratitude for finding those explosives."

She said nothing. Gratitude would not bring back her dad. Still, she felt good that she had prevented dozens, if not hundreds, of deaths of innocent people.

"Agent Doerr, I won't be available by phone for a while. If you have anything further, could you inform me by email? I'd appreciate it."

"I sure will. And if I can do anything for you, please contact me."

Just find the men who killed my father, thought Amy. But the man already knew that.

Amy dropped her phone into her bag. She watched her surroundings whiz by as Macy drove. She wouldn't be seeing these familiar sights for a while.

"Girlfriend, are you sure about what you're about to do?"

Craig had asked the same question. As had both of

her brothers and her therapist, Amanda Lange. Amanda in particular thought Amy's plan was a poor one, but Amy had made up her mind.

"I am. If things don't work out, I'll be back."

"I'm gonna miss you, girl."

Amy was stunned to see tears running down street-smart, hard-nosed Macy's cheeks. They triggered a similar response in her. She was going to miss her friend and the stories about all of her cousins and aunts and uncles. She put a hand on Macy's shoulder.

"I'm going to miss you, too. I won't be easy to reach, but I'll check into my email when I can."

"You'd better come back. I won't be able to hunt you down and save your butt if something happens."

Amy smiled. "Like that ever happened before."

"Hey! Who saved your—"

"Not now, Macy. You're going to miss the exit."

Macy swerved into the right lane in time to take the main exit to Lambert International Airport. She pulled into the departures area and helped Amy unload her bags from the back seat. Amy double-checked her bag and pockets. Traveler's checks. Phone. Tablet. Cash. Passport. Her carry-on bag was secure. She presented her ticket to the curbside luggage check and got them tagged.

She turned back to see Macy hurriedly trying to wipe her eyes, resulting only in worsening the smear of mascara across her face. She fought her own tears, hugged her friend, and said, "Bye, girlfriend. I'll let you know when I've arrived safely."

With that she turned, walked into the terminal, and headed for the security check-in. As she passed through the scanners and then picked up her bags on the other end of the X-ray conveyor, she thought she heard her name. She turned back toward the public concourse but saw no one and turned back toward her departure gate.

Lynch careened into the departure area of the airport and pulled into one of the unloading spots. He ran to the airport police officer who monitored the area and flashed his presidential transition team credentials.

"Officer, please, don't tow it. I need five minutes inside. Just five. Here're the keys."

He pressed the keys into the man's hand and ran into the entrance.

"Hey, get back here! You can't—"

Lynch ran along the cordon outlining the security check-in, looking through the lines of people at each scanner. He didn't see her. He couldn't have missed her. He had passed Macy at a stop light on Lambert International Boulevard. Amy *had* to be in line. TSA simply didn't work that fast.

He doubled back rechecking the lines. There! She was already picking up her things on the other side.

"Amy! Wait! Amy!" He saw people beginning to look his way. He didn't want to make a scene, but then realized he might have to do just that.

"Amy! Wait! Don't leave! I need to talk with you."

Now he also had the attention of the TSA and two airport officers. He waved to get her attention. She turned back toward him just as two TSA officers stepped between them, blocking his view of her. He stepped to the side and she was gone. He was too late.

A young, black male working the outside luggage check at Terminal A saw the woman walking toward him and quickly pulled his phone from his shirt pocket. He double-checked her appearance to that of a woman whose picture he had been sent weeks earlier. He had instructions to watch for her at the airport.

A rumor had spread that she prepared to leave the city, perhaps the country. Allah had blessed him. She had arrived on his watch and he would have the honor to inform lord Abdullah Said Abdi not only that the rumor proved true, but that she had been spotted. As he greeted her and accepted her bags, he realized he had one further honor—to be able to tell their leader her final destination.

Sneak Preview:
The Khmer Connection

CHAPTER ONE

The woman deserved death for what she had done to him. Now he would repay her, but not with so quick an end.

Abdullah Said Abdi glanced about the bay as the moon reflected off its calm waters. There was a serenity about it that he found disturbing, as if it could distract him from his mission. Life, for him, had never been calm. Calm had only predicted another rising storm.

The son of a warlord in Somalia, he had risen to that position after his father had died, but not without opposition. The man who dared to challenge him had never seen the knife coming. Still, the man had inflicted his own mark upon Abdi. He traced the scar that marked his face with his left index finger—forever a reminder that distractions could be dangerous, if not fatal.

It was the distraction of a woman when he was a younger man that had almost cost him his life before dispatching his opponent to Paradise. From that he had learned that women were to remain chattel—easily bought and sold for pleasure—and meant to be subservient. A woman's place was to serve her husband, or her master if she was a concubine within the harem. Cooking. Cleaning. Preparing her children for their appropriate roles in life.

Those things were expected. Not feminism, the workplace, or equality with men. Dressing indecently. Talking back to men. Bringing humiliation to a man.

Not what one Amy Gibbs had done to him.

The young girls of his tribe, both in Somalia and the U.S., must never see that she got away with dishonoring him. The members of his tribe would never assimilate into America and those values. It would be their pleasure to join their Islamic brethren in bringing down the American Satan. To regain face, he would have to deal with Amy Gibbs—even if it required going to the other side of the world to do so. There was more at stake than his small faction in America.

Thanks to his men working as baggage handlers at the airport in St. Louis, he had discovered the destination of that woman. Now he would see to it that she could no longer humiliate a man. She would soon discover the real destiny that awaited her for her impudence.

He sensed the trawler slowing. They did not want to be discovered by the local authorities, and he would transfer to a smaller boat for the rest of the trip. The captain approached him.

"We are at the transfer coordinates. You have fifteen minutes before we must depart. I cannot be caught in these waters."

"I have been assured that I have a boat to move to shore." He handed the captain an envelope. "Here is your payment."

The man took the envelope and nodded. "Fifteen minutes."

Abdi scanned the waters to the north. On his second

pass, he saw three flashes of light. He returned the signal with four flashes.

His twenty-hour ordeal was about to end. It paid to have money and connections, even if those connections were more likely to be seen on Interpol wanted lists than on social media. His trip back into Mexico followed the same path along the open southern border as had his entry into the U.S. years earlier. A wall back then would have kept him out, while a wall now might have corralled him in for authorities to round up. Once in Mexico, his cartel associates there assured him they had a way to confuse the U.S. authorities that sought him—a drone that could land and take off from water and also transmit a false radar signature. If it worked, the U.S. agents would see a Somali ship "parked" off their western coast and anticipate the potential of his escaping on it.

Instead, he transferred to a larger aircraft for the trans-Pacific flight, landed at another private airstrip in Indonesia, and bought passage on a small plane to the island where the Somali fishing trawler met him for the trip into the bay. No commercial flight schedules to meet. No airports and their security checkpoints. No customs or immigration hassles.

A man, to whom he had provided a steady stream of children and young girls, had a connection inside this country. That connection, in turn, had clients with expressed interests in a tall, attractive American woman for their harems. Upon seeing a picture of Amy Gibbs, he had become more than amenable to helping Abdi find this woman, whom they would capture and auction to the highest bidder. That suited Abdi's purpose. Death was too quick. Years of drugged imprisonment and sadistic abuse was the more appropriate lesson for this woman who must learn her place.

Abdi checked the clock on his phone. With allowances for the International Date Line, he estimated that he was nearly a full day ahead of her. He would be ready.

A quick note from Braxton . . .

I hope you enjoyed *Kidnapped Nation* and thank you for purchasing it. Please consider writing a review at Amazon, Barnes & Nobel, iTunes, Goodreads, or elsewhere. Reviews are crucial to Indie authors. It doesn't have to be lengthy. Just a couple of sentences will do.

Also, if you'd like to stay informed about my new books, book signings, and more, please sign up for my newsletter. You can do that at my website: **www.braxtondegarmo.com**. As my thank-you for signing up, I'll give you my eBook, *And Then One Day*—a prequel to the MedAir Series. If you've wondered how Lynch and Amy met, and what led to their breakup, this is the book for you.

And did you know you can purchase signed copies of my paperbacks at my website? With shipping included in the price, ordering them directly from me is typically cheaper than ordering them online.

ABOUT THE AUTHOR

Braxton can't lay claim to wanting to be a writer all his life, although his mother and seventh grade English teacher were convinced he had what it would take. A bachelor's degree in Bio-Medical Engineering led to medical school and a residency in Emergency Medicine. He served for a decade in the U.S. Army Medical Corps with tours such as the Chief, Emergency Medical Services at Fort Campbell, KY, and as a research Flight Surgeon at Fort Rucker, AL. Who had time to write?

By the 1990s, as a civilian, his professional and family life had settled down, somewhat, and his mother once again took up her mantra, "Write a book. You're a good writer." In 1997, a Valentine's Day writing contest convinced him that maybe he could write fiction. He spent the next fifteen years learning the craft of writing.

Now, twenty-plus years after that first hesitant start, he has sixteen novels published, as well as non-fiction books and a children's book, and can't find enough time to write. As a Christian, he writes "true-life" Christian fiction (suspense and thrillers) that many call "cutting edge," as he's not afraid to take on such issues as human trafficking, racism, and more. His characters are real-life as well, with all the flaws and blemishes real people have. As such, his books are never likely to gain acceptance by the Christian Bookseller Association. But then, he never intended to tell stories just to the choir.

Books by Braxton DeGarmo:

Still Here Series:
The End Begins - 1
The Shaking - 2
The Beasts – 3
The Trumpets – 4
The Mark - 5

Non-fiction Study Guides:
Still Here! Surviving the End Times
Still Here! The Apocalypse is Now
Still Here! Countdown Revelation

MedAir Series:
Looks that Deceive – 1
Rescued and Remembered – 2
The Silenced Shooter – 3
Wrongfully Removed – 4
A Zealot's Destiny – 5
Kidnapped Nation - 6
The Khmer Connection - 7
Resurrected Trouble - 8

Seamus O'Connor Thrillers:
The Militant Genome
Ten Seconds 'Til

Other Books:
Indebted

Children's Books:
The Toucan Who Can Can-can